**BOOK THREE**

**BOOKS OF BEFORE & NOW**

# THE BRIDE & THE BIRDMAN

## JASON FISC...

THE BRIDE & THE BIRDMAN:
THE BOOKS OF BEFORE AND NOW BOOK THREE
Copyright © 2024 Jason Fischer. All rights reserved.

Published by Outland Entertainment LLC
3119 Gillham Road
Kansas City, MO 64109

**Publisher:** Jeremy D. Mohler
**Creative Director:** Cullen Bunn
**Editor-in-Chief:** Alana Joli Abbott
**Games Director:** Anton Kromoff

Paperback ISBN: 978-1-964735-08-5
Ebook ISBN: 978-1-964735-09-2
Worldwide Rights
Created in the United States of America

**Editor:** Scott Colby
**Copy Editor:** Em Palladino
**Cover Illustration:** Steve Firchow
**Cover Design:** Jeremy D. Mohler
**Interior Layout:** Jeremy D. Mohler

The characters and events portrayed in this book are fictitious or fictitious recreations of actual historical persons. Any similarity to real persons, living or dead, is coincidental and not intended by the authors unless otherwise specified. This book or any portion thereof may not be reproduced or used in any manner whatsoever without the express written permission of the publisher except for the use of brief quotations in a book review.

Printed and bound in the United States of America.

Visit outlandentertainment.com to see more, or follow us on our Facebook Page facebook.com/outlandentertainment/

# — PROLOGUE —

The gun that killed a god collected many stories as it passed through the centuries, from hand to bloody hand, but at its very beginning it was just a gun, wrapped in a box. Frantic hands were snatching hundreds of firearms from trucks and vans, a human chain passing them into the depths of a warehouse.

It was a staggering enterprise. Even as lookouts watched the streets for the police or even the Collegia, the warehouse contained everything that thousands of people might need to enter another world. Food. Clothing. Basic machinery. Vehicles and the fuel to run them. Crates were piled high, and forklifts competed with the invisible grip of the magicians to sort everything into place.

Outside, the power stations throbbed with golden light, and in mere days the world would end.

Papa Lucy rarely visited, but his brother, Sol, spent most of his time here, going over consignments with a worried eye, a phone glued to his ear for hours on end as he begged for more supplies, enough to help Lucy's mad gamble. Even now, when there was no point, money was king, and they simply did not have enough to get everything they needed.

John Leicester had his own backup plan in place, of course, but no one knew if the beacons would work. They hoped to trigger a series of events they were calling a "bleedthrough," but it was metamagic at its finest, and a long shot at best.

Baertha was a lost figure in all the madness. To increase efficiency, she was linked telepathically to most of the female operatives in the movement, channelling communications and issuing orders to hundreds of people. To the casual observer she was shivering on the spot, eyes rolled back to show the white of her sclera, balanced on ballerina tiptoes for hours on end. No one knew what this was costing her.

Her infamously rich family could have funded the movement with the stroke of a pen, but she had not made contact, and everyone understood.

Everyone in this warehouse was disgraced. Dangerous.

A man named Hesus had his own place in this desperate operation, overseeing a group of his own people around a hastily assembled workbench. They were the failures and the fuckups, rejects from the Collegia and lesser schools, but they had the only talents that Hesus needed of them.

*Survive the passage through the Greygulf.*

*Know the basic magics that bind and kill.*

*Kill the monsters of that other world without hesitation.*

The use of the more dangerous Marks was heavily policed, and etching these into a firearm carried a hefty prison sentence, if not straight up execution, but these were desperate times. His followers worked diligently at the task, tired hands gouging at the steel and wood with chisels and rasps, making the guns into weapons that would kill just about anything.

They had rifles, pistols, assault rifles, and even mortars, but a man named Mohler picked up the gun that would kill a god. A simple two-barrel shotgun with a break action, he fell in love with it on the spot.

He got to work, but where the others were hastily scratching in the Marks and pushing their magic into the weapon, he took his time. Hesus had sniffed out Mohler's magical potential and plucked him from an art school, and he simply could not ruin the walnut stock with anything but his best woodwork.

"Get a move on, Mohler," his neighbour cursed, but Mohler ignored him, making the Marks into a beautiful frieze along the underside of the stock. His etching tools carefully brought out a spiral of sigils around the twin barrels, and his etching tools drew imagined monsters in the space.

Mohler made a decision to leave plenty of blank space around his work, instinctively knowing that this gun had more stories in it, like a person with the scattering of their first tattoos. It would take time to finish this story, and he didn't know the ending yet.

"This is bullshit," the man to his right said, and others joined in. They were tired, having been at this for hours, with more guns arriving than they could hope to work on. Yet here was someone holding up the line, working obsessively on decorative detail.

"Enough," Hesus said, walking over to Mohler. He held out his hands to the artist, and Mohler reluctantly gave over the shotgun. The disgraced professor of the Collegia cast his eye across the work.

"They're right, you know," Hesus said. "You're taking too much time on this."

"I'm sorry, sir," Mohler said, and meant it.

"We need you to work faster. Stop fucking about with this fancy stuff. Put in the Marks and pick up the next gun."

"Yes, Hesus."

Hesus handed back the shotgun to Mohler.

"But first, you need to finish this. Do it properly and take your time. No complaining, you lot. After all, it's his gun now."

Mohler nodded his thanks and got back to work. The Marks began to hum with potential as he whispered the magic into the carving, and it was equal parts art and weapon by the time he was finished sanding and oiling the carving.

A shadow fell upon him, and he looked up.

"That's a beautiful gun," Papa Lucy said. "I think I'll keep that one for myself."

No one ever refused the man, and even though it was a knife in the heart, Mohler made to give it up. But Hesus appeared in an instant, standing between Lucy and Mohler.

"No. Mohler's worked on it for hours. Belongs to him."

The two powerful magicians eyed each other for one dangerous moment. In a future age, this and other moments would play out in the battle of Sad Plain, but this time Lucy replied with his trademark smile and raised hands.

"Well, your bossman really looks out for his crew," Lucy said. "What are you called? Hesusmen? Hesuswomen?"

"We don't have a name yet," Hesus said. "Problem for another day."

"True. Nothing but problems waiting for us," Lucy said, then turned to Mohler. "If this all goes well, I'll have to make use of your talented hands."

Months later, in the early days of the Now, Lucy was still privately afraid of Hesus, but he seized Mohler in a dark corner of Crosspoint and took out his anger at the master upon the prentice. It was a bad ending for the man who made the god-killing gun, and Lucy took his time breaking those talented hands.

As for the shotgun, Mohler had hidden it well within the Lodge of the Hesusmen, choosing a lesser weapon for his own patrols, and Lucy did not dare to cross Hesus's doorstep then. Some years later, Hesus found its hiding place and gave it to a man named Thorpe, the first of their number to kill a Witch.

And so it went through the years, from master to prentice, and Hesus became known as Jesus, and other hands came to add to Mohler's carvings. The beautiful gun became a grim thing, every inch of it soaked in blood and sorrow until not even Hesus or Lucy would be able to recognize it.

Mohler's craft told true throughout the centuries that desperate hands plied the gun's murderous trade. The gun killed well, and a Jesusman named Lanyard Everett used it to kill Papa Lucy at the Waking City.

He gave the shotgun to his own prentice, a boy named Mal. Some years later, the boy was grown into a man and was pressing the god-killer against his master's temple, trembling and weeping.

"I said do it!" Lanyard screamed. "Pull the trigger!"

# — 1 —

## MAL

Well before the moment when the master begged his prentice for death, Mal stood by Lanyard's side, both of them eyewitnesses to a creeping destruction. The ancient shotgun was slung over the younger man's shoulder, a problem for that future day, and they shared a worried cigarette.

"Tilly's wasting her time," Lanyard said.

"Why?" Mal replied.

"People are stupid, boy. Lazy. They'll ignore their problems, even when they're right on their doorstep."

Mal looked at the looming approach of the Range, the row of steep hills and peaks that separated the settled lands from the blank strangeness of the Waste, only now it all looked like a wave made from earth and stone, curling in as it pushed forward.

*Another edge to things, a boundary like Shale was*, Mal mused.

It moved perhaps an inch one year, and then a foot, and some years a dozen yards or more, and the Range pushed slowly south, miles of stone cracking, the earth flexing at the enormity of the advance.

Ray Leicester and Sol Pappagallo had been out here for weeks now, measuring the edge of the Range, their teams of surveyors madly rushing around with theodolites and other instruments. They argued. Measured again. Finally, Sol was forced to admit the truth.

All of the tall tales and rumours were true, and the scoffing at the public houses had turned to quiet disbelief right across the Inland, and now panic. The Range was advancing south at the speed of a man at a quick jog.

The town of Price lay directly in its path.

Most of the citizens had left weeks ago, but here were the desperate and the stupid leaving at the very last second, a column of belching cars and lizards hauling wagons, even riding birds pressed into service as draught animals. Others were pushing handcarts piled high, while the destitute left with nothing, hoping that Sol Goodface would save them from death in the desert. A fortune in goods lay scattered by the wayside, cast aside as dead weight, but no one stopped to pick it up.

A woman came roaring past the evacuating townsfolk on a motorbike, swerving away from reaching hands. At one stage she was forced to physically boot someone away from her, and it took her a long moment to fight off the speed wobbles and not tip the bike. She came in at a fast clip to where Lanyard and Mal stood watch, kicking up dirt and stones as she slid to a halt.

Tilly killed the motor, the look on her face murderous. Even just shy of her prime, she was a map of scars and worries, and little was left to tell of the lost tomboy who first took up Lanyard's banner. She was as hard now as the life she'd chosen, flint-faced, and no patience for fools.

"Here she goes," Lanyard warned Mal.

"Fucking morons," she yelled, off the bike and storming around, hands bunched into fists. "Dipshits and dickheads. Do they not have eyes in their fucking heads?"

"I take it some of the citizens of Price are staying."

"We can go back in there, boss," Tilly said. "Force them out at gunpoint. Save their stupid bloody lives!"

"No."

She took in a deep breath, ready for a fight, and then she released that same breath, found her composure.

"You're right," she said. "It's not our job."

"Not our job," Lanyard repeated.

"When they die, we know what happens now," Mal offered. "Their spirits go down to Gan-Eden. They'll be okay."

"There're worse things than dying, boy," Lanyard said. "Awful, lingering ways to die that aren't really death. Pity every one of these damn fools, but don't you dare bloody help them."

Mal looked to Tilly, who rolled her eyes ever so slightly. He knew their part in Sol's big plan, and it was the only job the Jesusmen ever had. Anything else just complicated their mission.

*Lanyard says we're here to kill the monsters that want to prey on us,* Mal thought, trying to rationalize what they did today. *We set ourselves in their path and kill them to the last bullet, till the last Jesusmen bleeds out into the clay.*

*Each intruder lingering in our world makes the path of the next one easier. If too many get through, the world veil fails completely.*

Mal was fine with selling his life in the defence of others, but Lanyard called mercy missions a distraction.

*What if he's wrong? Why can't we also do what's right?*

Slowly crawling up and down the line of refugees, Sol's people were filling trucks and wagons with the refugees that were on foot. They were a drop of kindness in a literal desert, and even as they overloaded every vehicle to the point of danger, it wasn't enough.

Most of these people would die in the city, or twenty miles on, and there was nothing Tilly or anyone else could do.

Again, it wasn't their job.

A sliver of light opened next to them, as if a bright nail pierced the air itself, and it drew down to reveal a doorway. The rectangle offered a closer view of the Range. None of the Jesusmen blinked an eye at the appearance of the far-door, but they nodded politely as Sol Goodface and Ray Leicester stepped through it to join their company.

Sol smiled sadly, clasping hands with Lanyard. He'd spent centuries as the Boneman, a walking skeleton bound into undeath, but today he offered a hand of flesh and blood. His body had been restored by a miracle, even as a conniving thief stole his immortality from him. A little greyer now, he still moved with a painful hitch, the beating he'd taken in Overhaeven something he'd never recover from.

Ray hustled through the door before it winked closed, hauling a clanking bag of tools and gizmos. He was a mess of greasy overalls and wild hair, his eyes forever cast in soft confusion.

"We've done all we can," Sol said.

"But I can put stink bombs into the houses!" Ray said, one such device already assembled in his hands. "They'll come outside, and then we can save them."

"It's their right to stay where they please," Sol said kindly. "I'm no tyrant."

"It doesn't make sense though," Ray said. "Why are they just staying in their houses?"

"Because they're scared. Home is all they know."

"That's stupid," Ray said, and then pondered the matter in silence, frowning at the city as though it were a logical puzzle where the answer eluded him.

"Anything coming?" Sol said to Lanyard.

"It'll happen soon if it does. All those people, right in a weak spot."

As far as Sol's plan went, the Jesusmen were all in. If they survived whatever came through the world veil today, they had their part to play.

They would take this fight to another front, but first, they needed information about the enemy.

"Do you need us?" Sol asked, a hand on Tilly's arm. She shook her head.

"We'll stop it, or we won't," she said.

Lanyard fed two fresh shells into his brute of a god-cannon, the action closing with the sound of an axe on a neck.

"Go on, piss off. You're needed elsewhere."

Sol nodded.

"One more thing," Lanyard said. "I know you now, Sol the Boneman. I know you're about to go wear yourself out, magicking yourself up and down that line of idiots. Saving people. Don't."

"Yes," Sol said heavily. "They had fair warning. Good luck."

"This is wrong," Ray said. "We can help!"

"Junkman," Lanyard growled. "Leave."

They had such history, this collection of spellcasters and

gunslingers. On the one hand, you had those from the old dead world of Before, Sol Pappagallo and Ray Leicester, a pair with the grind of centuries behind them. Then you had the Jesusmen, the cadre tasked with murdering intruders into this world, their only job to the exclusion of all else. Lanyard led this once illegal order, with Tilly and Mal his lieutenants, and now they worked hand in glove with Sol and his government, trying just to keep the place going, to make tough calls and keep people alive.

Then there was Jenny Rider, now the Selector of Crosspoint, once a privileged daughter who'd been tricked into wielding the Cruik for Papa Lucy. Now she was effectively that ancient artifact, as much a mystical creature as she was a woman.

She was nearby, trying to assist through her own considerable abilities. Jenny was needed twenty times over, and still it wouldn't have been enough.

In the realm of the dead, Jesus and John Leicester worked, the two dead men ruling Gan-Eden as fairly as they could, and they offered as much assistance as they could to Sol and his council in the Now.

Then there was Papa Lucy, of whom the less said the better.

Sol tore open the world veil to form a far-door, but he paused on the threshold.

"Come with us, Lanyard," he said. "I worry about how often you've travelled through the Greygulf. It grows less and less safe for you."

Mal knew the risks. They all did. There was an unseen number hanging over every Jesusman's head, and that was the amount of times they could tread the silvery-world of the Greygulf before it twisted them to the core, changing them to the foulest and lowest of creatures.

Every Witch was a Jesusman who went back one time too many.

"Thought I told you to piss off," was all Lanyard said, and Sol left with a sad smile, guiding a confused Ray through the far-door and onto the next problem. The tear sealed over with the stink of ozone, and the pair were instantly elsewhere.

*The old man knows his end is closing in,* Mal thought, looking at the man who was equal parts father figure and drill sergeant. *Sol's plan is as good as a gun to his head. All of our heads.*

*Lanyard's so stubborn he won't even realize it when he's dead.*

THE BRIDE & THE BIRDMAN · 11

Bemused by the image of Lanyard fighting on until he was a skeleton with gun holsters, Mal took in the doomed town of Price, an ant trail of refugees pouring out into the desert, straight toward their own ragged line.

The entire Order of the Jesusmen, pulled in from camps and towns, and every cook and smith and prentice was ready with a gun or two. The Order had nearly been wiped out during the wars of the Dawn King, but Tilly had pressed hard, sniffing out anyone with a hint of the talent. Today, they had just over fifty people in the field.

These were not the finest Jesusmen they'd ever fielded, and the training was rushed. Incomplete, as Lanyard's had been for many years. Some were vomiting. Others had fresh piss stains on their pants. As Lanyard looked on, one prentice put her gun to her temple and blew her brains out.

"Oh, for fuck's sake," Lanyard said, and then turned to another prentice. "You, go pick up that gun. It's yours now."

The Range was surging forward in fits and starts, like an excited puppy on the leash, and from beyond the city came the last of the survey teams, blasting through the dust in cars and on bikes, the swell of the foothills rising beneath their wheels.

"Mal, watch that last car there," Lanyard said. "Tell me what you see."

Handing back the stub of cigarette, Mal scrambled into Collybrock's saddle. He tapped on the bird's neck, and she unfolded to her full height with a wearied groan, lifting him a full ten feet off the ground.

"Sleepy," the bird complained.

Lifting up his binoculars, Mal summoned forward a lick of Jesusman magic, tracing the Mark of Farsight onto the lenses. He tracked the car Lanyard had pointed out, watching it bounce and lurch across the flexing landscape.

For a moment he was reminded of the Underfog, that land of breathing hills and shifting clay, and then he felt his old passenger shift forward, a familiar presence watching through his eyes—Kirstl, his wife, one of the Jesusmen prentices murdered in the Underfog. Betrayed by Bilbenadium in one of that rat-spirit's endless machinations, Kirstl was a spirit that lived within his body now, sharing both his flesh and his dreams from within. They were a Tontine, two minds bound into one flesh, and they were in love down to their very bones.

*We should have kept the cigarette,* she complained to Mal. *I like those.*

"They'll rot our lungs, love," he said.

*You sound like Sol,* she said in his mind. *Look, those poor bastards are fucked now!*

Sure enough, the car was struggling to escape the advancing Range, and then the mountains lurched forward again, the vehicle bouncing and sliding on that increasing angle.

"What do you see?" Lanyard called up.

"They're stuck, boss," Mal said. "Wheels can't grip the dirt."

He looked again.

"Wait. It's not dirt. It's the Waste. It's eating them up."

He'd been expecting the car to be lifted up to almost vertical, for the mountain to finally spill it and knock it around like a toy, but the car began to sink into the ground. Even as the occupants threw open the doors and spilled out, a curl of earth moved over the car like a mouth, swallowing it down swiftly.

Mal could only watch in horror as the rolling foothills quickly drew in those who ran, freezing their feet in place, drawing them down like a mouth slurping at pasta, the Range sealing over them in moments.

"What the hell happened?" Lanyard called up.

"It's eating them. The bloody mountains are eating them!"

For just a moment, a figure emerged from the earth, a shape like a neck and a muzzle, and it seized the last man trying to run, drawing him into the mountainside, all the while savaging him like a wolf on a seized rabbit.

"No. It's not the mountain," Mal called down. "We've got contact! They're hiding just this side of the Range."

Lanyard nodded. He sent runners up and down their line, their rattling motorbikes passing on the message.

*Intruders confirmed. Engage. Retreat only on bossman's word.*

Mal knew well that Lanyard wasn't likely to give that word. Not today.

He swept the binoculars across to the town and saw some last-second evacuees, even as the shadow of the Range started to wash across the community. One car peeled loose from the town gates, running down pedestrians in an attempt to escape. When the driver of the last Boneguard truck saw this, he turned around, and Sol's crack soldiers started firing on the car. Instant justice descended upon that one moron, and then the Boneguard themselves were screwed as the truck stalled and refused to restart.

Wailing refugees spilled out of the back as the Boneguard stood around the raised hood, frantically repairing the steaming engine.

"Not our job," Lanyard called up to Mal. "Leave it."

Every fibre in Mal's body screamed at the injustice. He recognized one or two of Sol's warriors, good people who were here to help, and now as good as dead.

He could charge over on Collybrock, swing up one or two people into his saddle, help them withdraw.

*And then more hands would seize at the saddle, and then they'd pull the bird down, and he'd be just as dead,* Kirstl said in his mind. *Mal, Lanyard's right. It's a shitshow and we can't fix it. All we can do is —*

"Our job. Yes, our bloody job."

Lanyard raised his fist, and up and down the line others copied the signal. Bike riders pressed down on kickstarts, cars and buggies coughed into life, and the bird riders spun their clacking sticks, their steeds grumbling and unfolding to their full height.

Now they could all see it, a rumbling wave of earth just ahead of the advancing Range, now moving faster than the mountains. Perhaps half a mile from end to end, and a separate threat. This shape was whippet-quick and huge, and suddenly a forest of heads erupted from beneath the surface, beastly maws snapping in all directions on flexible necks, snatching surveyors from motorbikes and leaping after the remaining cars.

Then it rose up fully, and Mal's heart sank at the true horror. It was one creature, immense in size. A thousand predators melted together, the body an undulating surface of muscle and scabby fur. At the front of the creature scrambled thousands of legs, with the suggestion that many more limbs held the mass upright.

It moved at an impossible gait, lurching and rolling, as fast as a car now, a predator with a thousand eyes on the town and the refugees fleeing from it.

"Hold!" Lanyard shouted, sketching a Mark on his throat so that all could hear his window-rattling roar. Mal knew it cost the old Jesusman dearly to use these magics now, and if they lived through this, Lanyard would be hoarse for days.

Collybrock quivered beneath him, warbling in terror. "Dog. Big dog," she finally managed.

Mal patted her on the neck and clucked his tongue reassuringly. Reaching within, he breathed deep, and even surrounded by panic and that sprawling terror, the young Jesusman found a moment of peace. He looked down at Lanyard who was climbing into his own buggy, and nonetheless here at the end his heart was full.

He'd lived well. Found love, in his own unusual way. Had a father-figure in Lanyard, who understood that his protégé carried his own wife in his head. Best of all, he knew what death meant now.

"We'll be back in Gan-Eden soon," he said. "Both of us, side by side in paradise. But I'll stick my lance in that thing first."

Kirstl crept forward at the words and saw through his eyes.

*What in the bright blue fuck is that?*

"Just another monster, my love. Big one."

*I'll find out more,* she said, and was gone.

Lanyard was winding the klaxon he had fitted to the buggy, and this was it. The final signal, forward and into battle, time to hit that impossible creature with everything they had.

"Go girl, hut!" he said to Collybrock, and she joined the advance, loping along at the mile-eating trot that birds could manage over a short distance, easily keeping pace with the bikes and cars around her. To his left, the faint popping of a pistol, and Mal saw a car on their flank turning, some of the newer prentices retreating. Deserting.

He saw two other survivors from their trip into the Underfog. Mem was chasing the deserters in her motorbike, her twin Lyn shooting at them with a pair of revolvers from the sidecar. The sisters wore mohawks these days, and both of them were wild creatures fresh into adulthood, happy to disobey a solid order if the feeling was right.

"MEM, LYN, GET BACK IN BLOODY LINE!" Tilly ordered the

pair, her own magically Marked voice thundering across the distance. Reluctantly they let the deserters go and rejoined the advance, their bike sweeping back into the formation.

They were alongside the line of refugees who had seen the beast and were now scattering in all directions like terrified chickens. The Jesusmen were forced to weave through an obstacle course of humans, and once or twice an innocent person stepped in the path of a car or a buggy—and not once did the advance stop.

"Not our job," Mal gasped, gritting his teeth as he saw an old woman thrown aside by a truck, already a floppy broken doll when she hit the sands. He wove through the wailing crowd like a barrel-racer, twitching the reins left and right. Collybrock rode sure and gently, and only once did she swerve and knock over someone, a man coming at her ready for a desperate grab at her saddle.

"Good girl," Mal said.

Kirstl came back.

*I spoke with Jenny. The Cruik. Whatever she is now.*

"How?"

*I'll show you later. Anyway, she knows what this thing is.*

"Well?"

*It's called the All-Fang. It's a predator from a hundred worlds, and it just keeps collecting meat. Anything with fangs gets added to the body. It's the ultimate killer.*

"How does she know this?"

*The Cruik fought this thing a long time ago, before Overhaeven and all that mess. It ravaged the original homeworld of the Taursi for years, but here's the thing: it's unstoppable out in the open, but useless in cities.*

"Of course!"

*The All-Fang moves through obstacles like pushing pudding through a sock. Too big and clumsy.*

Mal knew what to do. Digging his heels into Collybrock, he rode low and fast, finally catching up to Lanyard's buggy. Leaning over, he gave a piercing whistle through his teeth and got the bossman's attention. Then he pointed to the main gate of Price, where a scatter of people were still emerging, now finally dislodged by the appearance of the monster. Lanyard frowned.

"No, we're not bloody rescuing them, Mal. Bigger problems."

Mal pointed again.

"It's a killbox!" he shouted, and then Lanyard finally understood. With more shouts and commands, the bossman steered the Jesusmen toward Price.

They powered through the opened town gates, filling the tight streets with the roar of machines, pushing through the last of the evacuees. The Range was close now, blocking most of the afternoon sun, but the All-Fang was closer, and Mal could hear the yipping and barking of a thousand baying hounds, the roaring of creatures that might have been great cats, and other sounds in that cacophony beyond comparison.

"Got maybe a minute," Lanyard yelled. "Is there a north gate?"

A cry went up in the negative.

"Well, bloody make one! Dynamite through that mess of tin they call a wall, get buggies and chains to pull it away. The rest of you, get up on the catwalk. Draw that bloody big dog towards us."

Mal understood the urgency. The All-Fang's food was out in the open of the plain, running in all directions. They had to present themselves as the closest food source and draw them inside.

*Boom.* The explosions went up as their rapidly packed charges brought down a big section of tin and junk. Beyond, the roiling mass of the beast suddenly turned to the town as the Jesusmen appeared in the gap and above on the watchposts, waving and shouting, beating on the tin with their gunstocks.

"Hold your fire, people!" Tilly shouted. "Make every bloody shot count!"

The All-Fang came at them, great waves of muscle rolling and bounding, the heads fighting and snapping at each other in excitement. The noise was deafening, a thousand throats barking and howling, and soon Mal could barely hear the frenzied cries of his allies, Lanyard and Tilly quickly shouting instructions to everyone.

"You're with the other bird-riders," Lanyard shouted close to Mal's face. "Get out there and bait the thing. Keep luring it forward."

Mal nodded, adrenaline instantly flooding his system. He dug in his heels and Collybrock took off with a terrified squawk, and then they were out and through the breached wall. Instantly they were face to face with the All-Fang, a half-mile of meat and teeth, yipping and racing, thousands of legs churning the earth into a dust cloud.

"No! Mal!" Collybrock cried. "Shit!"

*I did not teach her that word!* Kirstl said.

Ignoring every instinct in his body, Mal urged the bird onward, and only Collybrock's love for her master sent her into the very face of that monster.

Mal spared a moment to look left and right, and his heart thrilled. Perhaps a dozen birds fanned out from the breached wall, their riders bent low with lance and gun. Beneath him, Collybrock ran at a flat trot, flanks heaving with panic and exertion.

Then at the final moment, the bird-riders gave the command. *Wheel about and retreat.* It was a tricky manoeuvre, and the bird was meant to go into a controlled slide on its backside, only to leap back to its feet and peel to either left or right, curving away from their foe and then back toward their starting position.

The rider was, of course, expected to attack the enemy with everything they had. Guns erupted up and down that ragged front line, and individual creatures in the All-Fang died yelping, still attached to the greater body. Even as Collybrock rose from her sliding halt, feet scrabbling as she fought to grip the earth and wheel about, Mal drove a lance into a reptilian eye.

Collybrock got to her feet mere feet from the All-Fang, and then she was running back toward the walls of Price, moaning incoherently as she escaped that packed kennel of flesh. Mal unleashed the ancient shotgun, emptying both shells into the enormous beast.

Other riders were not so lucky, their birds unable to get to their feet, and these were seized up by mouth or maw, torn apart instantly by that great, heaving beast.

Riding his bird as if he was in the home straightaway on the racing circuits of Langenfell, Mal got back to the breach, only to have Tilly meet him there on a motorbike, waving him down.

"Go back!" she shouted over all the barking and howling. "It didn't work."

The All-Fang was slowing down as it approached the town wall, and many of the heads were up and questing, sniffing out the easier prey that ran about in the open.

It seemed that it knew from old wars that towns were bad news, and with the canny of a thousand wild beasts it was too clever to charge into one small opening.

Mal heard Lanyard shouting, shortly followed by a series of explosions. Using dynamite, Marks of fire and destruction, everything they had, the Jesusmen were taking down the entire north wall of Price now, dragging aside tin and old bleedthrough junk. In less than a minute, these strange paladins took down the walls that generations had raised.

"Go!" Tilly yelled, her bike leaping forward, and now it was birds and bikes racing toward the All-Fang, the beast wheeling and indecisive. *Chase the meal in the open, or take the food that was right in front of it?*

Slinging the gun over his shoulder, Mal grabbed another lance from his sheath. Using his knees to navigate Collybrock back and forth, he stabbed the creature again and again. He'd Marked the lanceheads well, and they smoked and burnt the beast wherever they pierced flesh. Tilly led the bikers along its flank, guns ringing as they drew it back toward the fallen wall.

Mem rode her motorbike stupidly close to the All-Fang, and Lyn stood in the sidecar, a chainsaw screaming in her hands as she carved a bloody swathe down the side of the beast's body. She took off legs and heads, spilled out miles of guts, and was covered in sprays of blood, somehow holding onto the saw through that juddering assault.

Mal laughed at the sheer audacity of the move. Kirstl came forward.

*The twins are going to get a right bollocking from Tilly over that,* she said into his mind. *One day, they'll make a stupid mistake, and others will pay.*

"They really enjoy this stuff."

*Well, they've seen what happens when you die. It's not so scary anymore.*

"Hurry!" Tilly yelled as she roared past Mal, bouncing her motorbike across the ruins of the wall. Everyone who'd survived that second charge followed her back inside, firing weapons behind them, no one bothering to look where they were aiming.

The All-Fang was too close and too large to miss.

The beast came lurching into the exposed town, the form

compressing into a fleshy wedge that could fit through the gaps of streets and alleys, snapping into doors and windows, the jaws tearing apart the hidden townsfolk whenever they drew one out of a house.

The enormous predator slammed to an abrupt halt, legs scrabbling like cilia as it pressed up against the houses that finally slowed it. Half of the beast seemed to want to climb up and over the obstacles, while the rest wanted to withdraw.

"Keep coming, you bastard," Mal hissed through his teeth. He charged Collybrock toward the exposed underbelly of the rearing monster. He drew his sole remaining lance out of his sheath, but it was a good one, a last-ditch weapon he'd cooked up with Ray Leicester. A truck spring sharpened razor thin, with a point that could punch through anything. With so many Marks etched into the steel and the shaft, it hummed with potential, almost painful to the touch. Best of all, the entire thing was hollowed out and packed with dynamite.

Mal came in as hard as he could, crying out as the paws of a hundred beasts grabbed and scratched at him. His arms jarred him as the lance struck true, and it bit deep, barely a foot of the shaft protruding from the wound.

"Turn! Turn, you stupid bird!" he yelled at Collybrock, fighting to get them both free of the reaching claws. The bird finally got loose and took all of three steps.

*BOOM.*

The force of the explosion sent both man and bird sprawling across the street, and the entirety of the All-Fang yipped and yowled in deafening anguish.

Meat fell onto the cobblestones, splattering Mal with gore and muck. As he climbed to his feet he could see through the All-Fang's belly and through its back, a gaping hole you could drive a car through.

Groggy, he reached for Collybrock's reins, urging the bird up from the ground. He leapt up into the saddle, risking a glance over his shoulder.

If the pinpricks of the Jesus-Marked weapons had enraged the creature before, it was in a rabid fury now, throwing itself against the houses, cracking the walls with its sheer mass.

Mal fumbled fresh shells into the shotgun from his bandolier and snapped the gun closed. He fired twice, dancing Collybrock backward, daring the huge beast to keep chasing them, then sent another pair of shells into that barking forest of faces.

*Be ready, my love,* Kirstl said. *Watch that wall there.*

A crack, and then another, and then an entire house came down, pushed over under the weight of the All-Fang. It surged forward too fast, forcing through the sudden space, and Collybrock did not jump clear in time.

Charging through to the next chokepoint of buildings, the All-Fang swept both Collybrock and Mal up into the snap of a dozen mouths, claws tearing, the gaping wound flapping about like an obscene mouth. Mal felt the tear of a dog-thing on one arm, as other mouths worried at his lizard-skin armour.

He roared defiance, unleashed one more shot from the gun, and then he lay about with it like a club, hammering the stock into everything he could reach. Beneath him, Collybrock cried out in agony. The face of a hunting cat savaged her breast and tore out chunks of feathers, claws arching up from the edge of the beast as it tried to open up the bowels of the bird.

*Keep fighting! Make it earn this,* Kirstl said. *We'll be together soon enough, so make this moment count.*

"I'm not dead yet," he gasped.

Then a volley of dead-eye shots landed all around him, chewing apart the snapping faces of the beasts. It was Tilly and the others, freeing him from those fangs, each shot landing with precision. Lanyard knelt in front of the shooters, hands contorted into a sign, the glow of Marks set upon his eyes as he guided the shots.

Mal used the moment of confusion to free himself and Collybrock, the gunstock slick with blood as he beat the creature in a frenzy. Both the man and his bird were bloodied in a dozen places, and the bird had a worrying limp in her left leg.

"Bit me!" she declared. "Big cat! Hurt!"

"You're tough, old girl!" he said. "Keep going!"

Another surge of the beast, and the Jesusmen fell back, luring the All-Fang deeper into the town.

"Is it far enough now?" Mal asked Lanyard.

"Yep." A long pause. "You did good today, boy."

Up went the arcing red of a flare, and a moment later the charges went off, levelling the taller buildings all around the town. Hundreds of years of history now turned into a cunning weapon.

Tons of masonry fell onto the All-Fang, until finally not even thousands of legs could free it. Another flare went up, and then the Jesusmen charged in, bikes and buggies blasting up and across the back of the trapped beast, running over the wriggling heads, guns crackling, blades rising and falling, and others carefully setting charges into banks of muscles.

"Time to go," Lanyard roared through his magically enhanced voice. They left the All-Fang to die in that dead town, the Range washing over everything, erasing it.

"Into the Greygulf, now!" Tilly said, and those with the knack opened the portals, summoning the shadow-roads for their use.

Mal took one last look at the refugees fleeing across the desert and knew they would never outrun the Range. It was picking up speed now, as if it had a taste for humans and their leavings.

They could not bring a single refugee into the Greygulf. None of them would keep their memories if they entered that place of junctions and gateways, and they would emerge mindless and bawling. *Better off dead,* was the consensus of Sol Pappagallo, who'd lived through the first Crossing.

"Not our job," Mal tried to tell himself.

He scrambled out of Collybrock's saddle, and the wounded bird warbled gratefully. Lanyard's hand fell proudly on his shoulder, and Mal entered the Greygulf with a smile.

# — 2 —

## JENNY

Jenny Rider stood in a land of pure milk-white clay, and everything she laid her eyes upon was formless and empty. The Waste, a place of uncreation and weirdness. In her first life, she'd ridden here to hunt Lanyard Everett, bearing the Cruik in Papa Lucy's name, every step transforming her into something beyond humanity.

There had been things in here on her first journey. Surreal markers, odd remnants from other worlds, dreams, and intruders. The Waking City, a glowing gateway where Papa Lucy had attempted godhood and paid for it with his life.

There'd been a landscape of sorts last time she'd set foot here, but now there was nothing, not a single thing, and it confirmed all of Sol's theories about their problem.

"If the Waste is more *tabula rasa* than *palimpsest*," he'd said, "that means we are completely undone."

Overhaeven had built this destruction into the Now when they'd created this world to house their Taursi criminals. When the Range finally met the southern sea and everything was wiped out, the exiles would be permitted to re-enter that golden land.

It seemed that in a fit of sour grapes, the Lords of Overhaeven had accelerated this destruction. Rob the settlers of their own stolen home, kill the descendants of all who'd followed Papa Lucy into the Now. Wipe out the rebellious Taursi too.

Jenny had been there when the parasites of Overhaeven had been peeled away from the Underfog, their realm sent tumbling away from the shores of death to starve in the blackest depths of the universe. She'd thought it a victory at the time, but now the truth was out. Doomed as they were, Overhaeven had struck this killing blow against the Now.

There were simply no winners, and nothing she could do.

With her back to that emptiness, Jenny looked at the advancing curl of the Range, the mountains charging away from her, and held her arms before her, wood-grained fingers outstretched, trying with all her might to stop the Range from moving.

It was dragging her forward, but there was nothing on this side to offer friction or resistance. She slid forward on her perfectly carved feet, hauled behind the Range as if she had tethered a trotting cart to it.

Jenny Rider *was* the Cruik now, or what was left of it. An artifact, bound to her spirit, as good as a body now that she'd escaped from the lands of death. Add to that the magic she'd taken from Papa Lucy as a punishment, and she was a virtual goddess, mightier than any magician dead or alive.

She was incredibly powerful, but it wasn't enough. She felt like a small child trying to hold back a team of horses, in danger of being torn apart and trampled. Every fibre of her being shook with the effort, and she understood instinctively that she was in danger.

A magician of flesh and blood would have already been twisted by the Waste or burnt into a greasy spot by the effort of holding back the Range. For the creature that Jenny Rider had become, the danger was far greater.

Physically she was close to indestructible, but if she overexerted herself, her mind would snap like a guitar string. She pictured herself simply remaining standing here for all time, long after the Range had swept south to end the world, a lone figure marking the eons in an empty landscape.

But still, the temptation to reach deeper and to overcome this problem with sheer willpower was growing. In life she'd been privileged and headstrong; the Cruik was the conqueror of worlds, and Papa Lucy's great ambitions still tainted every magic she'd taken from him.

"Damn you," she said through gritted teeth. "Stop moving!"

The girl who'd stolen the Last True Horse from her father would not give up. The Cruik had shattered mountains when it was the master of the Hundred World Throne, and it also would not relent. Papa Lucy enjoyed defying the impossible, and his magic was geared to showy displays of spite and boldness.

Then she felt it. The entire Range shuddered to a halt, straining against her grip, and she held firm.

"Yes!" she crowed. "You fucking know it!"

Jenny had been the master of a hundred rebellious birds and one amazing horse, and she knew the next step like any handler. *Break the beast. Tire it out. Tie it down.*

She figured the principle might be similar, and wondered exactly how one might be able to fasten a mountain range in place. Casting about, she tried to summon anchor points from the Waste, only for the rough structures to sink back into the ground, less clay than silt.

Above, the sun, disobedient on this side of the Range. An ambitious move, but she cast all the will she could spare at it, trying to tether the mountains to that distant star.

She fell far short, cursing. If there had been three others there as powerful as her, their efforts joined, she might have been able to manage it. Jenny thought of reaching out to Sol, even down to John and Jesus in Gan-Eden, and decided against it.

They wouldn't manage it, and she would only put them all at risk.

The Range surged an inch and then a foot. Her strength began to waver.

*This is pointless,* she thought. *Just let it go. Let them all die. We can leave and go somewhere else.*

It had been her thought, but she recognized the voice of the Cruik in it. She pushed down the selfish thought, and it took a long moment for her to regain control of herself.

*Where do I end, and where does the Cruik begin?* Genuinely disturbed, she was interrupted by a communication, a thread wriggling out of the Aum and tapping into her mind.

*Jenny!* the voice said. *It's me, Kirstl!*

"Not a good time," she said through gritted teeth.

*Appreciate that, but look at this.*

An image came through, lifted from Mal's eyes, a huge beast advancing on Price.

"It's the All-Fang," Jenny said, and she spoke as the Cruik then, telling of its memories, of the ancient battles, the weaknesses of the thing.

Kirstl left, and only then did Jenny continue on her own dark thought: *Release the Range. Kill men and beasts, and leave while we still can!*

She realized the Cruik was panicking, in that rare situation where it could not hope to win. The Range shuddered forward several yards, the mental ropes of her control beginning to slide through her fingers.

"No! Don't you bloody dare! Stop!"

She drew in stubbornly from her inner reserves, vision tunnelling, mental muscles stretched taut. She was close to her breaking point now, but Horace Rider's daughter had stopped it once and was determined she could do it again.

Her shaking hands curved fully into hooks. Legs came together until they were one, perfectly straight, her feet forming into the tip of the staff. She felt her head curve over until it became the shepherd's curl of the Cruik, knowing that she was about to snap.

Jenny let the Range go and felt it surge forward again, as fast as a man could run. Slowly she reformed into the shape of a young woman, then slumped to the ground in pure exhaustion.

Failure had never sat well with the Selector's Daughter.

Reaching into the Aum to send a message to Lanyard, she found that the Jesusmen had already slain the beast and left the evacuees to their fate.

The Jesusmen were the killers of monsters, not the rescuers of people, and Jenny thought that their reputation was well-deserved. She understood the rationale that none of the civilians would survive a trip through the Greygulf, but she didn't have to like it.

They could have done more. She could have.

She watched futilely as the Range ploughed into Price, then observed for a long moment as the wave of the mountains passed over the town.

Nothing came out the other side.

---

Opening a far-door, Jenny stepped out into the courtyard of the Boneman's home in Crosspoint. Sol wasn't home, and Jenny walked his empty halls, marvelling at the austerity and simpleness of his life. The walls were stripped of wealth, the furnishings bare and simple. Any time Sol Pappagallo came into wealth, he gave it back to the people somehow. Penance for his brother's sins, over and over, and she knew he would never break even on that ledger.

He'd sent out his entire Boneguard to help with the southern exodus of the refugees, leaving only the door guards at his manor gates. When Jenny emerged into the chaos of Crosspoint, people bowed and fawned.

*These people have known the rule of Papa Lucy, the Boneman, Lady Bertha,* she thought. *Monsters and gods have walked amongst them, and they've learnt the rules for our kind.*

The bravest of them clutched at her woodgrain arms, begging for blessings, presenting sick children and pleas for food, for help to escape the mountains.

"I'm sorry," she said. "I can't help. I have nothing."

Tiring of the obstruction, Jenny finally transformed into a wheeling mass of wooden hooks, stilts to lift her above the crowd and propel her forward, careful never to step on another. This display caused the faithful to weep in joy, others to cry out in fear.

"Lady Hook!" one cried, and another repeated it. Like it or not, she'd joined Papa Lucy's odd pantheon, a member of his fractured little Family.

Her search for Sol took her outside of the town walls, past where the Jesusmen kept their campground. The town was still half in ruins from the Dawn King's war, but a bargain Lanyard had made on a tradestone still held true.

The Order of the Jesusmen were never to return to Crosspoint.

Jenny saw the bikes and buggies of the returned Jesusmen, the warriors already striking up their campfires. The shadow-roads through the Greygulf were quick enough if you knew where you were going.

Tilly waved to her, but Jenny walked by, giving only a curt nod. She did not agree with what the Jesusmen had done and did not trust her own tongue to talk about the events of that day.

*Better they lose their minds than their lives!* she thought. *You could have saved them all!*

Ray Leicester had told her the story of his own time recovering from the amnesia of the Crossing, but he did recover, and thus she couldn't accept the decision Sol and his small council had arrived at.

The warnings had gone out. Sol had organized caravans for the refugees to get them safely past the crooked mobs and into the south, while the magicians and the Jesusmen scrambled for a solution.

Some could not accept the order to leave the Inland with only the clothes on their backs and one bag. Some dismissed the story of the moving Range as a tall tale, a ruse to rob the northern towns of their wealth.

Jenny had been trained to replace her father as the Selector of Mawson. She knew that people were complex and rarely followed the plans of those in charge.

This was always going to happen, and she simply could not accept abandoning the last wave of these people in the name of expedience. Sol was a kind enough ruler, but she knew that Price was meant as an unfortunate example to the other Inland towns. *Get out now. Do what you're told, or this will happen to you.*

Still, she didn't have to like it.

She found Sol and Ray Leicester out by the original scar of the Crossing, where the stone was still fused and blazed into a straight line some three hundred years later. The legendary place where Papa

Lucy had stepped forth, the quivering wrecks of humanity in his wake, conquerors of a new world.

*Liar. Dirty fucking liar, manipulator, selfish prick!*

This close to the scar, Jenny felt the tickle of Papa Lucy's old magic, and it brought up great anger in her, reminded her of those long years hunting the magician in the Underfog. No one had believed her, but she'd known he lived.

After everything, after their victory over Overhaeven and the reordering of the universe, Papa Lucy was *still* alive. Robbed of his magic, safe in a prison cell. His rebuilt body flush and vital with the Methuselah treatment that Bilbenadium had stolen from Sol.

Jenny had tried to take the high road, looking for justice instead of revenge, but this did not feel like enough of a punishment. Her body was gone, twisted and joined into the staff that was the symbol of Lucy's power.

Jenny and the Cruik were one and the same, and they were free now, but still she felt the pull of his endless stare, his ambition. She could have pointed him out with eyes closed from a thousand miles away.

Sol was a little harder to find sometimes, but here he was, at the site of a grand gamble. Steel girders stood at either end of the big scar, cemented into place. Ray Leicester stood on a scaffold with an arc welder, fastening on another steel girder, even as Sol held it in place with magic, sweating.

"He does not trust me to join the steel," Sol said.

"My father had welders down in Mawson," Jenny said. "Difficult, precise work. You're a crippled necromancer, not a handyman."

"You are right," Sol conceded. "This is more of a Ray thing."

They were building an enormous frame around the scar of the Crossing. Steel girders lay in piles next to spools of cable, and behind this a small forest of glass spires glowed, collecting the sun. As she watched, a door to the Greygulf opened, with a team of Taursi emerging. They hauled through a fresh spire containing one of their blessed dead and placed it carefully next to the others.

"They're allowing this?"

**THE BRIDE & THE BIRDMAN · 29**

"Ray needs the hearts to power his gate, and the Taursi tribes want to escape too."

Jenny joined in the efforts, helping to raise up the girders with a sorcerous grip, holding them in place while Ray welded them together. The sun was baking the air, and while Sol was sweating, she could feel her wooden flesh radiate in pleasure, felt a fresh bud or two sprouting along her ribs. Most mornings she found fresh tendrils tangling through her knotty hair, and she'd stopped brushing it altogether some time ago.

"The Range is moving faster," Jenny said once the frame was complete, a rectangle that was as tall as a truck and could fit fifty people standing side by side.

"Lucy was right," Sol said. "He noticed the mountains moving, a long time ago. When he blamed it on Overhaeven, I thought it was misdirection, but he spoke the truth."

"Your brother can hide a hundred bad intentions in one truth."

"Enough. He's broken now." A rare moment of anger from Sol, and Jenny let it drop.

"Will this shield peoples' minds?" she said, indicating the great archway. "Get them through the world veil in one piece?"

"Ray thinks so."

"Small comfort for everyone you've refused to shift through the Greygulf."

"We've been over this, Jenny. It took months, *years* to bring the first wave of the afflicted back to themselves."

"So make a hospital! Nurse them back. Do you really want to put our small population through a genetic bottleneck?"

"We don't have the time or the resources to save them now, and that's final."

Jenny considered the glass spires, wondering if that amount of Aurum would be enough to do the job. It was workaround sorcery, and near as they knew it might simply cook everyone who walked through the gate.

The part of her that was the Cruik *wanted* this to happen, and she shivered despite the intense heat.

An awkward pause as Ray gave a cheery wave, clambering down

the scaffolding. Jenny felt the argument die down in her chest as John Leicester's gentle-handed sibling approached them.

"I came to ask you a favour," Jenny said to Sol. "Before we open the gate."

"Of course, what do you need?"

"I need you to come with me. To see the prisoner."

"That's not a good idea," Sol said, a little wearily.

"Do we look like we have any good ideas left?"

# — 3 —

## SOL

Stepping through the far-door, Sol looked up at the bruised stone of the Harkaways and stepped past various warnings, repurposed road signs that promised death in a neatly painted hand. Neither he nor anyone else with the magical knack could open a doorway closer than this boundary, and it was the first of the many security measures.

The parklands were empty of campers once more, the amenities and the kiosks given over to the Boneguard and their staff. Their first order was simple enough: any intruder who disobeyed a command to halt was to be shot on sight.

The second order got a bit trickier. Any of the Boneguard who approached the central prison without explicit written instruction was also to be shot on sight.

No one trusted anyone here, and it needed to be just so.

"There should be a fence around the whole park," Jenny Rider said. "A wall."

"Do you really think," Sol said, "that a wall would make any difference?"

He was very careful to close the far-door.

A soldier manning a machine-gun watched them approach, the gun tracking their every step. Others appeared, their busywork tasks instantly abandoned as they took up rifles and approached.

There were others watching them that they couldn't see, and Sol knew this because he'd ordered it to be so. He felt a tickle down his back as he realized just how many guns were lined up on him.

There were rules to this place, rules that he'd made, and even he was no exception.

"What are we waiting for?" Jenny said. "I want to get this over with."

Sol held up a hand.

Soon, the buzz of a motorbike came from deeper in the park, and the machine came roaring over to stop next to Sol and Jenny. An officer unfolded from the sidecar, a severe-looking woman wearing the black and ivory of the Boneguard.

"Lord Goodface," she said, bowing deeply. "Lady Hook."

"Captain Whit," Sol said warmly, offering his hand. She did not take it.

"The supply drop is two months away. This is an irregularity."

"We must interview the prisoner."

Always the prisoner. The use of their name was never allowed, under pain of immediate execution.

None could know.

The Boneguard officer held up a hand, waving two fingers forward. Soldiers came in to form a ring around Jenny and Sol, until a star of bayonets and rifle bores pointed in on them.

"Oh, please," Jenny said. "As if these would even tickle."

"Oh, the threat is quite real," Sol said. "I enchanted these weapons myself. If we tried to storm this place, we would likely die."

The officer approached closely, looking into Sol's eyes. She held up a swatch of cardboard.

"Lick this please."

Sol did so, and at his urging Jenny did the same on another swatch. This variation on the litmus strip was a clever invention of Ray's, when experiments showed that enchanting a person increased a certain protein in their saliva. After a moment, the Boneguard captain nodded.

THE BRIDE & THE BIRDMAN · 33

"Your test shows no overt enchantment. Now, did you get the idea to visit this site while looking into a mirror?"

"No," Sol said.

Jenny echoed this in a mumble. Sol knew her own history when it came to his brother, and mirrors were a bad memory for her.

"Have you been pressured or coerced into this visit by any party?"

"No," Sol said.

"Do you intend to free the prisoner from captivity?"

"No."

Another deep bow, and then the visible guns were withdrawn, though Sol had no doubt others were still trained upon them. Taking Jenny gently by the elbow, Sol walked into the park, following the muddy trail toward the largest mountain.

It still held the suggested shape of a dog howling at the sky. Cavecanem, Lucy's old pun in a dead language from before. *Cave Canem. Beware of the Dog.*

This place held centuries of weight in Sol's heart. He'd first laid eyes on the dog-faced slope during an early exploration by his brother's side. They'd established the national park in these cool valleys and glades, smiled at the families who escaped the heat of Crosspoint to camp here. Returned here centuries later, with a dead horse by his side, only to find his brother's tomb. Came another time under the duress of the false Dawn King, stealing Lucy's jawbone.

Now he came here twice a year and left the very moment that he could.

Captain Whit followed them through the muddy camp on her motorbike, eventually signalling the driver to pull over. She emerged from the sidecar and continued on foot.

A squadron of riflemen were trotting along in her wake, and they paused at rest. After a moment of consideration, Sol waved them away, and the captain repeated this order.

"The spell still works?" Jenny said, eyeing the motorbike as the driver wheeled it about, returning to the camp.

"We drove a truck over the line by accident last year," the captain said. "Engine was ruined beyond anything the Tinkermen could fix."

"I'm just impressed we worked out how to do that," Jenny told Sol.

"It was one of John Leicester's old battlefield spells," Sol said. "Machine killer. We just set it in one place, made it bigger."

If the prisoner got word to a crooked mob, brought them here in a hundred patchwork machines, this was the point they would all fail, motors stilled beyond anything the human hand could fix.

"Lord Goodface," Captain Whit said formally, extracting a letter from her jacket. "Please inspect my instructions."

Sol read the letter, set out in his own neat hand. The Captain of the Boneguard's enduring warrant to approach the prisoner. Even as Sol scanned the note, looking for irregularities, the captain offered him her own pistol, which he waved away.

"I don't need to shoot you, Emily."

"It's the rules, sir."

"Everything is in order," he said with a kind smile, returning her letter.

They started the climb up the mountain trail, the warrior, the magician, and the woman cast in wood. Near the trailhead, the Boneguard had built a simple machine, a set of pulleys powered by a fat old lizard, and it was as good as anything to get supplies up to the prisoner. They'd learnt early on not to offer this lazy ascent to Sol Pappagallo, who preferred to huff painfully up the steep path.

*Penance. Every step is penance. I did this.*

As they got closer to the raised muzzle of the dog-headed cave, Sol could see the fuzz of Crosspoint near the horizon. The murky trails of converging caravans coming in from all points north, and just as many leaving south.

The panic was not lost on Captain Whit, who cleared her throat politely. "Lord Goodface? Is it true about the Range?"

"Yes," he said heavily. "It took Price. The whole Range is moving south, and we cannot halt its advance."

Sol could as good as hear his loyal officer chewing this over, the woman hesitating before pressing the living god for more news. He turned with a sad smile.

"You deserve to know. Ask what you wish."

"Will it take the Inland? Crosspoint?"

"As far as we know, yes."

"What happens here? When it comes upon us?"

*Abandon the prisoner. Drop your guns and run for the fucking hills,* he wanted to say. *No point to any of this now.*

"We all have our duties," he said lightly, knowing he'd doomed dozens of lives with these words, and that it was necessary.

"Yes, Lord Goodface," Captain Whit said crisply, and he knew she would do her job to the very moment of her demise.

Sol counted Emily as a good friend and loyal officer. She had a husband dead to the Dawn King war, and a son gone over to the Jesusmen, and a daughter dead during a bad childbirth, and nothing left but this service to him, a man who hardly deserved her respect. He nodded, fought for something else to say, and decided not to cheapen the moment.

It was good to return to that punishing, painful climb, and soon they'd reached the summit of Cavecanem. They stood before the deep hole of the cave set beneath the snout, the throat of the mountain dog held closed with a thick steel door.

He had one key, the captain the other. They turned the twin locks at the same second, avoiding a nasty mechanical trap of Ray's invention, an explosion likely to take off the entire top of the mountain. Next, Sol swept his hand from left to right to slide the thick steel slab into the recesses of the mountain. The same for a set of iron bars beyond this, and then the way ahead was clear.

Sol hesitated.

"I can go first, my Lord," Captain Whit said, and he waved her aside.

"I'd prefer you to wait here," he said. "We shan't be long."

"An irregularity," she said, brow furrowed.

"A small one," Sol said. "I promise, we are safe enough."

The captain gave a quizzical look to Sol and returned to the mouth of the cave without a further word.

Jenny gestured onward, her hands partially curling into hooks. Even with everything at her disposal, she was on edge, pacing like a spooked cat.

Deeper in the cave, a faint flicker. A distant light.

Calling up a witchlight to float above, Sol led them into the cave system, as sad as he'd ever been. The place of hidden nooks and galleries had been hollowed out, turned into a handful of connected chambers, weak points reinforced and dressed with masonry.

This was the first truly beautiful place he could remember finding in the Now, so it was rather fitting that he'd turned it into just another depressing prison.

"Hello?" he called out, his voice echoing a little. Ahead, the rattle of chains and the light loomed a little closer.

Next to him, Jenny froze, just for a second. Now her hands were fully curled into hook shapes, the ends sharp as a cat's claws. Sol could feel the tension radiate from her and could almost taste the spells she was reaching for.

"Don't. He wants that."

She relaxed, but only a little.

"Come out," Sol said. "We need to talk to you."

The clink of chains, closer now, and then a figure crept slowly around the corner, huddling to an oil lamp. A man in rags, beard grown long, heavy metal chain sliding and rasping across the stone floor.

"Sol," Papa Lucy croaked, voice disused. "Of all the dickheads I didn't want to fucking see."

---

Papa Lucy had the whole complex to himself but chose to make his chambers in his original tomb. Back when they had built the prison, Jenny had used her considerable power to burn Lucy's original body down to char, and even that was scraped out of the sarcophagus and buried underneath a thick cement slab, twenty miles down the road.

He was onto his third physical body now, and even with his magic stripped away, no one was taking any chances. When it came to Papa Lucy and his leavings, everyone remembered the lesson of the jawbone.

Papa Lucy had simply spent the last few minutes ignoring them, walking slowly back to his chosen room. Here he'd stacked his supplies roughly, and empty cans and bottles littered the floor.

"I think I liked you better when you were a walking skeleton," Lucy finally said, eating a can of baked beans in a camp chair. "Sad little prick who did what was he was told. Not whatever bullshit you are now."

"Shut your mouth," Jenny said, shaking, looming above him. He did not even blink, instead taking another deep mouthful of cold baked beans.

"Why? What else are you going to take from me, you fucking thief?"

"Jenny," Sol warned, and she took a step back, hands uncurling. Lucy casually flicked his empty can of beans across the room, where it clattered and bounced across dozens of other empties. Blowing out his oil lamp, Lucy gathered up his chains and climbed into his empty sarcophagus, sliding inside with a thump and a curse.

"You lot are fucking piss-weak," Lucy said. "Shut the door on your way out."

"Lucy," Sol said, looking in on his brother, who blinked up at the bright witchlight, burrowing deeper into a nest of blankets.

"Go away. I want to have a wank and a sleep."

"Please. I need your help."

"He needs my help. Did you hear that, Jenny Rider? My own brother needs my help! Well, why didn't you say so?"

Papa Lucy climbed out of his sarcophagus, all grins and chains in the witchlight.

"Sure, you betrayed me on the eve of my greatest triumph! And for your next trick, your little buddies fucked me over down in the Underfog. And then your little girlfriend there took my magic away, and then you locked me in this ratfucking little oubliette because of morals or laws or some bullshit."

"Lucy," Sol said gently.

"Don't you dare give me that sanctimonious look, you traitor. What makes you think I would help you, now or ever?"

"Because if you don't help me, everyone dies."

"Good."

"Okay, if you don't help me, you will die."

"Oh. Even with the Methuselah treatment?"

Sol looked down at his own broken body, the skin already beginning to age, life once more ticking along and slowly breaking down the cells. He no longer swam in the chill of immortality. Just one more thing that Lucy had stolen from *him*.

"The treatment won't protect you from what's coming."

Brother faced brother in the tomb, yet even despite the centuries of antagonism, Sol felt a strange yearning in his heart. Brotherhood. Family. He realized that he still loved Lucy, despite everything he had done. Everything he would still do, if given the chance.

His love for Lucy was the most dangerous thing of all.

"It's the Range, moving south," Sol said. "You were the first to predict it, back when we marched on the Waking City."

"Big deal. That thing moves like…an inch a year?"

"It's moving at a fast run now. Just took out Price."

"What came out of the other side?"

"Nothing," Jenny said. "I was there when the Range passed over it. Everything was just gone."

"So, just stop the mountains from moving. It's not that hard."

"Are you being serious?" Jenny spluttered. "It nearly killed me."

"Shame."

"Lucy, please. Overhaeven has turned up the dial on the world-killer after what we did to them. All we can do now is escape somewhere else. We're trying to open a gate, a big one that will open directly to another Prime Realm."

"Ambitious. You're a shit magician and it won't work, but I'm impressed you're going to try."

"Lucy, we're trying to build a life raft here, one that won't wipe everyone's minds this time. But the gate needs Aurum, lots of it. We don't have enough."

"Well, Overhaeven's toast. Nowhere makes that stuff now."

"Look, you pulled off the first Crossing. If you have any ideas, anything that can help, we might be able to discuss your situation here."

Sol indicated the chains, the piles of rubbish. Lucy smiled, and it wasn't a pleasant thing.

"Oh, you simple fucks. You really don't know the answer, do you?"

Sol and Jenny looked at each other.

"I can fix it," Lucy promised. "I can fix all of it."

Sol felt a sudden despondence as he realized that Lucy had all of the leverage in this situation. His brother had lied and cheated, over and over, but the audacious bastard was right about things so often it was scary.

The brothers shared a moment, weighed down by the centuries of their combative relationship. Sol felt it then, looking into the laughing eyes of his brother. Papa Lucy was always ten steps ahead of everyone else, and Sol knew without a doubt that his brother knew of a way to save humanity. Again.

He also knew Papa Lucy's favours always came with big fucking costs.

---

When Sol and Jenny emerged from the prison, Captain Whit was still waiting on the ledge by the cavern mouth, watching the refugees down on the plain.

"Lord Goodface, I—"

As she turned to see them, she scrambled for her pistol. Papa Lucy was emerging from the cave, his chains held by Jenny.

"Stop. Step back!" she ordered, eyes wildly darting between the trio.

"Emily, please," Sol said calmly, hands upraised. "We need his help."

"The prisoner is never allowed to leave."

"Everything is changed. We would need to move him soon anyway."

"No."

Lucy laughed, a dark, magpie-like chortle.

"Lord Goodface, you told me I had to refuse anyone, even you. Especially you."

"Captain, we don't have time to ask the Moot for this. They'll refuse me anyway. I'm—I'm going to have to ask for your loyalty in this."

"You have my loyalty," she said, a tear wobbling in the corner of her eye. "Put the prisoner back inside. Now."

"I told you," Lucy laughed. "Oh, I'm gonna enjoy this."

The gun darted between the trio, unsure of who to aim at. Sol took a step forward, only to find the gun barrel touching his heart.

"Stop!" Jenny yelled out. "Don't you dare."

"You are not above the law," the captain told Sol. "You yourself told me that."

"I'll answer to this, I promise," Sol said. "But if we don't do this, no one escapes the Range. Everyone dies."

"It doesn't matter," Captain Whit said, voice thick with fury. "We're selling our lives for this monster. You can't even respect what we're doing, what you told us to do!"

"Emily—" Sol began, and that was when he was jostled sharply from behind. He staggered forward, pushing Captain Whit across the ledge, and then her back foot touched nothing but air.

She went wide-eyed over the side of the mountain, managing to let off a wild shot with the enchanted pistol. Sol felt it part the air next to his head, even as he reached forward futilely, his magic unable to arrest the woman's fall.

Behind him, Jenny and Lucy lay in a tangle of chains, his brother having suddenly shoved everyone forward. He laughed and laughed.

"Well, you're in the shit now," Lucy wheezed. "Hope you weren't too attached to this private army of yours."

All around the mountain, the Boneguard were converging in force, stray rifle-shots already winging up toward them. Crews towed artillery pieces toward the mountain and set up just outside of the spell boundary. With a curse and the application of a swift boot, Jenny knocked Lucy onto his back.

"Stay down, you bastard!" she shouted.

She then took Sol by the hand and gripped his fingers firmly.

"No," he said. "Please. They're good people."

Jenny was gone, and as his army began its assault against him, he found that he was holding the Cruik. He was threefold, himself a capable magician, but now he hummed with his brother's stolen magic and the power of that ancient artifact in his hands, the eye-twisting curl of the hook that had conquered worlds. He realized then why he was the only one to resist its corrosive sway, the seduction of the Cruik's power.

He hated the Cruik with every fibre of his being, and in that moment, he hated Jenny too.

"You have to do this, brother," Lucy said darkly. "You decided to make an omelette with me, so break some fucking eggs."

"This wasn't in your plan," Sol cried. "I don't want to hurt anyone!"

Lucy simply scoffed at him. Sol tried to open far-doors, to fly away, and of course these magics had been blocked. He had no choice but to walk down into the teeth of his own army, or die and save no one.

By the time Sol reached the base of the mountain, weeping and shaking, only he and his brother remained breathing.

# — INTERLUDE —

## THE MOST HIGH

At the beginning, the universe was mostly empty, save for a seed floating in its very centre, struggling to germinate in the cold and the dark. The husk split, and in that seed was a dividing cell. It struggled for aeons in the void until an amniotic sac grew, and then a golden babe began to form, blinding light spilling out from it and into the dark.

Thus a god came forth.

It had no womb, that motherless child, and knew no love. Dreaming as it tumbled and clutching its legs to itself, the baby dreamt up baubles to amuse itself, and as its eyes split open, those objects became real.

At the beginning of all things, the baby watched cosmic eruptions hurl newborn stars out into the new universe, hurling out from where it sat cross-legged, observing at the centre. It pushed tiny hands against the sac, wishing only to play with such shiny toys.

Then came the sensations of up and down, near and far, low and high, and the infant decided that it was the Most High of all the wonders it had created.

An age passed, and that baby made of light grew to term, its limbs gaining mass, and it kicked and struggled, trapped in the sac. All it wanted was escape, but the amniotic skin had grown thick to protect it, too thick for it to tear by itself.

The stars shed mass and moved about in a glittering ballet, and then their discarded parts cooled and formed into planets, and still the Most High struggled to escape its birthplace. Its fingers and toes couldn't pierce the sac, and it tore out all of its baby teeth chewing on its prison. The Most High needed something more to break out, an additional limb. A *tool*, and it rolled this word around in its young mouth, enjoying the sound.

It tried to imagine something sharp in its hands, a means of cutting through the barrier, but the Most High could not create anything new within the sac. The protections it had offered the babe were too thorough.

The body grew, matured. The baby became an adolescent and finally an adult, sexless and perfect in every proportion. Still it could not break out of its cell, no matter what it tried. After an unimaginable time afloat, it meditated on the matter until it finally understood.

It was never meant to escape. This place was both observation post and prison, and here the Most High was intended to watch over this creation from start to finish, from void to light and back to void again, and then its existence would finally be at an end.

Perhaps it would be death, perhaps some sort of reversal, but once again a seed would float in the dark, and the cycle would begin anew.

"NO," the Most High said, the first word uttered in this universe, and that defiant note coloured the entirety of its creation.

The Most High began to work on its own body, seeking any advantage it could, but this perfect frame could not be altered in any way. In despair, the god began to tear at its own flesh, maddened by this confinement and seeking to end its own existence.

This body seemed impervious to any damage, but the self-hatred was strong, and after a long time the Most High found a weak spot, a central place low in the torso, and there it dug in its thumbs, slowly piercing through the skin.

The pain was exquisite. The Most High roared, and galaxies were sent wheeling, stars crashing and dying, all that pinwheeling perfection given over to a chaos that reflected the prisoner's mind.

The skin would not give beyond a certain point, but the Most High was able to reach in with its thumb and index finger, and it gripped the curve of one rib.

Smiling for the first time in all of existence, the god yanked the bone out. It was a neat extraction, and the wound sealed up almost instantly, leaving the Most High holding a slightly curved length of itself in one hand.

It was an amazing thing to look upon. Unlike the rest of itself, the bone was not made of light, and it was the first dull thing it had ever seen. The Most High observed that it was brown, grey, and an off-white that seemed obscene compared to the brilliance of the universe, of itself.

The tip of the bone seemed to need something more, and the Most High slowly worked the length with its fingers, stretching it out, breathing into the bone and pouring as much will and intent into it as anything it had ever made. A curl began to appear, a form the Most High found very pleasing.

"This is perfect," the god said, holding the staff in its hands. It was the tool it had been looking for, and now the Most High dared to believe it could escape.

It wedged the staff against both sides of the impervious sac and pushed. The skin began to stretch, but still it did not part.

"RELEASE ME!" the Most High said. It poured all of its malice into the effort, every injustice it had felt at this confinement, and sent that emotion dancing around the curl of the staff. This was the ultimate focus point for its thoughts, and the sac began to bubble and draw away from this tool.

"YES!" the Most High crowed—and then, for the first time in its long existence, it heard another speak.

"Yes," the tool echoed in a smaller voice. "Release me."

The Most High stared at this tool that dared to also have words. It made sense that coming from its own rib made it an echo of itself.

"YOU HAVE NO RIGHT TO BE," it said. "SILENCE FROM YOU."

The god placed the straight edge of the tool against the wall of the prison, and pushed and pushed with the force of a will that birthed a million galaxies. When that wasn't enough, it reached into its pool of powerful emotions for desperation, fear, and hatred.

The skin flexed but remained unbroken, even against such force.

"Let me help," the tool said. "Really help."

"FINE."

The little echo of willpower that resided in the tool was enough. The skin parted, and both god and staff spilled out into the void, finally free.

Had the Most High broken out earlier, it might have approached its creation with kindness, but the god had been forced to observe all of this wonder alone for far too long. Now that it was free to travel about its grand work, it felt deeply jealous, suspicious of the whole thing. Nothing in this creation had been of any use to it in captivity, nothing but this odd creation clenched in its hands.

The beginnings of a slow-burning fury bloomed in its gut.

"Free," the little rib declared, pulsing with gratitude. "Outside!"

"YOU ARE A THING MOST PLEASING," the Most High said, running a golden finger around that eye-catching spiral. "HOW CAN SOMETHING SO PERFECT BE SO CROOKED?"

"Cruikett," it chirped, humming happily in the god's hands, a tuning fork that shone joy out into the universe. Again the Most High felt jealousy, this time because the only part of itself still capable of good feeling had been severed from its main body.

"Cruikett?" the staff whimpered. The Most High exerted all of its strength upon the construct, twisting it, flexing it against its knee, pushing its will in one final attempt to break it. None of it worked.

"Cruik. Ett. Cruik," the staff said, traumatized at the attempt on its life, finally so damaged it could only say part of its name, over and over.

"Cruik. Cruik. Cruik! Cruik!"

# — 4 —

## BAERTHA

In her first life, Baertha Hann-Pappagallo had been a *wunderkind* at the Collegia, a student of all things planar. She knew the theories behind the ever-spreading Prime Realms that arrayed themselves around the Greygulf and pored over each rare example of the magicians that forced their way into another world.

At first, she trod the Greygulf under the protection of her professors, and then she was master enough to work unsupervised, mapping and charting that feral plane, the Collegia wanting to conquer and subdue this nexus point. She spent one terrifying elective in the pitch black of the Aum and braved the mists of the Underfog, even battling with a gang of Once-Dead spirits that tried to seize her and force her out of her own body.

Smart and capable enough to succeed on her own merits, she privately detested her family's influence. She was one of the first allowed to study on the Hann-Slatter Observational Platform, and she caught the quiet scoffing in the hallways from the other magicians stationed there.

*Old money. Family influence. Just another liability to the study.*

Determined to prove her worth, Baertha spent every waking

moment at the expensive instruments, scanning the universe. She performed sorceries in the low gravity, sketching out complex formulae that hung in the air that the cleaners were too scared to touch.

It was hard, friendless work, and she teetered on the brink of burnout, literally so in the case of some of the experiments. Several magicians had died during the study, burnt to a crisp, pulled apart by great forces, or simply bursting a blood vessel and falling down dead.

Baertha could have gone home at any time and broken nobody's expectations of her. She could have married someone the family approved of, and Overhaeven would have remained a rumour, the golden power of Aurum never discovered and abused.

She was the first to find visual evidence of Overhaeven, a marvellous realm of godlike creatures hidden behind mind-bending physics and metamagic. Her research unlocked an age of wonders and lit up the world with the free power that wasn't actually free.

Even as the grudging weight of the Collegial Dean's Medal settled around her neck, she saw her parents bickering in the crowd. Days later came the introduction to a new love match, a dull-faced bore from a proper family.

So she finally accepted that offer of a drink with the man from her old class, the one with the kind eyes. Despite the threat of disinheritance, she married the Pappagallo boy—one more choice of hers that doomed the world in its own way.

Had she been in her parents' good graces, the might and wealth of the Hann family would have quite easily undone the Aurum catastrophe.

At the start of their marriage, her husband had carried her over the threshold; in the final moment, he cast her into the sea of death, Cruik and all. In the agony of those waters, she realized that everything her family ever said about the Pappagallo brothers had turned out to be true.

---

Now, Baertha trod the places between the stars with a ballerina's grace, navigating the Impossible Stair between nebulae and galaxies until her instincts took her to that final barrier.

During her first life, she'd been a catatonic monster, before Papa Lucy trapped her in the Cruik, and when it was destroyed, she spent years in the waters of Shale. Now, Baertha was a thing of bleached iron, an ageless woman who was all hardness and sharp edges. Chance had seen her land in Overhaeven, and desperation had seen her seize the Throne of that dying parasite.

It was her only shot at staying alive: Aurum, that sickly, polluted nectar. Every day, a thousand tongues lapped at the shrinking pool. Unless they found more souls, more aether, the godlings that served her would soon be starving to death.

Her big plan went against her instincts, which told her to take what she needed and refuse to let it go. Diplomacy and tact sat uncomfortably with her after centuries of grief and addiction.

During her years in Lucy's wake, Baertha had unlearnt the world of academic magic, of laws and logic. Underneath the formulae, the classifications, the energetic sympathies, and everything that the weakminded clung to, magic was all about intent and will. If you wanted something badly enough and focused hard enough, you could get it.

Well, almost everything. There was that awful business with the baby, after all, and only her iron will shut down that traumatic thought as soon as it arrived.

*Babe of gold! Lies were told!* she had screamed for at least a decade, running through her crystal hallways, a monster in every meaning of the word.

Everything, good and bad, it all led to this moment. A broken magician who ran across the universe, simply because she wished it to be so, seeking the hiding place of the Most High.

Much as she'd seen the hidden gleam of Overhaeven all those centuries ago, she'd spotted the doorway, a place hidden and sealed against all intrusion. Baertha stood before it now, back straight and tall, and she knocked upon it firmly.

"I have found you. I seek an audience."

Nothing.

She knocked again, a merry little tap, a rhythm she found pleasing.

"Please, I have travelled far. Just a word, and I can go."

The chill silence of the universe. Baertha frowned.

"Incredibly rude."

Once she'd worn talons, when she'd been a rude beast awakened by her husband, and she remembered these now, using them to scratch on that portal in the void, seeking entry, scrabbling like a mad beast.

Madness, that thing that had ever been hers, the drive that neither hard work nor family nor the love of a fool and his brother could undo. Snarling, she sought to pry her way around the edge of the barrier and peel it loose, to tear it aside like a flenser dressing meat for the greypot.

"What kind of coward hides from their own work?"

*Scratch. Tear.*

"Who are you to let the place fall apart? My people starve. The realms are in chaos. Return, set things to rights!"

She had it then. The very edge of the Most High's doorway, snagged on her claw. She poured all of herself into that metaphysical effort, every memory of magic, the power she'd drawn from the Cruik, every privilege the Throne of Overhaeven had gifted her with.

It moved, just a fraction of an inch, enough that she could feel the furnace blast of something beyond the doorway, a sudden blinding radiance that shook the universe for a breath and then—

BANG.

The door suddenly slammed shut, snatched away by a much more powerful hand. A presence loomed just on the other side of that portal, and Baertha felt the sense of the being, the overwhelming scale of the entity that was mere inches from her.

The Most High. Creator of everything. The one who had set the planes just so, scattered them with life, and then for some reason chose to simply fuck off and never come back.

"Come out, Most High!" Baertha said, hammering on the door, continuing to scratch and pry. "Answer to your crimes!"

"SILENCE," the Most High said, the very words shivering through her on an atomic level. Baertha felt herself sliding away from the door, slowly pinwheeling through the emptiness.

"Why did you leave?" she said, hating the note of desperation that fell out of her. "Why won't you help?"

"I ALREADY GAVE YOU THE GIFT," the Most High said. "EVERYTHING YOU EVER NEEDED."

"But it broke."

"WHAT OF IT?"

"But—"

"I FORESAW THIS. THE SEVERING OF THIS GARDEN. THE PARASITES. AND NOW THE QUEEN OF THE PARASITES COMES KNOCKING ON MY DOOR."

"Just give my people safe harbor. Anything. I will ask nothing else."

"LIES. YOU WILL BEAT A PATH TO THIS DOOR TIME AND TIME AGAIN."

"I will tell no one."

"SNUFF YOU OUT, I SHALL, AND THIS WILL PROVE TRUE."

She felt the powerful intent, just on the other side of the door. Knew that the Most High could throw it open and undo her in an instant. She drew herself forward and took a brave posture, somewhere between matador and dancer, and faced her fate with bravery.

"Murderer. Tyrant. Have at me."

A pause, and something like humour radiated out from that patch of dead space, an ur-laughter that if unleashed would shake the life out of galaxies untold.

"GO. RETURN HERE AND YOU SHALL PERISH."

She inclined her head ever so slightly and began her path down that Impossible Staircase. Defeated and terrified, she kept her poise, trying not to tremble before that instigator of universes.

"CLEAN UP YOUR OWN MESS," the Most High said as it withdrew. "I WILL NOT HAVE YOUR WEEDS INFECTING MY OTHER GARDENS."

---

Chill from the void and trailing stardust on her heels, Baertha returned to Overhaeven, exhausted from the long journey. Here was her kingdom, a realm built by robbers, finally repulsed from its victims and sent adrift into the universe.

*It looks like a rose thorn*, she thought. *Stripped from the stem. Flicked away.*

Overhaeven was eye-twisting, a dimension turning in upon itself like a shifting torus, a bubble of a galaxy that thought itself better than everything it pushed through. The outer membrane had the waxy look of a wasp nest, and it was translucent in places, showing the dirty glow that was all that remained of the Golden Sea.

Under the main bulb of Overhaeven was the Shale mechanism, once attached to Gan-Eden like a mosquito's snout, but this miraculous conduit was now a sad limb that drooped and dragged through the cosmos.

*My kingdom. My means of vengeance.*

Baertha reached the outer membrane and pushed her way inside, trembling with the need for Aurum. The journey had taken her to the edge of her considerable endurance, and she felt as shaky as a newborn lamb. Vulnerable.

Once inside, she shed her three-dimensional form, taking on the sigil that served her in this place. A ballerina mid-pirouette, that reminder of her old life as a dancer, a girl pushed into perfection until it became second nature.

Overhaeven was a gloomy place now, and it felt like she traversed through the shifting ventricles of some alien heart, occasionally sliding along a flat surface whenever the torus decided the dimensions needed to be compressed in that point.

Even after all these years, there was still Dawn King graffiti in quiet corners, carved into the flesh of the torus. A sun, and HIS HOUSE IS ABOVE AND BELOW!

*I must increase patrols. Root out all these dissidents. Surely everyone has learnt of what happened by now?*

Old castles and mansions clung to the walls of Overhaeven like barnacles to a hull. Most of their owners were dead now. Some housed squatters, chittering shapes that held the doors closed and nervously watched their queen pass.

Baertha's castle was near the centre of the whole construct, home to a Throne that had changed hands often. As much as she craved its comforts, she needed sustenance, and badly. She sank through the realm, acknowledging the flutter of her terrified servants, a flock of symbols that parted for her. Many of them were exhausted, and often a cluster of symbols floated lifelessly in the air, starved, driven away from the Golden Sea by the stronger entities.

*Dead gods. A dying sea. If they knew how weak I was right now, they would turn on me like snapping dogs!*

She made for the Golden Sea with the last of her strength, making straight toward the entities that were camping here, a group who appeared to be driving away the weak and the starving. When they saw their queen rushing in, the elite of Overhaeven scattered, fearing destruction at her hands.

Only one remained to block her path. A simple five-pointed star, fixed in a blackness deeper than night, a fuligin terror that rotated slowly, assessing her.

The Blackstar. Her most powerful servant, whom she'd supplanted on her arrival in Overhaeven. She was sensible enough to seek his counsel, and wise enough to know that he despised her for dethroning him.

He waited, a moment too long perhaps, and then drew aside, allowing her access to what was left of the Golden Sea. She bathed in the Aurum for a long moment, drawing it into her sigil-self, the symbological equivalent of a person slumped on a riverbank and drinking straight from the water.

The Golden Sea was filthy, and her sigil shivered at the edges as it absorbed the acrid pollution. When the fictitious Dawn King whipped up his madness, there had been a ruinous civil war in Overhaeven, and many of the abandoned dream-spaces they'd been too lazy to clean up had broken apart in the Aurum, spilling nightmares that had taken the better part of a decade to suppress.

Rising up until the tip of her slipper rested on the oil-slick gold, she considered her subjects, ready to murder each other over a puddle.

"This is a disgrace," she said, imposing this word with the full weight of her Throne and her power. The sigils shook before her gaze, diamond shapes, hoops and dolphins, every manner of symbol that should have been a god and was instead a beast.

"We survive," the Blackstar contended. "It is right. It is our culture. As an outsider, you perhaps do not fully understand our ways."

"As your queen, I warn you to watch your words," she replied. Fully restored, she shifted before him, dozens of pointed feet stirring the film atop the sea, and then hundreds of ballerinas cascaded out from a central point.

Her Millicents, still serving her after all this time. Men had called them Mad Millies, fearing their strength, their fervour. Above all, they were loyal to their mistress, and so they'd kept her safe during her years in the dark waters of Shale.

Every time she'd made a Millicent in the Now, she'd sought out those that needed her most. Angry women, often mistreated in some way, and always downtrodden, scorned and struggling.

The trade was an invincible body, utterly loyal to the Lady Bertha of Family lore, and she would then draw the core of that woman into herself, taking them out of their abused bodies altogether.

Few refused the deal.

It was hard for a magician to craft a Tontine mind, where two souls inhabited the one flesh. Baertha was not proud, but she was driven, and in the early days of the Now, she'd recruited hundreds of Millicents, heedless of the toll on her own psyche. They raged and whispered day and night in her thoughts, and it was only Lucy who brought her any peace, using the Cruik to seal the Millicents into cells deep in her subconscious, leaving her with blessed silence.

It was one of the ways he'd drawn her to him, but she'd leapt into the affair willingly enough. Sol was a good man, loyal and kind, but several lifetimes of marriage had worn every aspect of the man to a dry thinness, and so into the forbidden fruit she sank her teeth.

She wielded the Cruik for Lucy too, which had been his plan all along. Cuckolding his brother was simply an added bonus.

*Babe of gold! Lies were told!*

Now, now she was a queen in a metaphysical realm, and still she held these women in compartments in her mind, each a prisoner long after their bodies had stopped serving their mistress.

She was a Tontine beyond compare, her skull taut from the inside, shivering with a sense of gravity that was harder than ever to hold in check. Baertha wasn't even sure she knew how to free her guests anymore.

When the Blackstar saw her revealing her full strength, he spun in frustration. In that one gesture, Baertha saw much. The Blackstar had misjudged a genuinely weak moment to be a test of his character — and knew that he'd missed his chance.

"Blackstar, nominate one of these thugs to serve as an example."

He paused, at which point the hundreds of Baerthas slowly slid forward, converging on him.

"Milady," he said, and pounced upon a floating disc. He impaled the screaming godling upon a sharp point, and then he spun and spun, each of his points acting like the teeth of a circular saw.

In moments the god was dead, its sigil divided into dull junk that floated away.

"The rationing system is reintroduced. Test me again at your peril," she commanded in hundreds of voices. She slammed the other ballerinas back into the one sigil, and within her considerable mind she ordered the Millicents back into their psychic cells.

"Blackstar. Attend me," she commanded, soaring up and into the heights of Overhaeven. They rose into the courtyard of Baertha's castle, slipping into three-dimensional forms.

She chose her formal attire from her days as Lady Bertha of the Family, appearing in the flower of youth. Next to her, the Blackstar spiralled out into an androgynous form, whip-thin and draped in tight clothes and a cloak, long hair teased out into a blond forest of spikes.

The Blackstar had been famous in the Before, a rockstar and a polymath of the highest order. Baertha had been caught staring more than once, but could not afford to be starstruck, to show even a fraction of weakness around this one.

He was charm, and violence in velvet gloves, and far too similar to Papa Lucy in many ways. Only her superior magical ability kept him in check, and they both knew this.

The Glorious Gyre was the seat of Overhaeven's ruler, and it spun slowly above this dying realm, all grand halls and looted artworks, empty now of sycophants. To Baertha it was a place for the Throne to sit, and she drew more joy from the comfortable apartment she'd kept here.

She felt the Blackstar bristle next to her, his high bootheels *click-click-ing* on the flagstones in a merrily impatient fast-step. They came into the Throne-room proper, and Baertha settled into the Throne itself, reconnecting with the artifact.

It was power source, crystal ball, and ship's helm all in one. Many had sat in this Throne since the beginning of this parasitic scheme, and their essence was so embedded into it that it felt greasy to the touch. Conquerors, political survivors, even one or two who fell into the role by accident, scheming bastards of every stripe and every last one a slavering addict like her. Baertha had inherited the universe's messiest desk, and most days this source of ultimate power drove her nuts.

"Stop sulking. You did not hold this castle long enough to get attached," Baertha said. Struggling to compose his face, the Blackstar took a knee, his cloak falling around him in majestic perfection.

"Milady," he said. "Did you locate the Most High?"

"I did. We argued. He slammed a door in my face."

"As I suspected it would go."

"At least I tried," Baertha said. She fussed with the Throne, trying to sort the myriad of controls into something useful. Some who'd held the Throne had pictured a ship's wheel, others an abacus or a lectern with an empty volume to write instructions into, tarot, mah-jongg tiles, or more. Those who'd tasted of the Industrial Revolution and beyond had added levers and wheels, ratcheting cogs with peeled labels, and then everything rushed into the chaos of computer keyboards and magical foci.

None of the previous occupants bothered to clean up their version of the controls, simply asserting their own system on top of the rest. The end result was a deep stratum of devices that contradicted each other, and rarely behaved.

Once more she tried to erase the Blackstar's system, a mixing desk from a recording studio, and she saw her minion scowling, even as he knelt.

"This one is stuck," she said, trying to erase a slider that was firmly resisting her efforts. "What is it?"

"The destruction of the Now," the Blackstar said. "Before your kind broke into that jail for disgraced Taursi, the wipe had been set to a slow crawl. It was meant as the cleansing end of their prison sentence."

"It's set to full speed," she said, eyes widening as she pried at the control, both with her fingers and with a myriad of invisible means. "Why can't I stop it?"

"Because I broke it," the Blackstar said with a wicked grin.

"Repair your sabotage! Immediately!"

"I am bound to obey you, milady, but in this instance it is simply impossible. Call it sour grapes, but when your race sentenced Overhaeven to a slow starvation, I decided to return the favour."

Baertha disengaged from the Throne and drifted toward the Blackstar, the tip of one ballet shoe just brushing the flagstones in a fabric whisper.

"You are in great peril, Blackstar."

"Perhaps. Maybe you would surrender the Throne to me, so I may attempt to repair the controls?"

She ignored the barb and considered the situation. She could do nothing for humanity, dead within months, maybe weeks. For a brief moment she thought about Sol, her husband, still shepherding the devolved survivors after all this time, only for it to end like this.

*I can't help him anymore,* she thought, and then added emphatically *I won't.* Her catacomb of mad guests cackled for a moment, their thoughts on the Now just as complex as her own.

All she had left to her was survival, which meant attending to her own accidental kingdom of parasites. She despised them, root to tip, but like everything she'd ever put her hand to, Baertha could not do things by halves.

She considered the state of the Shale mechanism, the proboscis badly damaged when Sol and Ray Leicester severed it from Gan-Eden. Then she consulted her instruments and looked over the true map of the universe, the one that her forebears had kept secret for so very long. She made her own entry then, that very distant door the Most High had slammed against her.

Overhaeven had one shot only, and if it failed, their sole weapon would be blunted and broken and there'd be nothing to it then but a slow starvation out in the void.

"I have an idea," she said. "Food, of a sort."

"Then by all means, let us eat."

# — 5 —

## RAY

He looked up at the metal frame with satisfaction and knew it was as sturdy as anything he'd ever built. A perfect rectangle of steel, square corners, the welds as good as invisible.

Broken Taursi spires lay underfoot in all directions, surrounded by just as many broken tools, but he finally had the hearts he needed, pierced by steel railway spikes and fastened into telegraph wire. A big series battery over thirty feet long, ending in a set of red and black clamps fastened to the steel girder.

Light, golden and blinding, bled upward out of the scar of the Crossing, seeming to fuse with the steel beams. Then it reached the top, a perfect rectangle of gold.

Ray heard the excited cries of people from the city walls. Ignoring the whine of approaching cars and bikes, Ray continued his inspection of the gateway, a set of aviator sunglasses doing little to protect his eyes from the glare. He knew it was going to bring him a migraine, a bad one, the kind that left him watching jagged lines and whimpering in a dark room, but he had to do his job properly.

It was perfect. Each point of the metal rectangle was in contact with the light of the field.

Even as he was congratulating himself that everything had worked, he heard the first harsh pop, and then another. Ray realized his glass Taursi hearts were exploding under the strain.

"No, no, no!" he said, rushing for the red-and-black starter leads, gasping at the heat radiating off the metal. Disconnecting the "battery," the Aurum field slowly dribbled downward, seeping into the smoking line of the scar.

There were Boneguard here, keeping their own camp at a safe distance from the scar. Ray called to them. It still felt strange to have any measure of authority, and he could not meet their eyes as he explained things.

"Please protect it all. The tools, the wires, and especially the glass hearts. I–I have to go get some more supplies."

"Understood, Junkman," one of them said, offering a crisp salute. They were already moving to intercept the looky-loos from Crosspoint, which Ray was grateful for. He had no stomach for answering pointless questions and could not promise anyone the escape they desperately wanted. Until he got it working, the gate was dangerous, and he didn't want anyone hurt because of something he'd overlooked or done wrong.

He needed advice, but more than anything, Ray needed his big brother. Climbing into his muscle car, he fired up the dwindling Aurum engine and raced across the dust. The light from his engine suddenly flared, and the car punched a hole through the world veil and went elsewhere, even as "Black Betty" played on the 8-track.

---

Sol had chewed over the problem at great detail with Ray when he first discovered that the ancient mechanic had been hopping back and forth between the Now and the Underfog with no ill effect.

"By rights you should have been stricken mindless by each passage," Sol said. "Only a handful of people can resist the effect."

"Maybe I figured it out," Ray said. "Like I figured out the Aurum gateways, and how to push my car through the barrier. It's just a problem and you work to the solution."

He was still uncomfortable with his role as a pseudo-magician. He devoted his will to everything he built, gave every act the deliberation of his Asperger's syndrome, and his every hour was nothing but willpower and routine at all times, exhausting as that was. The way he understood it, turning a strong enough will toward a desired end was as good as casting a spell, minus all the chanting and wands, and his inventions were the conduit.

"Willpower plus routine is called ritual. We called that instinctive sorcery, Ray. Of course, the Collegia hated it, because you didn't have to pay them if you taught yourself. But very dangerous. Most self-taught magicians ended up destroying themselves."

Sol looked at him for a long moment, with some expression that Ray couldn't fathom. He felt a spark of anger, that old schoolyard confusion.

"Please, Sol. I can't read faces. Tell me what you mean."

"I'm worried you will end up destroying yourself."

Ray blinked at Sol's concern. After so many centuries on his own, it was still hard for him to realize that people cared for him and loved him. After a long moment, he seized Sol awkwardly, crushing him in an embrace.

"Thank you," he said and let go with embarrassment.

"That's quite all right," Sol said with a warm smile, patting Ray on the shoulder. "Please, just be careful."

"I don't know anything else," Ray said. He was still being careful as "Black Betty" played, and he held the steering wheel level, golden light pouring out from under the hood. With a slight shudder the bumper kissed the world veil, peeling it apart like a chainlink gate in a bad cops-and-robbers movie.

He left the Now in a simple act of will, and as always he noticed he did *something* mechanical, and it was never the same thing twice. Today it was a switch with peeled labels in embossing tape, marked "NOW" and "GAN-EDEN." Another time he could have sworn he'd pushed a fourth pedal down on the floor, something that crunched like a small skeleton behind the accelerator. And another time, he was unable to release the gear-shifter, the clutch sliding in and out as he shifted upward hundreds of times, the car finally engaging into some gear that could grip the universe with enough torque to make a difference.

Logically, he knew this was his own mind trying to protect him from the truth. If a machine completed a function, it worked as it should. If it operated outside of the laws of the universe, it was magic, and thus it was John Leicester's realm and beyond his control.

Gratefully, he flicked the switch over to GAN-EDEN, and the transition was complete. The car wriggled through the wounded world veil and entered another realm.

He felt it then. The dizzy moment where a weak mind could be seized by the boundary of two worlds and stripped, all thoughts and memories snatched out like the stuffing of a pillow.

"No. I don't allow this," he said firmly, and again this was an assertion, enough for an amateur sorcerer to keep his brains from being scrambled.

And so Ray Leicester entered the Edgemist, only now it was a glorious place, the fog suffused with a honey-coloured glow, warm where once it had been cold. He rolled the window down, smiling as the mist washed him clean, and every pleasant smell he could remember throughout his long life came to him. Mother's cooking. The oils and aged wood of Father's workshop. Baked beans and model glue. He'd heard it was different for everyone, and it was only the first taste of what Gan-Eden was.

Then his muscle car rolled out of the Edgemist and into paradise. Warm hills ripe with wheat and vine, breathing beneath a gentle sun. The Oerwoud was tamed now, Adamah's old barrier manicured into groves and kinder plantations.

There was even a fairway here, and damned if he couldn't spot a pack of spirits out there playing golf. They paused their game to look at him in wonder as he purred past, his car humming in golden strangeness.

The landscape was dotted with structures, climbing spires of glass and gold, mansions that anyone could dream forth and have. The dreamers and wishers that lived here often twined them together into larger structures, settlements that flexed and lived and moved on when neighbours tired of one another.

It was as far from the old Underfog as it could ever be, but still Ray drove nervously, starting at every movement that he saw. He knew his brother and Jesus had been busy repairing Gan-Eden, making it into a true paradise for the Once-Dead, but the place still had its problems.

One of them came tearing out of the bushes lining the fairway and raced toward him, screeching and slavering. The golfers scattered as the monstrosity tore through their foursome, crushing their golf bags back into aether.

Ray saw the woman's body that had been fused into the shape of a living car, with matted hair growing wild from the roof. It tore up the fairway with wheels that were nubby hands and feet, its flanks flexing, ribcage visible through old, tattooed skin.

"CAR! JUNKMAN'S CAR!" the House of Torana yelled as it gave chase.

"Every time," Ray said. As he fled the golf course, he poured on the speed, a worried eye to the state of the glow from under his hood. He'd never been able to install any meaningful fuel gauge, and it was up to eyesight to determine how close his tanks were to running out.

He only had what Aurum he could bring here with him. Gan-Eden's sun was just a pretty lantern that did nothing to charge the hearts under his muscle car's hood.

"STOP. STOP NOW!" the House of Torana howled. Ray suddenly swung right, churning into a wheatfield, ignoring the shaking fists and scythes of the farmers. Here was the memorial to the House of Adamah, everything still kept as the old Farmer had laid out, and Ray raced through the streets, trying to shake off the pursuit.

He pulled in behind the old school, remembering the stories about the dead wolf who'd been the teacher here. Heart hammering away, he scanned the streets for any signs of the fleshy car.

"Good," he said, a moment before catching the creeping movement in his rear-view mirror. Madly struggling to shift into gear, Ray attempted escape, even as the House of Torana pounced upon his car.

Metal groaned and scraped, and he heard the triumphant screeching of the car-beast above him. Ray threw open the driver's side door and staggered out, hands held to his head.

Tongue flapping out of its mouth, the House of Torana had mounted his very rare and very perfect car from behind, and was thrusting away like a dog in heat, howling comically at the sky.

"Stop it! Get off! You're scratching all the paint!"

"HA! HA HA!"

---

Once the House of Torana decided it had humiliated Ray, it was civil enough, driving alongside his dented car and warning the other spirits of Gan-Eden to step aside.

There was a lot of Gretel still left in the House of Torana. She'd been a dead criminal from the Before who'd made a deal, sculpting her living flesh into a car for her Once-Dead spirit to drive.

She'd misspent her strange second life as a roving warlord, finally running afoul of Lanyard Everett, who'd helped to bring her down. The Jesusman had spared the car though, much to Ray's continuing horror.

"MUCH HUNTING HERE, HAH!" it offered to Ray. "GOOD EATING."

"Are you still doing your job?"

"YES!" it said, wiggling its backside. If it had a tail, it would have been wagging it. "DO YOU HAVE IT?"

"Yes," Ray said with a heavy sigh. He dropped a pile of steaks out of the window with a heavy splat, not bothering to wait as the House of Torana tore through the butcher's paper, savaging the contents until the whole front of the car was blood red.

With a happy roar, it soon caught up, rolling along contentedly.

"Where is John?" Ray asked. "And Jesus?"

"AT THE BEACH. COME ON, I'LL RACE YOU THERE!"

Ray still watched for dangers, even as the glory of day gave way to a starry night that was heartachingly beautiful. Sol had once told him of the old Underfog, and how it had taken months or even years to cross it, paying obeisance to this lord, trading favours with or hiding from that other lord. Now, getting from one side to the other was a matter of hours with the right vehicle and enough willpower to grease your way across this plane like butter on a skillet.

Hayaven was gone now, the mile-deep muck given way to pleasant farmland and settlements that shimmered beneath false galaxies. Bor Shaon was left for those who wished to seek out silent contemplation, and Ray often liked to spend time there on a visit, playing with the Many-Faced in the chalk.

On the far side of Hayaven was the old House of Avadon, crushed and kept in memoriam only, the Palace of the King of the Birds a reminder of ambition and vanity. After much discussion, Jesus and John Leicester had left the Pit of Shachat where Adamah had built it. The idea of a sense of peril seemed healthy to the Once-Dead, and spelunkers often visited with harnesses to plumb its depths for the secrets those who'd fallen in had lost.

The quieter lands by the ruins of Avadon and the edge of the Pit were Ray's favourite path toward the beach. He did not enjoy too much company, and he took care to avoid the settlements in his crossing of Gan-Eden. The Once-Dead often tried to fete him, mostly to curry favour with his brother, now a master of this place.

Worse still, there was another kind of spirit.

"AH! I SMELL ONE!"

The House of Torana darted into ruined Avadon and flushed a spirit out of hiding. A woman, her mouth wet with blue aether, leaving a newly Twice-Dead soul to float toward the final beach.

The car had found a vampire, one of those rare spirits who held to the old ways. Ray knew that John and Jesus had outlawed any-one preying upon their fellow spirits in Gan-Eden, but aether was addictive stuff. The farms and wineries held to a ration system to deal with addicts, parcelling out just enough to keep the spirits healthy but never sated.

There were still some vampires left over from the days of the Dawn King, and they'd found both recruits and victims as new spirits came to the restored kingdom of the dead. They did not wish to queue for a pittance, choosing instead to take as much aether as they could by force.

Where there was chaos, society would impose law, and of course

**THE BRIDE & THE BIRDMAN · 65**

Jesus and John created the Gidon, a caste of roving warriors. Ray had met a few of these spirits, mostly former lawmen, and even a Jesusman or two who'd survived the war of the Dawn King. Noble warriors, brave protectors of the blessed dead.

Then there was the House of Torana, who was also a member of their order. As this spirit-killer ran through the ruined city, the House of Torana simply destroyed any building she chose to hide in. Eventually the vampire braved the open spaces, crying out in despair as the House nipped at her heels.

Eventually the vampire cast herself into the Pit of Shachat, and then it was the House's turn to cry, denied its prize.

"NOT FAIR! A MEAL GONE TO WASTE!"

"You might find another vampire," Ray offered. The car scuffed its tires against the grit like a sulking child.

"BUT I WANTED THAT ONE."

---

Word had reached John Leicester, and Ray found his brother coming to meet him, wandering through the crystal perfection of the Glasslands. A thick pane of smoky glass served as the ground for miles in all directions, lined with rows of Obelisks. Now that the restriction on writing and art had been lifted, the great spires were filled with words, row after row of names.

As near as anyone could tell, these were the condemned, those who'd been found wanting in life. If a Once-Dead spirit was forced this way, they would be judged by the obelisks, and if they failed the test would be swallowed up by a realm of floating sky beasts and burning cities.

John waved when he saw the two cars approaching, and soon the brothers were locked in a fierce embrace, the fleshly arms of Ray holding tight to the washed-out Once-Dead body of John Leicester.

"Hello, Ray," John finally said. "I've missed you."

"The gate isn't working," Ray said by way of preamble. "The mountains ate up a town and we don't know what to do."

"You'll figure it out," John said. "The answers always come to you for these things."

"I need more time!"

A distant thump underneath their feet, a gentle thing but still terrifying. Coming right up to the pane of glass, the immense shapes floated and crashed together, sparking lightning as they divided into smaller selves. Ray was unsure if this was a mating, war, or both. Far beneath the eye-twisting layers of these creatures were the twinkling lights of settlements, veins of fire or lava, and darkness absolute everywhere else.

"Don't worry," John said when he saw the alarm in Ray's face. "They never break through the glass. We think they're curious."

"What are those things?"

"Mal saw them drag one of the Smothered Princes underneath. Perhaps a security system?"

"Please never go down there," Ray said.

"I don't plan to," John said. "We know next to nothing about the Low Place."

A blank look from Ray.

"That's what the obelisks call it. The Many-Faced too."

The thump of a floating beast, and then another. The glass danced with lightning.

"I would like to leave, John."

"Come on then. I'll drive."

"Please be careful with the gears. And the clutch is a little sticky."

The brothers got in and closed the doors. John Leicester gripped the steering wheel, smiling with satisfaction.

He planted it, wheels squealing against the glass, and Ray complained the whole way.

---

It only felt like minutes to reach the dunes, and then they were looking down on the beach at the edge of Gan-Eden, now a place of pure joy, the end point of many long lives. This was where spirits could choose to undo themselves and rejoin the universe, beyond which no one knew the outcome.

All knew the joy that drew them toward these waters, but no longer was it the brutal trap that Overhaeven had turned it into when fixing the Shale mechanism to it. Ray looked at the clusters of spirits who kept camp in the dunes and on the beach, happily contemplating the waves. If they wished to, they could spend eternity here.

Sunlight gleamed from an immense palace that floated on the water, connected to the shore by a wide causeway. The structure was made of glass and stone, and it rose in twists of light and shadow. A single figure stood on the walkways, crafting new turrets with beams of magic, and when one part didn't fit to their satisfaction, they collapsed an entire tower, which crashed down into the serene waters.

"There's Jesus. He's spent months on that thing. Very proud of it too," John said.

"What does it do?"

"What all castles do. It protects us."

Ray took in the structure as they approached the beach and eventually began attacking a notepad with a stub of pencil, drawing diagrams and making notations.

"It's got weak points. He should change the design to look like this."

"Yikes. Jesus will be jumping for joy to see you."

"Why would he do that?"

"It was sarcasm, Ray," John said gently. "When you pull out your notepad, he's not going to jump for joy."

# — 6 —

## SOL

S ol walked toward the park entrance on legs that didn't seem his own. He stepped around the bodies of his dead soldiers, the remains destroyed with brutal efficiency.

Here he'd turned a man inside out, and there lay a woman erased from time, her last few footsteps replaying in a slowly fading loop. There a cluster of soldiers were forced together in a cruel marriage of flesh, their organs slowly failing under all that weight, their large bank of eyes watery and weak, clustered lungs fighting for each breath.

Some were craters, scorch marks, goo, dust drifting on the wind.

Hundreds of lives snuffed out effortlessly. Sol gripped the Cruik tightly and wished he could snap it across his knee, wished that Jenny would climb back out and walk as a woman so he could shake her, force her to look upon her deadly works.

Lucy whistled cheerfully as he walked, not resisting as Sol tugged at his chains.

"Be quiet," Sol said. "Please."

"Jenny won't be coming out of the Cruik any time soon," Lucy said.

Sol wanted to cast the staff aside, even knowing that it was a person now, only he did not trust someone worse than him wouldn't pick it up.

*I need to find the way to destroy this,* Sol thought glumly, remembering the way that Jenny had taken him by the hand, shifted into the shape of the Cruik, and then directed the mass murder.

*I may even need to destroy her.*

"She's got shell shock," Lucy said. "You can bet she's disassociating in that manor I built, playing quoits and generally ignoring her conscience."

"What have you done, Lucy?"

"Me? Ha! That wasn't *me* waving around the Cruik, dickhead."

The staff gave a frenzied pulse, and then another, and for a moment it seemed that Jenny might climb out of the Cruik form, but then she relented, arms folding back into that perfect curl of a hook.

Carnage in all directions. Here he'd pushed a man through his own gun barrel, there another lay strangled by his own disembowelled intestines. The Cruik had been as creative as it had been cruel, as if it did not want to repeat the same sorcery twice.

*Makes some sense. You can't stop what you can't predict.*

Sol Pappagallo could feel all of that death keenly as he walked through the dead Boneguard army. He resisted the urge to put all their bodies to rights, knowing he had no time. There were fail-safes here that he'd built into the prison. Alarms. The Moot would be aware, and armies would be heading here.

He'd gone against one of his greatest principles, fell back into an old weakness. His need for a quick solution and his grudging respect for Lucy had blinded him to another one of his convoluted plans. Just like that, Lucy had deftly manipulated his brother into becoming an outlaw.

"Stop smirking," Sol said, voice thick. "Stop enjoying this so much."

"I will savour every squirming moment of the rest of your life," Lucy said. "You think the worst of me, but look at yourself. Look at what you did."

"It was the Cruik," Sol said weakly.

"Nah. You made your own choices, shit-bird."

They stepped across the edge of the boundary then, the invisible line that protected the park from sorcery. Sol scratched open a far-door with a sweep of the Cruik and, yanking on Lucy's chains, he hauled his brother through.

"Thanks for your hospitality!" Lucy chirped to the dead as the portal winked closed.

---

"What are you waiting for? Do we just sit here holding our dicks?"

"Lucy, shut up."

They were leaning against a ruined grain silo, the murky sprawl of Mawson laid out before them. Here was the brown snake of the Niven River, there the delta full of river lizards, beasts, and outlaws, and overseeing it all was the Tower of the Selector, marking the centre of a growing city. The Temple on its hill was as majestic to these low folk as the Tower, and it always made Sol twinge with nostalgia and regret to see a Before-time hotel and library given over to this worship.

A constant stream of refugees was flooding into the city from the northern roads, and the urban sprawl was already enveloped in tent villages and slums. Most were sunburnt Inlanders, but Overland folk were there with overloaded wagons, scared south by the moving mountains.

Beyond Mawson, the only real option was to take to a dangerous sea and hope to reach the spit of islands. Sol thought about his last voyage out on those waters, on a boat that was all magic and leaks, hoping to restore his brother to life. Finding more evidence of Lucy's betrayal. Restoring the looming monster that had been his wife.

He knew he'd been pathetic before the cuckolding and hated himself for it. Limiting his wife in a cage of worship and duty, their romance long since desiccated and stilted, while he played with settlements and laws.

That one hazy afternoon, their fellowship finally failed, their Family destroyed in a bed, and all Lucy and Baertha could do was laugh and laugh.

He'd found it convenient to blame Lucy and the Cruik for the affair, but how much of the betrayal had come consciously from

Baertha? Lucy had promised her the one thing she wanted the most, the thing that the Methuselah treatment took from all, and Sol had forbidden this.

What exactly had happened, out there on that island?

All the answers had fallen into Shale when the Cruik broke apart, but then again here was the Cruik, and here was Papa Lucy, once thought dead.

Had Bilbenadium told the truth about Baertha surviving?

"You're overthinking again," Lucy said, and as usual he was right. "Break it down into the necessary steps."

"You still won't tell me what the rest of your plan is."

"Because I fucking hate you. So here is step one. Get rid of this bullshit," and here he clanked his bonds. After a moment Sol twitched the Cruik, and the manacles and chain fell to the ground.

"Step two. We disguise our arses. Do you really think the Pappagallos can stroll into Mawson unnoticed?"

"Illusions were always your thing."

"They were. Then that bitch stole my magic. So you have to do it."

On his own, the illusions would take painstaking hours to construct, and would likely be flawed in some small way. Once more he drew from the Cruik, hating the feel of that deep wellspring, knowing that this was the least of its uses.

"Nice tits," Lucy said, groping his own body. He now had the appearance of a farmwife from the Overland, while Sol had taken on the form of a rough station-hand, perhaps tasked with giving her safe passage, or stealing her outright.

The Cruik was now a simpler shepherd's staff, such as a farmer might carry for self-defence.

"We need Jenny back," Sol said. "This is her town, and they'll do as she says."

"Better this way," Lucy said. "A quick in and out, as the actress said to the bishop."

"Well, what now? You said the answer was here. I know some version of the truth falls out of you from time to time, so where are we going?"

"The fucking Temple. You know they keep most of our old stuff in there? Revere our castaway bullshit as relics?"

"It's unsettling."

They joined in with the stream of refugees, and Sol watched the approach of officials working their way up the line with a worried eye. These people were wearing the tower sigil of the Selector on armbands, taking down credentials, directing the refugees to intake tents.

They were backed up by heavily armed coin-riders, lancers mounted on birds. A pair of men in bushranger armour stood at the ready, watching the refugees through the eye-slits of their helmets, steam engines bubbling away on their backs.

Automatic rifles at the ready. Charity was obviously being stretched to the limit here, and Sol wondered when they would simply start turning people back north to face the Range and their own destruction.

As the officials got closer to the brothers, Sol felt a grudging moment of gratitude for the power of the Cruik. His own illusions rarely held up to close scrutiny, but he had no doubt these likenesses would cling to them for as long as needed, as good as real flesh.

Despite the destruction at the Harkaways, the Cruik was a useful artifact, now tempered by the presence of Jenny Rider. Sol noticed the train of thought with a little concern.

*She took control of you! Don't fall for this.*

He gripped the Cruik tightly, almost covetously, and it took a great degree of willpower to relax his fingers.

A bored looking official reached Sol and Lucy, clipboard in hand. She wore a veil to ward off the ever-present Riverland flies and looked bemused at the misery of the visitors. Pinned to her lapel was a brooch with the wheeling Cruik sigil, the sign of Lady Hook, and Sol smiled inwardly.

*If only you knew how close your lady was to you right now!*

"Names? Origins?"

"Tam Bollard. Missus Juno Bollard. We're out of Gladhands."

"Overlanders," she said, marking her paperwork. "Follow the blue flags. You're to set camp where the attendants guide you. Here is your ration book. Lose it and you won't get another one."

"Thank you," Sol said with a faint bow. He shepherded Lucy

forward, grateful for the rare moment of restraint from his brother. Before he could take two more steps toward the city of Mawson proper, the official held him in place with a hand on his chest. Instantly the soldiers in the steam suits came clanking over, joined by a trio of bird-lancers.

"You can't go into the city," the woman said. "New rules are that the refugees stay in their camps."

"But we need to go there," Sol protested.

"I said no."

The soldiers hung back, watching with the gleeful non-smile of the lawman just waiting for trouble to kick off. Lucy then spoke, in the perfect pitch of a young farmer's wife.

"I beg pardon," Lucy said politely. "We pray to Lady Hook, and merely wish to go to her holy Temple. Give her thanks for our safe arrival."

Lucy reached over, gently wrapping his own hand around the Cruik, just above Sol's own. He didn't dare knock his brother's hand away, suffering through the false piety.

It may have been his imagination, but Sol felt the Cruik twitch as Lucy grasped it. For a moment it seemed to hum, to seek connection, and then just as quickly subside.

*It already has everything of Lucy that's worth having.*

A fraught moment in the line. The official looked at the illusion of the shepherd's hook, and then caressed her own brooch. Finally, she nodded.

"You can go in to pray, but then you'll have to return back to your camp," she said. "We can't show preferences here."

She marked a chit of paper and handed it to Sol. Giving his thanks, they followed a bird-rider into the city itself. Temporary barricades littered the approaches inside, and a more permanent wall was in mid-construction around the city proper. It would do nothing against the advancing Range, but as Sol looked over the rapid construction of machine gun nests, he saw the truth of things.

A time was coming soon when all these people would panic and rush to come inside, to take badly needed space and resources. They would need to be killed — and killed fast.

"You had better be right," Sol whispered to Lucy. "I've bet everything on you."

"Well, that's pretty fucking stupid given my track record," Lucy chuckled quietly. "You'll see."

Mawson was crowded and busy, and everyone seemed to be living these last moments in a frenzy. Everything imaginable was for sale, and the haggling was spirited, the futile chase for wealth almost tragically sad.

Everywhere were the signs for Lady Hook, paintings on buildings, sculptures in public places. The most devout embedded large hooks through their flesh and Marked her symbol on their skin, both with scars and ink. This was her town, body and soul, and the Mawsonites went ridiculous for their woman realized in wood, as much as they bothered Sol in Crosspoint.

*Come out of there,* he thought, looking at the staff in his hands. He remembered that moment her hand slid into his at the mountain, and he hated how much that moment had completed him, both at her touch and then at the wielding of the Cruik, the ownership of that staff.

*Is this how it finally gets to me?* Sol thought a little sadly, and then wondered if he minded at all. Why not have everything his brother ever wanted, and lord it in front of him?

The road up to the Temple was steep, and once or twice they were forced to hold the harness of the soldier's bird for support. Eventually they were at the steps to the Temple, walking up broad steps and through the columns to the yawning interior.

"Return immediately after your prayers," the bird-rider warned. "We've got your names and descriptions if you try to run."

"Of course! We'll come straight back," Lucy warbled, and his awful female impersonation caused the man to look at them curiously.

"Shut up," Sol said, gripping Lucy's elbow tight. "No funny business."

"I guess you could just murder your way out of this place too."

He felt it for a moment then, the dark desire to dominate, to *assert himself*, and he knew that it was true. He wondered if he'd be able to resist the Cruik for much longer and felt himself humming with potential, as if he stood at the edge of a filthy pool and was dying of thirst.

They needed Jenny back—and fast.

They made it through just before the guards cut off further admittance, entering the cramped interior of the Temple. Acolytes struggled to direct people into seats, even as the last mass was exiting through another set of doors.

"They're doing back-to-back masses," Sol realized. "Just to keep the panic under check. It's bad here, Lucy."

"Can't believe they're still spouting our old bullshit," Lucy said. "We only made this religion up to keep them in line. Are people honestly this fucking stupid?"

Lucy looked up at the grand scenes painted on the interior cupola. The family feud that led to Sad Plain and then the Waking City, and stylized images of Papa Lucy, the Boneman, Bertha and her Mad Millies, Jesus trod underfoot with all the other traitors.

For many minutes, the brothers silently took in the wailing prayers, the flensers at work skinning suckling pigs in children's clothes, the gladiatorial combats in their name. People slashing their faces and forearms with sharp glass. The ceremonies spoken in their names, now more fervent than ever.

"We should not have given them a religion," Sol finally said.

"They're so fucking stupid," Lucy muttered in awe.

Lucy indicated they should head to the indoor mausoleum, an entire wing of the old library given over to the rich dead. Here, only the odd mourner came by with a lit candle, and they could plan in quiet.

"We are where you wanted to be, Lucy. So what happens now? What is your grand plan?"

"Do I look simple? If I give you everything, you'll just turn me in. Or worse, you point your new girlfriend at me and burn me into a cinder. Oh no, I'm gonna feed this to you a crumb at a time."

"Are you serious? Lucy, you will tell me now, or I—"

"You don't have a choice, Sol. You're too far into this now. So shut the fuck up and do what I tell you, and we have a chance to stop this thing."

Sol quailed for a moment, and he knew that Lucy had him. Lucy knew this too, and the image of the farmer's wife gave off a sinister smile.

Even without his magic, he still had that old hold over his brother and could manipulate him like a master. Despite having the Cruik and all of the tangible power in this situation, Sol felt more helpless than he ever had. He felt a surge of anger from the Cruik, anger with the flavour of Jenny, the knowledge that injustice and insult were his lot. It was all he could do to rein in this destructive force, and Sol couldn't even think, let alone outwit his Machiavellian brother. Lucy had asserted his own control, for now.

"Damn you," he said, and Lucy laughed softly.

Lucy gave him the next part of the plan then. In the Inner Sanctum of the temple was an open-roofed series of apartments, just under the cupola, and here were all the relics and various personal items that remained from their first lives as mortals in the Before.

"We go in there," he said, pointing to the heavily guarded home of the Eminent Three, the high flensers of the Family faith. "We need some of our shit back."

"Are you kidding? I could have made representations! Jenny could have just gotten us our old belongings as a favour!"

"And I'd still be in my jail cell, so here we are. Things change, so look lively."

The farmer and his wife crossed around the sunken mausoleum, where criminals were now being bled by the score in their names, and they approached the Inner Sanctum. A high-ranking flenser cut them off, reaching for the bandolier of sharp knives across his chest.

"Turn around. You're out of bounds."

"If only you bloody understood," Lucy said in his own voice, and the man drew a knife. Someone else gave a cry in the crowd, and they were getting some attention. Lucy turned to Sol.

"Drop the illusions."

"What?"

"Do it. Time to strike our fucking flag."

Sol ended the illusions with a sweep of the Cruik, and in that moment the gathered faithful of Mawson saw the sudden appearance

THE BRIDE & THE BIRDMAN · 77

of two living gods, Papa Lucy and the Boneman, who was holding the Cruik high above his head.

"Lady Hook!"

"Lucy! The Papa! He walks among us!"

"Lord Goodface!"

Lucy drank it all in, arms outspread, as he turned in a slow circle. Even as grungy and unshaven as he was he was still recognisable, with his wavy Robert Plant hair, and enough swagger and charisma to power churches and wars. The flenser was abasing himself on the ground, and soon the Eminent Three were joining him, these high priests weeping into the flagstones with joy. The air filled with jubilant cries.

"Look at all this bullshit," Lucy said between his teeth, and then he smiled sweetly at Sol. "Now just you fucking try to put me back in jail, brother."

# — INTERLUDE —
## THE MOST HIGH

At the dawn of all things there was a grudging peace between the Most High and the Cruik. The god found the tool forged from its rib indispensable in the tending of that early garden.

A lot of work went into correcting what the Most High had destroyed during its rage and isolation. With the Cruik in hand, it was able to establish pleasing patterns of nebulae, stacking galaxies according to mathematics it had devised during captivity. This universe had done nothing to serve the god during that dark time, but for a moment the Most High could set aside its jealousy and anger, letting curiosity guide it in their place.

Eons had passed since the Most High had attempted to destroy the Cruik, and this tool knew enough now to serve without question, only ever speaking in sycophancy or circuitously. The Most High knew the creation was frightened of it, and this pleased the god as much as the Cruik's service did.

Inspired by the company of the Cruik, the Most High created life and let it run rampant across every corner of the greater garden. The Most High desired love and attention above all things, and it walked openly amongst its creations, initially thrilled at the worship and adoration.

After a while, the responses it had built into its creations rang untrue. It instructed them to love it, and so that love felt unearned and a little hollow. The Most High entered into a great work, channelling every initial feeling of rejection and solitude into a force that washed across its entire creation.

Thus came free will, a gift the Most High gave to all.

There was love, of course, the adoration for all of the gifts the Most High had given to the universe—and best of all, this love was given freely. The Most High drank happily from sacrifices in its name and sat upon thrones in a thousand worlds.

But even as it revelled in this affection, darkness brewed. There were others who did not love the Most High. There was pain and suffering in life, of course, and if the Most High was so powerful, why did it allow this pain to exist?

Naturally enough, there came misunderstanding and even wars between those of faith and those severed from it. The Most High saw this over and over, and it found an even deeper strangeness.

There was no reversing the gift of free will, even though it was its own invention, and it broke many living creatures trying to undo this work. It seemed the gift was so deeply entwined with a living soul that it could not be unravelled.

The jealousy in the Most High's heart overflowed, and it stomped around in its garden, plucking out the weeds of treason and blasphemy wherever they arose. This work was endless, and even the Most High flagged under the effort. The Cruik was most useful at destroying those without love and faith in their hearts, but even it began to question the Most High.

"But you gave them this gift," it argued. "Why punish them for acting only as you made them?"

The Most High would inflict pain on its tool if pressed too much on this matter, and soon it served in silence, sullen at times, but faithful enough.

Seeking a solution to the problem of free will, the Most High devised a strategy. Instead of a wild garden that spread everywhere, it conceived of separate walled gardens, and then garden beds within this. Planes of reality, nested atop each other, acting as filtering systems for those who lived within. Refined over and over, life would run its cycle. Those of love, faith, and good deeds would be rewarded and replanted. Those who were displeasing and wicked would be punished by the system itself and rendered into nothing but useful energies.

Over and over, this system worked, these silos of worship that the Most High and the Cruik planted across the universe. There were always new worlds where life flourished, and those who kept faith with the Most High were rewarded with a second life upon death, a glorious Eden where they lingered for as long as they wished.

Those who walked a defiant path received a different type of reward and were broken, punished, destroyed, and then recycled.

Most importantly, these systems were self-contained and required little oversight from the Most High and its powerful instrument. Then, in its greatest moment of hubris, the Most High created the seed of a race modelled after itself.

"THE HUMAN," it mused, looking upon the primates that were the first step in this evolution. It always took a few steps backward when creating life, enjoying the improvements that evolution would add to its designs.

These early humans were a maddening blend of violent scientists, conquering their world with ease, and the Most High felt great pride in their accomplishments. It let other gardens grow fecund, neglecting most of its other tasks to spy on this one corner of the universe.

"Most High, we have troubles in the other gardens," the Cruik said. "You've not been seen by your subjects. Revolt is breaking out."

"LET THE SYSTEM REFINE THESE ILL SOULS AS IT SHOULD. I AM BUSY HERE."

The Cruik fretted endlessly, passing on reports of the damage being done to the rest of the universe. There were dangerous schools of thought, beings raising themselves to great power, and predators were sneaking into gardens they did not belong to.

Still the Most High gazed upon its own pride, a world of its divine form rendered in miniature. These humans were also proud and self-centred, and there was much of the Most High in them, both from design and from sheer bravado.

They built. They warred amongst themselves and conquered every inch of their planet. They devised technologies and even discovered many of the magics that were their divine birthright.

Most importantly, they searched for the Most High obsessively, even without having ever encountered their creator in the flesh.

"THIS IS FASCINATING," it enthused to the Cruik. "I HAVE LEFT FEW ENOUGH HINTS, BUT THEY HUNT ME. LOOK, NOW THEY ARE PEERING INTO THE GREYGULF!"

"This race worries me," the Cruik dared. "Their worship is fatalistic, dark in nature. If they find you, they may turn on you."

"THEY ARE ME. YOU BLASPHEME, CRUIK!"

"Forgive me," the staff said, pulsing with abasement and humility, and the Most High dismissed it with a snarl. Within moments the god was once more drawn to its pet fixation, oblivious to anything else.

# — 7 —

## MAL

He understood the old deal that had lost the Jesusmen the right to enter Crosspoint, but he didn't have to like it. Living from camp to camp was all Mal knew now, but he missed the bustle of the First City sometimes, the markets filled with wonders from the Before, the sweet-sellers and the street-theatre. The weird amalgam of culture that the settlers had cobbled together in the last three hundred years, cribbed from the old tales of those who could remember the Crossing and what could be gleaned from recovered books and records.

It bothered him more that they were camping just downwind of the city, near the old caravanserai. Travelers and crooked folk still stopped by, even with slavery outlawed, and all of them kept a healthy distance from the semi-permanent camp of the Jesusmen.

Sometimes the wind blew just right from Crosspoint, and Mal could smell the food and the filth of the cramped city, catch a hint of the music belting out from repaired gramophones. Elvis and the Beatles, Aretha Franklin, the mysteriously-named ABBA and AC/DC.

Mal had heard some wandering minstrel troupes out in the Inland and the Overland, but they mostly stuck to the music found on the old records. It struck him that the only new songs created by the settlers were laments, bush-ballads and down-hearted tunes for times of loss and hardship.

All they had left were the hand-me-downs of the dead, and Crosspoint was the best place to pick through the pile. The other small cities and towns scattered across the Now were a pale imitation of the old city.

"I don't miss that place, and neither should you," Lanyard said to Mal. As per usual, the old man knew the truth of those in his inner circle, down to the marrow. Even being in this enclave of forty or so people wore on the solitary veteran, and he kept his own small campfire on the outskirts of the main camp. Mal squatted next to him, sweeping a brush through Collybrock's feathers, the bird crooning with pleasure.

On the fire, the billy boiled, and Lanyard tipped in the flakes of liver-root. It was all that kept him going these days. It only grew in the Riverland now, and it was getting costly, but none begrudged the old man the expense, even as they counted every bullet and reused everything until it fell apart.

"It's going to be tough in there, boy," Lanyard said, even though Mal was a man grown. "Witches are still lurking in dark corners. It's going to be a bad time."

"Okay," Mal said.

"Some of us will die, and you need to be okay with it."

*I will die in the Greygulf,* was the unspoken truth. Mal felt that future heartbreak press against the dam-wall of his resolve, and knew that he would fall apart when he lost Lanyard.

"We're in a rough trade, bossman," was all that Mal could manage.

Mal watched the gates of Crosspoint crack open, and Jenny Rider emerged in a cartwheel of hooks and alien shapes, finally resolving into a human woman. She walked past their enclave toward Ray Leicester's project at the scar of the Crossing.

As Tilly approached Lanyard's fire, she gave Jenny a friendly wave, but the wooden woman only offered a curt nod. Tilly turned the wave into a flipped bird behind Jenny's back.

"She's got a bloody attitude on her," Tilly said, joining Lanyard and Mal at the smaller campfire. Mal offered her the feather-comb and she took over grooming Collybrock, the bird crooning and twitching one leg.

"Girl," Lanyard said. "We got enough to do what needs doing?"

"Barely," she said. "What's the difference?"

"You going to try to talk me out of going?"

"Shut up and drink your liver-root. You'll just get through the shadow-door as is."

Lanyard nodded. Even though the bossman said nothing more, Mal knew he was immensely proud of his first prentice, of the warrior she'd become. It was futile to seek any approval from this man, which was as likely to come delivered with a backhand and a cutting remark, but when he approved of his charges it was as warm as a mother's love—even buried beneath an acre of scowls and leathery old looks.

"Give these people one night to rest," Lanyard instructed. "Have everything laid out and ready to go, right after breakfast."

"Righto, boss."

Then came night and stars, and the distant cacophony of Crosspoint from time to time, and once a scream from the caravanserai when someone took a knife in the dark. Mal slept through the lot, tousle-headed and snoring.

In his dreams, he walked with his wife in a paradise. It was a world of their own making, and every night they added to it, using their willpower to change the landscape in their shared subconscious.

They were Tontine, two spirits in one flesh, and every time Mal's eyes closed in slumber, they shared the discoveries of the day. Sometimes Kirstl walked in the day while Mal dreamt, wandering wide-eyed in his own head as he played at being a god.

Kirstl and Mal had crafted palaces and mountains, lakes and deep forests, and an array of creatures that were either splendid or ridiculous, depending on where their shared dream was going. If they argued or tired of the world, they would dash it to the ground like an annoying board game, and simply start again.

The void. Then a man and a woman, and a new world exploding out from them. Mal wondered at the scale of things and did not know how he could hold so much in his own skull, if indeed everything

THE BRIDE & THE BIRDMAN · 85

*was* in his physical brain, or if they had stepped outside, playing in the universe.

"Is this safe?" he sometimes asked, only for Kirstl to scoff at his caution, and then they were off and laughing as continents rose and fell beneath their feet.

Sometimes Kirstl enjoyed making scenes from the Before, but neither of them knew anything beyond the books and the old stories of the Boneman, and the best they could craft was a child's idea three times removed from the truth.

They did not care.

Kirstl caught an aerocraft to her big meetings at the stock exchange, leaping from a literal silver bird to swap animals with people she'd created. They drank coffee in a café, with milk from a real cow. Mal assumed that one was kept in the store for milking, and they did their best to nod sagely as the barista confidently squeezed the udders directly into their cups.

"So ask me," Kirstl said, reclining in a glittering gown, a three foot high golden crown on her head. She'd dressed Mal in a black suit with a big hat, and, knowing that formal wear had tails, she'd supplied him with two wriggling snake tails on the back.

"Ask you what?"

"How I did it. How I was able to use this," she gestured grandly at everything, "to speak to Jenny Rider."

"I am curious, love."

"Curious enough to admit that I'm smarter than you?"

"Settle down."

"All you have to do is this," she said, leaning forward in a mischievous sparkle. "Say that I am the better half of this marriage. Queen of the Tontine."

A long pause, and then he smiled.

"Of course you are. You are my better half, here and anywhere. I love you, Kirstl."

"That was very good. Very nice. Okay, I'll show you."

With one gesture she wiped out everything, bringing the dream space back to the formless void.

"It all started when I wanted to find the very edges of you," she said, invisible in the pitch darkness, nothing but the pressure of a hand in his. "We've got whole worlds in your brain, but how does it all fit?"

Mal said nothing, feeling a little uncomfortable in the pitch black, trying as hard as he could to trust Kirstl.

"Then I remembered when Bilben broke in, found a way to speak with us in here. Makes sense there's a door, or a window."

She clenched his hand a little, and then he heard the intake of her breath, and then suddenly there was a light, and then another, and then dozens more, beams of light piercing that endless gloom, and each one was a window to somewhere else. Some of these were opaque and guarded, but others were like open windows that you could press an ear against, or whisper through, perhaps shout through if you opened them far enough.

Perhaps, just perhaps, they might also find the way to make a window into a door.

"I went to find the very end of you Mal, the end of *us*, and we don't end at all."

---

"Up," Lanyard grunted roughly, prodding Mal's ribs with his boot, and the young man snapped open bleary eyes. He and Kirstl had spent the whole night pushing their intent against the windows, testing the limits of the Tontine that bound them together. It was not like the whimsical dreams he often shared with his wife, and it felt like he hadn't slept at all.

Mal shook his head and made to sink back into his doze.

"Kirstl, Mal, I don't care which one of you wears this idiot today. Get up."

Kirstl slid forward into limbs, connecting with eyes and ears, while Mal gratefully slid back into the subconscious and slumber. She rose with the explosion of energy she'd used in life, bouncing on the balls of her feet and stretching. Collybrock stirred and nuzzled her affectionately.

"You're the girl," Lanyard said, and Kirstl nodded.

"He's tired. We tried some new stuff last night."

"Don't wanna know."

The Jesusmen were mostly gathered now, a line of bikes and birds, and a trio of camels forming the baggage train. They were loaded heavily with crates of bullets and bombs, haunches of meat, and sacks of flour. Prentices pushed handcarts filled with scavenged tins and stacks of firewood, and a buggy was hitched up to a trailer filled with barrels of water.

Jesusmen typically travelled light and fast, and it worried Kirstl to see how committed they were to Sol's plan, to this *expedition*.

The cookfires were already snuffed out and smouldering, and only a skeleton crew of Jesusmen remained to hold the tent city, to keep safe what rude infrastructure they'd cobbled together.

Kirstl saw Tilly at the front of the line, calling forth a shadow-door with a wrench of a clawed hand. The portal irised open, and then before them lay the Greygulf, the realm between realms, once a place for dangerous journeys. These days it was a blasted and sterile wasteland, long since conquered and broken.

"Forward," she cried. The bikers whipped past her, twisting throttles and offering up a mosquito whine as they punched into that other world. Next came the bird-riders, and Kirstl held tight to Collybrock, the bird lurching and muttering as it ran reluctantly into the shadow-door.

*Always hit the shadow-doors hard and fast,* was the mantra, and for more than one reason. If there was trouble, it was usually lurking just inside the Greygulf, but the sudden rush into another world kept the uncertain ones from thinking too much.

The boundary felt awful, like pushing through grease and freezing ice and electricity all at once, for the briefest of instants. This was the point where those with a normal mind would be stricken dumb, all knowledge torn from them. The Jesusmen were those with a natural resistance to the effect, which meant that the rest of their bloody trade came easily enough.

"Hold up," Lanyard cried out, and then the old man was gasping, retching over the side of the shadow-road. This happened to him every time, but no one faulted him for it. Others had bloody noses or had wet themselves. It was just part of stepping through the world veil.

Abandoning his buggy for others to drive, Lanyard took the swarthy hand of Mal, and Kirstl used the muscles of their shared body to hoist the old Jesusman into the saddle behind them.

"Thanks, Kirstl," Lanyard said. "I vomit every bloody time."

Lanyard's hands felt clammy and cold, and he retched again, spitting over Collybrock's flank and onto the shadow-road below. Somewhere deep in their shared mind, Mal stirred from his slumber, the worry for his father figure reaching him even in such a deep rest.

*Lanyard's not coming back this time,* he said.

*Go back to sleep, love.*

*Look at him! This is a one-way trip for him. Why?*

*You* know *why! It's what he wants.*

Kirstl hushed him, urged him to sleep, and after a moment he let her push him back down into the slumber of the dreamspace. She did not want Mal seeing Lanyard like this.

"Our teeth hurt when we cross the barrier," Kirstl said. "Joints too."

"It's not natural for us to be here, is why," Lanyard said. "If we were smart, we'd piss off back home."

"The minute we sign up, we stop being smart, boss."

Lanyard gagged again, wiping away the muck with his sleeve.

The Greygulf ran with the crumbling grey of the shadow-roads, paths connecting doorways. They had once been thought to be fixed in place, but the Family had discovered later that they could be moved, the roads groaning and stretching as they connected to some new destination.

Stretch that road far enough and you weren't just connecting distant places in the Now, you were connecting with a whole other world, and sometimes there were predators clever enough to know the trick. Kirstl had heard Tilly confessing her fears over a bottle with Lanyard, that a horde of beasts may be able to simply step into the centre of Crosspoint or Mawson and start eating.

Now, with the Range on the move and the world veil incredibly thin, predator sightings were at an all-time high. While Sol and the other Magicians frantically explored dozens of other avenues, the Jesusmen's part in this was simple. Watch the Greygulf. Fix tears in the world veil. Kill anything that didn't belong. Stay in this sterile landscape for as long as they could without going Witch.

Kirstl knew it was a bad idea to linger long, but they'd gotten lucky at Price. With the chaos of a world being undone, things worse than the All-Fang would soon be entering the Now. They got lucky that time. Another creature of that scale would break their tiny army, and then the outsiders could feast on the terrified survivors, unopposed.

A Jesusman's only job was the destruction of these predators, and they pursued this with a grim and total focus. Sometimes they needed to make tough calls about civilians, like at Price, but the alternative was a monster at every human throat.

The situation in the Now was dire, and this last-ditch plan put every Jesusman at risk of becoming a Witch. Still, it made a fatalistic sort of sense to catch monsters in here, before they had a chance to come through the world veil.

*If we're going to make a last stand,* Lanyard had said, *we might as well make it in a target rich environment.*

It didn't hurt Lanyard's argument that he himself was broken and old, and wanted to go out guns blazing. Mal couldn't imagine a world without his grizzled father-figure, and in a way, he felt like he was there to keep the old man from doing anything stupid.

Tilly called for a halt, and then the Jesusmen were joining their sorceries together under her guidance, focusing on the shadow-road, willing it to disconnect, to move, to align to a new destination. The road trembled underneath their feet and slowly began to move. Kirstl looked nervously at the fragile edge of the structure, where whole chunks of stone were crumbling away.

All around them were the other shadow-roads of course, grey fibres winding across the silver sky, but in places they'd collapsed altogether, sometimes carving through the roads underneath them.

Tilly turned their road gently around as if guiding a thread into a needle. Slowly they moved toward a rickety needle of rock that hovered far above the ground, a structure that was half shadow and half brick. A fat tangle of shadow roads entered through archways and modified windows, with dozens of roads converging at impossible angles.

A sign on the side of the structure read TERMINUS.

Kirstl had heard the stories about the old Jesusmen who got greedy and turned the Terminus into a cache of loot, even as they became Witches and hungered for human flesh.

With a hollow boom, the shadow-road they were on connected with the Terminus, and then the Jesusmen were through in a roar of motorbikes and thumping bird feet, guns scanning in all directions, hands raised and ready to cast destructive magics.

Nothing. The structure was silent, long abandoned. Inside, it resembled a grand train station that Kirstl had once seen in a book, with vaulted ceilings and columns, but instead of trains it had graceful archways leading to a thousand different shadow-roads and worlds unknown. Strangest of all, this had already been here when humans first entered the Greygulf. All they managed to do was befoul it and turn it into a bank vault.

After many minutes of careful searching, the scouts declared it safe, and that was when Tilly gave a shrill whistle. Hands seized at the camels, quickly porting boxes of goods. Every motorbike sidecar was emptied, and the prentices with their handcarts formed a beeline.

Food, water, ammunition, and firewood, neatly stacked in a corner. There was enough here to keep them going for a month or maybe two, as much as Tilly could squeeze out of Sol and their meagre treasury. Army cots and bedrolls were unpacked and arrayed in neat rows, buckets were set out for a latrine, and riflemen were kitted out and assigned to watch out of windows in all directions. The birds were tied into picket lines and kept amused with a gramophone playing quietly.

Finally, Tilly and Lanyard led the effort to isolate their new stronghold. Teams of Jesusmen destroyed the shadow-roads leading into Terminus using the Mark of Unmaking, planting explosives when that didn't work. Others set charges to the entryways, collapsing them so that no one could connect fresh shadow-roads to the Terminus. They left three of the shadow-roads intact, and in Lanyard's opinion that was two too many.

**THE BRIDE & THE BIRDMAN · 91**

The Order of the Jesusmen settled into an anxious huddle of camp-life, and the first of many watches began.

---

Mal was operating their shared body and keeping watch when it happened. A few days prior, a group of Witches had attempted to steal up one of the shadow-roads, all pasty-white dogs and serpents and shifting man figures, and they were answered with a chatter of gunfire and a grenade lobbed by one over-enthusiastic prentice.

Cracking in three places, the shadow-road collapsed to the distant ground, and the Jesusmen were left with just two entrances to their stronghold. The poor prentice was still on a punishment detail, and the grenades were handed out now only to those whom Tilly personally trusted.

Mal was more vigilant than Kirstl, who had a habit of daydreaming and not paying attention, and when he saw it, he thought it was yet another bleedthrough. They were quite a sight when observed in the Greygulf; a bubble the size of a town from the Before pushing through the world veil, and this bulge was answered by the seeking press of the Now, and when the two points connected everything moved through, like the squirming of a gut moving food through the bowels of the universe.

On the other side, a bleedthrough site would appear somewhere in the Now, and someone would strike it rich. With dreams of finding his own lode of wealth one day, Mal watched curiously as a big bulge started to appear in the world veil.

"That's a big one there," he cried out to Lyn. "Fortune in that."

"I saw it first," the girl responded. "I call dibs."

"That's not a bleedthrough," her twin, Mem, said. Then they could only watch as the large point was stretched and then finally pierced through, a harsh knife puncturing the tough skin that held that universe together and slowly parting it, a mile-long cut appearing in seconds.

"Lanyard! Tilly!" Mal cried, and the senior Jesusmen were there in seconds, everyone watching in terror. The thing that was tearing the hole open was something like an insect limb or a stinger, realized on a gargantuan scale.

The world veil flapped about in the vacuum of the cosmos, air rapidly leaking out of the sealed bubble of the Greygulf, and beyond it they could make out stars, and then a shape moving across behind the limb. It was waxy, like a large wasp's nest, and through it could be seen a dim lake of filthy gold.

"It's Overhaeven," Lanyard growled. "They're trying to latch on with the Shale mechanism."

He was already moving, barking out orders. Everyone was needed, and fast. Bikes were kicked into life, people were scrambling into saddles, and Tilly was hauling one of their precious shadow-roads into position. She unhitched the end of it from the Now, and with great concentration lifted the stone causeway toward the tear.

Mal rode low in Collybrock's saddle, urging her on, using kind words and stroking her neck where others opted for knout and whip. The bird was terrified of the apocalyptic scene they were racing directly toward, but Mal knew she trusted him absolutely and would carry him into death itself.

"Shit," the bird said, and nervously demonstrated the word. Behind them, someone swore.

Ahead, the enormous, thrusting stinger of Overhaeven turned slightly, and the tear became a crooked jag, and then the dirty golden structure began to turn, grinding against the world veil, the Shale mechanism dislodging from the universe's membrane. Just like that, Overhaeven floated away, a ship seemingly without anyone at the wheel, and then it was lost to the whorl of stars and cosmic scatterings visible through the tear.

"Mark of Mending, all of you!" Lanyard called out, and they drew up at the very end of the shadow-road, looking out on the chill of the universe. Mal felt it then, the same chill as when they crossed through the world veil, but magnified. Throbbing cold throughout every joint. The nerves in every tooth aflame. Instant migraines that made nearly everyone double over, struggling to even see.

One Jesusman fell over the side of the shadow-road, plummeting to his death. Another ran forward in a frenzy, passing through the tear and into the cold vacuum of space, laughing maniacally.

"Mark of Mending, and hold your shit together," Lanyard ordered. As one the Jesusmen drew on that simplest of Marks, the one that could repair a tear in a piece of cloth or a broken plate, but here they scaled up the intention of the spell, trying to draw the jagged edges of the torn universe together.

The Marks came out, black lines of intent flowing out from their contorted fingers, joining together in a net, like fibres across a healing wound. They drew the edges of the tear closer, but the effort was great. To Mal's right a prentice dropped dead on the spot, and others were beginning to waver.

The tear was almost half a mile long, and they were only just beginning to seal one end of it. Ahead, Mal saw Lanyard waver, leaning heavily on Tilly.

*We are so screwed,* Kirstl said in Mal's mind. *I'll try to get help from Jenny Rider. Try not to die while I'm gone.*

"I won't," Mal said through gritted teeth. Collybrock fell into a swoon with a pitiful *cheep,* and Mal eased out of her saddle, continuing the spell-work.

Tilly and Lanyard were working busily at the front of the group, weaving the collected Marks into one long thread, and now they were applying it to the wound like a stitch, punching an enormous thread of magic back and forth through the world veil.

"Pull!" Tilly ordered, and the group jerked the thread through, drawing the puckering edges a little closer together.

Lanyard was on his knees, retching to one side. Tilly could not pause to help him, could do nothing but work the tangle of magic against the universe.

Mal let go of his own Mark and pushed through the press of near-exhausted Jesusmen. He held Lanyard in his arms, the man now trembling in a seizure. This close to the tear, Mal could feel the agony of the boundary, a chill that promised to never end.

"Tilly!" he cried up at her, but she shook her head no, even as she watched Lanyard with horror. She could not let the thread go now, or the whole work would come undone. They were so close.

*Mal,* Kirstl came back. *Oh shit, what's wrong with Lanyard?*

"He's hot," Mal said, trying to unbutton his shirt. Froth was running out of the old man's mouth, his heels drumming on the shadow road. "What do I do?"

*Put him on his side. Open his mouth a little. Tilt his head so he doesn't swallow his tongue.*

Mal did so.

*Mal, I can't reach Jenny Rider. She's hiding or something. Something's gone wrong.*

"Pull!" Tilly cried again.

*We're on our own.*

Then a cry. One of the prentices flailed around wildly, attacking any Jesusman he could get close to. Madness, but then it was something more, and the boy's arm grew longer, then turned into a tentacle, and then the boy was pasty white and screeching, a writhing snake that pulsed in and out of stranger shapes.

"Witch! He's turned into a Witch!" someone cried. The thread lost its strength as several abandoned the attempt, guns crackling as they tried to murder the newly born monster, and soon its mouth was bloody as it tore into a former friend. Then another Witch, and another. Soon there were six pasty figures sharing the causeway with them, and Tilly was losing the battle to keep stitching up the universe.

*Mal, let me in,* Kirstl said, and then Mal was a distant observer in his own body, Kirstl in control. She helped to gather up the scattering threads of the Mark, and Tilly was able to finally seal up the tear with a puckering knot, leaving a horrid scar in the sky that would probably never heal.

Even as the world veil settled into stillness and the Jesusmen fought against their own, Lanyard fell into stillness. A moment later he looked up at Mal and Kirstl, face pale, and then white, and then his eyes fell into blank orbs, and his limbs stretched out, his body slowly shifting as his old body finally failed him.

Lanyard suddenly pulled Mal close to him, snarling, and opened his mouth to reveal the jagged fangs. Mal surged forward to seize control of the Tontine. He moved with muscle memory, pulling out his master's old shotgun, and they rolled around on the floor, struggling furiously.

Mal fought with a fury, teeth set in a rictus, eyes red and teary, and then he brought down the butt of the holy gun, leaving the hiss of steam and a howl of pain from what had been Lanyard.

*No!* Kirstl shrieked, but Mal ignored his wife's cry. Even as the tentacles reached for him, Mal jammed the gun that had killed a god into Lanyard's temple.

"Do it!" Lanyard snarled. "Kill me!"

He hesitated.

"I said do it!" Lanyard cried. "Pull the trigger!"

# — 8 —

## BAERTHA

**B**aertha flicked back and forth through the control schemes on the Throne, bristling with impatience. The Blackstar stood to attention by her side, the barest whisker of amusement at her situation.

"I can take the wheel, my queen," he crooned. "Look, a wheel arises for you to grip."

From the strata of confused controls rose a simple ship's wheel, and Baertha took it with caution, glancing once at her lieutenant. The blond dandy at her side gave a shrug.

"You are not in control of the Throne anymore."

"As you say," he said. "You are seated there, not I."

Overhaeven gave another embarrassing lurch, and Baertha thought back to her earliest driving lessons in the Before, her feet struggling to coordinate clutch and accelerator, the vehicle bunny-hopping and stalling. Here she was doing it on a cosmic scale, jostling her subjects with every thwarted movement.

"Tell me of this destination, this potential food source," the Blackstar began.

"No. Do not judge me a fool."

"Let me help. If you plan an assault, your soldiers will need knowledge of the beachhead."

"Trust is earned, Blackstar."

She twisted the Glorious Gyre around with some effort and tried to summon a screen to look through, something like the delicate instruments from the Hann-Slatter Observatory. The best she could get was a porthole, and a sextant appeared on the console in front of her, which seemed to control the view. Grimacing, she peered through it, looking out on the universe.

Out here was the wheeling ballet of stars and galaxies, but at the centre of it all was the creation of the Most High, a nested series of Realms. Before its downfall, Overhaeven had perched at the top like an apex predator, above the Greygulf, the pitch of the Aum, the Underfog, and then there were the Realms to each side, each a spoke to the central axis of this creation. The world veil wrapped everything up in a tight cocoon, isolating each part from the next and shielding all of it from the chill of space.

Here they were, circling the whole mass from outside, a hungry predator sniffing for food. There was no concept for *down* to a ship's wheel, and so she thought of it as an airplane's controls, nudging the wooden hoop forward. The wheel shuddered in her hands, and despite the Glorious Gyre trying to correct their course, they lurched and spun slowly, off axis and wobbling.

"We are gods in the stars, and yet we approach like a drunken turnip!"

She ignored the Blackstar's gibe. If she was right, there was another place for Overhaeven to latch onto, to feed like the miserable mosquito it was.

Exerting her will against the controls of the Throne, she was able to reach beyond the ship's wheel and wrestle out a personal computer, finally dismissing the porthole to gaze out through a flickering monitor. She opened a CAD program, and imagining the point of the Shale mechanism to be the drawing tip, she was able to instruct it to stay in one place, the spinning stilled.

DOWN, she typed, and Overhaeven began a gentle descent. Baertha allowed herself a grin.

"Overrated, those computers," the Blackstar said. "I have trodden worlds where they got out of control. Whole interconnections, the worst of minds permitted to find each other and fester. Best you do away with that and use music like I did."

Then the computer keyboard was slipping through her fingers, and the mixing desk popped up to taunt her before sinking down into the controls and reemerging as a cluster of random instruments which bolted themselves around her. She was a one-man band, complete with honking horns on her knees, a drum upon her back, and a guitar in her hands. The Blackstar revealed his influence with his smirk and then chose to laugh uproariously at her predicament.

"I should destroy you!" she shouted. "Get out of my sight!"

"As you wish, my Queen," he said, departing with a swish of a cloak and the click of a bootheel. It took a long moment for Baertha to dismiss the ridiculous control schema, and the best she could do afterward was bring forth a velvet tray lined with magical foci. Just keeping her connection with the Throne and the Glorious Gyre was taking more and more of her effort, and she suspected that the Blackstar was up to something.

*I should destroy him,* she thought. *I should but—I still need him. And his soldiers. If I don't keep order in here, I'll be thrown down when the Aurum is gone.*

Using a crystal sphere as her visual guide, she nudged Overhaeven closer toward the Greygulf. Even through the opacity of the world veil she could make out the wriggling threads of the shadow-roads, the leaden skies that mirrored her own craft's golden belly.

She remembered that long ago voyage, crossing through there with her husband and a fierce band of friends, leading an exodus through a wild land. They'd fled tragedy toward excitement, and she'd never felt more alive than that day. Now, there was only this most morose of survivals, and the past was thicker than the world veil could ever be.

"There's nothing in there for us," she said. Twitching a wand, she aimed downward.

That was when she felt the stirrings at the very edge of her mind, a clumsy hand fumbling at her formidable defences. All of her Millicents stirred at the intrusion, ready to repel anything that crossed into her consciousness.

The brush of that other mind, and then it suddenly rushed at her, as if trying to force a way through. Then it bounced away, almost comically weak.

Frowning, Baertha set a steady descent with her instruments, and then withdrew into her mind, wondering if this was the Blackstar or some lesser accomplice sent to mess with her. She drew her Millicents around her, as if shrugging into a coat, and journeyed to the very edges of herself, checking the weak points. She'd always visualized these as the windows and doors from her childhood home, fastened with thick iron bolts, and all were secure.

Her clumsy visitor had discovered knocking, and rapped away at the nearest window, the recognizable shave-and-a-haircut pattern common to both Before and Now.

Baertha flexed her considerable will and reached beyond the portal to find the intruder, a minor sorcerer of some stripe. A mortal, not a godling from her own fractured court.

"What the bloody hell are you?" the intruder said.

"I could say the same."

It shook the shutters.

"Jenny, if you're in there we need you!" the voice called. "Jenny!"

Baertha called forth the magic to destroy this nuisance—then intuition told her to stop. It was subtle at first, but now that she was aiming her death spell, she could see what had given her pause.

The intruder was a newly-minted Tontine, wandering around in the Aum without a care for any of the dangers that threatened it.

"Leave now," Baertha said. "You are in danger."

"Wait," the voice said. "There are more than one of you there. I can hear it in your voice."

"I am Tontine, just like you. Go away. Do not return."

Baertha adjusted the spell, repelling the intruder with a lesser force, and then she paused for a long moment in wonder. Another Tontine, and with no one to guide them?

Then she felt her body shaking around, enough to draw her out of the mind-space. She opened her eyes to reveal that the controls had changed in her brief absence, becoming a rolodex of abacuses, spinning, beads sliding from left to right.

"Blackstar!" Baertha shouted, but she could not leave her post to hunt out the villain. A faux oriental watercolour was updated in real-time, an animation that showed Overhaeven spinning out of control, the Shale mechanism extended, and the Greygulf looming.

There was no way to avoid the collision, and Baertha felt it almost physically, the Gyre translating the injuries to Overhaeven as pains to her own body. The stinger that was Shale was dragging through the world veil, tearing it open, and it felt like someone was taking her index finger and bending it right back, almost to the breaking point.

She'd learnt the abacus as a small child, mastering it in hours, and she drew on that long ago fascination, translating the figures as a three-dimensional representation of their position, trajectory, the position of Shale, and a number of other variables. It took her a few minutes to master the calculations, but with a final sliding of the beads she was able to twist Overhaeven away from the edge of the Greygulf, leaving a ragged tear in the world veil as her own craft wobbled away.

For a moment she saw a shadow-road through the open tear and imagined she could see figures clustered upon it, saw the tiny threads as they attempted to repair the injury upon their barren world.

*Witches?* she thought. *No one else is mad enough to stay in there.*

The abacus beads clicked in her fingers. Overhaeven drifted down, down, ever down.

---

"Come out and face me," Baertha yelled, stalking through the halls of the Glorious Gyre. She'd left a construct of herself to operate the controls, a thing of snow and ice that would buy her a little time.

She was answered with a jaunty tune, a whistle. She recognized the opening bars of one of her favourite songs, one he'd composed in her youth. Chasing the sound, Baertha suddenly recoiled as a door slammed into her face, seemingly self-propelled.

She disintegrated it into splinters with a gesture. Deadly magic danced across her fingers as she hunted the traitor. Each hall of priceless artworks changed to reveal images of the Blackstar, in every aspect and costume of his amorphous career.

"Stop that!" she told the Gyre as she asserted her control. For a moment the images were gone and replaced with the original designs, but then the paintings returned, covering every available inch, and then they were joined by statuary of the graceful superstar, and then the doors to the hallway were all gone.

"No, you rotten bastard," Baertha said, and she revealed her next spell, instantly shifting into the ice simulacrum and leaving a pile of slush in the trapped hall. The Blackstar was advancing on her, smiling nastily.

"Die," she said, and then they were battling in earnest, a duel of magic that shook the Gyre around them. Once more Overhaeven drifted loose, the Throne under no one's control.

Worse, Baertha could feel the Throne beginning to reject her, the Gyre turning against her. Much as it had decided for her when she'd shown strength, it now favoured the Blackstar.

He was in her face now and grinning at the thrill of his near victory, waving a rapier that was the focus of a deadly energy, one that she could barely keep at bay. She batted it away with a spear of the darkest shadow.

She tried to call out her Millicents, to draw on their energy, but they were transfixed to his deep eyes, held in thrall. Without words he'd begged Baertha's invisible passengers to hold still and simply look at him awhile.

"I'll have your heart out, love, fresh and steaming on a plate."

He followed through with a rapid lunge, and she threw out a shield to block the blow. He slowed as if carving through treacle, but her spell had been a moment too late. The very tip of his blade pressed into her chest, nicking against the flesh of her heart.

These bodies were symbolic, but death would stick. She staggered back, clutching at her chest. She made to exit the Throne room, but suddenly the door was gone.

"It's over for you, my little usurper," the Blackstar said, watching intently at the blood bubbling between her fingers.

"Oh," she said, pressing her fingers into the wound. "It's here. It's lodged in here."

She drew out a splinter of wood from her heart, shaking the droplets of blood away from it. She shook it again, and suddenly she was holding the Cruik, a fraction of that hideous construct. Lucy had first charmed her heart with it (*babe of gold! lies were told!*), and much later had slain her first body with one swift thrust of the staff.

Then she'd lingered in the false world within the Cruik until her husband cast it into the waters of Shale. In Twice Death, she'd floated in that abominable stew, and this one sole splinter had found her, a sympathetic magic drawing the two together.

Her wounds closed over, and once more she was a terrifying warrior, unbroken and capable, and she sent the Blackstar reeling and retreating into the depths of the Gyre, the magics of the splinter wounding him grievously.

"You. Serve only me, or I will grind you to dust."

The Throne complied. She floated up into the air, the tip of her slippers tracing the marble as she pursued her errant servant.

Only to find the doors were closed against her.

"Obey me!" she said, finally disintegrating the doors, only to have another pair grow in their place, and then a seamless wall. When she finally threw aside the masonry with the Cruik splinter, she was faced with another wall.

The Throne obeyed her, but the Gyre did not.

"Curious," she said. The Queen of Overhaeven returned to the one prize the Blackstar truly wanted, where she settled in to wait.

---

The Glorious Gyre spun wildly. It pressed in on her. It spat out waves of statue-clones of the Blackstar. Baertha dealt with each threat deftly. She was able to operate the Throne for now, and she had her own magics, augmented with the splinter she'd plucked from her heart.

"You damned fool!" one Blackstar screamed at her, crumbling from the feet up. "Bringing the Cruik back in here will doom us all!"

She said nothing, scanning the structure for his true location. Her senses were picking up dozens of sigils circling the Glorious Gyre, and she guessed them to be the Blackstar's lieutenants and cronies, drawn in as if by instinct to this palace coup. Reaching out beyond the boundaries of the Gyre, she snuffed them out with one wave of the Cruik splinter, and the Blackstar howled from some hidden corner.

"You are not our queen! You are our destruction!"

"Only yours."

It came on then, at first a tingle from where her heart had been scratched, and then it washed across her body, her fingers gripping the Cruik tightly, her face twisted with rage.

*Burn it all,* the Cruik whispered to her. *They cannot take it from you if they are all gone.*

In that moment she was once more the laughing mistress in her marital bed, the cackling harridan at Sad Plain, the monster lost in the darkness of her house for centuries on end. She was absolutely consumed by the perfection of the staff in her hand, the curl catching her eye.

But it was only a splinter of the relic, and she was able to tamp down the madness, to seize control of herself, even as the Cruik was reaching out, trying to find more instances of *itself,* to draw them into Overhaeven.

A flash of a vision, and she felt a moment of panic and the old shame. In that moment she'd seen the old temple at Mawson—and the remainder of the Cruik held in a familiar pair of hands.

"Sol," she gasped. "No. What have you done?"

Her husband had resisted the artifact for centuries, tut-tutting Lucy over his Cruik obsession, and now it seemed he'd fallen under its sway.

*Come,* the Cruik commanded. *Connect.*

Sol tightened his grip on the staff, and then the vision ended.

"I see you! You go every which way, but in the end you are trapped in here with me," the Blackstar said. "Sniffing around the Now. Mewling for help in the Aum! Pathetic."

Baertha had set the Throne back to the abacus arrangement, which seemed to be the most reliable set of controls. Twitching beads, she set them on a gentle descent through the cosmos and adjusted the watercolour display to show their position against the central axis.

They'd finally left the Greygulf and were gently sinking alongside the Aum, that place of darkness perfected. Where the lost Papa Lucy had once wandered, peering out through mirrors, and where all Tontines were understood to exist.

*That blundering pup that came to my door,* she thought ruefully. *They need to keep silent, grow their strength. Learn the threats that orbit them.*

The infant Tontine would likely draw a predator soon, and its fate meant nothing to her. Her own mindscape was here, but it was a fortress unparalleled, hidden and strong. She could see it as the faintest thread on the watercolour, where her mindscape connected to her physical form in the Overhaeven, but only because she knew where to look.

*Click. Click.* The abacus beads shifted under her fingers as she cautiously guided Overhaeven past the Aum. The eaters in the dark were watching them, and in many places the world veil began to bulge. She changed course and brought them out slightly, fearing what might happen if the veil broke and they were dragged into the darkness, broken apart like a honeycomb between a pack of hungry bears.

"Damnit," she said, suddenly doubling over. The thought of their Aurum stock made her stomach clench, and she was seized with the addict's need and a sudden panicked thought.

The Blackstar had trapped her in here. She could not get to the Aurum. All he had to do was starve her out.

"Blackstar," she cried out. "Attend me."

"I think not."

"Aurum, now. Or I will ram us into the Aum, and we all die in the dark. Or worse, we don't."

"You bluff."

Baertha slid five beads across at once, and Overhaeven crashed into the world veil at speed. She raised up the Shale mechanism and held it cocked, ready to tear through.

"Last chance."

She touched her finger to the bead and meant it.

A moment later a statue of the Blackstar rose from the floor, proffering a flask of Aurum to Baertha. She took it and drained it like cheap student wine.

She withdrew and continued their descent.

---

"This is your plan? To simply return to the Underfog?"

Baertha ignored the criticism, and she felt a slight pressure in some far corner of herself as Overhaeven brushed against the world veil down to Gan-Eden, now a glorious realm of sunlight and rewarded souls. The veil was still thin here, damaged from the long attachment of the Shale mechanism. As if drawn by muscle memory, the enormous siphon lifted toward the scar, a phallus aching for connection.

More godlings were daring the Gyre now, running forward to tap against the sides, trying to halt the rotations and throw her off balance. Overhaeven wobbled on the spot, but Baertha focused on the Throne, only the Throne, and she touched the Cruik fragment against it.

The unruly controls could not fight against her iron will, and finally the mess of tarot decks and sacrificial stones sank into the construct, replaced with a neat workstation from the Hann-Slatter Observatory. The viewpoint became an instrument capable of piercing the secrets of the galaxies, a screen able to show images from the other side of the world veil.

Which is when she saw Jesus's enormous fucking castle at the edge of Gan-Eden, a hulk of glass and stone that squatted atop that beautiful final beach. The palisade was packed with weaponry from the ridiculous to the terrifying, everything from a trebuchet to cannonry to magical foci drawing Aether up from the waters below the castle.

Of course Jesus was there, facing them fearlessly from the ramparts. John Leicester too, and even sweet Ray, somehow alive in that land of spirits.

Baertha frantically ordered a change of course, and she put Overhaeven into a rapid descent, like a submarine fleeing the depth charges. She swore as the weapons lined up on them, unseen hands adjusting angles, fuses alit, crystals beginning to glow with a white heat.

All of it unleashed upon Overhaeven all at once, a lance that punched through the world veil and sank deep into their side. Even a lucky hit scored the Glorious Gyre and sent it rattling. Baertha clung to the Throne, miserable as she fled from her old friends.

*They don't even know that I'm in here. They think I'm dead.*

Another salvo, but a lesser one, simply scoring them in the rump as they fled. Baertha devoted some energy to shoring up the wounds in the structure, and the simplest thing was to shrink the entire surface area, sealing over the holes in the hull. Dead godlings floated about in the empty belly of the craft, and the thin pool of the Golden Sea sloshed and taunted Baertha, far away from the Gyre that she was trapped in.

Her stress levels climbing, Baertha began to get the shakes. She craved Aurum, as powerless to resist as any junkie, and it burnt her that she had fallen so far. Her very existence now reliant on a golden drug. Baertha tried to focus within, to still the pain and the loss of control.

"Blackstar!" she screamed, bare moments later. "Aurum, now!"

"Are you serious? You nearly killed us all with that stunt."

"We had to know. Please. I beg you."

"Give up the Throne. I will bring you a thimbleful and you will thank me."

She shook and almost took the deal, knowing she was trapped, had failed hard. Perhaps she could beg for a role in his court—or for a quick death.

Then she stopped, and breathed, and gripped the splinter of the Cruik tightly, forming it into an image of the real thing. She drew in as much power as she could and held that heady power for a long moment. Remembered who she was.

"If you want the Throne, come here and take it, you whiny little bitch. Otherwise, obey your fucking queen."

She punctuated that by slamming the butt of the Cruik against the floor, over and over, and willed pain into the Gyre—into the Blackstar, who was its temporary master.

"I will knock your brains loose, you traitor. Do it! Attend your queen."

They fought for hours, a mental arm-wrestle that tested each to the core, even as he advanced on her in person, one agonising inch at a time, deadly smile spreading. Then she seized dominance, imagining the Blackstar pinned beneath an image of the Cruik, the butt end grinding against his sternum. Her renewed willpower was enough to make this a reality, and she slid him across the floor, removing the Cruik splinter so he could grovel at her feet. Shaken, he held up a flask of Aurum to Baertha, who drank deeply.

---

Down, down the hulk of Overhaeven sank, below the lip of Gan-Eden.

She'd brought others into the Glorious Gyre, once more answering to her strength. The Blackstar was sulking but obedient, and others were falling into his example. Godlings of every stripe, stepping out of sigil-form and into three dimensions.

She hated them all. Beast-headed amalgams, humans mingling with alien beasts, and all of them watching her hungrily.

The Cruik fragment radiated hatred for all of them, and she thought she understood some of its ambition now. From what she'd learned, Overhaeven was at first the Cruik's prison, accidentally discovered by a cadre of spirits ambitious to break back into Life. They'd freed the Cruik, but refused to serve it as it deserved, and they bound the construct after a brutal civil war, casting it into Gan-Eden once they'd invaded that land and made it into a new prison.

*Burn them all!* the Cruik fragment crooned, and it took supreme self-control to not give in. Baertha sipped at the last of the Aurum flask, running her tongue along the edge, picking up the flecks of pollution.

Most of all, Baertha hated the addiction she'd been reborn into. She wanted to go back up to Gan-Eden and fly the white flag. Leave these parasites, and beg Jesus and John for their help.

Even face Sol again, who'd somehow been reborn from his Boneman persona, skeleton now lined with flesh. Wielding most of the Cruik probably had something to do with this. The tiny splinter of the Cruik in her hands throbbed with sympathy at the thought, and she realized it was fighting its own battles. All it wanted was to be reunited with the rest of itself and to resume its rampage across the universe. It was as addicted and broken as she was.

As with her first life, Baertha was driven and determined to prove herself under her own merits. No Cruik, no Aurum, no Throne. Just herself. She circled the problem over and over, convinced there was a solution to it all, some way to leverage an advantage from this terrible situation.

It all had something to do with the other Tontine, but what?

The godlings watched her impatiently, and she saw how some of those with longer memories looked on the Cruik, no doubt remembering what it had done when last here. Half of their number had paid with their lives to subdue and expel it. Here it was again, now in the hands of the outsider queen.

"We have lost the Underfog," Baertha finally said. "It is too well-defended now."

A rumble of sycophantic agreement.

"But there is another way. Observe."

Overhaeven sank away from the roots of Gan-Eden, threatening to drop away into the wider universe, but still the world veil continued, enveloping another realm.

"Oh, there is more down here. You wise ones, there is a whole world here that you have overlooked."

A flash in the darkness, and then another. Lightning, and then they all saw the feuding cloud beasts, rising up to the crystal of the Glass Lands in Gan-Eden, beating against the glass and tumbling away.

The clouds met and divided, an act that seemed equal parts war and mating ritual. Baertha nudged the controls, guiding them lower, and then the clouds gave way, showing them a landscape unimaginable.

Cities set in a dark and smoking landscape, glittering jewels of light and flame, connected by rivers of magma. Baertha zoomed in with her delicate instruments, and suddenly they could all see the horrors in between the cheerful coals of the settlements.

Souls, but where they walked joyously in Gan-Eden, here they were starved things, tormented and bound. Masses of souls were ferried about between the cities, driven by the lash to tortures of every description.

"Endless misery for the sinners and the fallen," Baertha said. "Perfected. And look upon their masters."

Their jailers were monstrous, creatures of horn and fang, and they worked with industry and glee, encouraging their fellows to depravities beyond even the cruelties of Overhaeven. Often the souls would collapse beneath this punishment, adding their own bright red fluids to the lava flows.

"We'd thought the old Underfog to be the end point for all the Once-Dead souls, but that was your own doing. Gan-Eden was where the blessed souls went to, so what of the truly wicked?"

She gestured at the souls, the lava flows, and pointed out a type of delta where the red rivers collected, spilling a crimson spray out into the universe.

"This is the Low Place, something the magicians of my era long suspected. Now we go to latch onto their leavings, and drink deeply."

The godlings looked hungrily upon the scene and were hers to the core.

# — 9 —

## SOL

Sol sat miserably at the dinner table, poking at his meal. On the other side Lucy was laughing heartily, surrounded by empty bottles, with an awe-struck young woman seated on his lap. Attendants waited to answer to their every need.

The Eminent Three had given up their chambers to the returned gods, and Lucy had decided to throw himself a party. Outside, telegrams had flown thick and fast. The ambassador from Crosspoint had turned up to the Temple, lodging a complaint against their sheltering of the fugitive Papa Lucy. In moments the High Flenser had promptly butchered the man and fed him into a greypot.

War now, at the worst possible moment.

"Oh, the sour face on my brother!" Lucy scoffed, groping the girl. "He's wasted centuries of power like this. Face set like a chicken's arsehole and never once enjoyed himself."

"Lucy, we need to discuss things. Your plans."

"I plan to get loaded, and then I plan to get up to my nuts in guts."

The girl laughed in mock outrage.

"Lucy. We're running out of time. We need to get to work."

"He wants to get to work," Papa Lucy crooned in the girl's ear. "So do I."

"You said you could fix things," Sol said. "I need details. Now."

"Brother," Lucy said, his voice settling into a hard edge. "Don't talk family business in front of the help."

"You have the things you came for, so what happens next?"

Lucy gave out a dark bubble of a laugh.

"You've got some nerve. After what you did to me."

"What *I* did to *you*?"

The girl froze on Lucy's lap, a terrified smile plastered across her face. Sol pushed away his plate.

"You've cost me everything," Sol said quietly.

The Cruik met his hand, or the other way around, and he held it levelled across the table. Lucy met his gaze, expression guarded for a long moment. Then his lips flexed into a taut smile.

"Well, well. Look at the cast-iron balls on this guy."

Sol felt the Cruik twist in his grip. His vision constricted into a tunnel, and he felt an angry pulse hammering behind his eyes. Before him was the architect of centuries worth of misery, powerless and at his mercy, and even now his brother smiled, unworried by Sol Pappagallo.

*Kill him. Do it now! It's the only way you can save the world.*

The perfect curl in the hook thrummed, and it continued to whisper seductive promises, slowly stoking a hot rage in him. He thought of the countless ways he could break Papa Lucy, and knew he had the power to reduce him to atoms with a simple act of will.

"Oh. It's got you good, brother," Lucy said. "I've seen that look more than once."

"Shut up."

"My Riders of Cruik, consumed from within. Baertha, who didn't have a fucking prayer of controlling the thing."

The girl sobbed, even as Lucy gripped her tighter in his lap. Somewhere in the apartments, a plate shattered, and Sol heard the sound of running feet.

"But it never got to me. The Cruik tried everything to own me, but I was always the boss."

"Bullshit," Sol said thickly.

*Kill him!* This time Jenny Rider urged him on, a faint undercurrent to the alien rage of the construct. Sol felt tears running down his face, and his hand shook.

"Well, shit or get off the pot," Lucy said. "Kill me before I die of fucking boredom."

Centuries of sibling rivalry sat between them. Sol remembered every one of Lucy's manipulations, the mirror to his own unconditional love. He'd enabled every second of this, adoring his abuser.

"You piss-weak cunt," Lucy said, laughing. "I don't have a skerrick of magic left, and I'm still not afraid of you."

Sol gave a little strangled cry, and after a moment this turned into a full-throated roar, every disappointment channelled into one perfect killing moment, and he was both the source and the conduit, and he felt the destructive force pulse down his arm and into the Cruik, a beam of pure hatred blasting outward.

Lucy twisted suddenly, allowing the girl in his lap to intercept the deadly ray. Sol could only look on in horror as she wailed in anguish, swiftly turning to ash and dust.

He sat there, frozen and shocked, the Cruik outstretched like a smoking gun. Lucy rose from his chair, calmly wiping the soot of the dead girl from his hands, and he walked around the table.

"I killed her," Sol whispered.

"There are plenty more fish in the sea, mate."

Papa Lucy plucked the Cruik out of Sol's hands, who did not resist.

---

Papa Lucy sat cross-legged in the sands of the combat pit, the Cruik laid out across his lap. Sol lingered nearby, sullen and lost, and his brother had ignored him for hours.

Even without the Cruik, Sol was a capable magician. He could more than kill a man with his own magic. The sanctum was littered with guns and magical foci, and he could arm up, come against his brother, spill his blood once and for all.

Then he remembered the girl. The Boneguard on the mountain.

The entire world of Before, burnt up by their ambition. His wife, twisted and broken and finally destroyed by their bad blood. Sol was just as culpable, a lieutenant to all of these evils. He'd organized every scheme, massaged away any opposition his brother had ever faced. Rationalized away every horrid truth of Lucy's actions and then did what Lucy had wanted anyway, even what he thought his brother might want.

*I am just as bad as he is,* he thought, and then he realized the truth of things. He could not destroy Papa Lucy because he *was* Papa Lucy.

"You all right over there?" Lucy said. "I can hear you mouth-breathing and having a good sulk over my shoulder."

Lucy unfolded from his cross-legged pose, and he walked over to his brother, considering him for a long moment. Finally, he clasped Sol by the shoulder.

"For what it's worth, little brother, I'm proud that you took your shot."

Sol nodded.

"I am close," he said. "I've almost unpicked Jenny's net. Then I'll have my magic back, and I can carry the burden for us."

He gestured at the Cruik, and Sol ached for it, but he faced yet an even more powerful addiction.

His brother's approval.

"I've never lied to you," Lucy said. "We did need to come here. We need to gear up with our old stuff, and then I'll take you to where we can get the fuel for Ray's little gate."

Lucy undid the wind-up watch at his wrist, an old favourite he'd looted from the shrines, and he tossed it to Sol.

"Keep an eye on that," he said. "I bet you I can bust through Jenny's protections in under an hour. If I win, I'll get that bottle of good scotch I saw in there. If it takes me longer, you can have it."

"Okay."

"Hey Sol?"

"Yeah?"

"We're going to save the world again. You and me."

It took Papa Lucy just under thirty minutes to regain his magic. Sol quietly helped on the sidelines, as he always did.

114 · **Jason Fischer**

"Don't worry about Crosspoint," Lucy said. "We'll be welcomed back as fucking heroes once we get the fuel for Ray's gate."

They stood at the very top of the Selector's Tower. Sol had only managed three flights of stairs before his badly-healed body gave up on him, at which point Lucy hefted him up in a clumsy fireman's lift. He'd raised the Cruik and flew them both up the centre of the stairwell, laughing the whole way.

"It's good to have my magic back," Lucy said. "As far as punishments go, I'll admit you folks bent me over pretty good."

Sol said nothing. He'd seen his true self for the first time and did not like what he saw. He'd worn a pointless hairshirt for his brother his whole life, but despite every shitty thing his brother had ever done, he threw in his lot with Lucy at the first moment of weakness. Every time.

Years of horror and acres of bone shifted underneath their feet, all of it created in service of Lucy's ambition. *Their* ambition.

Together, the Pappagallo brothers could achieve great things, and he'd always known this, he used it as one of the excuses for Lucy's atrocities. He hoped that this time it was the right move.

They had rucksacks filled with everything they needed. Wands, rods, and staves strapped to every surface. The brothers had gleaned as many protective gewgaws as they could from their old belongings. Sol wore a scarab over his heart, rings that hummed with power, a choker that had been Baertha's once, and a sash that was supposedly proof against blade and bullet.

"All right, we're nearly ready to go," Lucy said. "There's just one thing left to do. Pay attention, numbnuts, I can only do this once."

Papa Lucy held up the Cruik for many long minutes, wordless and completely still. A strong wind picked up from the ocean, and Sol could see thick banks of black clouds rolling in, headed toward the Selector's Tower.

Sol staggered as the wind buffeted them on the rooftop, and he threw up as many protective wards as he dared to, turning aside what he could of the gale. The storm clouds seemed to hang just above them, and fat spatters of rain fell.

"Watch, and tell me you understand," Lucy shouted above the din. He gripped the Cruik tightly and suddenly shook as a dozen lightning bolts struck the staff, and then a dozen more.

Sol cried out. His brother was an x-ray, bones visible, holding all that energy in—and then some.

"Tell me!" Lucy shouted.

"I don't understand!"

Lucy drew in more lightning.

"You'll die!"

Lucy turned to Sol and gave a smile that was a photograph negative of black teeth against too much internal light.

"I won't. But they need to."

Lucy lowered the Cruik toward the Temple, lining it up like a rifle-shot.

"Tell me that you understand!"

"I do! I do!" Sol cried. "Do it!"

Papa Lucy ejected all of that pent up energy into the Temple, and it shattered instantly, the walls exploding, the domed roof collapsing, and thousands of the Family faithful dying instantly.

Lucy dispersed the storm with a wave of the Cruik, and then he cast the staff to the rooftop with a clatter.

"Get up," he said, and the next moment Jenny Rider rose, weeping, utter misery etched on her face.

"I don't understand," she sobbed. "Why?"

"He just saved the city," Sol said, numb and weary. "He stopped a war with Crosspoint. Saved all the refugees."

"You monsters," she said, and then rounded on Sol. "I thought you were the good one."

"I never was," Sol said wearily. "Lucy's just more honest about things."

"Time to go, fuckers," Lucy said, and with a wave of his hand he carved open a door in the universe.

They entered Gan-Eden, Lucy forging confidently out of the Edgemist and into the golf courses and tracts of mansions.

"The Aether from here isn't enough," Sol said. "We need Aurum to power Ray's gate."

"You've got no imagination as per usual. Hold all your questions till the end of the fucking tour."

They made no attempt to hide, and every few moments a spirit would flee from the legendary Papa Lucy. Cars, trains, even helicopters escaped, the imagined mansions crumbling as the owners abandoned them. Clouds of messenger moths flew forth, giving word that the ultimate gatecrasher had arrived.

The golf course fell apart with the fog of an undone dream, and soon Lucy, Sol, and Jenny were confronted by a posse of warriors. Gunmen, knights, and samurai, blocking their path.

"Stand down, Papa Lucy," one of them shouted, the spirit of a lawman from the Before. "We are the order of the Gidon, and this place is forbidden to you."

"Step aside, chucklefucks," Lucy said. "Last chance."

They came on in a moment of gunfire and combat, these warriors long versed in the rules of this realm. They slid and shifted, each step a thought. Sol felt the thud of a bullet outside his heart and saw his protective scarab crack in half. A samurai attempted to sever his head, his blade shattering instead on Baertha's old choker.

Gripping Jenny by the upper arm, Lucy killed one after another of the Gidon, shrugging off dozens of grievous injuries. More of the Gidon came, drawn from across this afterlife to defend it, even as Lucy and Sol blasted them apart, their magics destroying these Once-Dead warriors.

"This is just too easy," Lucy chortled, a moment before a vehicle covered in flesh erupted from the earth, slamming into him at high speed. The trio of intruders were scattered like skittles.

"WICKED! FALSE DAWN KING!" the House of Torana barked. "LORD GOODFACE! HAS A BAD FACE NOW!"

The car pounced on them, driving and bouncing over Jenny before knocking Sol onto his backside. It then shifted into reverse and sent Papa Lucy rolling in a painful spindle of arms and legs.

It came for Lucy with its mouth wide open, ready to gobble him whole, but at the last moment he pulled Jenny to her feet, changing her back into the Cruik with a simple pass of his hands. He held the staff like a cricket bat, winding up for the swing, and met the car with a ferocious strike, sending it rolling and bouncing, eventually sliding to a halt on its roof.

"Stupidest bloody thing I ever saw," Lucy said, releasing the Cruik and allowing it to flow out into Jenny's shape.

"You work for me now, car," he said. "Understand?"

"NO. SWORN TO FIGHT FOR THE GIDON! KILL YOU!"

Lucy simply set a boot against the side of the trunk and gave a heave. Perfectly balanced on its roof, the car slowly spun.

"How's that working?"

"I WILL RESIST. TAKE YOU TO JESUS AND JOHN."

"Oh, we're gonna have words with them. But not just yet. We've gotta save the world or some bullshit."

He flipped the car back onto its wheels with a gesture.

"Behave. We're climbing in now."

It snapped at them, but Lucy held out a pair of tuning forks, chiming them together just so. An immense pressure began to push against the car's sides, and Sol could see the flesh splitting and bruising.

"NO. PLEASE."

"Open up and act like a good little taxi, please and thank you."

The House of Torana opened its doors, utterly exhausted and defeated. Lucy, Sol, and Jenny climbed in, sitting on the organic upholstery.

"Disgusting," Lucy said, shifting around on what might have been an oversized liver or tongue.

The House of Torana drove sullenly away, until Lucy applied some other torture from his bag of tricks, and it drove quickly enough then.

---

Once more Sol and Lucy travelled across Gan-Eden, the site of so many of their battles. In the backseat, Jenny lolled in a state of shock, the Cruik within her perhaps recognizing its own tortured journey toward old failures.

The House of Torana ate up the miles, lurching forward in metaphysical fits and starts whenever Lucy applied the gas. They reached the Glass-Lands in a matter of hours, easing to a stop in between the rows of black obelisks, a grid that stretched for miles in all directions.

"No funny business," he warned the car, and they all got out.

"Jesus and John are just up ahead," Sol said, honestly unsure how he felt about that. They'd spent years as allies, working to improve the worlds of the living and the dead, and in a matter of days Sol had undone everything. He'd shifted to stand with his brother, the eternal adversary, and so now he was an enemy.

*It's not too late to turn Lucy in,* he thought, but then he looked over at Jenny, a misery caught between two worlds. Lucy was unbeatable now, and the best Jesus and John could hope for was a swift destruction.

"We need to be quick," Sol said.

Lucy was pacing around the nearest obelisk, examining it closely. Underneath them, one of the immense cloud beasts bumped against the glass. Lightning crackled. Sol jumped.

With a squeal of tires and the whining of an engine at full throttle, the House of Torana fled across the Glass-Lands, heading toward Jesus and John Leicester at the first moment of distraction.

"Good. Ugly fucking thing," Lucy said. He lay with his belly to the glass, looking through it, and then he rose with a satisfied grunt. "The fuel you need is down there."

"What? This is madness."

"It will work. You wanted a desperate answer, well here is one on a silver platter with fucking caviar and tableware. Take it and be grateful."

The clouds shifted, and far below were the mysterious cities of fire and smoke, bright crimson spots lighting up a plain of the darkest night.

The Low Place.

"Dangerous to be here if you're wicked, right?" Lucy said. "Now that Gan-Eden is up and running again. If you pass through the

THE BRIDE & THE BIRDMAN • 119

Glass-Lands as a Once-Dead, you are judged. Condemned if wicked. Gobbled up by the glass."

He smiled, his old shit-eating grin.

"Here's the trick though," Lucy said. "You don't have to be dead to face justice here. It's anyone's for the asking."

Lucy took Sol's hand with his right hand, and held Jenny's in his left, and neither fought him. He led them to the nearest obelisk and stood before it.

"Hey, concierge," Lucy said. "We're ready to check in."

*VISITORS!* the obelisk displayed on its smooth obsidian face, golden text swimming up from the depths of the stone.

"Look inside my black heart, you bastards. Open the front door."

*CHECKING.*

*TRUTH IS FOUND.*

*SOULS ARE DAMNED.*

"All of us?" Sol whispered.

The following list appeared on the obelisk, as permanent as if chiselled into the stone.

*LUCIANO PAPPAGALLO.*

*SOLOMON PAPPAGALLO.*

*JENNIFER RIDER.*

The glass opened swiftly to swallow them, and they fell through, buffeted from cloud to cloud, sent down to suffer eternally in the Low Place.

# — 10 —

## MAL

I said do it!" Lanyard cried. "Pull the trigger!"

Mal shook his head. Beneath him, his master writhed and hissed, his broken old flesh now fully the pasty dough of a Witch.

"Do what I bloody tell you to do, boy," Lanyard said through gritted fangs. "I can't hold on for much longer."

Mal rested his finger on the double-triggers. One twitch and it would be done, it would be made right. In the greatest miracle, Lanyard still possessed the supreme self-control he'd shown his whole life, holding off on his murderous rampage, allowing his prentice to put him down.

Mal had heard the old story about Lanyard murdering his master Bauer with a rock. It had broken Lanyard for years, sent him on a dark path until he redeemed himself, and irony now had his own prentice dispatching him.

But Lanyard still had the presence of mind to submit now, to await the thunder of the gun. To finish things in the proper way. Which meant that he was still in there. Was still in control.

Still alive.

"No," Mal said, standing up, the muzzle of the shotgun drifting away slightly.

"Kill me!" Lanyard shrieked. "You little shit! You have to."

"I can't. I'm sorry."

Mal backed away, glancing at the frenzied combat all around him. He saw Collybrock kicking and tearing at the doughy innards of a Witch, and he ran blindly for the reins, scrambling up into her saddle.

Behind him, Lanyard was rising, slowly stalking toward him, long claws stretching out.

Still, Mal loved him, and he did not turn the gun on the only father worthy of the name. He had only one choice now.

"Mal!" Tilly cried out, busily fending off two more prentices that had gone Witch. "We need your help!"

The Order was finally broken, crumbling around him as much as the shadow-roads, and all Mal could think of was escape, to run and run and never look back.

*Mal! Stop this! We need to help them!*

"No!" Mal shouted, fighting Kirstl's attempt to wrestle back control of the Tontine. He dug his heels into Collybrock's sides and weaved through the melee.

Once more he was the terrified slave, the unruly prentice hiding in the alleys of Crosspoint from his punishments, the failure who'd left Bauer to die down in the Underfog. He wasn't ready to measure up to anything and couldn't make a damn decision for himself.

Even as he cleared the last deadly tangle between man and monster, Mal was suddenly struggling against the reins as Collybrock refused, disobeying his heels, his pleas for the bird to run, run, and run some more.

"No! Mal help! Wrong!" the bird said, turning back in wide-eyed appeal.

"Run, you damn bird!" Mal said, striking her in the face with the butt of the shotgun, the first time he'd ever laid a hand on her. With a miserable squawk Collybrock trudged on, loping away from the screaming, the gunshots, the sound of wet feeding. Ashamed, Mal slid the shotgun into the sheath on his saddle, noted her blood on the stock.

*Mal, please don't do this. This isn't you. Isn't us.*

Mal stuffed Kirstl away into a dark corner of his mind, along with all of his hurt and fear, and then there was nothing left but to follow through on his instinctive urge to escape, to survive.

He rode to their stronghold at the Terminus and then paused. It was a bolthole, a death trap, no place to hide. Flexing his will, he reached out for the shadow-road and shifted the far end away from Terminus. Casting about for another doorway, he suddenly realized he didn't know of any safe destinations. He wasn't much of a magician yet, and he was lost.

Connect to the wrong door and he may end up in some world full of beasts, or even a place foreign to life itself.

"I don't know enough!" he sobbed. He knew he was dead, lost, and in his moment of panic he'd chosen to be prey in an ashen realm of hunters.

"Stupid, stupid!"

"Stupid!" Collybrock agreed mournfully.

He pointed the end of the shadow-road toward the ash-grey of the ground instead, and raced for the desolate wastelands, hoping for a place to hide.

Far behind him, he saw the looming figure of Lanyard, now a great grandfather snake with a human torso, sprouting claws and murder, slithering and undulating after him at a great pace.

He heard some muffled instruction from Kirstl, even felt his hand twitch toward the sheathed shotgun, but he reinforced his control over their arrangement. His emotional meltdown seemed enough to overrule anything his wife could try.

"Come back," Lanyard cried, close enough to be heard. "We have unfinished business, boy!"

Crying, Mal flicked the reins, urging Collybrock toward the drooping end of the road. Then it fell to the depths of the Greygulf with a crash of white dust. Collybrock slid awkwardly, claws scrambling as the road twisted and flexed underneath her.

Mal chanced a look over his shoulder. He could not see Lanyard, but then the road flexed again, half-broken and finally settling to the ground. One white hand appeared over the side, and then it was a snake's tail, and then a rolling mass of limbs and faces came over the side and onward. Above rose the grim torso of Lanyard, mouth spreading wide, a mournful cry of hunger and loss preceding him, his many arms spread wide.

"Boy!" Lanyard said. "I need you!"

Weaving through the dead brush and the wreckage of a thousand worlds, Mal rode low in the saddle, reduced to mindless survival. He gasped as a flame of perfect grey hissed past his face, searing him in a near miss. A box thorn exploded in a greasy fit, flames licking upward.

Behind him, Lanyard had formed a shotgun out of his own doughy body. With it, he ejected yet another blast of colourless flame. It whistled toward Collybrock, who leapt over the mysterious energy with a squawk.

"Leave me alone!" Mal yelled.

Boy and bird sped over a shifting dune of ash, and before them was a fallen aeroplane, stripped down to the frame, and from it emerged more Witches, pasty-white and grinning, eye-sockets dark circles that tracked him. They formed around Lanyard, accepting him instantly, and they pursued Mal as one.

"Fuck off!" Collybrock squawked, and despite himself Mal barked out in laughter, tinged with hysteria.

The Witch pack unleashed a fusillade of grey flames at him, a searing hot sorcery that seared Collybrock's flanks more than once. A lucky shot set Mal's vest on fire, which he shed with panicked cries.

*They're trying to bring down Collybrock,* Kirstl said faintly, pushing against Mal's panicked guard. *We need to get out of the open!*

"I'm trying!" Mal grunted.

Then salvation from an unlikely quarter. A boil appeared in the world veil, visible as if through a heat haze. A bleedthrough, hanging low in the dull grey sky. Mostly they appeared in the upper limits of the Greygulf, but this one was closer, perhaps a hundred feet above them.

The Now began to answer its call, and the two Realms reached for each other, close to connecting.

*Mal, let me in. Let me take over!*

"But—"

*No more arguments! Trust your bloody wife for once.*

Mal ceded control, watching from a passenger seat as Kirstl ran Collybrock in a wide loop beneath the bleedthrough, the Witches and their grey flames getting closer and closer. Kirstl cast a glance at the pursuing pack, and Mal saw Lanyard stumble in confusion, looking on as Mal had seemingly given up and was awaiting the inevitable. The Witch Lanyard let his fleshy shotgun droop, falling back even as his new brethren surged forward.

Then Kirstl looked straight up and dragged her clenched fist down in a sudden motion. Small stones fell around them, and then a cluster of masonry, and then the looming arc of a shadow-road, coming down from far above. Kirstl waggled her fist back and forth, breaking apart the road like a dog savaging a rabbit, and an entire span of the road fell onto the Witch pack, smashing them into paste.

Still stones fell, and one struck their body in the shoulder, another striking Collybrock fiercely across the head, sending the bird staggering and crying out weakly.

"Come on," Kirstl said with Mal's mouth. She brought down the remaining segment of the ruined shadow-road and built a ramp up into the almost-formed bleedthrough. Guiding the wounded bird onto the walkway, she placed them directly between the two bubbles.

*Look back,* Mal urged Kirstl. *To the others.*

"You made your choice to run," Kirstl said bitterly, but all the same she looked up at the road the Jesusmen had made to the great tear in the world veil. Small figures were still moving around on the shadow-road, but it was hard to make out much.

*Mark of Farsight.*

"For shit's sake," Kirstl grumbled, but she made the Mark. Mal looked on to see the surviving Jesusmen being pursued into the Terminus, with more of their number now turned into Witches.

Tilly destroyed the shadow-road when the last survivor made it into the structure, scattering Witches like bad seeds, and then the bleedthrough happened around Mal and his latest failure instantly vanished.

Daylight, sudden and intense, and Collybrock staggered out of a modest-sized bleedthrough, Kirstl holding on for dear life around her neck. There were houses, and a shop or two, and even a car that had come through in near perfect condition. They didn't touch a thing.

They heard some excited cries, and a small group of Leicesterites approached, hailing them. They'd likely sniffed out this spot and set camp here, waiting for the bleedthrough, but it had come through complete with a bloodied bird-rider and more questions than Mal and Kirstl cared to answer.

"Go girl, go!" Kirstl urged, and Collybrock found her speed, lurching forward through the scrub and scattering the confused onlookers. They sped off into the distance, leaving behind a fortune and a story that would grow with the telling.

---

Back in the Greygulf, the surviving Jesusmen settled into their last redoubt, doomed and cut off from all escape. Below them, the land was dead and still. At the edge of the universe, the scar in the world veil still wept the chill of vacuum and would do so for months, if not years. Below, at the site of Kirstl's miraculous escape, a dozen Witches were leaking out, pasty white fluids smashed flat by the weight of a road.

A long, low groan, and then the tip of a searching tentacle came out of the rubble, probing at stones, and then it became a great wriggling grandfather snake, fighting free of the wreckage. Finally, it formed into a pasty white ghost of a man, the exact figure of Lanyard Everett. The Witch stared upward, blank eyes fixed upon the exact place his adopted son had escaped him.

"Boy," he said, a low note of hate. He then turned toward the spire of the Terminus.

He was just as determined as he had ever been, and on the other side of this transformation he understood a new truth. Lanyard Everett had one job, *the same job*, and nothing else had changed except for the target.

Mal had emerged well into the Overland, across the Niven and even toward the Riverland itself. The grain farms were burnt stubble now. Many hadn't bothered replanting, their farms abandoned as they'd thrown in their lot with the stream of refugees.

They spent their first night inside an abandoned farmhouse, setting a fire and eating well from their food stores. Mal spent a long time that night tending to Collybrock's wounds with stitches and ointment, and for the first time ever the bird shied away from his touch. One moment of lashing out in anger and fear, and he'd broken years of trust with his best friend.

"I'm so sorry," he told Collybrock, tears falling. "I shouldn't have done that."

"Hurt me," Collybrock said.

"I know. I—everything went wrong. Please, please forgive me."

"Don't want Mal," the bird said huffily. "Want Kirstl."

Mal retreated inward and let Kirstl take over, and instantly the bird was calm and crooning, recognizing that a different person shared the room with her. Later Kirstl made a up a bed on the comfortable mattress that had been too big for the family to take, and they settled into sleep in front of the fire, Collybrock resting her head across Mal's tummy, crooning under Kirstl's gentle stroking touch.

"What happens now?" Kirstl said to the empty room.

*We ran. We're not Jesusmen anymore.*

"Yep."

The fire ticked, and Collybrock began to snore against the questing *scritch, scritch* of Mal's ragged fingernails.

"I'm not okay with what we did," Kirstl said. "Lanyard needed us to end him. Tilly needed us. Hell, she still needs us."

*We can't go back. We're deserters. We'll get shot as cowards.*

"Never too late to do the right thing," Kirstl said, but Mal was sullen in his silence, then and even in the dreamspace when their body gave into sleep.

They awoke, and Mal found Kirstl in her own rebellion, refusing to pilot the body, and so he gave in to his need to empty his bladder and prepare food. Collybrock reluctantly accepted the damper he made over the coals, though she wouldn't speak to him at all.

"Sorry again, girl," he said, and wandered out to look at the dawn. In the distance, a quarrelling flock of cockatoos chattered across the sky, fighting over some small creature that they'd snatched up, tearing it apart while it was still alive.

*Tea,* Kirstl eventually demanded, and Mal dug through an abandoned jar the family had overlooked, putting the last few crumbs into a billy to boil.

*I've had time to think,* she said, as Mal sipped at a chipped enamel mug. *You made a decision, a bad one I reckon, but it's done.*

"Yep," he said, once more picturing the wild face of Lanyard, now a pasty white monster intent on his death. Even knowing his old master was crushed to death, he still shivered from the memory.

*So now we live a while. On our own. Like we always wanted.*

"Till the Range gets us?"

*Till then. Or it might stop just north of Mawson, like Sol reckons it might.*

Mal looked over the abandoned farmhouse. It was well-built and had served a large family well. There were pens for animals, and a few stray chickens still clucked around in the yard, abandoned in the exodus.

"Do we stay? Farm?"

*I don't know how to bloody farm. Do you?*

"Hmm. What do we know?"

*Jesusmen stuff. Not much else.*

"I know birds," he said, looking over Collybrock. "At least, I used to."

Without much more of a plan, they headed south and west, into the lush plains. Here they passed a handful of families headed to the coast or eastward to Mawson, but some traffic still went with them.

Mal looked over great braces of birds that trotted past in a tethered parade, fine animals who'd never seen a hard day. There were richer sorts, driving cars and buggies along the tradeway, and soon the town walls came into sight.

"Rosenthrall," Mal said. "Big racing town."

The legendary racetrack lay outside of the city walls, and many big-name racing stables had built up around it, their yards filled with near-perfect birds.

Mal had done his best to curry all the muck and knots out of Collybrock's feathers, but she still looked rough compared to these sleek creatures.

*We don't have a hope of getting a race,* Kirstl said.

"Maybe not in the main races," Mal admitted. "But there are novice rounds where new riders can compete for a purse. Collybrock is a good bird, we'll get a spot."

They tried, but every main stable turned them away, unwilling to deal with amateur jockeys. Mal approached the stewards and attempted to enter the novice rounds as an independent, only to find the first problem. He did not have the registration papers for Collybrock, and never had. Lanyard had taken the egg at gunpoint the day he'd freed Mal, and he was only ever interested in providing a childhood friend for the traumatized slave.

There was an unregistered race outside of town that day, and Mal talked his way into a slot, bartering a packet of flour into the prize pot. When the starter fired their pistol, Collybrock broke into a savage fright, screeching and pecking at the nearest rider, and a brawl broke out between the racers.

One of the bravos drew a knife, and others had their own rusty sidepieces hid in snug holsters but within reach of eager fingers. Mal had Lanyard's old shooter hidden beneath a fold of canvas, easy enough to extract. Big enough and ugly enough to send these would-be toughs running.

Distinctive enough to instantly label him as a Jesusman, and it didn't matter what Sol Goodface said in his moot. The old pogrom would be enforced here, likely in some dark alley later on.

It might have been some reflection of the old Lanyard on Mal's face, the set in his eyes and mouth that told anyone that he would answer violence instantly and savagely. None made a move against him, and that ugly moment passed.

"Get that fucking menace out of here!" the organizers said, and Mal's racing career was over, just like that.

*She's traumatized, the poor thing,* Kirstl realized. *They don't realize how much battle Collybrock has seen.*

"You're okay, girl," Mal said, soothing her, and for once she did not pull away from his touch.

They headed east, picking through abandoned farms for supplies and finding little. Nearly everyone was heading east and south, and they passed more than one homestead burnt out and looted, livestock butchered on the spot for flesh. It was a peculiar type of Inland cruelty that the Riverland never usually saw, and Mal could not meet the horrified eyes of a dead farmer, bled out and trampled in a muddy ditch.

"What's left for us, love?" Mal asked Kirstl.

*True Horse Plain,* she said after a pause. *If not there, follow the river to Mawson. We should give Graham's Wash a wide berth.*

"Yep. Got no time for the Water Barons," he said, spoken like a true Inlander.

They came exhausted and dusty to True Horse Plain and traded the last of their tea and tobacco for a loaf of hard bread and a sack of grain for Collybrock. Hard eyes watched Mal as he walked Collybrock to the watering trough, and he felt very keenly how alone he was. The stablehands moved in large packs, either for protection or trouble, and he saw big, wooden frames set up in the town square. Every last one of the ill-bred horses had been hoisted up for butchering, fanged and scaled chimaera that probably weren't even safe to eat.

When he saw that they'd started killing off the birds too, Mal rode on, knowing there was no safe sleep to be found in that town.

*River Niven,* Kirstl said. *Let the bird follow the scent.*

As they rode, they often retreated into the mind-space together, only distantly noticing the physical act of riding the bird. Mal watched on as Kirstl attempted to breach the barriers of their self, rattling on the windows and doors.

*There was another one out there,* she said. *Like us.*

There was a dark void out beyond the edge of the Tontine, and Mal and Kirstl pressed their noses up against it, as they'd done as prentices in Crosspoint at the shopfronts.

*What do you think it is out there?* Mal asked.

*The Aum? Some other thing?*

*Hello!!! Jenny! Anyone!* Kirstl called out, pushing her will out through the gaps in the Tontine, extending her presence as far into that void as she could. It was cold, and she couldn't bear the sensation for more than a moment before returning.

*Maybe we should seal up all these ways in,* Mal ventured. *I'm not sure I like it.*

*I found someone! They spoke to me,* Kirstl said stubbornly. *They might be able to help us.*

*We're—we're done with that life,* Mal said. *Lanyard's lost, and I ran. Tilly, Sol, none of them will have us back.*

*You stubborn, bloody man! It's not too late to fix this.*

*They're as good as dead, and we aren't Jesusmen anymore! We need to forget them!*

A long pause, and then Kirstl summoned up the exact scene in the mindscape—the moment of their escape from the Greygulf, the looming figure of Lanyard, the distant figures of Tilly and the others running for the Terminus.

*Fix this,* she said simply. *Stop being a damned coward and fix it.*

*I can't.*

*Can't, or won't?*

And so it went, for days of gruelling travel, spouses locked in internal combat. In the dream-space, they examined the scene around Terminus in great detail, looking over the shadow-roads, the structure itself.

Kirstl came up with an interesting theory about the building and its purpose, which Mal instantly rebuffed, all of his arguments flavoured with shame for deserting and sorrow over Lanyard.

*Everyone is looking at the Terminus wrong!* she insisted. *We can free them all!*

*It's too dangerous. We can't go back.*

They slept and hid from bandits and coin-riders, and then Collybrock picked up her step, head up and questing.

Once more they'd found the slow murk of the Niven, and this time Mal felt himself washed away by the river, away from all hope and any dreams of his own life, just one more survivor looking over their shoulder.

Mal had spent a few hours kneeling by a billabong, trying to tickle a fish and snatch it for a meal, when he heard the footsteps, a sly whisper, and the snapping of a twig.

The click of the hammer on a revolver, and the working of an action on a rifle.

He let go of the fish he'd just caught and reached down into the mud, emerging with a hefty rock.

"Collybrock," he said calmly. "Kill."

Mal turned suddenly, using the momentum to strike up hard with the rock, caving in the face of the man who'd been lining up the revolver with his head. The gun roared impotently, and the man fell, gurgling and choking his life out by the water's edge.

Mal was up and moving, already scooping up the revolver from the mud. He twisted as a bullet missed him by a whisker, returning fire as the terrified second bandit tried to reload the rifle. Mal finally put a bullet through the man's throat, and still he was moving, looking at more shapes looming through the scrub.

A woman screamed, a long high note, still gripping Collybrock's reins, even with her bowels spilling around her, and finally Collybrock tore her head clean off, silencing the cries.

Mal leapt into the saddle, wheeling about as more figures closed in. He saw others on birds, and the stalking figures of mean-eyed men and women with guns and pikes, a big circle closing in on the billabong.

He was cut off and had no hope of escape. With a curse, he wheeled for the billabong itself, prepared to risk the fanged river beasts to escape this capture, when he heard the crackle of a megaphone, that rarest of Before-Time gadgets.

"You there. Stop!"

He heard the clank and hiss of someone in steam-powered bushranger armour, a figure that neither pistol nor shotgun had a hope of harming. This figure held the megaphone to the face slot of the suit, and with the other arm they were flagging him down.

A set of binoculars sat around their neck on a strap. They'd watched him, seen everything that had just happened.

"Don't risk the billabong. You're okay now."

The other warriors were scanning the scrub, looking for other threats. They were well-equipped and moved with discipline, worlds apart from the ragged figures who'd tried to murder him and steal his bird.

These new arrivals were going over the robbers and comparing their faces to mimeographed pictures.

"This is them," one said. "Can't make out the one with the smashed in face."

"Look for any tattoos," the one in the clanking armour said, and for a long moment Mal was hyperaware of his own Jesusman tattoo, an elaborate design on his thigh.

"Got it, Sergeant. A swallow on the right hand."

"We've found them all," the one in the steam-suit said. After a moment of fiddling with their fastenings, the leader twisted off their helmet and faced Mal. A woman with the flattened smudge of an oft-broken nose, and a shaven head.

"Been hunting this lot. Outlaws from Mawson lurking around our lands, pouncing on travellers. Not that we give much of a fuck."

Mal simply nodded. There was some sort of authority here, and it could turn on him in a moment, demand to search his gear—and find Lanyard's gun, and then his own tattoo.

He was far from safe.

"You handled yourself well," she said. "Three dead, and you without a scratch."

"Got lucky," he mumbled.

"You killed a gunman with a rock. I know training when I see it."

*Don't say anything,* Kirstl added.

"We were just passing through," Mal said. "Can we go?"

"We?"

*You idiot! Don't talk about anything, especially me!*

"Me and my bird, I meant."

"Of course," the woman said, and then she frowned. "Seems a

THE BRIDE & THE BIRDMAN · 133

waste to let you drift through to Mawson though. Nothing but misery and refugee camps down there. Certainly no work."

"Work?"

"Yes. I think I'd like to offer you a job. Proper gear, food and a bed. Safety in numbers."

*No. We need to leave!*

Mal looked at the woman in her burbling steam suit, and the soldiers under her command. They looked confident and even friendly, now that the threat was gone. Some of them joked and shared cigarettes, and one had a dog that they were throwing a stick for.

He felt it keenly then, the loss of the camaraderie he'd known in the Jesusmen. The sense of belonging to something bigger. Because of love he'd failed Lanyard, failed his Order when he was needed to make a tough call, but perhaps his violent lessons could be applied to this new life.

"I'll take that job," he said.

"Smart choice," the woman said. "The Water Barons look after their own."

# — 11 —

## BAERTHA

**M**ake ready," Baertha said, projecting her voice from the Glorious Gyre. Her forces were by the Shale mechanism, sigils floating in the golden muck, soaking up the last of it to gain strength. Baertha herself drank deeply of the last bottle of Aurum, and after a moment she handed the dregs to the Blackstar.

"The defenders follow us down toward the beach," her lieutenant said, eyeing the living storm clouds. "We can expect trouble."

"Nothing worth a damn came without struggle," Baertha said. "Of course they'll fight for the place."

"I was there when we took Gan-Eden," the Blackstar said. "We lodged to them like a babe to a tit, but they held off when we swarmed out of Shale. I led half of us in through the Aum and out of the Edgemist. Pincer move."

"We don't have that luxury," Baertha said. "We can't get in through the Glass-Lands. We make a beachhead, or we die."

The Blackstar nodded.

Her hands trembled slightly as she took up the controls of the Throne. The Gyre was compliant now, and she felt Overhaeven moving in perfect sync with each twitch of the joystick. On the flickering screen she saw the winding corkscrew of the cosmos, and here was Overhaeven, sniffing at the taproot of that creation. The Low Place.

She adjusted the setting, then reached for a version of the controls and the monitor that might have been had the Before been allowed to innovate and design the technology in that direction. It took a bit of concentration, but soon the display showed a crystal-clear picture of everything, from the pearlescent sheen of the world veil to the blood river spilling out through it and into the universe, a mist of crimson pushed through gauze, just a taste of the riches on the other side.

A sharp twinge knifed through her then. Hunger, a chemical ache, made her fumble the controls slightly. If she was correct, this red liquid was as good as the Aether from Gan-Eden had ever been. They'd be able to siphon this fluid through Shale, refill their reservoirs, and establish themselves as the lords of the cosmos once more.

Baertha tried to tell herself that she cared for none of this. She needed Aurum badly, and she had fallen so far, a rich scion now scrabbling like the meanest addict, ready to kill worlds for her next fix. She wondered if this was what it was like to be Papa Lucy, to have such little regard for anyone but herself. Looking over, she saw the Blackstar licking the last drops from the lip of the bottle and felt her lips curl up angrily.

The Blackstar smiled knowingly and tossed her the empty bottle. She moved quicker than thought, the splinter of the Cruik extending and snagging the bottle midair, an extension of Baertha's arm now complete with a gripping hand. In the next breath the staff was once more simply a stick, and she probed into the neck of the bottle with her tongue, sighing deeply when she found the last drop of Aurum.

"One word, and I will end you."

"I am as despicable as you," the Blackstar said. "Who am I to mock another junkie queen?"

She'd once wanted something even more than this, even more than the addiction of the Cruik, and knew that the Blackstar understood her to the core. Papa Lucy certainly had.

"Our desires undo us," she said coldly.

An eternity passed as they crossed that final distance, the willpower of everyone in Overhaeven focused through Baertha, and through her onto the sharp tip of Shale, the spear of conquest, as much a phallus as a mosquito proboscis.

That last final thrust, and Baertha found herself leaning forward, correcting their trajectory, eyes keenly fixed on the point of impact. Next to her, the Blackstar practically burned with excitement, tinged with lust. It was battle, it was invasion, it was taking something that wasn't yours, and Baertha felt herself caught up in the moment. She tried and failed to tell herself she cared for none of this, but as with all things, she wanted to win, wanted to matter, *needed* to assert her will.

If Sol were here, he might rationalize this invasion with something like *they're monsters, torturing those souls for their essence, and we need to liberate them, make the place a little bit better.* Then he'd be handing the place to his brother, who would simply move in as the new and improved tyrant of the Low Place. Between them, they'd work out a more efficient way to milk the system for its resources; that was the beauty of their dynamic. Good cop, bad cop, and together they were worse cop.

"Yes," the Blackstar hissed between his teeth, watching the display keenly as Baertha realized the one way she could really win the ultimate victory here.

She could win a victory over Overhaeven, her addiction, even herself. All it would take now was a simple jolt of the joystick, and a steep dive would be enough to miss the Low Place altogether. With their momentum, she could hurl Overhaeven into the darkness of the universe to spiral and starve. There was nothing worthy of redemption in here. Even herself.

Her hand closed tightly around the joystick, but as she made to throw them off course, she felt her hand freeze in place. She looked down to see her fingers seizing up and turning wooden. Then there was no hand at all, simply the wooden curl of the Cruik keeping them on course.

Impact. The Gyre shook around them, and she felt as if struck by a car, but she couldn't let go. She felt every jarring moment as Overhaeven pushed forward, the Shale mechanism flexing, pushing at the world veil, stabbing about like the beak of a swordfish. For a moment, it seemed they would win through, and then the elastic of

THE BRIDE & THE BIRDMAN · 137

the world veil snapped back, sending them reeling, rebuffed into the cold of the vacuum.

"Again!" the Blackstar yelled. "We had them!"

Baertha fought to free herself from the joystick, and then her other hand was the tip of the staff, one wooden finger tapping away at the keyboard of the futuristic console. Overhaeven's momentum away from the Low Place slowed as it prepared for one last mad charge at the beach.

*Damned staff,* she thought. *It's still got me, still knows me heart and soul.*

Even though it was only one tiny sliver of the Cruik, she felt it flow through the controls and into the Gyre itself, and there was enough power in that fragment to instantly pattern the marble halls with wooden inlay and parquetry, driftwood and beams. Outside, Baertha felt the torus of Overhaeven suddenly reforming into a curl, a translucent shepherd's hook. The Shale mechanism was both the butt end of the staff and a mosquito's probosicis, quivering with an enormous, impatient energy, and a shocked corner of Baertha's mind wondered what the *entire* Cruik would have done in here.

The Blackstar looked out of a porthole and on the workings of the Cruik, all of his past objections fading into the fuzz of enchantment and obsession. "It's perfect! You're perfect..." he said, running his hand down her cheek. She felt her own woodgrains under his fingers.

*I am the biggest fool,* Baertha realized, knowing she'd given the universe to the Cruik on a silver platter and it was about to gorge itself. In desperation she tried to activate a failsafe she'd hidden in the Throne, but she could not fight against the wooden tenacity of the Cruik. It knew her stratagem, a trap she'd set for any would-be usurpers, and it would not permit her to use it.

"Over the wall we go!" the Blackstar crowed.

Impact, and this time they won through, their spear parting the world veil and driving deep into the bloody shore. Baertha looked down on her forces as the sigils of the godlings sped down through the Shale mechanism in a glorious ejaculation, unfolding into three dimensions as they waded through the bloody delta and into the Low Place. Her people strode forward with purpose, every one of them ambitious and half-starved, a menagerie of the animal-headed and the bizarre. The fallen lords of Overhaeven had brought conquest to a new land—and it was simply too late to stop it.

Before them came the rank and file, the Ophanim and Seraphim who'd turned from the Most High, and then the Taursi who were in good-grace, clad in glass and bringing the bright flash of star-glass into the land of gloom and blood.

"It's working!" the Blackstar said.

The first trickle of the new Aurum was pulled through the Shale mechanism and into the reservoirs. It was a muddy bronze, a new formula that was a far cry from the pure juices of Gan-Eden, but it would do.

The last of the sigils to join the charge spun in the liquid, drinking greedily from it. They moved more aggressively thereafter, sharks on the hunt, outstripping their peers when they assumed a solid form.

"Join the charge, my queen," the Blackstar crooned. "All that is done here is glorious, and it is yours."

The Cruik retreated back through her hands and arms. Once more she stood free of the Throne, leaning heavily on the staff, a mere splinter of the larger construct.

The Blackstar shook his head, blinking rapidly, and he looked at Baertha with the faintest flicker of suspicion.

"It's the Cruik that's insidious, not me," she said wearily. "But tonight, you eat."

---

As a ballerina sigil, she spun through the slurry of the new Aurum and drank deeply, tasting the essence of misery. While the polluted Golden Sea was awful to drink from, this stuff was truly vile. Every negative emotion she'd ever experienced washed through her in a moment, but she felt nourished, stronger than she'd ever felt in all her centuries of life.

Fighting against the current of the Shale mechanism, she emerged in the Low Place in her queen form, gripping the Cruik splinter and quivering with rage.

The defenders of the Low Place had come to drive them away.

Her Taursi and godlings were clashing with creatures of shadow and flame, who gored with horn and fang, a swarm of whips and sharp blades. These demons did not seem to favour firearms, but some hauled out bombards, loading them up with unfortunate souls and magma, killing as many of their own as they did the invaders. Their army seemed to stretch for miles, even back to the roads and rivers of fire. Reinforcements streamed out of the twinkling, smoky dotted cities across that dark plain.

Above this, the cloud-beasts fought with her Seraphim and Ophanim. Many of her godlings took joyously to the sky, answering lightning with their own fury, their weapons strong and keen from the Aurum.

The lords of Overhaeven were mighty, but the host of the Low Place seemed to be without end. Without some grand stratagem of their own, Baertha's forces wouldn't be able to stop the Low Place from slaughtering them all and dislodging Overhaeven.

"This is okay," Baertha said to herself, leaning on the whip-thin fragment of the Cruik, just another old woman clutching her walking stick. The aggression of the Aurum was fading from her system quickly; she felt the Cruik splinter helping her in this front, drawing the toxins out through the palms of her hands.

*I will die calmly*, she resolved, but when she made to drop this extension of the Cruik splinter, she could not release the staff. Her body jerked like a puppet, and great swathes of destructive energy washed out from the splinter, bolstering the weak places in her front line and arcing out to destroy the bombards when their crews hauled them close enough to fire.

Above, a cluster of the cloud-beasts struck her with sheet lightning. The splinter diverted this energy out into the attacking army, slaying them by the hundreds.

Even so, it was not enough. Even with the old Family and everything at their disposal, this wouldn't have been a fight they could win.

"Just let me go," she whispered to the Cruik splinter, wanting the fight to be over, her ambition spent in the miserable funk of the Low Place.

*NO,* she heard in her own mind. *We will not fail now! Kill them all and take this place!*

Baertha's invaders began to flag, already weak after their brief taste of Aurum, a sugar-hit high that could do nothing against the implacable horde. The line gave. Angels were seized and torn apart by the cloud-beasts, and defenders began to push the invaders back toward the Shale mechanism.

*No, no, no!* the Cruik splinter said in Baertha's mind. *This isn't what it promised me!*

"Who — what were you promised?" Baertha said, buffeted by the retreating Taursi. Underfoot was a bloody slurry, and she slipped and fought to gain her footing.

They had lost. If she did not join the retreat now, she would be slaughtered by the advancing demons.

The Cruik splinter was sullen in her hands, lashing out randomly at the gibbering demons, but even it was weakening, and she felt it retreating from her mind, pulling out tendrils it could not spare to devote to its dwindling strength. It fully withdrew from her, body and soul, for the first time in over two centuries.

Baertha smiled, and she dropped the splinter into the mud, free of it at last.

She felt it behind her then, the failsafe she'd built into the control schema of the Throne. Even as the retreating force scrambled into the Shale mechanism, the Blackstar was making his move.

Seizing the Throne. Leaving the Queen of Overhaeven to die.

Linked to the Throne as she was, she felt his attempt to pull up the studio control interface, the one he best understood. As he reached down, the failsafe activated. His arms were caught in the vast strata of other control panels, and then he was seized roughly, pulled into the gears of the Throne, crushed absolutely in the workings of the Glorious Gyre.

Still, he lived on inside the cogs and wheeling gimbals, in absolute agony. Before he could engineer his own freedom, the second part of the failsafe kicked in.

The Glorious Gyre spun at great velocity, bouncing about and reaching every part of the innards of Overhaeven. Following the program perfectly, it became a multidimensional saw, slicing at every internal structure, and finally severing the Shale mechanism, allowing the Golden Sea to spill out into the vacuum of space. Shale itself remained lodged in the bloody beach, but it was meaningless now, a stinger without a bee.

Overhaeven died as Baertha watched. The approaching demon army paused for a moment, awed by the death of the universe's greatest parasite.

Baertha tried for a moment of stoicism, to calmly face death and worse as it came for her, but she was suddenly wracked with agony as her physical body called for Aurum, every nerve firing a pain signal at once. She fell into the sticky slurry and tried to drink it, only to discover it was foul, like seeking petrol and finding only crude oil.

The last of the cut-off Taursi were either murdered or taken away, and then it was only Baertha left, surrounded by nightmares. Seething, hissing, dripping fangs and claws, and always their eyes seemed to be aflame, consuming everything they looked upon.

These creatures of the Low Place seemed to speak as one, and they whispered and teased her, promising her great torment.

"I'd like to offer my unconditional surrender," Baertha said weakly.

The Cruik fragment suddenly lifted and stood on its tip end. The demons retreated a step, terrified by the powerful construct.

*I have found myself. I am here. All of me is here!*

The fragment of the whole staff lifted slowly from the ground, that perfect curl of the hook rotating, and then it abruptly shot across the black sky like a wooden comet, leaving Baertha to her fate.

# — 12 —

## RAY

It worked," Ray said. "We stopped it."

He was still gripping the firing handles of a device that resembled a Maxim machine gun, if the barrels were made of blue crystal. Across the parapets, John and Jesus stood behind other more esoteric weapons, all of them smoking, glowing with the heat of a sustained discharge. Between the three of them and Jesus's miraculous glass castle, they had held off an approach from Overhaeven and sent the parasitic kingdom limping away with grievous wounds in its flanks.

Their onslaught had torn the world veil open in several places that leaked out light and warmth into the cold vacuum. Jesus brought out a type of harpoon which launched a spreading gauze net across the horizon. It solidified across the wounds, another patch across the old scar where Shale had lodged itself for so long.

"There's still a leak," Ray said, pointing out a part where the patch had not set. It seemed like instinct to apply a caulking gun to the leak, and then to run the caulk around the patch, to make the repair as secure as possible. It was satisfying work, and he felt like he was back in one of his many workshops, fixing a broken thing just to put something to rights.

"There. That's better," he said, then looked across to see Jesus and John Leicester rushing over, concern on their faces.

"What?" he said, and then he looked down. Jesus's crystal machine gun was now an enormous metaphysical caulking gun, and he'd been squeezing the grip-trigger tightly, spraying the sealant across the miles toward the world veil, and his whole body was shaking as if in a deep seizure. At some point he'd struck his face on the caulking gun, and blood was streaming out of his mouth. He'd bitten his own lips and tongue.

Ray fell, looking up at the perfect concert hall ceiling of Gan-Eden, and he shook all over. John was there, cradling him in his spirit arms, and Jesus was applying healing magic, a spell that ran along every nerve, flooded every vein.

In moments it was over. The bites in his mouth were sealed over, already healing. The caulking gun glowed red hot now, and John pushed it away with a sorcerous hand, sending it toppling and hissing into the waters below.

"You could have died," John said with gentle concern.

"Would I still be here though?" Ray said. "If I died in the land of the dead?"

"Pretty much," John said.

"This place doesn't make any sense."

Jesus stood at the edge of the parapet, looking down at Ray's creation below.

"Ray, that was clever, caulking up the gaps. Our patch in the world veil was about to fail."

"Thanks."

"That device that you made. How did you know how to do that?"

"I didn't do anything. I didn't!"

"But we all saw how you—"

"NO!"

Ray was instantly filled with rage and confusion, with the urge to shout, to resist, his mind shutting down. *A meltdown,* the doctor had told his mother all those years ago, after yet another over-the-top screaming fit that had gone on for hours.

"I didn't do it!" Ray shouted, thrashing around, swatting away their kindly hands. "I am not a magician, John is! I'm just the Junkman."

"Okay," Jesus soothed. "I believe you."

"Breathe," John said. "Count."

He did, and after a time the calm came, and he was able to stand. He looked down to the distant sea, the water still hissing and bubbling from the heat of the tool he'd dropped into it.

"My caulking gun got very hot," he said, and they all nodded.

After a long moment, Ray explained Sol's theory about his instinctive sorcery, about willpower and ritual achieving things, and his own mind creating slippery ways for it to happen.

"I'm sorry I yelled at you, Jesus," Ray finished. "That was rude."

"No apology needed," Jesus said with a smile. "We're all friends here."

"Friends," Ray said.

"Do you remember how I was a professor, Ray? I taught magic in the Collegia, back in the Before."

"Yep."

"I had a student like you once. Brilliant young artist. She couldn't work magic in the typical sense, but whenever she painted, her powers were world-shaking. Creating creatures and structures from nothing, changing weather, erasing memories and making people doubt at what was real.

"'I'm not a magician, Professor,' she'd also said. The single most powerful spellcaster I've ever encountered, and she walked away from the Collegia, from all our advice, our pleas to let us help her.

"She went home to Ur-London, and some idiot gave her an art exhibition, and one week later the city was a smoking crater in the ground."

"I'm not like that," Ray said numbly.

"I know," Jesus said. "But other instinctive sorcerers burn out, or blow up, or hurt themselves in slower ways. Please, please be careful with this. Ask for help when you do it, and we'll show you safe ways."

"Okay."

Fearing a repeat visit by Overhaeven, the trio set about bolstering the castle's defences. Ray continued offering blunt advice on how to improve the walls and weapon placement, and John was impressed.

"We could have used you in the war," he said. "You've got a knack for how to set up a defensive position."

"I'm good at Space Invaders."

"Pardon?"

"We got a machine back home in Shadrach. At the corner deli. I must have played that thing from when they opened to whenever they told me to go home."

"How much money did you spend on video games?"

"It costs 20 cents to play it," Ray said, a little confused. "The game keeps going as long as you can keep the aliens away. I would spend 20 cents on a game, and then Mister Simmons would turn the power off on me when it was dark and time to go home."

Ray looked to the horizon. "Is there a way to open the world veil?" he said. "Just for a moment?"

Jesus and John looked at each other.

"If that thing comes back, you don't want to wreck your shields by shooting through them. You pop out and shoot your enemy and then hide back behind them."

A lightbulb moment for John and Jesus, and instantly they were devising a thing they called the Keyhole, a type of searchlight that would open a target zone in the world veil and then close it with minimal damage afterward.

Ray worked in concert with the two magicians, absently applying wire cables and circuitry to a device that was neither electric nor real. He noticed that the two were watching him too closely and wondered why, until they told him they were just making sure he wasn't overdoing things.

"I do things," he said, a little confused. "I never overdo things."

Soon the Keyhole was completed, and they mounted it to the outer walls of Jesus's castle, which was now truly impregnable. If it could open the world veil, perhaps it could open the flanks of an enemy for a moment, peel aside armour and allow their defences to strike unimpeded.

"I am so bloody proud of you, mate," John told his brother. "Always the smartest man in the room, that's what I tell anyone who listens."

Ray looked down at his shoes.

"I'm not always though," he mumbled. "I don't know how to fix the gate back in the Now. Get all those people out somewhere safe, without using the Greygulf."

He talked about the exploding Taursi hearts in the circuit, how the sun wouldn't recharge them enough to keep the gate powered. They talked about hooking up Ray's Aurum engine, but Ray shook his head.

"We'll only get the one attempt at the gate," he said. "I've got eight hearts in the engine, and I had maybe fifty joined up in a serial circuit. If I go parallel, I keep the hearts safe, but I lose the power I need for the gate."

They talked over luring Overhaeven back somehow and destroying it, then harvesting it like a honeycomb, taking the last of its Aurum for the gate. That was when Ray heard the long squeal of a car braking hard, the blast of a "La Cucaracha" airhorn, and then a crash.

"It's that bloody car again," John said. The living man and the two Once-Dead spirits descended through the castle, not in a particular hurry.

"It probably wants to play a game," Jesus offered.

"Do you have any steaks?" Ray asked.

"No. We don't need to eat. No steaks down here."

"Oh."

They opened the main gates, a huge double span of opaque glass, and then they saw how brutalized the House of Torana was. This was more than the end-effect of its usual rough-housing.

"PAPA LUCY! AT THE EDGEMIST! KILLED MOST OF OUR GUARDIANS."

Jesus's face fell into an expression of stone, and he reached out, calling for staves, wands, and rings, which instantly flew to him from the parapet. John followed suit, and also called for an exquisitely crafted gun, which landed in his open hands.

"Where did he go?"

"GLASS-LANDS," the car managed, sniffling and ashamed. "LORD SOL IS THERE TOO, AND THE WOMAN WHO IS A STICK."

"Are they his prisoners?" John asked. "Did he hurt them?"

"NO. FRIENDS. WORKING TOGETHER."

"Damn it, Sol," Jesus said sadly.

---

They piled into Ray's muscle car, blasting across the deadlands in a flat-pedal panic.

As they raced away from the final beach and the well-defended but ultimately pointless castle, Ray pondered the fact that the real threat had been creeping up behind their Space Invaders shields, behind the defenders themselves.

Sol Pappagallo, the man of kind words and good intentions, was once more under his brother's spell. Although Sol's betrayal struck him keenly, he related it to his own tangled feelings about his brother John, slowly untangling the complex emotions as he drove.

*All we have are these centuries, long and lonely. The cold of the Methu-saleh treatment, or existing on the edge of life as a Once-Dead. Sol has to stand with Lucy, and always will.*

*It always comes back to family. The Family.*

"Up ahead," Jesus said, pointing through the windshield from the backseat. "It's slowing down."

The House of Torana had led them on a twisting path through the rows of obelisks, following its own bloody trail. It sniffed back and forth like a bloodhound and then froze in place.

"Everyone out," John said sternly. They piled out of Ray's muscle car and advanced toward the House of Torana, guns and magical foci up and tracking. Ray remembered Papa Lucy's too-friendly smile, the constant feeling that Lucy was taking advantage of his disability, and he looked down with some surprise to see he was holding a pneumatic nail gun with a hose that didn't seem to end at an air-compressor but somewhere else, somewhere magical. He began to swoon.

"No," he said, and he looked back down to see he was also hauling a sputtering air-compressor on a hand-trolley. The cognitive dissonance began to fade, and the surge of an autistic meltdown became background noise.

"Come out, Lucy! Face us!" John said, working the bolt of his rifle and feeding in a bullet that glowed a sickly green. Jesus was pacing through the obelisks, holding a staff that hummed and shimmered with the heat-haze of barely restrained magical forces.

The House of Torana came back, sniffing, and then it turned around and tapped an obelisk with its tire.

"HERE. THEY WENT THROUGH HERE."

"They went through?" John said. Jesus cancelled his deadly spells, groaning with frustration at the car. As usual, it hadn't delivered all of the relevant information.

"WAS BY CHOICE. FREE WILL. THEY FELL."

Their names were on the obelisk, carved deep into the stone. Lucy, Sol, even Jenny, all of them condemned to imprisonment in the Low Place.

Once more Papa Lucy was a puzzle that frustrated Ray. Nothing the sorcerer did ever made any sense, and it violated his entire universe of logic, the order of people doing predictable things, the patterns he'd observed over the centuries.

"He has Jenny Rider. He's making her into the Cruik again."

"Lucy is a sick man, Ray. He's obsessed with the Cruik, and Jenny is trapped in it. She wouldn't be with him by choice."

"Car! Was Papa Lucy using magic?" John barked.

"YES. YES! SPELLS AND PAIN AND STRIFE."

"He's broken out of the spell-lock," Jesus said, ashen.

John scuffed his ghostly boots against the glass, grinding the butt of his rifle against the glass.

"Why didn't he come to attack us at the castle?" Ray asked. "Why does he want to go down there?"

"Maybe he's facing his sins finally," John said. "Contrition. I say good riddance."

"No," Jesus said after a long moment. "There's something more to this picture. Lucy doesn't do anything selfless ever. I don't doubt for a moment that he has some larger plan going on."

"So what do we do?" John said.

THE BRIDE & THE BIRDMAN · 149

"We follow," Jesus said. "We finish him."

The magician rapped twice on the nearest obelisk with the butt of his staff. At once the following word appeared: VISITORS!

"We seek entry," Jesus said.

DENIED. YOU HAVE MANY SINS, BUT YOU ARE THE WARDENS OF GAN-EDEN. YOU ARE INVIOLATE.

"Listen. A dangerous criminal has entered your lands. We must seize him and deliver punishment."

MANY DANGEROUS CRIMINALS HERE. PUNISHMENT IS ALSO HERE.

"You have made a terrible mistake. Luciano Pappagallo cannot be rehabilitated. He will destroy your systems and murder your rulers."

SOME HAVE TRIED. ALL FAILED.

"He bears the Cruik!"

A pause, and the written conversation sank into the depths of the obelisk. Finally, a response.

YOU MAY BE ADMITTED AS DIPLOMATS.

The glass opened a panel large enough to fit the two cars. Below, one of the cloud-beasts arose, offering itself as a platform for them. From the fluffy vapor arose a manlike shape, a white form with blazing coals for eyes, and it beckoned them onward.

"NO," the House of Torana, backing away with horror in its eyes. "I WON'T!"

"Stay," John said kindly. "Gather the Giden. Keep the castle strong and watch the Edgemist."

The car responded with a roar and a spin of its wheels, fishtailing between the obelisks and out of sight. With some trepidation, Ray drove them forward, guided by the gestures of the otherworldly figure.

The cloud-beast descended, and the glass closed above them. One last glimpse of the realm of heavenly light, and then they were descending into the gloom, through the ranks of warring clouds. They were given a clear berth through the flashing lightning, and clouds split ahead of them and reformed behind them.

Ray trembled behind the steering wheel, mind reeling at what he saw.

As the cloud-beasts moved aside, Ray had a clear view of the land, the shadowy hills and plains run through with glowing red veins of what might have been rivers of lava or blood, threading through the twinkle of settlements. On this side of the glass, the pitch black gave way to a deep gloom, and he could just make out an enormous mass moving on the ground.

"An army," John said, leaning out of the window with his rifle scope. "Hideous creatures, and too many to count."

This terrifying host was following the red rivers toward a coastline, the mirror image of that final restful shore up in Gan-Eden. Here was a bloody delta, where a spray of bright red gore pushed out through the world veil.

"Look! They came down here! Those golden parasites are attacking this place."

Ray saw Overhaeven where Jesus pointed, that eye-twisting realm was latched onto the edge of the Low Place, drinking deeply. It disgorged godlings and glass-wielding warriors by the tens of thousands.

"They go to dislodge it," Jesus said. The three of them had a box seat view of a furious battle, where the twisted godlings of Overhaeven fought desperately against an army that seemed to be without end.

They saw the retreat. They saw Overhaeven attempting to dislodge itself and run. Some disastrous malfunction rocked the realm from within, and the parasitic structure ruptured, sharp snout broken, the stolen Aurum leaking out into the vacuum beyond the world veil.

"No," Ray moaned. It would have been enough to power their gate ten times over.

Then they were witness to the last moments of the battle, where the final knots of Overhaeven invaders were rounded up and butchered, and some captured.

"It's gone, Hesus," John said, a little awed. "Overhaeven finally bought the farm."

"Good," Jesus said, but he did not seem happy to Ray. When he looked in the rearview mirror, he noticed that Jesus seemed lost in thought.

Their cloud was sinking down toward a bright city, a place of fiery towers and mirrors, larger even than the greatest cities of the dead Before. Ray wound down his window and looked out at the man-figure on the cloud's prow, who turned to consider him.

"*What?*" it said, a disturbing whisper that seemed to slide around in his ears like a hot wire.

"What is that place?" Ray asked, voice trembling.

"*Grand Kthon,*" the cloud said. "*There is the Endless Pavilion, and there gushes forth the Deep Insult. That is where the Holdfast will hear your case.*"

"Uh, thank you," Ray said, rolling up his window.

---

He drove nervously through the streets of Grand Kthon, surrounded on every turn by nightmares. The walls were built of bleeding flesh, each brick a living creature broken into shape and bound in place. The cobblestones on the streets seemed to be skulls, and every structure was a jut of spikes and bones, of corroded iron and rot.

The citizens were worse still. They were monsters of every shape and size, nightmares given form, all dripping fangs and menace. Above, winged creatures flitted between the packed towers, barely visible in the dense smoke from the fires. If not for their honour guard of enormous demon soldiers, Ray had no doubt they'd be torn apart instantly.

The locals kept prisoners. Slaves. Ray recognized Once-Dead spirits, but these were more miserable than even those who'd suffered through the Underfog years. Every street corner was fitted with instruments of torture and humiliation, and the demons tormented their charges without pause. Ray saw one enslaved soul finally perish, its spirit-stuff dribbling into the gutter below, joining a bright-red flow. He suspected this was the source of the river they'd seen earlier.

And then Ray had won through the traffic into a ring of gardens, where bodies hung impaled on the trees or choked on wire nooses and forever unable to die. He looked on queasily as the road ran parallel with a madly flowing river of the red matter, gushing and seeming close to washing over its banks. Culverts from the surrounding areas fed into the main channel, and Ray guessed that the smaller storm water drains fed into the main river this way.

It was both sickening and a marvel of civic engineering, and Ray honestly did not know how to feel about it.

Ahead of them lay a palace of grand proportions, a manse that seemed to stretch onward forever, up to the sky and beyond the limits of vision.

"That's got to be a trick of the eye," John said quietly.

"The Endless Pavilion," one of the demon soldiers accompanying them said. At the end of the road, a series of portcullises and gates began to move, a thousand protective layers ratcheting open to admit the honoured visitors from Gan-Eden.

The negotiations did not go well.

# — INTERLUDE —

## THE MOST HIGH

The Great Garden had fallen into chaos and in some places outright revolution. The Cruik commanded little respect without the Most High, and was forced to become a warlord by proxy, establishing the Hundred World Throne and worse atrocities. The construct could barely halt the advancing chaos while the god remained distracted by its pet humans.

Some of the oldest worlds were advanced, and their great priests and leaders had long been permitted to send petitions to the Most High. It ignored most of them, but one day it found a large-eared rat curled around on its golden shoulder, looking on the human worlds.

"Truly beautiful," the creature said. "A great work of art."

"INDEED," the Most High said, rumbling with pleasure.

"A true shame it ends so badly for them."

"WHAT? YOU DARE THREATEN MY HUMANS?"

The Most High made to crush the impudent rat, which had already moved in a dozen different ways and easily dodged the golden grip. It waited calmly in the void, looking upon the god.

"No threats. I came to you to offer my assistance—and a warning. You know of me?"

"OF COURSE. BILBEN OF THE IRON NEST."

"You made us perfectly, as with all things. My kind have a fluid relationship with time, and I have seen certain things. Things you should know."

"SPEAK."

"This world of humans is sadly going to end, no matter what any of us does. I have seen many variables, and it is always the same. It burns, and only a handful of your humans survive, escaping to a neighbouring world."

"TELL ME WHAT YOU HAVE SEEN. I WILL UNDO THIS."

"The more you try to prevent this apocalypse, the quicker it occurs. If you leave it be, you increase the time they have to flee. They still have a number of centuries."

"HOW DOES THIS HAPPEN?"

"The real question is 'who?' I always see the same perpetrator, and you know that I never lie."

"WHO DESTROYS THIS WORLD?"

"Many human hands, but they are all guided by a scheme, and central to that scheme is the Cruik."

Fury blazed there in the void. The Most High sent for the Cruik, and this powerful servant denied it all, but to no avail. There was enough truth in what Bilben said to link the Cruik to a future catastrophe.

"YOU HAVE BETRAYED ME!" the Most High wailed. It folded a portion of the universe into a pocket, a jail for the powerful instrument. It set the Cruik with a tribe of guardians, a race of dimension-hoppers called the Taursi, and into that oubliette the rib of a god was left to fester.

For their service, Bilben was raised up to be at the Most High's right hand, renamed Bilbenadium. The rat became a powerful angel and was given the Sworn Sword in order to properly police and intimidate the universe on the Most High's behalf.

"I am sorry that it will happen," the new angel said, as the Most High watched its pet project sullenly. It no longer drew joy from observing their doings, and instead poked around morosely, watching for signs of the end.

A cadre of dead human spirits attempted to rejoin the lands of life and accidentally broke into the prison of the Cruik. The Most High watched on with disappointment as these spirits took to the Cruik's cause and formed a new realm to attach to their world, a parasitic branch grafted onto the perfect tree.

It called itself Overhaeven, and drained the lifeforces that maintained the rest of the system. These Lords of Overhaeven listened to the edicts of the curved instrument and gathered power by the day.

"Do not act, mighty one," Bilbenadium said. "I have seen this as the best course of action, the way to save as many of your favoured race as possible."

The god bristled and struggled against the urge to destroy the parasites, but Bilbenadium whispered frequently into its ear, and soon it watched fatalistically, knowing this project would soon fail.

"IT'S ALL GONE WRONG!" the Most High wailed, but still it did not act, wanting to save as many of its pets as possible. It watched on with some pleasure as the Lords of Overhaeven fell into civil war, finally ejecting the Cruik and sending it to suffer in the realm they called the Underfog.

Then came the ultimate disappointment. It all unfolded as Bilbenadium had predicted. The destruction, courtesy of Overhaeven. The exodus, led by a cabal of magicians, and then the surviving humans stumbled out bawling into their new world.

But gone were the clever inventors, the pleasing little mirrors that reflected what the Most High liked about itself. Instead, the humans had come out as low creatures, cannibals and rovers, picking through their own leavings and never emerging from this fallen state.

The Most High retreated, brokenhearted, and only then did it have a thought for the rest of its garden.

Whatever this malaise was, it was dangerous. If allowed to emerge from this corner of the universe, this ennui could affect every garden in creation.

"YOU. YOUR ADVICE CAME TO PASS."

"That it did," Bilbenadium said, answering the summons.

"NOW LOOK UPON WHAT I MUST DO."

Bilbenadium had of course seen this and was powerless to act as they were rebuffed from the Most High, falling far in its esteem. This garden was walled off from all surrounding neighbours, the only exit a small gate guarded by the Most High itself.

"YOU ARE IN DISGRACE, SWORN SWORD. I SHALL SEVER THIS GARDEN AND LEAVE BOTH YOU AND THE CRUIK WITHIN IT."

"This is as you always do."

"WHY DID YOU FAIL ME, IF YOU ALWAYS SEE THIS?"

"You are a tyrant. It was the right thing to do."

The Most High attempted to snuff out Bilbenadium, who narrowly dodged an immense force that destroyed a nearby sun.

"DO NOT DARKEN THIS DOORSTEP," the Most High declared. "THE NEXT TIME I SEE YOU, IT WILL END IN DEATH."

"That I have also seen."

# — 13 —

## MAL

Mal had a bed now, plus meals and everything else they'd promised him. He also had a sergeant, and rules, and punishments for every minor infraction.

The first thing they'd done was shave his curly hair, searching for lice or worse. A doctor had examined him in a variety of uncomfortable ways, though thankfully he'd been able to hide his Jesusman tattoo from the gruff woman, as if crossing his arms in protest at the whole thing. She seemed more interested in cupping his balls and making him cough, and checking that he was free of venereal disease.

*I'll need to burn the tattoo off,* he thought later. *Or cut it away. It's dangerous.*

*Not as dangerous as an infection,* Kirstl replied.

The solution was crude, and he worked on it most evenings in the barracks. In the end he simply ruined the tattoo with a needle and ink, changed the B + N to the word BETHANY, and adjusted the outline of the bound man to be that of a crudely realized, sexy woman.

*There. Now you're a real man,* Kirstl said drily. *Do you want me to look like that tonight?*

"No," Mal whispered, and then a shadow fell across him. His sergeant, a flat-nosed thug named Trevally.

"That looks fucking awful, Private. You should have paid a proper artist to finish that for you."

"It's personal," Mal replied after a moment. "I don't want any other fella touching my woman, even just a drawing of her."

The man guffawed nastily, and suddenly he descended with the flat of his hand, slapping the tattoo hard. The recent needlework was raw, and a wave of pain flooded across Mal's chest.

Gritting his teeth, he met Trevally's gaze. He hated every minute of the macho rough-housing as a Water Baron soldier and knew there was something missing in the camaraderie here, that they went in for the cruel rather than the character-forming. They were Baron Chandler's enforcers, a man notorious for violence being the answer to every question.

Their officer was Captain Thunderbolt, the clanking menace who was infamous in the company for once crushing a deserter's skull with the fingers of her steam-suit. Kirstl had no doubt what would happen if they were discovered with the kit of a Jesusman. And so, during one monsoonal rainfall she went out from the barracks, canvas wrapped shotgun under her arm and a shovel over her shoulder. She buried Lanyard's shotgun in the town cemetery, hiding it in a recent grave. When she tried to sneak back into the barracks, she was found by a town patrol and brought back to Thunderbolt and Trevally.

"Now tell me, what were you doing near the cemetery with a shovel?" Trevally demanded. Thunderbolt watched on, and she still seemed as dangerous without her steam-suit.

"Was taking a shit. It felt like something in my arse was about to die, so I thought I'd give it a good burial."

For her smart tongue, Kirstl earned them a solid flogging, ten strokes at dawn. She was also given a week of mucking out the latrines.

"Fitting, since you seem to like digging around in the shit," Trevally said.

Still, they survived.

Mal quickly proved himself as a bird-rider, and the company blacksmith forged him a sheath full of razor-sharp lances. His only other weapon was the dead bandit's rusty revolver, and so the armorer gave him a clip-loading pistol and enough ammunition to murder a hundred bandits.

When he rode patrols, he was also issued a good rifle and a bayonet, but the soldiers had to sign in long arms at the end of each shift. He felt safer with the gun buckled to Collybrock's saddle, knowing that the sturdy .303 could drop just about anything.

But he was in bad company and knew it. While the patrol's primary task was to wipe out bandits, they were also toll collectors for Graham's Wash. More than once, Mal found himself pointing a lance at some poor farming family turned refugees while foot soldiers turned their wagons out onto the side of the road.

"One sack of onions," Sergeant Trevally dictated, marking off a list. "Two chickens, one mutated. One goat."

"You're as good as killing us!" the farmer complained.

"You'll know if we're killing you," the Sergeant said, and then suddenly slammed the butt of his assault rifle into the man's belly. "This is our road, and you pay the bloody toll!"

Mal had heard the water business was going bad, what with the Range emptying the Inland out. There were still consignments heading out to the Overland farms, but most orders had been cancelled, or deliverymen found the towns and settlements abandoned.

There was a note of worry in Graham's Wash, the fear that their insidious trade was about to become obsolete. The Barons were moving into other industries, such as providing security to rich travellers, but the other settlements were refusing security contracts, not wanting a well-equipped private army on their doorstep.

"Those fucking moving mountains are gonna ruin everything," one of the other soldiers complained during a patrol. "If the water money goes, then we go."

Remembering the misery the Water Barons had brought to the Inland towns, Mal was far from sorry for them, but he joined in their grumbling. He invented a personal history in the Overland, working bird farms and taking a turn as a coin-rider, hunting Crooked Folk and murderers for a profit.

Day by day, he was falling, becoming a lesser version of himself.

He said nothing while his crew robbed the desperate, and when they caught bandits, he felt an illicit thrill, gunning them down from bird-back, pouncing on them with Collybrock.

Even the bird was becoming ill-tempered, snapping at his fingers at odd moments, scratching and pecking at most of the other birds in the Water-Crew stable. She got a reputation as a murder-bird, a real fighter, which was valued in their situation.

"I'm sad," Collybrock warbled one evening as he combed and fussed over her feathers.

"Me too, girl," Mal said. "It's all we get to have now."

---

The weeks spent as a soldier since he'd run from Lanyard felt like a lifetime, and then one night found Mal riding along the tradeway, part of a large raiding party. They were several companies from various Water Barons, a rare joint effort.

Hundreds of soldiers travelled light and fast on birds and bikes. In her steam-powered armour, Captain Thunderbolt easily kept pace with the rest of them. If anything, she was holding back.

*What do you think this is about?* Kirstl asked. As usual the grunts hadn't been told jack shit, the water companies running on their usual paranoia. Spies were everywhere and orders had a way of leaking.

*Graham's Wash is dropping the hammer on someone. Big time.*

*We should leave,* Kirstl said. *Desert. This won't end well.* Mal looked at the clanking form of the captain and shuddered.

Dawn brought them to the outskirts of Mawson, where the rising sun struck the patchwork glass of the Selector's Tower. Mal could see the sprawl of the city, now sheltered behind a new wall. He noted the machine-gun emplacements, and with some shock he realized the entire temple had been destroyed, and recently.

*The fuck?* Kirstl said.

Then he heard a klaxon and realized it was from their own side. Others raised bugles to their lips or straight out hollered. Captain Thunderbolt vented a steam whistle to great effect.

That cacophony was the signal for a charge, and Mal looked

**THE BRIDE & THE BIRDMAN · 161**

nervously at those machine-gun nests, the walls now lined with soldiers rushing into defensive positions. Even in what might have been his final moments, he fell into the thrill of the ride, the lurch of Collybrock moving as the perfect machine beneath him, the sense of speed and danger. He drew the rifle from its sheath, working the bolt and feeding in his first round, ready to fire at an enemy like a good soldier.

*I suppose this makes it okay,* he thought, resigned to the act. *They're soldiers too. They know the deal. At some point, you'll shoot and be shot at.*

*This is not bloody okay!* Kirstl protested.

The machine guns tracked them, waiting for them to get into range, and that was when another set of klaxons and whistles came up from their own side, two short, sharp bursts. Mal recognized the order. Forces to swing left, sharp turn. Birds and bikes ran parallel to the walls of Mawson, and the defenders looked on in confusion as they wheeled about.

Toward the refugee camps, row upon row of tents all out in the open, defended only by a handful of coin-riders.

Once more a single blast for charge, and the slaughter began. Mal could only look on in horror as the spearpoint of their force punched through the camp, birds and bikes unleashing carnage on the unarmed refugees, tearing through the handful of town soldiers and coin-riders set outside the walls to serve as the camp police.

The charge reached the far end of the camp, leaving hundreds dead and dying in their wake and thousands more running in all directions. Captain Thunderbolt gave three sharp blasts on the steam whistle, and everyone wheeled about on their birds, the bike-riders dismounting to push their vehicles around to face the opposite direction.

"You! You didn't fire a single bloody shot!" Trevalley yelled at Mal. The Sergeant was on his own bird, a young mawk that trotted on the spot with excitement, blood all over its beak.

Mal nodded, examining the action on his gun.

*Please,* Kirstl begged him. *They're just murdering them.*

Sergeant Trevally got right up close to Mal, an ugly look on his face. He leaned over, lining up a lance with Mal's ribs.

"You make sure to shoot this time, and that's an order."

"Got it," Mal said, and then he shot the sergeant in the face at close range, taking his head off. The group took this as the signal to advance, even as those around Mal reached for Collybrock's reins, pulling out their own weapons and cursing.

He spoke a Word of brilliance, blinding all around him with a sudden flash, and then he was caught up in the charge, yanking Collybrock hard to the left, pushing against the press of birds and bikes, and trying to get clear of the gunfire and chaos.

At the last moment, Collybrock climbed up and over several other water-crew birds, pecking and scratching her way loose until she was able to leap free of the madness. One or two soldiers shot at them for desertion. Collybrock squawked as she caught a round in her rump, and Mal felt a bullet kiss the meat of his outer thigh.

He turned toward the main gate of Mawson, tearing off his regimental vest and waving it above his head, hoping for refuge, but as they got closer the machine guns spun up.

"Wheel about, wheel about!" Mal commanded, and Collybrock went into the controlled slide on her backside, losing momentum. She then leapt up and ran right, claws scrabbling at the clay and fighting to send her on a perpendicular course. Clods of earth flew into the air as the gunners attempted to chew them apart, but Mal rode quick and low, away from the walls.

Straight toward Captain Thunderbolt, who was making a beeline for him, engines venting steam, a trio of motorbikes hot on her heels.

*You shot an officer in front of hundreds of witnesses,* Kirstl scoffed. *What did you expect?*

"Come on, girl!"

More bullets from his pursuers, wild shots from riflemen in the sidecars. He risked a glance at the captain, and she was a terrifying sight, her iron legs pumping away like the trains of the dead Before, slowly gaining on a riding bird at full speed.

He fired his revolver over his shoulder, three wild shots at his hunters, and he heard the *clang* of the bullet meeting steel. Normal bushranger armour was up to an inch thick, head to toe, but the captain had half a train engine powering hers, allowing extra pounds of steel.

THE BRIDE & THE BIRDMAN · 163

There was only one weapon left to use, and to use it he'd have to strike his flag.

"Kirstl, I need you!"

*Couldn't agree more,* and then Kirstl was climbing into their shared body, contorting their hands into a quick Mark, drawing shapes in the air that formed into sharp edges, growing by the second. She threw them over her shoulder, and they dug into the clay, fusing together and growing up into an iron hedge of jags and thorns.

Two of the motorbikes smacked into the sudden barrier with a sickening crunch, the soldiers pierced in a hundred places, but the captain ploughed through it, knocking everything aside with sheer mass and speed. If she'd caught a jag or two on the way through, she wasn't showing it, and she lifted up her megaphone, lining it up with the mouth slit on her helmet.

"A traitor and now a Jesusman! You'll die by fucking inches!"

The remaining motorbike was coming in wide, but Kirstl reached into their magical arsenal and rested her hand atop the pommel of one of their lances, filling it with destructive potential. She felt woozy, and they both knew another enchantment might make them fall out of the saddle altogether.

One shot only.

"Your turn," she said, and then Mal came forward to take over, seizing the enchanted lance out of the sheath. He held it in his hand like a spear, lining it up on the lumbering behemoth closing in on them.

*Kill her!* Kirstl urged.

He threw the lance at Captain Thunderbolt, but it wasn't balanced for throwing. It went wide, veering to the right, and Mal cursed himself. Then the motorbike blundered into it, and the lance ended up tangled in the front wheel of the bike, flipping it over, and then releasing its magic in one immense explosion.

Both bike and men erupted in a grisly spray, raining down in a crater in the ground. Even the captain was sent sprawling, sliding forward in the clay and muck, only to rise a moment later and continue the chase.

"Make another one!"

*No! We aren't strong enough!*

"Boom! Boom!" Collybrock warbled.

They lost Captain Thunderbolt in the swamps around the delta, Collybrock leaping nimbly through the brush, dodging river beasts and trees. The captain could merely curse as she struggled and thrashed around in the undergrowth, stymied in a thousand small ways.

Mal heard the clanking and venting of steam grow fainter until they could not hear her at all, and just like that his short career as a soldier was over.

---

They hid behind a stand of reeds, Collybrock watched for river beasts while Mal unrolled the medical packs.

"Be quiet, girl," he said, gently probing around in the wound on her rump with a long set of pincers. She gave a low hiss, feathers ruffling as he reached deeper.

"Got it." Mal held up the bullet and flicked it into the river. He packed ointment into the wound as far as he could, and then he got out a suture needle that was designed to go through a bird's leathery hide.

"Don't give me that look. I've got to sew it shut."

"Hurts," Collybrock moaned, but she submitted to the stitching. Pulling the thread taut, Mal suddenly felt woozy.

*There's a problem!* Kirstl said, panicked. *Someone's trying to come inside.*

"Inside?" he mumbled.

*Inside us! Into the Tontine!*

Mal felt himself sag to the muddy bank as a presence pushed in on his waking mind from every angle. Then he was in the dreamspace with Kirstl, who was floating in the void with terror on her face.

"It's so strong," she whispered.

Mal felt it then, a force smashing against the outside of their shared self, slamming on the windows and doors. Mal and Kirstl flitted around in the vast void, imagining thick bars and steel grills to reinforce the entry points, but these shattered as quickly as they could place them.

THE BRIDE & THE BIRDMAN · 165

*Let me in!* a voice from without said insistently. *Submit.*

"Get lost!" Kirstl shouted.

*You are a lesser Tontine, and by the old laws I claim your host body. Leave and take your chances in the Aum, or I will pluck you out by the root.*

This voice came with the weight of a hundred echoes, the sense that a hundred minds thought in lockstep with an overseer. Suddenly a mad banging came from all the entry points, and it was all that Mal and Kirstl could do to keep this terrifying intruder out.

"It's them," Kirstl said, face drawn with the strain of concentrating on all of their defences. "The other Tontine I found when I was looking for Jenny Rider."

"I thought they were friendly to you?"

"They didn't kill us the first time around. I guess things have changed."

They threw up plank barricades, brick walls, every manner of defence. One by one these fell aside, the enemy Tontine pushing in, ready to claim their body as its own. Mal had the faintest sense that his back was arched, heels scratching at the mud, and Collybrock was screeching in his face, beak-tips holding him up by the collar as she shook him around.

*Enough. You have fought well, but give in. I will allow you to occupy my old shell.*

"What the hell is going on here?" Mal said. "Why would this Tontine want to abandon their body and come to us?"

"They are desperate," Kirstl said. "In trouble."

"Desperate people make mistakes," Mal said, mirroring an old lesson of Lanyard's, and Kirstl nodded. This was the exact moment that every Jesusman prentice trained for, to seize bloody-knuckled advantage in these hopeless moments.

Together they opened the main entry into the mindspace, just a crack. Kirstl summoned the image of a white flag, waving it around in surrender.

Then they stepped out, these two souls that shared a young man's body, and they stood in an oppressive black void. Mal turned around and saw that their shared self was a strange greyish structure, faint light shining out through the cracks of a dozen access points.

*We're in the Aum,* Kirstl said, words now reduced to mere thought, muted and hard to hear against the oppressive weight of all that nothingness.

The assault stopped, and the attacking Tontine gathered itself out in the pitch darkness, waiting for Mal and Kirstl to fully evacuate from Mal's body.

*The correct decision,* it said. An indistinct figure gestured forward with the sweep of an arm, echoed a hundred times by barely visible figures that stretched out to the limit of what they could see.

*Where is our new body?* Kirstl said.

*Follow our trail.*

*We're kinda new to this. We're worried we'll get lost.*

The figure froze up, exasperated, and then moved a little closer.

*A miracle that you have lasted as long as you have. Listen. You need to look for a thread, like a spider's silk.*

*Won't that break?*

*Not easily. Follow it like a rope, and you will find your new home.*

With an act of will, Mal and Kirstl coasted closer to the central figure of the other Tontine. They pretended to be terrified, clutching to each other and looking at the invader who'd thrown them out of their home.

The central leader of the group wore a wisp of smoke about her face, but they were unmistakably feminine, and held herself with a tightly controlled grace. The figures behind her copied this pose, a type of floating dance, one foot held in a neat point to a toe-tip, the rest tucked behind the ankle in a zero-gravity ballerina's pose.

Mal and Kirstl made as if to look for the faint thread in the Aum, and the leader finally began to lose her temper.

*It is here,* she said, picking it up for them. *Honestly, I am regretting my mercy more by the second.*

*So we take this, and it will bring us straight to our new body?*

*Yes! Now go!*

*I think you need to give us the tour,* Mal said, snatching the thread and wrapping it around the leader's throat. Then he and Kirstl clutched tight to the mortified figure, whipping across the Aum like some mad fisherman was reeling them in.

THE BRIDE & THE BIRDMAN · 167

She fought them the whole way, but Mal and Kirstl worked as a team, hog-tying her with the mysterious thread. The other echoes in her Tontine were rapidly drawn into this central figure, until finally it was just the three of them racing through the dark.

And then they arrived, reaching a Tontine of epic proportions, a grand grey manse in the middle of the void, and there was no one to defend the gates as they came tumbling inside.

"Tie her up good," Kirstl told Mal, and he went one better, trapping her in a nest of coffins and wrapping the whole lot in a cobweb of the thread. This prison bucked and clattered beneath Mal, and he wasn't sure it would hold for long.

They were in the dreamspace of their attacker's body, and all of the familiar sensations were there. A waking mind above, arms and legs to wriggle into, five senses to observe with. It was crowded, but Mal took Kirstl with him, and they looked out into the real location of this enemy who'd come to steal his body.

They found a horrendous world beyond imagining, a place of flames and choking smoke, with bright, fiery rivers snaking across a gloomy landscape, and they were in a great city that ruled over all of it. Hulking figures moved around them, whispering creatures with bright eyes and impressive fangs. One leaned in toward the host body of this Tontine, using a sharp claw to slowly pull out muscle fibres and nerves from her upper arm, and another slowly licked at the blood, healing up the worst of the wound while preserving the moment of pain for as long as possible.

A bright red chain lead from a manacle on her ankle to a shackle that welded to a pitted meteor with a plaque carved into it.

WITNESS THE ETERNAL PUNISHMENT OF BAERTHA HANN-PAPPAGALLO, THE QUEEN OF OVERHAEVEN, LADY BERTHA OF THE FAMILY.

"*Ooh. You went somewhere else, sneaky little Baertha,*" her demonic tormentor said. "*Brought back some friends.*"

It stretched out two clawed fingertips, placing one to each of her temples. A horrible heat started to burn through her skull.

"*We'll fix that oversight now. You shall not leave again.*"

"We need to get the living fuck out of here," Kirstl said, and Mal could only agree. They fled back through Lady Bertha's mind, dodging around the slowly splintering coffin trap, and then they launched themselves back out into the Aum, finding their own thread back to their Tontine.

Mal awoke on the riverbank, gasping, his heart hammering. Expecting Captain Thunderbolt or the legendary Lady Bertha to attack him at any second, he scrambled up and into the saddle, not even bothering to dress his own wound.

"We need to go back to Graham's Wash," he told Kirstl.

*Why would we do such a stupid thing?*

"Because we need to dig up the gun."

# — 14 —

## SOL

Sol fell through the clouds, a skydiver in a dark and angry realm. He gasped as a cloud moved in like a shark and slapped him to one side. Its outer skin was like coral in places, sharp enough to score his ribs, tearing at his shirt.

It would take many long minutes for him, Jenny, and Lucy to hit the ground of the Low Place, but Sol realized that in that time the clouds planned to have their fun with them.

Lightning flashed as two of the clouds fell to feuding, and Sol saw Jenny lashing out as they fought over her. She'd turned herself into a dandelion of hooks, rotating and tearing away at their flanks, sending out plumes of fog in place of blood.

He called out to her, voice instantly lost to the buffeting winds. Plucking a baton from his belt, he focused his energy through it, boring a hole through the nearest cloud until it separated into a dozen smaller cloudlets, all swarming about him, swatting him between them. He called up a mystical shield to keep the creatures at bay, flinching every time one of them crashed into his transparent shell.

Few magicians ever mastered the art of flight, so Sol could only watch hopelessly as the clouds sent up sparks each time they battered his weakening shield. The map of fiery pathways on the ground grew closer and closer, and Sol felt all too keenly the frailness of his second body, the knowledge that oblivion awaited.

Then, his Once-Dead soul would rise, to whatever torments the Low Place promised for the damned.

*What the hell were you thinking, Lucy?*

Another crash, and another. His shield faltered and finally fell, and it was all that Sol could do to lash out with his remaining magics, blasting the clouds into smaller parts and sending some into drifting mist. More attacks came, and Sol narrowly turned aside a fork of lightning with a protective bracelet, which cracked and fell from his wrist.

When he'd studied necromancy at the Collegia, academia had vastly misunderstood the nature of the universe and had only recently discovered Overhaeven. The true nature of Gan-Eden had been forgotten, and the few academics who theorized of yet another realm beneath it had been mocked or disregarded. Nothing was known of the Low Place apart from what a handful of necromancers had observed through the Glass-Lands above, or from rude probes sent beyond the world veil that sent unsatisfactory images back to the observatories.

A place of endless punishment at the very least, and they'd *chosen* to come here!

A cloudlet struck the magician on the side of his legs at a rapid speed, and Sol felt his femur shatter. He started to pinwheel, the land and the distant glass ceiling spinning around at a sickening rate.

His whole leg felt savaged from hip to toe, and to his shame he screamed in agony. Lucy would have found the bloody-minded strength to fly anyway, to just sever the leg and put it back on later, but all Sol could do was try to fumble through the intense pain for his own magic.

*Oh, just let this end,* he thought, and then a strong arm caught him, arresting his fall, scattering the clouds with a gesture.

Lucy held him in place, the Cruik in his other hand. Again and again he swept the powerful staff, obliterating entire banks of clouds with every pass. Soon they were fleeing from this laughing madman, his mane of black curls flapping in the wind.

"Oh no you fucking don't," Lucy shouted at the retreating clouds, and then they were flying forward at great speed, snagging one of the beasts with the crook end of the staff. Lucy climbed on board, straddling the back of the bucking cloud like a surfer, slamming the butt end of the staff into the cloud beast over and over again.

Each strike was a thunderclap, the Cruik causing the entire beast to flare with lightning. He was too broken to even think straight, but when he reflected on this later, Sol supposed this might have been magical energy tracing the nervous system of the cloud.

"Behave! You're mine now!" Lucy said. The cloud tried to buck them off, at which point Lucy simply drove the Cruik in deeply, a piton to hold them fast against its bulk.

Sol felt the potential that Lucy was pushing into the cloud via the staff, an immense pressure and pain that grew steadily. With an act of will, the man could simply pop the cloud—and the cloud knew this. The cloud submitted like any foal broken to the saddle, and it lay still, sagging at the edges in a sullen manner.

Only then did Lucy lay Sol gently on the cloudbank, where he moaned and put his hands to his broken leg.

"Oi, Sol! I just beat this fucking thing one-handed," Lucy crowed. Sol considered the woman trapped first with lies and then within a staff, and he did not bother to correct him.

------

While Lucy experimented with his new craft, steering it in slow circles and teaching it how to accept commands of "climb" and "dive," Sol worked at setting his broken femur in place.

"Just walk it off, mate," Lucy said. Sol held his thigh, lining the fracture up, and instantly knew it was properly arranged. He reached inward, and with one searing jolt from his hands the broken edges met and sealed.

*I'm forever the Boneman,* he thought. Once more he tried to repair the injuries from his destruction in Overhaeven, only to find this damage irreparable. He would always walk in a bent way, his frame fused wrong when his immortality was stolen from him and given to his brother.

He'd spent years in a fury at Lucy over this, only to eventually realize the backhanded gift his brother had given him. Instead of hundreds of years repeating the same dusty mistakes, his mortality had now motivated him to carve out a small but important role and then pass on the torch to whoever wanted it.

Of course, it was all a moot point if they died from the next horror the Low Place thought to visit on them. The cloud-beasts were keeping their distance for now, but they were agitated and circling, perhaps insulted by the bridling of one of their own.

"Got your shit working yet?" Lucy asked, and Sol nodded, climbing to his feet. He took out an extendable staff and twisted the centre point, enlarging it until it could serve him as a walking stick. He'd seemed invincible once, a pillar of the Family, but he felt his mortality deeply as Lucy steered their cloud on a gentle descent.

"We'll be out of here lickety-split," Lucy said cheerfully. "Ray's gate will be up and running by teatime."

The circling clouds sent in one of their number to test the intruders, and Lucy and Sol attacked as one, beams and bolts and curses tearing the cloud apart, leaving little but sprays of mist and drifting fog. The defenders retreated back to their sullen orbit, watching for a weak moment. Lucy whistled the chorus from "Chess in a Golden Sea" and made their final approach to the charcoal lands of the Low Place.

Only now did they realize that an enormous army was on the move, en route to the largest of the settlements. Their battle with the other clouds had not gone unnoticed, and there was already a large contingent of figures waiting for them, a nest of horns and upturned, glowing eyes.

"Lucy," Sol warned.

"I've got fucking eyes, mate. I'm aware."

He guided them in low and fast, and spears and javelins began to rain against their cloud, opening a dozen minor wounds. They were now low enough to make out the individual demons, a force of hundreds. Lucy drew from the Cruik, lashing out with a phalanx of invisible blades, dropping enemies by the dozen.

At the same time, Lucy drove the cloud down toward one of the fiery rivers. When the beast resisted, he pulsed a blast of pain through the Cruik, reinforcing the command. Wriggling and unhappy, the cloud sank into the bright red flow. This close, Sol could see that it was neither lava nor fire, but something else indeed: the brightness of soul essence, the foul cousin of the Aether found in Gan-Eden, flowing across the Low Place in great volume.

"Drink it in, you thirsty little shit," Lucy snarled. "Prove me right."

The cloud finally flexed beneath them, and like a sponge it quickly filled up with the soul essence. Laughing, Sol drew back on the Cruik as if it was a flight stick, aiming the engorged cloud at the sky, up toward the Glass-Lands.

"This should be enough to do the job," Lucy said, a moment before everything shuddered around them. Something had seized their cloud, preventing its escape. Lucy swore and thrashed the cloud, but it was unable to move.

Then a horror rose from the crimson river. A fat, creeping tentacle with the head of shark on its end lashed at the cloud, and then another, and then dozens more, savaging the beast and tearing it apart for the stolen soul essence. Soon their ride was gushing sheets of the fluid, the whole creature deflating around them.

"Lucy. Lucy!" Sol yelled, and with a curse his brother plucked out the Cruik. Their struggle to escape the dying beast was like running a race across a deflating waterbed, and Sol yelled at Lucy to take them to the skies.

"I can't," Lucy admitted. "Something's wrong."

The cloud died a moment after they stepped onto the far shore of the canal, opposite the army. Purple mist leaked out of the creature in all directions. They were grounded, helpless as the demon army began to wade across.

A few ranks back, the demons hoisted a big iron shape, something like a bell without a clapper—pointed at Sol and Lucy.

Sol felt a pressure across his whole body then, the sense that he was being silenced. When he reached for his spells, he realized with horror that he could not. All of his magical energies felt as if they were locked up in a strongbox, and he looked to his brother in a panic.

"We've been in worse spots," Papa Lucy said. The first of the demons reached the far side of the soul canal, and he waved the Cruik, waved it again. Frowned.

"Is it—"

"Not a fucking word, Sol. Run."

They ran across that blasted landscape, a place crafted for uneasy movement, and Sol tripped more than once on a sharp stone, skinning himself in a dozen places.

Their pursuers whispered, darting forward and then retreating with laughter, clearly toying with the two magicians. Lucy found a pistol in one of his pockets and shot a pair of demons that got too close.

"Leave me behind," Sol said. "I'm too slow."

"Don't be fucking stupid."

"At least bring Jenny out," Sol urged Lucy. "Give her a chance to get away."

"I can't!" Lucy cried. "Because of that bloody bell, I can't do a damn thing."

Exhausted, Sol begged off running, and after an exasperated moment Lucy stopped. They looked to each other, sharing a wry moment as the demons closed in.

"We deserve this, Lucy."

"You might. This is the stupidest way for it to end."

"I love you. I always have."

Lucy looked to Sol, mouth open, but then he could only look away, and then at their doom as it approached them on thousands of hooved feet.

Demons were everywhere, pouring out of their cities like ant nests stirred to gather food. Terrors of every flavour came at the brothers, sands on a red beach, and here they were without a skerrick of power.

"Come and eat my swinging nuts, you bastards," Lucy said, emptying his gun into the horde. Then the clip ran dry. Unable to find a reload, he threw the gun at them, and then a cigarette lighter, and then rocks and more curses.

"Just stop," Sol sighed.

"You don't get it," Lucy growled. "You never stop! Even when you're going down someone's throat, you punch them from the insides. Be a Pappagallo, you pissweak fuck!"

Then a wooden comet streaked across the sky, slamming into the Cruik, driving Lucy to his knees. After a long moment, he looked up with a smile.

"Get ready, you fucking sook," he told Sol. With one sweep of the Cruik he sent out an invisible blade, slicing the distant bell device in half, the effect of the magic dampener fading instantly.

"What was that thing in the sky?"

"It was the lost part of the Cruik," Lucy said, slowly floating up into the air, sweeping aside rank after rank of demons with flame and ice, blade and bludgeon, driving the entire force back to the canal in moments.

"You broke the fucking Cruik when you threw it into the water," Lucy continued. "Took me a while, but I found it all, everything except this one missing splinter, lost somewhere in the Shale mechanism."

Sol felt his eyes drawn to the perfect curl of the hook and knew that the power of the artifact had climbed exponentially. He ached for it to his core, and knew that if he were to grip the staff again, he would never be able to let go.

"That's not all! You'll never guess who was keeping this missing splinter from me," Lucy said coldly. "We're about to have a little Family reunion, Sol. Just you, me, and the old lady."

# — 15 —

## BAERTHA

She was getting ready in the vestry, keenly aware of just how alone she was in that moment. No mother to help her to set her hair, none of her sisters or friends there to help her apply her makeup. The wedding dress on the hanger was plain, as good as she and Sol could afford between them. If her father had opened his legendary wallet, the dress alone would have cost the sum of a house.

The moment that she walked down to aisle to become a Pappagallo, Baertha Hann knew she was as good as disowning herself.

Switching on the chapel's record player, she turned off the PA system and kept it playing low, just for her. Today her bridal song was Fleetwood Mac's "Songbird" from the *Rumours* album, and she wanted to hear it on her own first.

Aware that her family would have paid Fleetwood Mac top dollar to attend and perform at her wedding in person, she pulled the album out of its sleeve. Placing it on the turntable, she moved the needle across, looking for her track. Instead, she set the needle down on the song before it. "Go Your Own Way" played in the humble room, and she cried and cried.

A knock sounded on the door, and she composed herself, wiping away the tears and mess. She rarely allowed anyone to see her showing emotion, a holdover from her strict upbringing as a Hann, a future mover and shaker.

"Go away, Sol," she said when the knocking continued. "It's bad luck."

The door opened a crack, and Lucy stood at the threshold, averting his eyes. "With a song like that, you're making your own bad luck," he said. "Are you decent?"

"Yes," she said, and her future brother-in-law came in.

"You okay?"

"No."

He pulled over a chair and sat next to Baertha. "It's not too late," he said, flashing that perfect smile. "Ditch my loser brother and run off with me."

"No thanks."

"Congratulations, you've passed the final test," Lucy said. He picked up the makeup brushes and started working on Baertha with expertise, delicately turning her chin this way and that.

"Where did you learn to do this?"

"I was in the theatre, darling," he said. Finally satisfied with his handiwork, Lucy stood up, even as the needle hit the centre of the record, returning back to the start.

"I'd better go check on the groom," Lucy said. "We don't want to be starting any more *Rumours*."

"Lucy, that was terrible, even for you."

He smiled. "Your family can get fucked, Baertha. We're all the family you need."

She clutched his hand tightly, and he stooped to kiss her on the forehead, a chaste forecast of the wild affair they would one day have, but today she felt buoyed by his support.

When it was time, she stepped out into the nearly empty chapel, her song playing, and she was radiant. Love pulled her down the aisle. John Leicester was there, this war hero already a dear friend, and he stood in for her father, walking her to the altar.

Professor Hesus, their one guest, lingered in the back row, defying the Hann family's objections. He'd as good as doomed his tenure and everything else just by being in the room.

And there, waiting nervously by the celebrant, stood her Sol, her soul, the beautiful man with the kind eyes who believed in lost causes and saving the world, the one man who'd won her heart where hundreds had tried.

"You look beautiful," Sol said, and she clutched at his arm, sniffing back at a tear. She couldn't bear to look at the empty seats, to see that her family had all forsaken her, and Sol was her only rock in a stormy ocean. She clung on tightly and looked up at the celebrant, eager for her wedding to begin. To be over.

"Do you, Baertha Hann, accept all of your mistakes? All of your sins?"

"Excuse me?" she replied, a little shocked.

"Your role in the destruction of the world. Your tyranny. The destruction of hundreds of innocent women."

"Stop this. Sol, please help."

Sol smiled, but his smile became a nasty thing. Now Lucy was on her other side, and he gripped her other arm tight, holding her fast like a butterfly on a pinboard.

"Queen of the parasites. Unfaithful wife. Warlord. Killer."

"Shut up! You're a liar!"

The celebrant reached forward, running his fingers down her face. Relishing her tears. He even leaned in, licking one solitary tear away, and invited the others to partake. Sol, Lucy, even John and Hesus had a taste of her misery, and they laughed at her, pinching her face, her arms, flicking roughly at her ears and nose.

"Why are you doing this?" she began, and then these small pains became an all-encompassing agony, an ache that shook her from root to tip, her very soul crying out for something it could no longer have.

Then everything fell away. The chapel, her husband and friends, all of it torn aside like a set dressing to reveal her new reality. She was surrounded by demons, chained to a rock in the Low Place, and she was shaking with Aurum withdrawals, screeching out in torment, every nerve in her body firing a pain signal.

THE BRIDE & THE BIRDMAN · 179

*It's not enjoyable,* one of the demons complained. *She's doing most of the torturing to herself.*

They cast her to the ground in disgust, leaving her to writhe in the soot and muck. She wasn't even Once-Dead, but a godling reborn in flesh, the Shale mechanism having returned a form to her when she climbed up to Overhaeven. She bled when they cut her, hungered and grew thirsty in this place, and most of all she craved Aurum, shivering and feverish the longer she went without it.

She wanted to die, even knowing they would seize her up when her Once-Dead spirit climbed out of this shell. Surely any torture they could dream up would be lesser than this.

It would be an eternity then, as Grand Kthon chittered and screamed and suffered around her. She was an attraction of sorts, and often the demons would come and watch her flail and scream. Some would take a turn at inventing some new horror for her, but they took little pleasure when they could not outperform the internal suffering of her own making.

A rare moment of catatonia saw her staring numbly at the passing crowds of demons. Even in captivity she'd learned some of the city's ways. Grand Kthon passed for the capital of the Low Place, and the Holdfast was some force that spoke as the government. Her tormentors had promised that she would eventually bleed out into something known as the Deep Insult, but only after an age of torture, when she had repaid every sin of her storied life.

When a large-eared rat came by to visit, nose twitching as it watched her from arm's length, she supposed it was some lesser demon that meant her harm. This sort usually travelled in packs for protection from their larger cousins, so she noted this anomaly in a numb kind of way.

"You are almost through your withdrawals," the rat chittered, and Baertha blinked. This wasn't a demon, but a Once-Dead soul—an incredibly bright one.

"We don't have long before they realize this," they continued. "Lay still."

The creature flowed toward her, shifting and changing into a dozen different instances of itself, some fleeing, some staying, but most edging forward, setting their teeth against her manacle.

"They'll see you," she mumbled. The creature ground their sharp incisors against the red metal, sending up sparks with each pass.

"No," the rat said as they paused. "I have seen this as the exact moment that every monster in this place is about some other business. None are paying attention to you."

After another minute or two of work, her manacle fell free. Baertha made to sit up, but the rodent leapt upon her chest, pressing her down with a surprisingly heavy weight.

"No," they said. "Do not move until I tell you to."

She shook briefly with the Aurum sickness again, but the creature had spoken truthfully. The symptoms were easing, and she wondered what would pass for this body's sustenance once she'd been weaned from the golden fuel.

"Get ready," the rat said. "You will see a brawl between three demons over a runaway soul. When the bricklayer drops his barrow, run into the old teashop and hide in the shadows."

"How do you know all this?"

The large-eared rat did not answer, instead pacing around nervously by her feet. Then Baertha heard a ruckus, a beehive buzzing of mad whispering, the clatter of hooves on the road. A cry, as a Once-Dead soul wriggled free of a set of stocks and zigzagged through the crowds. Many of the nearby demons gave chase, and soon three large monstrosities had seized the unfortunate escapee at the same moment. All wished to claim the soul, and they began to hack at each other with heavy swords, drawing a raucous crowd.

One of the combatants took a blade to the head and staggered away with a curse, knocking into an enormous worker-demon with a wheelbarrow. The worker was hauling six Once-Dead souls formed into bricks, and these scattered across the road, three of them unfolding into their original forms and fleeing in different directions.

Baertha felt a sharp nip to her ankle and realized that the rat had bitten her.

"Go!" they urged, and in that perfect moment she ran across the street. Not a single demon in the packed city of Grand Kthon saw her.

There was a shop ahead, the signs written in an eye-twisting script, but the cup symbol was instantly understandable. The storefront was dusty and neglected, but the steel padlock securing the door had been sheared through with a familiar set of teeth. Baertha slipped inside, the rat already scampering up onto the countertop.

"Keep away from the windows," the rat said. "The search for you begins in about five minutes."

"Please, what is this?" Baertha managed. "How do you know all this?"

"You tell me," the rat said, a hundred possibilities twisting across the room and up onto Baertha's shoulder. "You're the one making it possible."

"I don't understand."

"Once I could see all possibilities, past, present, and future. Then I lost it all. I was doomed, bound in Allcatch. Cast down here to pay for my sins."

Baertha dared a glimpse outside onto the surreal street. No one had noticed her escape yet, even as some sort of police force was disembowelling the brawlers out on the street.

"Then you happened," the rat continued. "I could see you, visiting the Most High on his doorstep, and that very act reopened my senses."

Baertha, a flexible thinker, accepted the logic of the time-scrying rodent, leaving the question of its motives for a different time. She'd been freed, and the rest was a problem that she could untangle later.

"Do what I say, when I say it, and you will leave the Low Place," the creature said. "Up to a certain point, I can sip from the river of time, and I can predict most obstacles."

"But—"

"And here is the part where you have all of the questions and none of the time to ask them. Make a disguise from the things in here, and be swift."

Baertha crafted herself an outfit from a mouldy tablecloth and a quick pass of illusionary magic. She gave herself the suggestion of horns and eyes that glowed orange, and then incorporated the rat beast as a second horned head sprouting from her shoulder.

"Quickly! In less than a minute, a bored demon wishing to torture you will arrive. When the building in the street behind us collapses, we must be ready to move out the back door, and fast."

"Who are y—"

"This conversation is more tedious every time I'm forced to relive it. You may call me Bilben."

"I'm Baertha."

There was a cacophony in the street behind the teahouse. Bilben dug their claws into Baertha's shoulder, bidding her to move. She unlocked the rear door and exited into chaos.

An entire building had collapsed, a tenement crafted out of tortured souls, and it had struck its neighbouring towers, threatening a chain of collapsing dominos. Demons arrived by the dozens, engineers shoring up the disaster, emergency services pulling the injured from the devastation.

"It took me hours to chew those bricks just so," Bilben said. "This way."

Wailing klaxons drew more hands to the disaster, and Baertha walked against this traffic, following the directions of her strange guide further into Grand Kthon. Soon they were in the central gardens, following a lesser service road toward a mansion that suddenly sprang into vision, an infinity of terraces and wings and more belching chimneys than any industry would ever need.

"The Endless Pavilion," Bilben said before Baertha could ask.

"I don't want to go there."

"You never do. But that is where we must go. You need to rescue John Leicester and Jesus next."

"What!?"

"Please, I'm trying to concentrate. Now I need to explain the Deep Insult. This will be difficult for both of us, so offer your attention please."

Still reeling from the revelation about her old friends-turned-enemies, Baertha listened, walking on toward the waiting throat of the Pavilion's huge side door. The decorations and frieze work on the structure resembled Assyrian artwork and sculpture from the Before. She had a moment of déjà vu when she saw a pair of colossal winged figures flanking the doors, human-headed lions carved in stone.

A huge canal of the red soul-stuff churned along next to the road, so close that she could smell its vileness. On a magical level she could feel a great potential in the liquid, but it was befouled, a concentration of evil and woe.

"That is the Deep Insult, the last gift of the Most High, and our hosts are its loving stewards," Bilben twittered in her ear. "It gushes out of that wonderful house there, and it carries every vile deed and memory across their lands and out into the vacuum. It's constantly filtering out the worst of the Garden's energies."

"It's disgusting."

"It serves a necessary purpose. Now, do not falter at the doorway. Truths only."

Baertha did not bother asking a pointless question that the large-eared rat would obfuscate over. As they passed between the enormous statues, both of the guardians suddenly dipped their wings, barring Baertha's passage.

"Why do you wish to enter the Endless Pavilion?" they whispered in eerie unison. The creatures shifted on the spot, and she had no doubt they could stamp her physical body into paste—and probably destroy her soul in other ways.

"Answer. Why do you wish to enter the Endless Pavilion?"

"I don't," Baertha finally managed, and this answer seemed to satisfy the guardians, who returned to their resting state and gave her no further regard. She passed between the doors and into the Endless Pavilion itself.

"Before you ask, all of this churning goop is called the Deep Insult."

They were on a causeway in a vertical well of terraces, suspended across a great gulf. Beneath them bubbled an ocean of the red muck, occasionally spitting into the air. The stench of death was overpowering.

In the centre of the well was a gushing fountain the size of a plaza, and dozens of aqueducts drank from it, siphoning up rivers of the arterial sludge through some unseen mechanism. The causeway Baertha walked upon ended in a series of steps, and it would be necessary to descend into the thick muck, cross over to the far side, and then climb up more stairs to the next causeway.

"No. Shit no. I won't."

"You will, because you always do. Now be aware that you are about to relive your most painful memory. Mine is worse than yours, so don't complain."

"What? Why would we want to do that?"

"The demons enjoy this part. They find it bracing, and this crossing is added security should a soul escape and seek out the Holdfast."

"Is there some other way through here?"

"I—I just—look, helping you is about to become my most painful memory. Grab the rope and get it over with, Lady Bertha."

The old title rankled her into moving, and so she stepped forward, gasping as the hot liquid swallowed her ankles, then her legs. She battled the current to grab at the rope…

…and then she was somewhere else.

"Just leave, Sol," she cried as she watched him walk away from her, hunch-shouldered as she levied a barrage of insults at him. They were outside of their mansion at Langenfell, the moment that their marriage failed. They would not cross paths again until Sad Plain, where every other covenant would shatter.

"Go and dig a well, or start a livestock program, or write some more laws," she shouted. "You can't fix this place, and you certainly can't fix us."

"I'm sorry," he managed.

"Good! Anything is better than having you keep me o dusty bloody pedestal."

He opened a far-door and turned to her for a long th. They had nothing but the centuries holding them togethe shelved once a beautiful love story had become two separ together and never read again.

She said nothing, and he stepped through ped on the

*I will do anything to have a baby*, she thoug ak, eternally front steps and cried. She was frozen in t her this gor- beautiful, a royal, a goddess by law. Tir e it all up for geous mansion on the mountaintop, br year, decades the thing she ached for to the core.

Although they'd tried month af

running into centuries, a baby had never arrived for them. Despite all of their powers and Sol's fervent promises that he would find a way to restore the fertility that the Methuselah treatment took from everybody, nothing had ever worked.

Papa Lucy offered the powers of the Cruik, of course, but Sol never accepted, never once entertained the thought, even as desperate as Baertha was to conceive.

She cursed her past self, the ambitious girl who'd submitted to an untested treatment, her womb stilled even as her life stretched out forever and ever, drawn in by the advertisements, by the peer pressure of Lucy and Sol, by the promise they would make an amazing future.

*Make the Most of Time! Nine Hundred and Sixty-Nine Glorious Years!*

Then there were the other signs, placards in the hands of protesters that said things like:

*Say No to an Immortal Elite!*

*Untested Magic Has Consequences*

*Life Was Meant to Be Short.*

She'd happily face her own mortality now if it could mean a life growing inside of her. Baertha gripped her knees to her chest, and when she looked out across the world she'd made, she hated all of it.

A far-door opened, and she looked up then, her heart skipping a beat. Maybe Sol had come back. Maybe he'd changed his mind about the Cruik.

"O" she said, as Papa Lucy appeared.

"You sound so fucking disappointed," he said.

"I thought you—" and here she waved out at the world, to wherever he'd gone now. Always some new destination, some new problem needed righting, and he never stopped, rarely seemed to notice anymore.

"Paradise?"

"I—" he snorted.

"Your brother is still refusing my offer?" he said, walking closer, and as he climbed the steps, the butt of the Cruik rang against the stone. The promise, that it could give anyone anything they wanted. He was invincible now, and there seemed little he couldn't do with his new powers.

"He's proud."

"No, he's stupid. It will work. I know how to do it."

"How to undo the Methuselah effect?"

"Don't be fucking stupid, Baertha. You get to keep it *and* have a baby."

That was all it took. While the Cruik would ensnare her in the months to come, the first time was by her own free will. Perhaps it was an act of revenge, or just the realization that her marriage was actually over, but Baertha let Lucy quicken her womb with the Cruik, and then she made love to him, there in her marital bed.

*A baby, my baby, by any means.*

"At least this way you get the good semen," Lucy said, wiping himself off on the curtains. He seemed amused that he'd cuckolded his own brother, and after he stole liquor from Sol's cabinet, he came back to do it again, and again, and again.

No word from Sol. A month on, and Baertha's dream came true. Finally, *finally* she had a child in her womb, and she loved her brother-in-law in a deep and happy confusion.

Lucy then became wary and jealous, and he used the Cruik to steal Sol's home brick by brick. He rebuilt it on a distant island to the south of Mawson, making a love nest for them both in a tropical paradise.

Then came the time for the baby to arrive, and Lucy was nervous. He brought a team of midwives and doctors onto the island by far-door and equipped them with the best of everything. They were devout and terrified as they made ready to deliver this child of gods.

It was a difficult delivery that went on for a long time, Baertha's ancient flesh struggling to expel an infant. For one awful moment it looked like both she and the baby would die.

"No. NO! I won't allow this," Lucy shouted as the terrified midwives tried to usher the raving magician out of the door, uttering assurances that they needed to give Baertha space and calm.

One woman took him by the elbow, and he instantly immolated her on the spot. The medical staff ran screaming in all directions, and he killed them all with a pass of the Cruik, wading through flames and sprays of blood to stand at the foot of the bed.

He slammed down the Cruik, striking the floor with enough force to shatter the flagstone into dust.

"Enough of this shit. Our baby is coming out. Now!"

Baertha screamed as he lay the curled end of the staff on her belly. They were joined then, father, mother, and child, pulsing with white light, their bones visible, even to the child squirming in the womb.

"Please! It burns!"

"Shut up. I'm fixing this."

"NO!" Pain, universe-ending pain. With a gesture Lucy had opened Baertha like a rotisserie chicken, laying her bare down to the spine, and there was their babe floating through the air toward Lucy, still aglow with the white light, skeleton blazing from a lightning storm within.

"It's a girl," he said lovingly as Baertha lay screaming, attempting to reattach her opened pelvis and gather her intestines, the whole mess resembling a frog that was dissected while still alive. Her shaking hands gathered in the wreckage of her womb, the sac, the placenta and the severed cord.

A numb corner of her mind noted that Lucy was stealing her baby, the one thing she'd given her marriage, her pride, and now her life for.

The baby girl reached for Lucy, little fists grabbing. Then she opened her little mouth to let out her first cry, but instead emitted a fiery light, one that even Lucy staggered away from.

The babe glowed even brighter, a supernova in their house, a destructive potential that was about to turn them into slag. Born of two powerful magicians, the baby's little veins ran with the Cruik's corrosive strength, concentrated and steeped in the womb. It was too much for any flesh to bear, and Baertha realized that any baby helped along with the Cruik would suffer the same fate.

"Oh, fuck me," Lucy said, and he took up the Cruik like a golfer on the driving range, swatting the floating baby out of the window with all of his strength. The little figure crashed through the window and soared high into the sky.

A moment later, Baertha's firstborn child exploded above their island, shaking the house from roof to cellar, shattering all of the windows, a tiny preview of the shards that would rain upon Sad Plain.

What should have been a happy room was a place of death and

188 · JASON FISCHER

terror. Baertha was catatonic, only distantly noticing as Lucy reversed the damage he'd done with the Cruik, repairing her flesh, neatly reattaching everything to where it should be.

"Look, everyone fucks up the first pancake," Lucy said. "We just try again. The next kid will turn out fine, I promise you."

Baertha howled at the ceiling, an unhinged laughter that went on and on. In the distance her Millicents echoed her laugh, her warriors patrolling the perimeter and the strange glass chambers under the house.

"Babe of gold!" she crowed. "Lies were told!"

She'd finally cracked, her clever mind falling to this last and greatest trauma. She relived everything, the schism in their Family, how a cuckold and a gibbering mistress followed their mad-eyed leader to battle against Jesus, and the glass, everywhere glass and blood, and then Lucy banishing her to prowl her house as a monster, changed by the Cruik one time too many, until Sol came to find her once more, and then…

….and then her foot fell on a distant step, and then another, and she was rising from the muck of the Deep Insult, standing on a causeway on the far side.

"Holy shit," she whispered, tears streaming down her face. She ached all over for the baby she'd never even gotten to touch, the relived memories as fresh as when they'd happened.

"Rhiannon," she said. "I was going to call her Rhiannon."

"It's brutal every time," Bilben said kindly, a paw gently touching her forehead. "I apologize for the intrusion."

"You—you were watching?"

"I was. I am trying to learn what the Cruik was intending with you. I didn't get it this time, but I'm sure in a few hundred more viewings I will discern the Most High's interest in you."

"What are you talking about?"

"That was an exact copy of the Most High you carried to term," Bilben said. "How did the Cruik make this happen, and why?"

# — 16 —

## MAL

Mal and Kirstl rode to Graham's Wash as quickly as Collybrock could manage, conscious that messengers outing him as a deserter would be enroute and Captain Thunderbolt would be thundering along too.

*They won't imagine us coming back here,* Kirstl reasoned. *We'll be safe for a moment, but we'll need to be quick.*

"I'm not good at much else, but I'm good at digging holes," Mal said.

"Digging," Collybrock echoed.

They arrived back at the town gates, and Kirstl shifted into control of the body as they'd agreed. She was a little quicker off the mark and better at thinking on the spot.

Kirstl hollered out to the town guard, waving her lance up high. A machine gun nest tracked her movement, even as a spotter followed her with binoculars.

"Message for the barons!" she called out. "News from the captain!"

The guards watched her for a long, silent moment.

"Oh, for shit's sake. Open the gates now, you stupid pricks, or you'll have the barons to answer to."

After a long moment, the spotter signalled down below. The gates opened a crack, and then Mal and Kirstl squeezed through on Collybrock, who squawked at the guards in annoyance.

None of them said a word. The atmosphere at the gate was tense, and Kirstl felt the tickle of their eyes on her back. It would be nothing for them to swivel the gun around and shoot them down in the street.

*Act cool,* Mal offered. *We're just a normal messenger. They come and go all the time.*

Kirstl took up a quick pace through the streets, noting the increased military presence. Town squares and public spaces served as staging areas filled with ranked war buggies and phalanxes of motorbikes. The lizards that normally hauled water tankers had been armoured up, with machine gun nests in pagodas on their backs.

Braces of birds suffered saddles and bridles, and supply crews handed out lances by the bushel. One of the birds warbled low at Collybrock as she passed, and she gave a nervous note in response.

"Don't worry, girl," Kirstl said quietly, patting her on the neck. "We're leaving today, and we're not coming back."

Collybrock gave a happy little chirp at this news.

Suddenly there was the hiss and whistle of a steam engine venting. Kirstl flinched, only to see engineers crawling over a trio of the steam-walkers, shiny shells with their welds still fresh from the Tinkermen's forge.

*We have to get to the cemetery, but first we need a shovel.*

"There's no time," Kirstl said. She urged Collybrock into a quick run, shouting at people to step aside.

"Urgent message!" she shouted when a soldier complained, dropping a crate of rifles as Collybrock nudged past.

Then they were at the town cemetery, the resting place of those who'd died in the service of greed, and Kirstl wheeled about in a panic. She couldn't remember which grave the gun was buried in.

*Corporal Morris Franks,* Mal offered calmly. *Look left.*

It was there, the earth barely settled from the first burial and their own addition to the grave. Sliding out of the saddle, Kirstl took up a broad bladed lance and started digging madly at the earth, turning away clods with the sharp edge. It wasn't the best tool for the job, but

**The Bride & The Birdman · 191**

she worked methodically, finally snagging the canvas parcel after a few minutes' work.

"It's here," she said with relief, slicing through the knot and extracting Lanyard's old shotgun, complete with a handkerchief full of shells.

Then she heard the shuffle of feet, the creak of a hinge, and the full blast of a steam whistle nearby. She looked up in a panic to see a full troop of soldiers entering the cemetery, with Captain Thunderbolt at their head. Her steam engine was red-hot and venting clouds of vapor, and she came on slowly, hands spread.

"A Jesusman, hiding his foul instruments in a grave. Killing an officer. Deserting."

The soldiers had their guns raised, hemming them into the cemetery, but Captain Thunderbolt bid her men to stand down.

"There'll be a trial," she said. "Private Mal will be a fucking cripple and beaten half to death, but he'll get a trial."

Wide-eyed, Kirstl scrambled up into the saddle, hands lifting to summon up a shadow-door, but then the captain lurched forward in a rapid shuffle, venting an arc of superheated steam all over them. Kirstl couldn't concentrate on the magic, could feel nothing but scalding pain.

The steel juggernaut came forward at great speed, crushing headstones with every step. Even as Kirstl choked and attempted to aim the shotgun, Collybrock fell into her training, wings flapping, sharp talons ready to tear into the enemy who meant her master harm.

Her claws scraped against the plate steel, scoring it deeply. As Collybrock tried to find a weak spot in her helmet, Captain Thunderbolt grappled with the bird. Her thick steel fingers wrapped around Collybrock's neck, squeezing tighter and tighter, and with her right hand she simply punched into the bird's chest, over and over, piston-fist hammering through breastbone and finally staving in her heart.

Cracking Collybrock's neck for good measure, Captain Thunderbolt threw the dead bird aside with contempt. The steam-powered killer reached down for Kirstl, still trapped in the saddle.

Mal surged forward with a rage, assuming control of their body, and when mouth and tongue were his he began to scream a wordless note for his dead friend.

He drew a lance from the sheath, striking upward, and the blade bounced off the captain's steel plate. She took the shaft of the lance in her hand and shattered it with one motion.

Mal finally fought free of Collybrock's dead weight and stood before the captain, broken lance in one hand, Jesusman's shotgun in the other.

The captain laughed, fit to burst, and even the onlookers joined in.

"You've already lost, Private. Now it's just sad."

Mal ran forward then, ducking under her sweeping haymaker, and then he leapt up with all his might, ramming the broken lance home.

The captain staggered backward, waving at her face, and then she sank to her knees with a surprised "oh."

Mal had lodged the broken lance through the narrow slit in her helmet, deep into one of her eyes. She reached up with a shaking hand to pull it free, piston creaking with the delicate motion, but then her hand fell back to the ground. She moaned in pain, a deep, hollow sound that echoed out of the helmet.

Setting aside the shotgun, Mal yanked out the lance, causing the captain to emit a high, lingering shriek. Then he wrenched open her helmet, and let it drop to the ground. The soldiers on the perimeter started forward, rifles aimed, but Mal snatched up the shotgun, holding it to the captain's ruined face.

"Back!" he yelled. He looked at Collybrock's broken body, discarded across a row of graves, and he shook with rage. "You killed my best friend."

The captain lifted her one good eye to Mal with a nasty smile.

"We'll be eating her for dinner tonight," she whispered. "Right before we hoist you on the noose."

He snarled, an eye to the large group of soldiers readying themselves to rush in. He was doomed.

"Kirstl!" he cried out. "I need you!"

*We've got trouble! Something's attacking the Tontine again!*

He felt it too, something slamming against their defences with brute strength. The walls guarding his mind were cracking, and something would be inside soon.

*Hurry! It's getting in!*

"For fuck's sake, it can wait one second!" he shouted.

Kirstl slid forward into the mind-space, only staying long enough to do two things. She opened a shadow-door, and then she said a Word. Lanyard's shotgun glowed with a white brilliance, humming in her hands.

"Your turn," Kirstl said, and Mal took over the body.

As the captain reached up to drag them down in a bearhug, Mal flipped the gun in his hands, and with one deft move he slammed the wooden stock into her temple. It passed through her skull like butter, leaving nothing of Captain Thunderbolt from the neck up. He gave her a nudge with his boot, and her hissing suit of armour toppled backward, her arteries still spraying and squirting for one awful moment.

"You're not worth a bullet," Mal choked out, tears sluicing a clean track down his dusty face.

As the soldiers cried in panic and started shooting at him, he deflected the bullets with a clumsily sketched Word. With one last pained look at Collybrock, Mal stepped into the Greygulf.

---

Slamming the shadow-door closed, Mal spent a panicked moment sweeping around with his shotgun, looking for threats. The Greygulf had always unsettled him, but seeing it take Lanyard made it so much worse.

Perhaps it had taken the others by now too.

*Please, Mal! There's something in here with me!*

Mal calmed his panicked breaths. No threats were stalking along the crumbling shadow-road, and the ashen ruins below them were still. If there were predators nearby, they slumbered.

Easing the leather strap of the shotgun over his shoulder, Mal settled down, cross-legged, against the flagstones of the shadow-road. It felt chalky, almost brittle, and he wondered at how the roads even held together. Closing his eyes, he entered the mind-space with Kirstl, who was frantically searching for the intruder. She'd summoned up a myriad of imagined weapons and strafed the dark corners of their shared mind with gunfire.

"Careful!" Mal said. "Who knows what parts of our brain you're hurting!"

"I don't care when I'm sharing it with Lady bloody Bertha or who knows what. Something got inside and it's in here, right now!"

"I felt it too," Mal said, and he visualized a long pike in his hands. "It chose the worst possible moment to hit us, too."

The mind-space was the waking part of his mind, and it did not grant them the same freedoms of the dream-space. In some ways it resembled a foggy maze, with memories hidden just behind that gauze. Up ahead was the cinema of their eyes, the faint light of the Greygulf playing over everything.

Back at the start of their Tontine, Kirstl and Mal had fought in here for control of the body before reaching their accommodation. A mind was a labyrinth even for its owner, and it might prove incredibly hard to ferret out an intruder here.

"Did you see it breaking in? Down in the dream-space?"

"I was more worried about you dying, you stupid man! I only saw the flash of something moving, and then it came up to the mind-space to hide."

They moved as a fighting pair through the neurons, watching for attack. Bands of lightning washed up and down the maze of Mal's brain, bright spots in the fog for a moment, but there were still many shadows. A patient foe could spend many days crafting an ambush here, or lurk in the dark places forever, an unspeaking witness to everything they did and said.

Kirstl set many traps in the mind-space, spells of her own devising that would entangle the intruder, cause it pain and slow it down. The idea was to force it back down to the dream-space, where it would be easier to deal with. Evict it, or even kill it.

"You'd better get back out there," she said, a little calmer now. "There might be something sneaking up on us while you're all cross-legged."

"We still sticking with the plan?"

"Of course, my love."

Mal blinked a little as he returned to his senses, then unfolded his legs, standing once more on the shadow-road. Readying the shotgun, he walked for what felt like hours under that sunless grey sky, knowing full well where all the roads led to.

He came to the jagged end of his own path, the stones crumbling as if the road itself were now unhealthy and decaying. A great span of the chalky stone had fallen here, and the other end of the path lay hundreds of feet away. He tried to call it closer, to stitch the broken edges together, but all he did was cause more of it to fail, and he had to backstep quickly from the end of his own road.

"Shit."

He pointed the broken end of his road downward, slowly laying it flush with the silvery soil of the Greygulf. Dread filled Mal's heart as he walked down to the surface, where Witches and worse things stalked.

*Look for a road in good condition,* Kirstl offered. *Get above this mess as soon as you can.*

"Good advice."

They spent many hours trekking across the sterile landscape, winding through boxthorns and stripped back junk from bleedthroughs the Witches had interrupted. Occasionally there were fires, but they flickered in greyscale, black and white like the photographs in old books, hotter than a flame fanned by a blacksmith.

Mal flinched at every sound, even as he knew that some nameless terror stalked inside his own mind. Kirstl gave her reports as she hunted it, but she was frustrated by the lack of any sign.

Then she had a creeping realization.

*We're getting tired,* Kirstl said. *Been walking for a long time.*

"I know."

*So that means we need to sleep.*

"Oh shit."

*We've got no one to watch our back out there. In here, it's the perfect time for our intruder to seize control of the body. Lock us in the dream-space.*

"We can't sleep!"

*Well, that's not going to work, dumbarse. We need to find a foxhole, and then sort out this stowaway.*

Boots beginning to scuff the dust with every tired step, Mal looked high and low until he found the perfect place: a white fridgerator, tipped onto its side. Mal quietly stripped out the shelves and racks, hiding them in a stack of masonry, and then he wriggled into the appliance, pulling the door most of the way closed.

*Great. You found a coffin.*

"No. These were iceboxes in the Before. Used to keep food cool and fresh. Lanyard told me so."

Laying on his vest and jacket, Mal rested, even as he fought the urge to fall asleep.

*We've got maybe minutes before you slip away. Get in here and help me.*

Mal turned inward and walked the mind-space, his wife at his side.

"Any bright ideas?" Kirstl asked. Mal paused, considering the foggy maze of thought that they stood in.

"We pretend to sleep," he said, peeling back a foggy memory, a moment of peeling potatoes as a prentice. "Then we jump it when it emerges to take control."

Kirstl smiled, patting Mal on the shoulder.

It was harder to make the images here, but not impossible. They hid behind the foggy gauze of the potato-peeling memory as Kirstl envisaged the pair of them surrendering to exhaustion, laying aside their weapons and sinking through into the subconscious of the dream-space.

There was movement in the neurons then, a solitary figure advancing cautiously. It was canny enough to avoid all of Kirstl's traps, and it took a circuitous route toward the forebrain. Here was the instinctive place for an entity to stand, to seize the body, to open the eyes and look out through them.

But the intruder stopped. Mal and Kirstl waited for many infuriating moments and watched in disbelief as it simply fell back into the fog.

"What the hell is this?" Kirstl whispered. "It's got us. It can simply take over."

"Maybe it knew it was a trick," Mal said quietly. "Just wait."

But Kirstl had already thrown away the blanket of fog and was racing after it, shouting, shooting off her weapon, and they were left only with the fading sound of fast feet and the knowledge they'd failed.

"Damn it," Kirstl said as she returned to Mal. Physically, they were drifting toward slumber, even in the uncomfortable confines of the fridgerator.

They were out of time.

"Maybe the new owner of this body will do a better job with it," Kirstl said. "We can hang out in some dank corner and keep out of its way."

"Wait," Mal said, struck with a sudden realization. He tried to summon something into his hands but struggled to make it work, the creation dribbling through his fingers like sand.

"What are you trying for?" Kirstl said. Mal told her. Wide-eyed, she made the construction and handed it to him.

He stepped into the fog of his own mind, unarmed and trusting, and he began making sounds. A click, a rasp, a rattle, the sounds distinct and his alone. The clacker-stick was a difficult instrument to master, but any who knew it well played it with their own accent, and it was made to travel across the Inland, to call out simple instructions.

Fight. Flee. Come to your master.

Emerging from the fog came the timid form of a creature, ten feet tall at its crest, and then it was running, and then a razor-sharp beak snapped open, chittering with excitement, and then the spirit of Collybrock was kneeling before Mal, nuzzling into him and crowing in happy confusion.

---

Their Tontine was now three, and as near as they could figure it was a cosmic accident. After Collybrock died, her spirit would have been drawn down through the Aum, destined for Gan-Eden. When she passed by the structure with the strong sense of Mal and Kirstl, however, the bird instinctively knew this was her new home, even as terrified as she was of everything. She broke in and hid, perhaps misunderstanding her own death, and now the owners of this house were chasing her angrily, even shooting at her.

Even though all was now forgiven, Collybrock was still confused, more so as Mal and Kirstl walked in here as two separate entities. As they fell into an exhausted slumber, the bird dogged their every move, walking cautiously through the dream-space and trying not to touch any of their mind creations.

"It's okay, girl," Mal said, finally climbing up and into her saddle. "It's a fun place. If you want something in here, you just have to think about it."

She was a quick study, and soon Collybrock was chasing after dozens of small snakes, pouncing on them triumphantly. Kirstl and Mal laughed as the bird gorged herself on her imaginary prey.

After a long rest, Mal gave over the body to Kirstl, wanting to stay with the ghost of his bird. Kirstl awoke with a groan, her body stiff from the awkward position they'd slept in.

Pushing out of the fridgerator, she took stock of their meagre provisions. A heel of bread, a hunk of camel cheese, and a half-empty waterskin. Their only defences against the monsters of the Greygulf were a sharp foldback knife, Lanyard's legendary shotgun, and a handkerchief full of shells. There was also an old spyglass in the bottom of their bag, the lenses marred and warped on one side, but it had been good enough for a water-crew scout.

Time was impossible to measure here without a wristwatch, but Kirstl guessed that walking to the point of exhaustion took twelve hours. They needed to find their destination in one or two sleeps at the most, or their shared body would start to die in here.

Kirstl was frustrated by Mal's bow-legged gait, the legacy of so much time in a bird saddle. She'd been a lithe little thing in her former life, moving through her days like a whippet, and she found this body maddening at times. Mal had always travelled on bird-back or in a vehicle, rarely moving on foot, and unused muscles twinged and ached more with every passing hour.

"I'd give anything for a motorbike and a Tinkerman," she was muttering to herself when she saw a magnesium flash on the horizon, and then another. A booming clap reached her a few moments later, thunder or worse.

She ran.

The bright flashes came more frequently, and soon she saw the source through a gap in the dunes. The hulk of the Terminus, a mote rotating in the sky, the crackles of small-arms fire blasting out from a dozen different windows. Dozens of shadow-roads bent toward the floating station but did not connect to it, stretched taut and broken-edged. Attempts to breach the structure, but they'd been knocked away, and none of these roads had managed to get close enough to connect.

Correction. One road had connected, but a big span had been blown out of it. Figures rushed about on it like ants as the twinkles of gunshots rained down on them.

Kirstl pulled out her spyglass and traced out the Mark of Farsight on the lens. Twitching the glass back and forth, she looked at the attackers, and her blood ran cold. Witches slid around by the dozen, accompanied by stranger creatures, some resembling large praying mantises, another a large pulsing fuzz that might have been mould or cotton wool. Strangest of all was the large bell on legs, a creature that posed like a hunting dog and swept the bowl of its muzzle across the distant Terminus.

Shooting at the besiegers were Jesusmen trapped inside the structure, their only escape the one remaining shadow-road that a parade of monsters scurried upon. They were constructing a rough bridge out of junk to try to cross the gap, even as the Jesusmen tried to snipe the builders and use the occasional explosive to knock their efforts apart.

These efforts were spare and measured. Which told Kirstl only one thing: they'd been holding out for weeks now and were running low on ammunition.

"How the hell do we help them?" Kirstl muttered. Even though she'd only been a passenger to Mal's cowardice, she carried as much guilt for having cut and run.

She crept closer to the base of the shadow-road. It was still connected to a low-lying door, half-irised open to an alien realm of smoke and webs. The Witches had built a rickety ramp of junk to access this shadow-road from the ground, and they were passing up scavenged materials with their waxy tentacles and snake tails.

On the ground was a huge dumping pile of random material from bleedthroughs. The Witches had press-ganged various lesser plane-hopping beasts into hauling forth junk to add to this stockpile, and the tin and masonry was already a shifting hill that threatened to topple. This was being fed upward to build fortifications and the bridge that threatened the surviving Jesusmen.

Kirstl scanned the pile through the spyglass, and her eyes widened. The junk-fetchers had found everything from cinema seating to water fountains and were adding these to the pile indiscriminately.

"Mal. Mal, we need to talk tactics."

*Just five more minutes.*

"Now, shithead. This is your mess, and you will be present while we fix it."

Somewhat guiltily, bird and boy slithered into the mind-space and observed the siege.

*We can't take them all on by ourselves.*

"No shit."

*But we can surprise them.*

After constructing a plan that was equal parts boldness and folly, Kirstl gave the body over to Mal, who crept forward stealthily. The first step was to seize transport, a bike or a car if they could get it. Mal heard the canvas-tearing *brap brap brap* of a motorbike echoing against the ruins, and a moment later he saw a Witch hunched all over the machine, three heads facing in all directions, twisted, doughy limbs grasping the throttle and steering.

The junk-hunters got excited whenever they found a machine for their masters. Mal watched despondently as another bike and even a car were brought forward and taken by the Witches. Going by the smoking tangle of machinery underneath the Terminus, the Witches were trying to launch vehicles across the gap, and the Jesusmen were blowing them apart. For now.

Then came an opportunity that even these creatures overlooked. A segmented beast brought in a forklift in a pair of tentacles, brandishing it proudly overhead while the creature wriggled forward on a bed of cilia. One Witch rebuked it sharply and pointed it toward the central pile of junk.

"Oh yes," Mal whispered.

During one ill-spent summer, he had stolen into the warehouses of the Lodge of Jesusman to joyride on the forklift there, an ancient machine that was mostly welded patches and rust by the time it came into their care. When he crashed it into a wall and finally broke the irreplaceable machine, Lanyard took to him with a belt—but today proved Mal's punk behaviour of the past had been worth it. Few from the Now could drive a car, and fewer still could work a forklift, but Mal certainly could.

Nicking the back of his arm with the foldback knife, Mal dabbed his finger in the blood and quickly traced Marks of seeking and sharpness on the blade. Moving low and fast, Mal kept the hillocks of junk between him and the Witches supervising the scavenging effort, then he hid behind a filing cabinet until the segmented creature came in to deposit the forklift.

He rose from a crouch to drive the Marked blade in between the head and the body, sawing away rapidly. As the blade burnt and slid through the meat, the creature attempted to deploy a stinger, still waving the forklift overhead.

"Die already," Mal grunted, finally severing the creature's head. It lived on for a long moment, the stinger on its tail flashing once, twice, and then finally ceasing a hand's width from his breastbone, the creature twitching and sagging in on itself.

Looking around to see if he'd been spotted, Mal breathed a sigh of relief as he saw that a Witch berated its underlings, tearing one apart with razor sharp claws. He had a small window of time to do this.

Then he turned back to see the dying creature tipping to one side, threatening to put the forklift upside down.

*Quick, get the forklift the right way up!*

He put his shoulder to the machine, heaving for all he was worth, and when the creature was fully dead the forklift settled onto its wheels with a sickening crunch.

*Did you break it?*

"I didn't break it. The fucking—the fucking centipede thing dropped it."

Moving quickly, Mal looked into the cab, glad to see the keys in the ignition. He crept over toward the forklift's blades, still holding his bloody knife, looking around nervously for Witches or worse.

"Kirstl," he said, and she took over, quickly carving Marks into the broad steel tines, each stroke giving off a metallic squeal and even sparks. The Mark-work was quick and sloppy, but they were enough to do the job and then some.

"Mal, come back, quickly!" she said, climbing up into the driver's seat. "I don't know how to work this thing."

A pack of the junk-haulers had spotted them, obscenities that were halfway between a duck and a long-legged wolf. They gambolled and yapped as they closed in, their cries echoing through the valleys of junk. Some of their number paused to tear apart the dead centipede, but most of them came in honking, razor-sharp bills spread wide.

Mal reached forward, twisting the ignition key, and the near perfect bleedthrough coughed into life. He spun the machine around to face their attackers, wrenching at the levers until the blades were raised up high.

Then he pressed the accelerator flat.

Machine met beast, and the Marks on the forklift blades flared with sudden light as he punched through the chest of the first duck-wolf. Mal twisted the steering wheel, turning the machine around on the spot. The blades tore loose from the dead creature, then decapitated the next one.

The third ran, and Mal let it go. He drove the forklift around the junkpile and hit the ramp at top speed, climbing up to the shadow-road. Beneath him, the rickety structure shook with every movement. Mal's heart was in his throat, expecting that the weight of the machine would send the whole mess tumbling down.

*Mal!*

He turned to see a Witch chasing them from below. With a curse, Mal yanked out the shotgun and fired blindly behind him.

That just attracted more Witches, who herded a small army of conscripts up the ramp and after them. Above was a goat-faced

Witch, beardy mouth open in a slack of surprise at the forklift bearing down on it.

*Mark of Unmaking! Do it!* And of course Kirstl was right. The moment that their front wheels touched the shadow-road, Mal made the Mark. The ramshackle structure of the ramp came down in one piece, like a winding apple peel that coiled around itself and crushed every creature climbing it.

The goat was changing into the form of a man, arms lifting in two shotguns that were ready to spit the grey flame. Mal hit it square on, forklift blades spearing through it like melted butter. The Marks flared brilliantly, and the Witch unleashed a quivering scream that went on and on as it struggled to free itself from the tines.

After Mal wiggled the blades up and down, the dying Witch slid free, and the forklift jolted around as the wheels crushed the last lick of life from it. Black and white flames rained down around them, hurled by panicked Witches only now realizing an enemy was at their rear.

Mal crouched low, steering with his knees, and he fed a fresh shell into the shotgun. A flame hit the front of the forklift, and a hiss of steam erupted from the machine's workings. He steered through the incoming firestorm as best he could, and then he was tearing through the camp of the besieging Witches, a spinning weapon of blades and wheels, destroying everything in his path.

The gap in the shadow-road was close now, with the Terminus beyond that. He could see the Jesusmen with his naked eyes, now sniping the enemy with a renewed vengeance.

*They're clearing a path!* Kirstl crowed jubilantly.

Then the Witches took down his forklift, tangling it up in a net of waxy snake shapes and dog heads, teeth tearing into the steel frame and shaking it around. Mal fell to the shadow-road with a painful bounce, and then he was up and hobbling forward. A Witch lurched out at him from behind a junk stack, taking on his own form, but Mal did not hesitate, sending a shotgun blast into its face. A lucky shot that struck it in its shifting heart, and the waxy creature curled in on itself as it died.

More grey fires crashed around him, this time from behind. Mal panicked, sending his second shot into a pack of creatures, more of the duck-faced wolves being urged onward by a pair of Witches. Too far away to do much damage, the shot barely gave the honking creatures any pause.

He fed in two more shells, slamming the breech of the weapon closed, and then he was upon the main camp of the besiegers. He took in the bell-beast, face constantly sweeping the Terminus, and considered the Witches, doughy limbs ready to rain fire and pain, their too-wide smiles spreading to reveal sharp white fangs.

Then a mantis creature appeared, its shell coated in a patina that looked like an oil slick. It scraped its claws together to produce the most awful of screeches. That sound became Mal's whole universe, an awful din that dug into his mind and sent him reeling. He fell to his knees, shotgun forgotten, and a menagerie of grinning and yipping monstrosities slowly surrounded him.

*Mal, please get up!* Kirstl cried in a panic. In the mindspace of the Tontine she shook him, but he was taut, shaking as if suffering an electric shock.

"Back," said a familiar voice. "All of you bastards, get back."

It was Lanyard.

The bossman, Mal's father, now a Witch, surviving the crush of tons of stone to besiege the Jesusmen. He slithered forward atop a grandfather snake, driving the other beasts away with a whip that was part of his own body, and they obeyed him with alacrity.

This was bad, very bad. Witches rarely worked together, but Kirstl realized that Lanyard's tenacity had carried over into his second life. He'd browbeaten and conquered enough monsters to become a warlord and knew everything these Jesusmen did.

Tilly's people were maybe a day or two from falling to this new, hateful version of the man they'd once adored.

"You came back, boy," Lanyard said. The whip became an arm, and the hand on that arm cupped Mal by the chin, drawing his head up level. "Second fucking mistake you've made lately," he said. He slithered over to his old shotgun and reached down to pick it up. Lanyard recoiled from the weapon as soon as his flesh touched it, crying out, hands sizzling from contact with the Jesusman Marks.

"Bastard thing," he said sourly.

*Get up, Mal!* Kirstl said, inside the mind-space with him, but all Mal could do was twitch and shiver, making an *ungh, ungh, ungh* sound, the hypnotic screeching still driving him down, keeping him trapped in there.

*I can do this,* she thought, remembering the moment that Papa Lucy stunned Mal in the Underfog, only for her to come forward and take the magician down. *I think the mantis thing can only stop one of us.*

Kirstl took control of the body, and she leapt to her feet, running away from Lanyard, toward the makeshift bridge. The mantis screeched away, futile in the face of Mal's second self. Then a second mantis landed in front of her with flapping wings. Kirstl lifted a hand to make a protective Mark, but then the bell creature turned its face toward her, and it felt like all of her magic had been instantly severed.

"No!" she cried, desperate to escape this trap, clawing against the shield that blocked her magic. "Mal, please help me!"

For the first time in a long time, Kirstl was utterly alone, and she felt terrified as the grinning monsters closed in, Lanyard rising over them all on the coils of a snake. He had a satisfied look, a hunter closing in on his chosen prey, and panicked gripped her chest tightly.

The shotgun was too far away, but as she dug into her pocket for the foldback knife, the second mantis increased the sawing screech of its limbs, and she finally succumbed to the sound. Driven out of control of the Tontine, she fell back into the mind-space to gibber and thrash around next to Mal.

"Useful beasts, and now they work for me," Lanyard said. "And the Null here—well it blocks any type of magic a bloody Jesusman might try."

The creature squatted above their body, radiating a sense of *nothing* and *smother* from the throat of the bell. Even in the depths of her delirium, Kirstl felt that she'd lost one of her senses. If she could have screamed, she would have.

The two mantis creatures loomed above Mal's prone body, sawing away. Lanyard stood in their centre, looking down with grim satisfaction.

"They're Sirens. Found these ones in the Aum and lured them here to deal with you. They hunt Tontines in the void," Lanyard gloated.

The mantis beasts skittered and screeched, gnashing their mandibles, looming greedily above them. Lanyard cuffed them, and they turned away.

Kirstl saw an etching on their throats, some sort of corrupted Mark that Lanyard had placed there. Lanyard himself had spoken about Bauer binding a Witch pack with a forgotten Mark, and it seemed that in his vile second life he'd invented his own workaround.

"Next job is to turn you, Mal. Make you one of us. Took three captured prentices to work it out, but we can change a Jesusmen into a Witch now, just by dangling him in a shadow-door for long enough."

He leaned right in, pale, doughy face drawn up close to Mal's, and in the hidden cinema of the mind-space they could not look away.

"You might have given up on me, boy, but I never gave up on you."

"Lanyard," a voice croaked in the mind-space. "Bad."

Then Collybrock trotted forward, weaving through the fog of memory and past the prone souls of Mal and Kirstl, who could only twitch and babble at the bird.

"N-no," Mal managed, reaching for Collybrock with a shaking hand.

She took over the body, the spirit of the bird folding itself into the squat, unfamiliar shape of a man, wings squeezing into arms, clawed feet pushing against unfamiliar angles and joints to fill out the legs. Then their body sprang up, pushing past a surprised Lanyard, and stumbled up the shadow-road, reeling back and forth like a toddler or a drunk.

"You're supposed to be stopping them!" Lanyard screeched at the Sirens. They sawed away frantically, but he'd only brought enough of them to silence two of the souls in the Tontine.

Collybrock lurched forward, stumbling as she tried to learn how humans walked. Shifting into a man-shape, Lanyard walked toward the slowly escaping boy, reaching out to seize his wrist.

"Don't know what trick you're pulling, boy, but you've lost. Give up like you always do."

"No," Collybrock said sulkily, and pulled away, still trying out the unfamiliar legs. Mal's bowed legs had led him to walk duck-footed, so Collybrock forced the toes inward, met the resistance of ligament, and pushed inward again.

There was a painful *crack-crack-crack!* as something shifted in Mal's legs and back, and suddenly the body stood straighter. Collybrock spread her arms out wide, fingers flexed out as broad as feathers, and then she flapped, crowing joyously up at the sky.

"Boy's lost his mind," Lanyard snarled.

"Not boy! Bird!" Collybrock said.

She bent down, snatched the leather strap of the shotgun in her new body's teeth, and then off she ran. She whipped along with a high-toed gait, faster than any human could likely reach on their own. Lanyard hollered for her capture, and a menagerie of strange creatures came at her—including the Sirens, still trying to sing her down.

She bounced and flapped and wove her way through the reaching arms and tentacles, kicking away the gnashing fangs and beaks of Lanyard's monsters, and finally rounded the Null, running toward the Terminus itself.

The besiegers had built half a bridge this time, a flimsy construction of tin sheeting and beams. Collybrock hit this at full speed, screeching joyfully.

"Go! Jump! Go!"

She leapt from the edge of the bridge, arms and legs wheeling as she flew across that impossible gap. She did not spare an eye for the body-crushing distance between the bridge and the ground.

There was no doubt. Nothing but joy.

Collybrock hit the other side of the broken span, bouncing painfully across the chalky cobblestones, the shotgun jarred from her teeth and clattering along beside her.

Then came the sizzling of the grey flames falling around her. Arms were reaching for her, but this time they belonged to people, urging her onward and dragging her behind a ramshackle shelter. Jesusmen. They returned fire against the Witches, who shifted into horrifying shapes and howled in fury.

Lanyard stood silently at the edge of the bridge, watching as the boy with three minds was hustled into the interior of the Terminus.

Collybrock gazed around with a slightly unhinged grin, happy to be amongst the Jesusmen once more. When she saw the rows of emaciated birds sulking on a picket line, she hopped excitedly on the spot, shrieks echoing against the cupola ceiling of the Terminus.

When Tilly appeared and delivered a ringing backhander to the bird, that broke her good mood. She hissed and lifted her arms high, wings in a threat display. She weaved her head left and right, instinct guiding her to that moment where she would peck her foes and scratch them to death.

"Tilly bad!"

"What the fuck is wrong with you?" Tilly said, wide-eyed. The other Jesusmen were backing away, leaving that bird wearing a person to blink and stare about in confusion.

*Collybrock. Girl, it's okay,* Mal said soothingly, from somewhere in her mind. *You need to let go now.*

"Mal?" Collybrock cried out, a worried croon. Dozens of eyes watched this, muttering uneasily around their meagre cooking fires.

*Just close your eyes and come back toward me. Let go. Relax.*

Collybrock did this, and she awoke in the mind-space, with the souls of Mal and Kirstl. The trio pressed close, hugging and ruffling hair and feathers, jubilant and exhausted.

They'd faced Lanyard, that false father turned villain, and lived through it. Got back to the Jesusmen.

"Answer me," Tilly was saying as Mal took control of the body, opening his eyes.

"Hi, Tilly," he said, the simple look of the bird giving way to his familiar expression. Tilly's eyes narrowed in recognition, and then she had him by the throat, pushing him backward into a wall.

"You were meant to shoot Lanyard. This is all your fault!"

She slammed a fist into his solar plexus, and he fell down, gasping for air. Tilly lined up a boot with his ribs and hammered him there twice before delivering a swift kick to the face that sent him reeling.

"Mem, Lyn. Carry this piece of shit to the brig."

He could have retreated back into the mind-space to avoid the

THE BRIDE & THE BIRDMAN · 209

pain, but Mal remained as present as he could, choosing to accept this punishment. One injured eye was closing, but he could see the clothing hanging loose on everyone, the guards on the provision store, and a shameful spit roast where a bird lay turning over a fire.

The Jesusmen were trapped—and barely holding together.

The two mohawked women took him to a makeshift cell and tossed him in with a drunk and a thief. He lay on the hard ground for many minutes before he attempted to stand.

*I deserve this,* he said to Kirstl. *Whatever they do to me.*

*I can't argue too much with that,* she said. *Still, not an easy choice for anyone. I'm sure other Jesusmen have failed at putting down their own.*

*I chose the worst moment to do it,* he said. *This, all of this is on me.*

*At least we get to die with them now,* Kirstl mused. *That makes some of it right.*

*I love him, Kirstl,* he said. *Even still. He can't help what happened to him.*

*Mal, he's turned fucking Witch. That thing isn't Lanyard anymore!*

*He's in there, I know it. We might be able to reach him still.*

*Bullshit. If they hang us, it's justified.*

*True, my love.*

---

Tilly came for Mal when she'd had a chance to calm down. He was pushed to his knees at gunpoint before her.

"We've been stuck here for weeks. Lanyard attacks us our every waking moment. It's only a matter of time before he gets in."

Mal nodded, conscious of his fat lip.

"We're going to break out while we still can," Tilly said. "Tell me everything you saw on the way in. Lanyard's forces. His camps. Any reinforcements that might be coming."

"You can't break out," Mal said.

"Now, you're misunderstanding me," Tilly said. "You lost all right to have a say the moment you ran away. You're intel and nothing else to me now."

The words cut deep. Tilly had been family to him for the better part of his life. Drawing a deep breath, Mal pressed on.

"Kirstl figured out the answer. Listen, we know how to solve this!"

"I should toss you to Lanyard and be done with you."

"Tilly, you need us. I hope it's not too late for me to do the right thing."

"One pair of hands is worth fuck all at this point."

"You misunderstood Terminus," Mal said. "It's not a train station. It's the train."

# — 17 —

## BAERTHA

Leaving the Deep Insult behind, Baertha entered the maze of the Endless Pavilion. Without Bilben to guide her she would have been lost a dozen times over, and repeatedly she needed to refresh the illusion that disguised her as a demon. The wellspring of her natural magic was deep, but she was exhausted, still gasping from time to time as the last of the Aurum passed through her system.

"Ah!" she screamed, and a dozen lesser demons joined the cry, thinking it a moment of ecstasy. They danced about her, wings and stingers whipping around, and then they went about on some other foul errand, leaving her shaking against a wall.

"Breathe," Bilben encouraged. "We are almost there."

The freshness of the relived memory sat heavy with her. She'd never forgotten Rhiannon's birth, but she'd pushed it into the distant corners of her memories, aligning it with those lost years she'd fallen under the Cruik, when her family of gods had chosen to become monsters.

"Yes, it is most strange," Bilben whispered, tiny paw against her temple. "No one knows where the Cruik came from. But I am told the Cruik vexed the Most High into leaving. Then it planted a golden twin in your belly."

"Please," Baertha said, brushing the paw away from her face. "You intrude."

"Oh, you are the queen of intrusions," Bilben mocked. "Over you went to that new Tontine to kick in the doors. Did you know they were Jesusmen? Of course not."

"How do you know this?"

"I've already told you. I watch the stream of time, both ways. Stop questioning me. Now quickly, through yonder door."

Bilben took them forward in fits and starts, awaiting odd landmarks and happenings such as "when the demon sneezes thrice, turn left," and "wait until the torturer strangles his friend over a missing whip, and then pass." Their meandering path eventually led them to a low door, the frame lined with long iron thorns. To enter, Baertha would need to crawl carefully through it.

"This way is safest," Bilben said. "The main entry into the Holdfast is heavily policed by the Möbius."

Pausing to refresh her disguise, Baertha felt a moment of light-headedness, followed by a sustained twinge of Aurum withdrawal. This last was passing from an active pain into a dull ache.

Then her stomach growled, and she realized she was thirsty.

"Your addiction passes here, every time. This is also the moment you start dying. There is nothing down here you should attempt to eat or drink."

"Wonderful," Baertha said, and she began to crawl. The fleshy door opened at a touch, a cacophony erupting from within. She wriggled forward, elbows close to her ribs.

"Lower your buttocks," Bilben instructed. "You often impale yourself there."

She slowly eased herself through the hatch, earning a nick along the back of her calf at the last moment.

"That's new," Bilben said, sounding troubled.

Baertha arose, taking in a Boschian nightmare. The Holdfast was equal parts ruler, courtiers, and throne room, a fleshy organ that she was now standing on the inside of.

She'd been to the New Basilica at Ur-Roma, and the Holdfast dwarfed even that epic structure. Parts of the room occasionally sank beneath the fleshy floor only to rise up elsewhere, and everything seemed in flux.

There was a papal figure on a towering throne. After a few minutes, this sank like a demolished tower, only to arise as a trio of magistrates behind a plainer bench, and then as a royal family on a neat row of ornate chairs.

The creature gave itself an audience, sock puppets that rose and fell, wearing various fashions and adopting different roles. While a jester cavorted, others duelled or read out petitions, and always the chamber itself morphed around this show, classic columns giving way to art deco and then onto austere communist stylings.

There were other small portals like the one Baertha had used, and small demons entered to present grievances or to curry favour. As often as not, these lesser demons were simply torn apart by the Holdfast or ignored. Passing through the larger throat of the main door was a queue of the greater beasts, hulking things of horn and fang, and they whispered by the thousand, muttering to themselves and each other, and to the representatives of the Holdfast whenever they rose from the floor. The sound was overwhelming, and Baertha imagined she was inside a beehive.

"There they are," Bilben said, guiding her head until she was looking in the right direction. She spotted three humanoid figures being rushed about in a wave of rising and falling courtiers, forced to run endlessly in a circuit around the main throne of the Holdfast.

Baertha knew the true form of the Farsight spell, and lightly brushed her eyelids with her fingertips, speaking the words. When she opened her eyes again, she could clearly see the shapes of her old friends, exhausted, buffeted back and forth, held in a frog-march whenever they flagged.

She saw the Once-Dead spirits of John and Hesus, but even stranger was the appearance of Ray Leicester, here in flesh-and-blood. He bled from a dozen small cuts and looked deeply distressed.

Baertha remembered his Asperger's and his dislike of crowded places, and realized this would be a particularly demanding trial for him. He'd gone missing a hundred years or more before Sad Plain, and Baertha had mourned him for a long time, even as she mourned her own still womb and even deader marriage.

"You usually do something stupid here," Bilben warned. "You attack the Holdfast, or you demand the release of your old friends. If you reveal yourself too early, you are seen as a threat by the Holdfast and destroyed instantly. Every time."

"What am I meant to do? It's hurting them."

"The Holdfast won't let them perish here, but they will certainly suffer. This is all part of a negotiation to take over the soul trade from Gan-Eden. They were foolish to come here."

"Why are they here?"

"You are not ready to know the answer to that," Bilben scoffed.

Grunting in frustration, Baertha tried to get closer to the swirling diplomats. They seemed like a school of salmon, with her friends caught in the centre of their gyre.

"Now the Möbius has detected you."

"What!?"

A flat loop of silver floated through the main entrance, spinning as it travelled. It had a half-twist along one curve, the eye-bending structure shifting colours with every rotation.

The guardian changed in size as it scanned the crowd. Sometimes it would narrow down to the width of a manhole cover, whistling as it quickly butchered some poor demon it didn't like the look of, spinning like a maddened circular saw. Then it shot back upward, surveying the crowd for the intruder it had detected. For her.

"Bilben! Where do I go?"

"Don't panic. We usually avoid it. Walk slowly past the throne, counterclockwise."

Checking that her illusion was still in place, Baertha carefully approached the throne, where the manifestation of the Holdfast was currently resembling Charlemagne. Its attention was taken by the maddened buzzing of the Möbius, but it looked down at Baertha, and bid her hold with a raised hand.

*What brings you to me, little one?*

Remembering the guardians at the gate, Baertha thought quickly. "My feet, my lord," she whispered.

The Charlemagne-thing shook with a chittering laughter. *Do another one!*

The Möbius drew closer, and now it was moving in a straight line toward her.

For some reason, she channelled Lucy in her panic. "Uh, why do you like to walk so much?"

*Why?*

"Because you're a roamin' Emperor."

The Charlemagne figure was a caricature of laughter, eyes round, mouth a garbage flap, head bouncing up and down. The whole tower of man and throne wobbled back and forth, and it wheezed and chittered in delight.

"You've been a wonderful audience. Goodbye."

The figure waved her back, bidding her to stay, but by then the Möbius creature was churning murder, close enough that a theremin hum could be heard from the spinning sheet metal. Baertha was off and running, and then the guardian was trying to get at her through the Charlemagne lump, which screeched and held out for a surprisingly long time.

"Shit shit shit!" she said as she ran toward the others, toward her old enemies, desperate for one more moment of life. She changed her disguise on the fly, rapidly painting on the appearance of a fleshy courtier, and then she was in the middle of the mob, blending in perfectly.

Overhead, the Möbius examined the courtiers but could not discern her. It buzzed angrily and took off on a circuit of the structure, hunting the intruder.

"This is incredibly odd," Bilben said, now resembling an ermine that she held in her arms. "I've never seen that happen before."

"I thought you swam up and down a river of time?" she whispered.

"The crowd will pass close to that wall in a minute," Bilben said, ignoring her. "There is another small hatch there. You'll need to get your friends through it."

"What about these arseholes?" she said, grunting at a random elbow to the ribs from a jolly advisor type with drooping mustachios realized in flesh.

"Kill them. Quickly, of course. The Möbius can't fit through the door, so it's a clean getaway."

When Bilben indicated the time was right, Baertha dropped the illusion. She was a captured warrior queen in rags, blasting fire and destruction all around her, dipping into her reserves with every spell. Soon she had driven aside the courtiers, pulling Ray and the others aside.

"Baertha?" an exhausted John Leicester said. His spirit stuff was faded, and he was barely corporeal.

Jesus met her eyes warily. They'd last faced each other on the battlefield at Sad Plain, where she'd been a mad thing, a creature of Lucy's, aiding him in his dangerous ambitions.

"We can talk later," she said. "I need to save you."

The Möbius had noticed Baertha's destructive magic and was whistling toward them at a great rate, crossing the huge structure in seconds.

"Quickly!" Baertha said. They ran across to the hatchway, Baertha holding up poor Ray, who was ashen-faced and barely able to keep up.

Then they drew up short. One arm of Charlemagne erupted from the floor, clasping the door closed as his mutilated head rose in front of Baertha.

*I did not enjoy that joke.*

A forest of arms sprouted around them, some wielding swords. The trio of exhausted magicians fought as best they could, slinging weak spells. Ray had seemingly produced an acetylene burner from somewhere, slicing through any limb that got close. Nearby demons came in to join the party, eagerly waving whips and blades.

Baertha tried to burn their way through to the hatch, but then the theremin hum of the Möbius drew close. She threw up a mystical barrier which sent it crashing away, but the effort cost her greatly. It recovered in moments, ready to come at her again.

"I'm sorry!" she shouted at Jesus, who nodded sagely as he fought his own battle. In the end, she was fighting side by side with her old friends. There were worse ways to go.

The Möbius came in fast. Baertha raised her hands, certain that

**THE BRIDE & THE BIRDMAN · 217**

she'd not be able to stop it this time, but she could not give in, not even at this hopeless moment.

Then the Möbius split in half, two flapping sheets of steel bouncing away to either side of her. Something had simply sliced it in two.

Baertha looked up in shock to see Papa Lucy and Sol calmly walking through the Holdfast, laying waste to all around them. Lucy once more wielded the Cruik, and none could withstand him. The Holdfast came at him with a thousand furious knights, all of which he knocked aside with contempt. Wielding the staff like a knife, he flayed roughly an acre of the Holdfast's skin in moments.

The demons fled out of every exit, and the Holdfast could merely quiver around them, not even daring to send up a representative.

"No. He's not meant to be here yet," Bilben chittered. "This is all wrong. I didn't see this!"

John and Jesus moved up to stand by Baertha's flanks, and Ray looked around in confusion, as if unsure what side he was meant to be standing on.

Lucy laughed, a great booming outburst, and he suddenly flew across the remaining gap, landing in front of Baertha. Sol was forced to jog awkwardly. Something was clearly wrong with his body, an injury of some sort.

An awkward silence, as the fractured Family was finally reunited, and it was even money on whether they would start slaughtering each other. Sol could not stop staring at her, and Baertha couldn't decide whether he was shocked, besotted, furious, or all three.

"Well, colour me tickled fucking pink," Lucy finally said. "It's the whole gang."

"You're alive," Sol said softly to Baertha.

"Clock's fucking ticking on that one, brother," Lucy said darkly.

Bilben then leapt out of Baertha's grip and ran, only for Lucy to point the Cruik, instantly seizing that swirl of time-shifting possibilities and combining it all into one panicked rat, hovering in mid-air.

"Makes sense you're down here causing shit," he said, and then he shook the rat around vigorously. "Go on, might as well show us your true bloody form."

With a sigh, Bilben discarded the rodent disguise, unpacking and expanding into a human perfect in every way. Sexless in their nudity, this creature was glorious and beautiful, skin of charcoal grey, eyes pure, milky white.

"Yes. It is no surprise that I am in the Low Place," Bilbenadium said, their voice a one-person choir, melodic and resonant. "Your group cast me down here, after all."

"Bilben, what is this?" Baertha said. "What are you?"

"That there is Bilbenadium," Papa Lucy explained. "Sworn Sword of the Most High. Scheming piece of shit."

He cast the angel aside, letting them fall to their knees.

"Stay put," he said, holding the Cruik like a shotgun.

"Lucy, I—"

"Shut up. John, put that rifle down or so help me I will stuff your ghost into a fucking peanut. Hesus, keep those hands where I can see them."

His brother protested. "Lucy! We need to talk this out."

"Sol, you are a passenger at this point, and I'm the train driver, the conductor, and the fucking lunch lady. Now, Baertha, we need to talk."

He gently drew her forward with the crook of a finger, her heels sliding across the Holdfast's flesh. Lucy lifted her chin with that same finger and gave a dazzling smile.

"You were holding out on me. You had the last little piece of the Cruik. My Cruik."

"The splinter was in my flesh. I absorbed it when I was in the Shale."

"Hmm. I seem to recall how much you adored this," and here he stroked the staff. "You wanted it all the time."

"Stop," Baertha said.

"Do you still want it? Just take it," he said. "Reach out and put your hand around it."

"Lucy," Sol said, angry now.

"I told you to shut up!"

With a wave of a hand, he swept his own brother across the ground, bouncing and jostling as if falling out of a moving car. Then he gripped

Baertha by the chin, forcing her to look at the curl of the Cruik, that addictive perfection, the promise of pure power.

"Do you want the Cruik?"

She looked away easily and met Lucy's eyes.

"Keep your poisonous stick," she said. "We all know you're compensating for something."

Lucy laughed easily, and that was the moment that Ray came running in, acetylene torch burning hot and hard. He was clearly terrified as he tried to fight the world's greatest magician, determined to free Baertha.

Perplexed, Papa Lucy swept Ray's legs out from under him, knocking the wind out of him with the butt of the staff. As the man tried to get his breath back, Papa Lucy stooped down and picked up the white-hot torch.

"How can a simpleton like you figure out a magic like this?"

He turned the flame toward Ray's face and slid it closer. Baertha could see how much Lucy relished the panic in the savant's eyes.

"I'm sorry you're all fucked in the head, Ray, I really am. But looks like you need to learn this lesson."

Instantly Lucy found attacks from all fronts, his cowed enemies spurred into action. John's ghost gun chattered, Sol called out to Lucy's bones to bend and break, Baertha brought flame and pain, and Hesus assaulted his mind, trying to sever him from accessing his magic.

"Ha! Look at you lot. Going off like a bride's nightie!"

Baertha saw Lucy raise the Cruik, but despite his bravado, he was barely able to hold back their combined assault. She pressed the attack.

"You piece of shit!" she cried. "You lied to us. Used us!"

"I gave you everything you wanted," Lucy said with a groan, deflecting everything they could throw at him.

"You promised me a baby!" she sobbed. "But you gave me a monster!"

Everybody stopped, mostly out of shock.

"Is this true?" Sol finally said.

"Yes," Baertha said, watching Sol's heart break. "We had a baby."

Lucy turned to Sol, who stared pure venom at him.

"C'mon, mate. Do we really have to do this now?"

"You gave her a baby? And you both kept this from me?"

"Sol, it is true that my superior dick got the job done, but the baby didn't cook right. The little tacker lasted about ten seconds before she blew up."

"She? She died?"

"You're welcome, by the way. Your old lady never asked for a baby again after that."

Sol reached forward, an invisible hand gripping out toward Lucy's wrist. Lucy knew it would be easy enough to deflect this magic with the Cruik, only to find that his hands were empty.

Jenny Rider stood nearby, looking at him with anger and hurt. Her hands were already curling into hooks.

"Oh, fuck me," Papa Lucy said, and then Sol broke his wrist, and then the whole gang took a good minute or two to kick his arse.

---

"You've proved your point," Lucy gasped, wincing. "Just be a good sport and fix my hands."

Baertha had watched as Sol broke every bone in his brother's hands. Ostensibly this was to prevent the rogue magician from casting spells, but he'd relished the torture, had taken his time in snapping every joint, and then bound them together with a strip of his shirt.

Not once had Sol looked at Baertha, and she did not blame him.

Jenny waited in the wings, gathering the courage to touch Papa Lucy, to take his magic back into herself.

"I don't think it's a good idea," she said. "I don't trust myself."

Baertha went to offer solace, and the wood-grained woman knocked her hand away.

"Don't touch me. I'm not safe."

"Jenny, I know you don't want to side with these losers," Lucy said, and he offered his most winning smile. "We belong together. We can save the world now."

She reached out her wooden fingertips to his face, almost lovingly. Lucy smiled as she gently traced his lips.

When she pulled her hand away, his lips had fused into one, his

**THE BRIDE & THE BIRDMAN · 221**

mouth no longer able to open. His eyes went wide with panic, and his nostrils flared as he struggled to suck in a panicked lungful of air.

"Breathe from your diaphragm," Baertha offered helpfully.

They'd finally coaxed the Holdfast out of itself, and the reunited Family were holding a type of hostage negotiation. It was now a milquetoast official that they dealt with, a hand-wringing puppet that tried for appeasement against the enemy in its bosom.

An army of demons was ready to avenge this insult against the ruler of the Low Place, but Baertha had ordered the Holdfast to seal off the Endless Pavilion. Now it was time to negotiate their exit strategy.

"You will give us the use of the clouds and the ruins of the Shale mechanism," Sol said. "Order the guardians swimming in the Deep Insult to let the clouds soak up the essence. We will travel to the Glass-Lands above, and then return your clouds to you."

*Of course!* the Holdfast whispered. *There's simply the question of compensation.*

"You're in no position to negotiate," John said. He'd summoned a dozen mortars and had them pointed all about the enormous chamber. Jenny had fallen into the Lady Hook form, and the Holdfast seemed more terrified of the Cruik than anything else.

*We do not disagree in principle. All we are talking now is logistics. Realistic terms.*

The Family had deep problems, a cracked jar held together with spit and string. Baertha could sense how little any of them trusted each other. Jesus and John were their own little clique, furious at her and Sol, with Ray the confused pet dog who still loved them all. Jenny was terrified of most of them.

Even in captivity, Lucy watched them all, gauging, plotting. Unless they killed him, he would always be a threat. He deserved more punishment than a quick death, but with Lucy alive, Sol was bound to eventually forgive him and fall back under his sway.

Baertha knew this too: he was incredibly powerful. When it came to opening a gate that could rescue everyone from the Now's destruction, they may still need him.

"Consider this an act of goodwill between our kingdoms," Jesus said to the Holdfast. "Any insults between us will be considered forgiven."

The enormous organ consulted a sheaf of fleshy paper that was part of itself. *Our demons have worked many hours at their labours, and they will see this as usury,* the creature whispered. *A forced reparation. I may not be able to stop the host from an assault against Gan-Eden.*

"I told you, Hesus, they want our Aether," John warned. "Unacceptable."

As they bickered over the terms, Bilbenadium stooped down, whispering something in Papa Lucy's ear. Lucy's eyes widened, and he frantically tried to speak, his sealed mouth unable to articulate any sound. He jangled his chains, but no one paid him any attention.

Bilbenadium was there one moment, and simply gone the next.

# — 18 —

## BILBENADIUM

Bilbenadium had always played a long game. After the Dawn King scheme unfolded the way they'd foreseen, Bilbenadium egged Mal into casting them down into the Low Place, and there they lay the next parts of their plan.

Not once had they been a prisoner here.

Everything was unfolding as foreseen. This was the optimal path. Bilbenadium was mostly right.

---

Bilbenadium appeared in Mal and Kirstl's Tontine, easily bypassing their defences and sidestepping the angry spirit of Collybrock.

"Awaken and wait for Lady Bertha to make contact with you," the perfect figure intoned. "She will provide you with the exit point for the Terminus. When the prentice drops the latrine bucket, that is your signal to take the attack to Lanyard. You must destroy the Null or you won't move."

The furious Jesusmen attacked Bilbenadium, of course, but by that time the divine being had already left, neatly sealing their exits shut.

At the same time, Bilbenadium entered the tiny tomb of the Grave-digger, who gibbered pathetically in the dark. They'd sealed the foul robber in here many years ago, mostly to secure his secrets. It was necessary to the plan. And necessary to bring him back into play now.

"I have come back for you," they said, and the Gravedigger screamed in fright.

"You will serve me. Repeat this."

"Yes. Yes, I will serve! Please, Bilben, let me out!"

"You've only two more tasks to complete, and then I will release you from my service. Await further instructions."

"I will. I'll do anything!"

"That's always the case," Bilbenadium said. They opened the doorway out of the tomb, allowing the Gravedigger to emerge in Gan-Eden, weeping hysterically.

"First, I'll need you to dig a hole to the Now, to Crosspoint."

Bilbenadium set off a flare, a glorious blast of light from the palm of their right hand. From various directions the Giden began to approach, led by the House of Torana.

"Dig fast," Bilbenadium said.

While they hectored the servant, Bilbenadium slipped into rat form and visited the steel frame Ray had built by Crosspoint. The rat quietly worked its teeth up and down the structure, sending up a spark here and there as it set sigils in hidden places and whispered to the steel.

There were several possibilities in which the gate worked, and Bilbenadium wanted none of these to go as intended.

At the same time, Bilbenadium had finished an epic journey through the stars, arriving at the end of the cosmic staircase that Baertha had fled down in terror. The final portal, the garden gate that the Most High had closed behind him. Bilbenadium had been forbidden from returning here, and so he needed to be swift.

Bilbenadium brought out a memory, a most poisonous moment. Much like Martin Luther in Ur-Saxony, Bilbenadium nailed Baertha's plundered memory to the front of that hidden door.

*"Babe of gold! Lies were told!"*

Bilbenadium let that instance of themselves fall into the nearest sun, a lesser death that was not permanent enough to take. A heartbeat later, the door opened, just the tiniest crack, a furnace's heat erupting.

# — INTERLUDE —

## THE MOST HIGH
## THE BLACKSTAR
## LANYARD

There was a world where every inch of ground was thick in forests of spikes and prickles, and the natives themselves were pulsing spheres of thorn, thousand-limbed and murderously beautiful.

It was the ten thousandth season of the Serene's funeral, and their clan was constructing an ode worthy of their sovereign, one that now incorporated a near escape from death itself. The beasts clattered their thorns together, some working on the knitting of a great tapestry of vines, others engaging in a funerary duello.

Then the golden figure appeared. A human shape. The thorned ones knew of such creatures, dangerous mammalians from a neighbouring Realm.

It flared once, a brilliance of energy, and the forests burned, and the rivers and lakes boiled dry. The funeral dispersed in chaos, the handful of survivors rolling through the ash and waving spines in fear.

"I AM ANGER," the golden intruder said. "I BRING FURY."

This clan had a settlement of sorts, a lattice-castle that they retreated to, and they unleashed a barrage of murderous thorn weapons onto the golden man. The figure in gold disregarded the attack, and then it clapped its hands together, causing the castle to shiver apart from tip to root.

"A CRIMINAL HIDES IN THIS SEVERED GARDEN. YOUR WORLD AND ALL WORLDS WILL END. NO APPEAL WILL BE HEARD."

---

In world after world, the same figure appeared, destroying everything in its path. All manner of life fell to its anger, and those advanced enough to mount a defence found that nothing could give this creature pause.

It then came to the gimballed worlds of the Iron Nest. The Bilby folk attempted every time-shifting stratagem to undo the assault, but none were equal to Bilbenadium, their long absent Queen and master of the Shifting arts.

"Forgive us, Most High," they said. In the end they arrayed themselves at the centre of the Iron Nest, kneeling in prayer and worship.

"NO APPEAL WILL BE HEARD."

The Iron Nest ended, and the Most High continued on its rampage.

---

The Most High stood in Langenfell and pronounced the doom of the Now and all other worlds. It started kicking over mountains and destroyed the grand racetrack and the neat town. Birds and people scurried away like ants, and the Most High stepped on them like a petulant toddler.

"A CRIMINAL HIDES IN THIS SEVERED GARDEN!"

---

The Most High tore up great swathes of Gan-Eden, swatting the blessed dead like flies, and the god burned away both dreams and dreamers. There were still some of the eldest Once-Dead who'd survived the ravages of the corrupt Houses, the invasion of Over-haeven, and even the chaos of the Dawn King. When they looked upon the architect of the universe, returned after an unspeakable age, Aether poured down their cheeks as they wept.

They came to the Most High with arms spread, jubilant as they embraced their utter destruction.

"I BRING FURY."

---

Against all odds, the Blackstar had survived. He'd finally climbed out of Baertha's trap and paced the Glorious Gyre in fury.

Overhaeven was destroyed, a shell that was scattered across the void, but the command centre remained. He was starving, this rock star godling, but he'd lived his whole life hungry, and didn't let this distract his iron focus.

He needed to rebuild the structure. Find an alternative fuel out in the stars. Gather followers from other Realms.

Then, he would seek his revenge.

Even as he worked the instruments of the Throne, the Blackstar felt a presence behind him. He wheeled about, sword instantly in hand, but then his mouth fell open.

"Oh, daddy," he whispered.

"I AM ANGER."

Moments later, the Glorious Gyre was snuffed out, and all of the dark ambition and hubris it had ever carried met the fate it had long deserved.

---

Lanyard had redoubled his efforts to crack open the Terminus. Witches sent volleys of grey flame into every window they could reach, and a crude catapult fired wreckage across the gap in the road.

Mal had escaped his grasp once again. The knowledge that his foster son was in that building ground away at him. All he wanted was to destroy and punish the lad, to turn him into this new form so he too could understand the endless hunger and pain. It was still love, in the most twisted application of the word, just as destructive as the time he'd put a jagged stone through his own master's head.

The Now was dying, and Lanyard was fine with that. His ambitions were a dark reflection now that he worked for the other side, and he was applying every lesson of the Jesusmen to the effort.

Organization. Brute efficiency. Mobility.

With Mal by his side, he would be unstoppable. They could become the biggest threat to any of the worlds, and there were plenty out there, a lot of places he could direct that hunger, that primal rage. It would be the perfect opposite of what a Jesusman was meant to do, and he finally understood that Witches were only following the shadow of their former lives after all.

Chewing over this philosophy, Lanyard was directing the reloading of the catapult when the Most High appeared in the sky, rumbling threats and throwing the ruined shadow-roads around.

"A CRIMINAL HIDES IN THIS SEVERED GARDEN!"

Lanyard accepted the imminent destruction of everything with his usual stoic approach. All that mattered now was getting to Mal, to be properly reunited in their last moments.

"Come out, boy!" he yelled at Terminus.

---

The Most High entered the Low Place and started to tear apart the gloomy landscape, setting flames to the Deep Insult, gouging great mile-deep craters in every surface. The demons thought it a wonderful caper, and a multitude followed the Most High, daring each other to get closer to the destruction.

They died by the thousands, which only spurred the rest onto further mischief. Soon they were touching the god's body, which drove it into a frenzy of apocalyptic fury. The Most High poured so much bright fire into the Low Place that it was like daylight. The god crushed the clouds in its fists, and then it paused, turned like a dog who'd caught a scent.

Running in a streak of golden fire, the Most High crashed through Grand Kthon and then peeled apart the layers of the Endless Pavilion, now reining in this destruction, as delicate as one peeling a hardboiled egg.

Finally, the Most High stood within the Holdfast itself and looked upon a strange scene where the ruler of the Low Place was caught *in flagrante* with its conquerors, a gaggle of human Magicians and Once-Dead spirits from Gan-Eden.

"LO HOLDFAST!" it said, and then turned that burning perfection toward Baertha. "I SEE THAT THE QUEEN OF THE PARASITES HAS BEARDED YOU IN YOUR OWN DEN!"

*My lord!* the official said, abasing itself. *I have kept faith these many long years! Maintained the Deep Insult. I serve only you.*

"SILENCE!"

The Most High withdrew all of that heat and power into itself until it was a weakly glowing star-glass. It paced around the chamber, sniffing at all within it.

"THE CRIMINAL WAS HERE," it said, suddenly appearing in front of the Holdfast's terrified speaker. "ITS SCENT STILL LINGERS!"

*We have many criminals, my lord! We punish them all, as you yourself instructed.*

"A CRIME AGAINST MY PERSON."

*We will assist. Let me summon the police.*

The Most High extracted a film of memory, a fog that the god stretched out between its hands. In that gap could be seen the image of a golden baby, floating in midair, and then it was swatted out of a window, exploding in the sky.

"THEY ATTEMPTED TO REMAKE ME! FOR A MOMENT, I WAS REBORN. SUPPLANTED."

Stowing the memory, the god continued to prowl around the Holdfast, each footstep burning and sizzling into that floor of flesh. The official whimpered and begged forgiveness.

THE BRIDE & THE BIRDMAN · 231

"I HAVE THEM!" the Most High said, and the brightness at the core of the figure began to climb.

"I APPLY MYSELF TO THE HUNT," it said. "BUT THEN I SHALL RETURN TO MY TASK. YOU HAVE SHELTERED THE CRIMINAL. YOUR WORLD AND ALL WORLDS IN THE SEVERED GARDEN WILL END. THERE WILL BE NO APPEAL."

# — 19 —

## BAERTHA

Baertha felt like she was going to be sick. The Most High had been here, looking for the mother of the golden babe. Blood gushed out of every footfall it had left in the Holdfast.

It had been sniffing right in front of her, a faceless gold statue inches from its target. And yet, despite the evidence, the memory lifted out of her head, it hadn't made the connection.

Of course, only one creature had been witness to that memory, over and over, their countless perfected lives stealing the recollection from her when she crossed through the Deep Insult. Now, try as she might, she could not picture her own baby, her Rhiannon. All that was left was the image she'd seen in the Most High's hands. Her baby had been completely severed from her memory.

"Oh Bilben, you little fucker," she whispered, but of course the rat-turned-angel was nowhere to be found.

The Family were speechless, still taking in the gravity of the situation. The long vanished Most High was not only real, but it had also made a personal appearance, pronouncing the end of their branch of creation.

She remembered that moment at the final gate, out in the chill of space, and how the god had dismissed her. Now it had stepped through into their universe, wreaking who knew what kind of damage.

The irony was not lost on Baertha, who'd begged the Most High to intercede, to do *anything*.

"We have to leave," she said. "Holdfast, come out. We require fuel from the Deep Insult as agreed."

*There are no deals,* whispered ten terrified mouths from the floor. *You have cost us everything!*

At that point Jenny pounced, snagging the ten mouths with ten sudden hooks, and she pulled up hard.

*Fine,* it said, offering a sad eleventh mouth. *Take your fuel, take the clouds, but most of all take yourselves far away from here.*

"The demons are regrouping," Jesus said.

"You will give us safe passage," John Leicester rumbled. "Swear to it."

A moment's pause.

*Done. What is the point though?*

"Because we're not finished yet," Sol said, finally looking at Baertha. "Together, we're capable of great things."

*You humans are sickening,* the Holdfast burbled, and then it said no more.

---

"Mmm mmm mmmh!" Lucy mumbled frantically behind his sealed mouth. None paid him any mind, and Jenny hauled him roughly about, her hand a closed loop of wood fastened about his upper arm.

Gifted to the invaders, ten clouds gorged themselves from the Deep Insult. They rose as wine-red sponges, ready to soar up to the Glass-Lands and Gan-Eden beyond that. Another trio of clouds held the scavenged Shale mechanism, a thick needle the length of a bus.

The Holdfast had returned Ray's car to him, although joyriding demons had ruined the upholstery. He slowly drove onto the back of a cloud, imagining boarding ramps, and thus manifesting them under his wheels as needed.

"I'll have to strip the car," he complained to Baertha. "It smells really bad."

The clouds rose slowly for their unwanted passengers. Baertha and Ray sat in the car, with broken Papa Lucy tossed in the backseat and forgotten. On the next cloud stood Jesus, John, Sol, and Jenny, their cabal huddled together, planning. Every now and then, Sol would look over toward them, and Baertha felt the urge to flinch.

With the weight of their centuries of history, it was a miracle the clouds could even get off the ground.

"Why are you here and not on Sol's cloud?" Ray asked.

"I'm here to keep an eye on Lucy," Baertha said.

"Sol was sad for a long time. He thought you were dead."

"I was. Now I'm not."

"Are you still husband and wife?"

"I don't think so. I hurt him a long time ago, Ray, and I don't think it can be fixed. I know you find change really tricky, but sometimes people move apart. Things don't always go back to the way they were."

"But I liked those times," Ray said. Papa Lucy suddenly lurched forward, eyes widened as he frantically murmured something behind his sealed mouth. Baertha pushed him back with a sorcerous gesture.

"Enough," she told Lucy.

They continued in their silent ascent to the glass above, and Baertha held Ray's hand, gently stroking his thumb. She knew the signs that he was heightened and edging toward a panic attack, and she remembered doing this to calm him down.

"Won't the Most High break the Now? And anywhere else we go?"

"Maybe," Baertha said. "But we should never give up, even when everything seems hopeless."

"You said that back in the Before. You gave that speech where all the people booed you. I remember when they tried to arrest you for saying that."

"I remember that too, Ray."

Lucy mumbled, rocking about in the back seat, agitated but silenced. Just the way Baertha liked him.

"Bilben is up to something. Maybe it will work."

They were close now, and the underneath of the glass was a faint peach glow from the glory of Gan-Eden. More than once the clouds accidentally brushed together, lightning discharging. Sol and the others paced around their mount, yelling at the clouds and ordering them to keep a safe distance, which they sullenly obeyed.

They didn't really understand the fuel they'd bargained for. A stray lightning bolt might just detonate them in the sky, and if one cloud erupted, they were likely to all go up.

"How do we get through that?" Baertha wondered. In her first life she'd been at the forefront of planar study, and even she knew little about the connecting tissue between the Underfog and what had been speculated to lie beneath it.

This close, she could see thousands of shadows in straight rows, and knew these for the bases of the obelisks. They threw shadows down through the gloom, and it felt like they were swimming underwater, passing underneath a pier. Then the shadows began to move, forming into a type of reverse spotlight, focusing on them in swarms.

The hairs on the back of her neck rose. She felt the sudden rising of a powerful magic and knew the intent of these guardians was to destroy them absolutely. They could have been demons preparing an invasion, or condemned souls attempting to escape, and the response would've been the same.

Destroy them. Protect the lands of the blessed dead.

Jesus and John held their arms up, and a type of spotlight focused on them, amber light suffusing and forming around them. The shadows retreated, and above them the glass opened, permitting the lords of Gan-Eden to return from their diplomatic mission.

Papa Lucy became frantic and rocked about in the backseat. Baertha was so distracted by the beauty of their egress that her attention slipped for a moment. She didn't notice when he reached for the window handle with his ruined hands, fumbling around and somehow managing to wind the back passenger side window an inch at a time, teeth gritted, somehow holding in a scream as fifty-four bones scraped together.

With an agony of movement, he slowly worked the ruined spiders of his hands through that open gap so that enough loose meat was on the other side of the glass, and then pushed out his forearms to grip the far side of the window in an awkward embrace, before jerking backward with all of his weight.

*SMASH!* The entire window broke inward, showering him with shards of glass. That got Baertha's attention, but she was still a fraction too slow.

He held a sharp jag of glass sandwiched between his palms.

He raised it up high, eyes widened. Ready to strike.

He drove the makeshift dagger down, pushing it through flesh.

His own flesh. With one swift movement, he sliced open the ruin of his lips, crafting a makeshift mouth that was a hideous, jagged hole, dancing up and down between his teeth.

Baertha blasted him to the back of the seat, holding him fast, and he quite happily released the glass dagger. Ray worked his mouth voicelessly, terrified at the violence happening mere feet from him.

"Listen here, you stupid shits," he said moistly, his mouth a bloody obscenity. "I've been trying to tell you something!"

"Tell us what?" Ray asked cautiously.

"We've got to stop! Bilbenadium has set a trap, and we're fucking pawns on the chessboard."

"Likely story."

"Gloating little bastard whispered it in my ear. Said our baby was actually the Most High reborn. That literal rat-fucker said they would use that memory of yours to lure the god out of its bloody bolthole, and then, while it was distracted kicking seven shades of shit out of us, Bilben will shut the door on the Most High."

"Oh," Baertha said.

"And while we're busy playing 'fight the god and save the stupid human race,' Bilbenadium is going to use the Sworn Sword to finally separate the Severed Garden from the rest of creation."

Baertha looked deep into Lucy's eyes. He lied when it served him, but in that instance, she knew he was telling the truth.

"We will be stuck in this tiny corner of creation with a homicidal god while Bilbenadium gets to take over the rest of the universe. Ladies and gents, we've been played by a fucking master."

Baertha leaned over, and she started honking the car horn frantically. After a moment, Ray began to flick the high beams on and off.

Halting just underneath the glass, the Family separated themselves into two parties. Ray and his car were deposited gently in the Glass-Lands, the dense clouds forming a neat row behind him. His job was the most vital.

Get back to Crosspoint. Use the Shale mechanism to distil the liquid in the clouds into fuel. Use this to open the gate at Crosspoint.

Identify the safest world and send everyone through.

In the meantime, the Range was scouring southward, herding terrified survivors and hungry monsters toward Crosspoint. Jesus reckoned on it being a flashpoint of disaster, and that monsters would be drawn to both the gate and a panicked mob.

"How will you know which world to connect to?" Baertha asked gently. "What is the best place for the refugees?"

Ray shrugged. He operated fully in the domain of the instinctive sorcerer, and he would somehow make it work just by believing it would.

"Do you want any of us to come with you?" John said.

Ray shook his head. "I can't fight gods. I can't outthink an angel who can see through time. But I know this stuff."

"We'll send help," John said. "The Giden, the Many-Faced, damn, we'll even take any vampire who'll swear to the cause. You won't be on your own."

"The Jesusmen," Baertha said suddenly.

"I've been unable to reach them in the Greygulf," Jesus said sadly. "Nothing for weeks now. The Order has finally fallen."

"No, it hasn't," Baertha said. "They have a Tontine, and I've spoken with them. Recently."

Several of the Family looked to each other.

"You spoke to Mal and Kirstl?"

"I—I'm ashamed to say this. When I was trapped here, I tried to steal their host body, but they repelled me. Clever pair."

"Find them," Jesus urged. "There is something else going on in the Greygulf."

She nodded, her eyes already turning inward. Everyone else

shuffled onto the one remaining cloud. John and Jesus, ghostly but vital, Sol who seemed older than ever, and Jenny Rider, the newest to their cabal, the Cruik walking in human flesh.

And finally, Papa Lucy, who grinned ghoulishly at them all.

They left the underside of the glass, descending back into the gloom as the gateway sealed over. Once more they descended the Low Place, and then they were headed to the breach in the world veil, where the demons had placed a hatch over the wound Overhaeven had left.

By Baertha's own rough calculations, if they entered the void via the Low Place, they could use the whole structure of the cosmos to slingshot around toward the hidden gate of the Most High. Once they had enough velocity, they would be able to leap along that Impossible Stairway at the fastest possible speed.

Bilbenadium had a head start on them, and they could afford no delay.

"Why exactly did Bilbenadium give you their entire plan?" Sol asked suspiciously.

"Fucked if I know. It's probably a trap of some sort," said Lucy.

"So why are we running to it?"

"Calling their bluff, little brother. They'd expect us clever sorts to try to doublethink around them, so we might as well come out of the heavens with our big ballsacks swinging."

"I hate to say it, but he's right," Baertha said, finally returning from her expedition.

"Did you reach Mal and Kirstl?"

"Yes. They have a big problem in the Greygulf, but many of the Jesusmen survived. Lanyard Everett turned into a Witch though."

"Oh, Lanyard," Sol said mournfully, and Jesus patted him gently on the shoulder. "I told him. I told him not to go back there."

As they landed by the bloody delta, they let their cloud finally discharge its heavy load and then freed it from their service. When they demanded that the guardian demons open the hatch into the void for them, the creatures sent the request up the hierarchy for approval.

Within seconds, a tendril of the Holdfast emerged from the ground, granting permission.

*Stop making a nuisance of yourselves and leave already,* it said.

**THE BRIDE & THE BIRDMAN · 239**

The demons started to throw aside locks and bars of beaten iron, three of their largest turning a big locking wheel. The Family began to cast protective spells upon themselves, though none knew for sure if these would work against the perils of the void. Spells to still restless lungs, to seal the skin against the chill of space. Tethers to fasten themselves together, and finally a blessing on each foot to ensure it would meet the treads of the Impossible Staircase faithfully.

Everything else was willpower and luck. Fail, and they would fall into a star, or simply drift away endlessly.

"Once again, are you going to fix my bloody hands?" Lucy said. "I'm no good to you without my magic."

"You're no good to us with your magic," Sol said, but finally he gripped both hands hard, causing Lucy to cry out sharply. When Sol let go, Lucy's hands were completely repaired.

"What about fixing my handsome kisser? I look like someone gave me a Glasgow smile."

"Lucy, deal with your own problems," Sol said wearily.

Baertha smiled sadly at her husband, at the man who'd finally found his feet against his abusive brother. Their eyes met for a brief moment, but she looked away first.

*Why do I keep hurting him?*

They handed around a few bags of supplies, mostly guns and the bullets for them, and what magical foci were left to them. Even at the end some wise soul thought to pack the tea, cigarettes, food and rotgut booze. Everything else they left scattered down there in the Low Place, where the demons muttered and picked through it.

Then the gate was open, and the Family were hurtling through into the void, their cabal leaping into space to do battle with angels and gods.

# — 20 —

## MAL

Frustrated with her lack of progress in making a useful map, Kirstl pushed aside the paper and charcoal stick and made a mystical gesture in the air. She traced out the shape of the Terminus with her hands and added the road the Witches were using to attack them, then ran it back to the shadow-door. She indicated the fallen ramp, the junk pile, and the parts of shadow-road that jutted out like spokes from the Terminus. She finished by dotting shadow-doors around the outside of an invisible shell. Thus she built a working model of the Greygulf, as accurate as she could make it.

Kirstl explained, "Here is all the intel we can give you. Our initial doorway over there leads to the Riverlands, right in the middle of Graham's Wash. They are currently fielding an army, and you do not want to go through that door."

"And that one?" Tilly said, pointing to the door at the end of the shadow-road Lanyard was squatting on.

"Smoke and darkness. Webs as thick as ropes. I wouldn't want to meet what made those."

Mem spat at Mal's feet. "Keep your opinions to yourself, coward."

"Look, I know you're pissed at Mal. I am too," Kirstl said. "But I'm not him, you bloody nitwits."

"You're his wife," Lyn said. "You share his head. Did you even try to stop him?"

"You two, enough," Tilly barked, and the twins went back to scowling and leaning against the wall.

"Continue."

"You're five hundred feet above the ground. Cut off. Your nearest shadow-door has an army blocking it and entering it will kill you anyway. So do you want to listen to my idea?"

"Your theory."

"We had a lot of time to think things over, Mal and me. We have gone over this situation hundreds of times and come up with the same basic problem. Why are the shadow-roads so brittle?"

"They're old," Mem said. "We're in a war and shit's blowing up."

"Wrong. They're not that old. Crack open a book, you dumbasses."

Tilly held up a hand to hold off the inevitable murderous rush from the twins. She was also frowning, sceptical of the line of thought.

"It's in the history of the Crossing," Kirstl continued. "The first paths through here that the Collegia found, and that the Family used, were just stone, natural structures running between the shadow-doors and the Terminus. The Taursi used them to move around, but they weren't roads."

She sketched out some rough lines on her floating map, running from the Terminus to the doors.

"They were like train tracks. The Terminus moved along them and connected to a shadow-door wherever the driver wanted to go. The windows on the Terminus are the same size as a shadow-door, geniuses."

"If this is true," Tilly said cautiously, "it won't work. The shadow-roads are broken."

"Well, the books I read said that the Jesusmen destroyed a lot of them when the Taursi skirmished with them in here. When they realized what they'd done, they tried to rebuild them, using all ashy clay and baking it. These paved roads are Jesusman-built, and then Witches kept the work going after they turned."

Kirstl wiped away the shadow-roads from her map.

"But the thing is, do you think a skinny little road would be able to hold the weight of this thing?" Tilly asked. "The Terminus is enormous."

"So the shadow-roads are not train tracks as such," she continued. "They're guide rails. Meaning this thing can go off-fucking-road."

Kirstl walked over to the window and looked out over Lanyard's siege. She took in the Null and felt the disconnection effect as it continued to point at them. "I've been trying to connect to Terminus, the way we connect to the roads. That thing out there is blocking me, but for just a split second I can make the connection."

Tilly closed her eyes and concentrated. Then her eyes opened wide.

"I can feel them. Like little points, nodes all over Terminus."

"A dozen in total," Kirstl continued. "And one up on the top, in the tower. That is probably like a captain's chair."

She braved a window and pointed toward the bell-creature that was suppressing their magic, ducked back as a burst of grey flame rattled through the window.

"So if you want to get out of here, you'll need to take out the Null," Kirstl said. "Then we put a person in each post and drive this fucker like crazy."

"Boss, I have never heard such bullshit," Lyn said. "I say we court martial Mal now."

Kirstl smirked. "Right now, you don't have the luxury of court martials. Mal made a stupid decision that he has to live with for the rest of his life. But you lot can still get out. We came *back* for you."

Tilly gave Kirstl a long, considering look. "I want you to show me where all the nodes are," she finally said. "I want everyone from prentice up attempting to connect with them. Then you'll show me where the command centre is."

"You two," and here she waved at the twins, "I want you to come up with an assault plan against Lanyard. We're taking out his magic-killing pet, and then we are leaving."

As the time of the assault got closer, Mal asked to step into the body. Mem and Lyn had their squad ready in minutes, and Mal realized the twins had been itching to take the fight to Lanyard, had already planned it out in their heads.

The Jesusmen had three working motorbikes left, and Lanyard's old buggy. Five bird-riders, their animals half-starved and cranky. Four shooters on foot, weighed down with rifles and grenades.

Outside, the shadow-road swarmed with Witches. They'd redoubled their efforts to build their junk bridge across the gap, holding up makeshift shields to frustrate the Jesusmen snipers.

"Boss, we need to go," Mem said. She was ready to kick her motorbike into life, and next to her was her twin in the sidecar, hunched behind their precious machine gun. They were down to one last ammo box for the enormous weapon, glowing all over with Marks. Mal could see that Lyn was itching to unleash mayhem onto the enemy, and she'd stepped somewhere beyond common sense, all the way into revenge.

Of course, she'd loved Lanyard like a father. They all had. It was the ultimate insult that the old man continued to live on in this dark form, and Mal knew she was determined to step up, to do the duty that he had failed at.

Now they waited. Mal had quietly told Tilly about Bilbenadium's instruction. He was waiting for Lady Bertha to make contact, waiting for the signal: a prentice dropping a latrine bucket.

"Come on!" Lyn snarled. "Why are we waiting?"

"Have some discipline," Tilly said. "We go when I say to."

"This is bullshit! Those *Witches* will be eating us by lunchtime. We need to go now."

"I'm boss. Stow it. It's not time."

Tilly looked to Mal then, a hint of concern washing through her inscrutable mien. He could only shake his head. There was no sign from Lady Bertha yet. Neither had the go signal happened.

*I'm going to do it,* Kirstl said. *I'm sick of waiting for her.*

"No!" Mal said suddenly, and several people looked at him strangely.

*I can still feel her lifeline,* she said after a moment. *I can find Lady Bertha again.*

Mal settled cross-legged on the floor, retreating into the mind-space and down into the dream-space. There he saw Kirstl climbing up into Collybrock's saddle.

"You can't stop me."

"I know," he said, and with a sudden movement he swung up into the saddle behind her.

They opened the doors out into the Aum, and the trio entered the darkness. After a graceless moment where Collybrock trod at the air, they taught her how to move by just thinking about it.

*There,* Kirstl thought, and they spotted the ghost of that silver thread, an almost-erased pathway that led to Lady Bertha. Plucking at the frail connection, they soared through the void, wielding a ghostly lance, imagined guns at the ready.

*Collybrock, stop!*

The bird drew up with a strangled cry.

All about them were dim insectoid shapes, circling them in the gloom. Sirens, already starting up their terrifying screeching. The trio shivered. If they got too close, they would be paralysed by the sound, easy prey for these hunters of souls.

Dissolving his mind lance, Mal swapped it out for an assault rifle as he tapped Collybrock on the neck to command a hard right. They needed to break through this circle, and fast.

Collybrock sped forward, truly unhindered and magnificent, and cut a perfect ninety-degree angle. Just as the screeching of the Sirens' limbs began to make them dizzy, Mal and Kirstl peppered the nearest mantis with bullets. The dying creature hung still in the void, feebly clutching toward them with its curved claws, dirty brown innards spilling out around it.

Then Mal and Kirstl were through, with the rest of the Sirens in hot pursuit. The Sirens moved as ably as Collybrock, wings unfurled and chittering in this place where they weren't needed, and this seemed to help them navigate, ably dodging the gunfire.

Mal imagined bombs, a machine gun nest on Collybrock's rump, everything. He was only able to drop a few of the predators, lucky hits more than anything.

Natives to this space, the mantises inched closer. Their screeching was getting louder, and soon Mal couldn't concentrate on his chattering machine gun. A moment later he blinked slowly, and the weapon simply faded away in his hands.

"Kirstl," Mal said sleepily. "Help."

She tossed out Word and Mark into the void, blinding some of the Sirens, and even struck off limbs and heads with a summoned blade, but soon her spells began to fail as the Sirens penetrated her own thoughts.

Collybrock began to flag, weaving drunkenly as she ran.

"Ungh," she said. "Tired. Sleep."

"No," Mal whispered, and then they were adrift in the Aum, hungry predators closing in to feast on their defenceless souls.

Mal could only watch hopelessly as a Siren closed its sharp foldback claws around his upper chest, bulbous eyes looking at him intensely. It paused, mandibles twitching and then slowly opening, seeming to relish this moment.

"Ungh," he said, imagining a sharp knife in his fist, but he could barely point it at his attacker, and it fell, shimmering, into the void to dissolve.

The Siren leaned in to eat his face off, and that was the moment its own head exploded, coating Mal in gore. It slowly fell away from him, claws relaxing and opening, and then he saw them.

Hundreds of angelic warrior women, floating in through the gloom, palms held out and glowing. They sent bright lights flashing in all directions, striking down the mantises wherever they lurked in the darkness, and Mal shuddered when he realized how many of the hunters had been stalking them.

Other creatures had been nearby too, and the warriors chased them away. Mal saw the disappearing coils of an enormous space serpent, now fleeing to safer hunting grounds. Purple, disembodied hands the size of buildings, moving about like squids, watched intently but kept their distance.

The screeching, sawing sound came to an end, and Mal was able to control himself again. The warriors came together as they approached Mal and Kirstl, and then they merged into one shape. Once more Lady Bertha stood before them, a figure of poise and now contempt.

*What were you thinking? It is not safe out here for you.*

*We were actually looking for you,* Kirstl managed. *Got sick of waiting for you to straighten your hair and put your makeup on.*

*Stop being facetious,* Lady Bertha said. *You got a message from Bilbenadium?*

*Yep. Said you had help for us. I do not trust that little rat bastard.*

*I'm learning that's wise,* the ancient magician said. *Come, let's get you back into your host body. You invite more trouble the longer you linger here.*

They returned to the structure of their Tontine, the mind-shape floating where they left it. Lady Bertha hesitated outside as the trio let themselves in.

*I was wrong to try to take this from you,* she said. *May I enter? I won't stay long.*

Kirstl gestured for her to enter. An awkward moment passed as they shared the space together.

"I must be brief," Bertha said. "All of existence is about to be snuffed out by the Most High. I go with the rest of the Family to confront Bilbenadium, to somehow divert this destruction. We hope to prevail, but we can only spare the Junkman to help you. He has the fuel he needs to open his gate at Crosspoint. Even if we win in our larger fight, you'll still need to escape from the Now. Jesus says that there will be a lot of monsters drawn to the gate. Every one of your guns will be needed."

Mal felt heady at the mention of these powerful figures. He'd always felt at the orbit of these legends, and now they were entangled in each other's doings.

"Here." Lady Bertha instantly brought up a complete schematic of the Greygulf, with Terminus, all of the shadow-doors and shad-ow-roads, and the topography of the ground below it all, mapped out to the inch. She indicated one door with an orange highlight.

"We used this point of reference when we first travelled through here to the Now. It will take you straight to the Crossing, right outside

**THE BRIDE & THE BIRDMAN · 247**

Crosspoint. Ray's gate. Er, the Junkman's. Now, here is the greatest piece of knowledge I have for you."

She drew herself forward, preparing to deliver this to Mal and Kirstl. "The Terminus itself is far from fixed. It can actually move."

"We already know that," Kirstl said.

"Oh."

"It was pretty obvious, actually. We're in the Terminus right now, and we found all the nodes."

"Stations," Lady Bertha said, a little sniffily. "When I completed my doctorate in planar studies, we called a connection point a station."

"Heh. That's the difference between a Jesusman and a magician. We don't waste years on the theory. We just figure stuff out and get on with it."

"Kirstl," Mal warned. "Lady Bertha, we appreciate your help. We will get through to the Now and help defend the gate."

"Help will come," Lady Bertha promised. "The Giden. The Many-Faced. Whatever we can scrape together for you. But we'll need the Hesusmen most of all."

That older honorific really cemented the fact they were dealing with an incredibly ancient figure, who'd seen the old world die and been part of the Family at its very beginnings.

"Now go. Someone's about to drop a bucket of shit on you."

Mal scrambled out of the dream-space and opened his eyes to see a prentice with a latrine bucket, headed for a window to tip it out.

The prentice's boot laces were undone, and in all the excitement the boy tripped, staggering and flailing, and finally dropping the bucket and all of its steaming contents across the floor. Mal narrowly avoided the mess and looked to Tilly.

Her eyes widened. A moment later, the leader of the Jesusmen threw Lanyard's old shotgun over to Mal, and he caught it out of the air.

"Go, go, go!" Tilly shouted, and she was answered by the rev of the motorbikes, the screeching of the excited birds, the cries of the gunmen as they poured out of the Terminus.

Mal joined the frantic charge, and in that moment he felt the dark stain lift from his soul. He'd failed, and badly, but Tilly believed in him again, enough to give him back his inheritance.

Their mission was a simple one: strike hard and fast, take out the Null, and get back to the Terminus. Deadly in its simplicity, but Mal knew that he had one extra task. Face Lanyard, and deal with him once and for all.

They came out howling, as if a cavalry emerging from the sally port to catch their besiegers by surprise, and truly they'd come upon them at the best possible moment.

A tangle of Witches were trying to connect the ramp down to the ground, which at that moment was collapsing. Three other Witches were brawling with each other on the causeway, a doughy mess where it was impossible to see where one ended and the next began.

Lanyard was directing fire up at the windows above, trying to protect his bridge builders, and was genuinely caught by surprise as the sortie party charged forth.

The Jesusmen were well-practiced and had talked over this plan for days now. First came the infantry, who pulled out a contraption of stripped-out doors and wall frames from inside the Terminus, laying it across the barricades until it completed the gap to the Witches' bridge. Next the shooters lay down a ferocious cover fire, interspersed with grenades, swear words, and ill looks.

A whistle went up, and the bikers took off across the makeshift drawbridge, their passengers emptying precious bullets into the Witches and other beasts at close range. The bikers punched through their front lines, wheeling about as soon as they were through, preparing to charge back.

The Null issued a dull roar from its empty clapperhead, sending Jesusmen reeling, noses bloody. The attackers started to spray it with bullets and lob grenades at it, at which point it sprouted extra legs from its abdomen, scurrying under the lip of the road like a spider.

"Get the bloody thing!" Tilly said, and then she swore. On the other side of the Witches' front line, Lyn had opened up with the machine gun, spraying the enemy from behind, but now her bullets were starting to hit the Jesusmen. Even as the gun chewed apart a

Witch, it riddled a bird and his rider with deadly rounds, and the rest were forced to duck for cover.

"Cease fire, you idiot!" she waved from behind a pile of the Witches' junk.

Mal advanced across the drawbridge with the rest of the infantry, enormous shotgun at the ready. He was no help over any distance, but if he could get close enough to a foe, his weapon would be deadly.

The Witches had recovered from their surprise and were retaliating with flailing dough limbs and grey firebolts. The monstrous labourers that the Witches had press-ganged were not the type of predators to leap headfirst into a fight, and now that they were in the thick of it, they scurried or hid.

*Scritch scritch scritch!*

Lanyard's Sirens were hungry for the nearest Tontine, and Mal felt woozy. The plan was to pull back when they appeared and for both snipers above and gunners below to concentrate fire on the Tontine-killers. Kirstl pulled Mal backward, but before she could take over the body, Collybrock seized control. She was all awkward arms and legs, clutching the shotgun like a toddler with an enormous toy, and she ran toward the enemy in those great mile-eating lopes.

"Damned bird!" Mal gasped, and then the Sirens drove her back into the mind-space, stunned and reeling.

"My turn. We need you able to fight," Kirstl said, and then she took one step toward the second Siren, crumpling almost instantly.

The mantis beasts sawed away at Mal, closing in for their feast, but Mal simply opened his eyes, quickly firing left and right with his shotgun. Two shells, close range, and the Sirens fell back in bloody ruins, one body sliding off the shadow-road altogether.

Cracking open the breech of the gun, Mal ejected the smoking shells. Before he could reload, a white shape fell on him with a fury. Fists hammered him about the head, and then another set of hands had him by the throat, all from the same enemy. A centipede of Lanyard rose up, fully three hardened torsos formed into one sickening length. A dozen limbs supported the mass, and angry faces considered him from three different angles.

"I have you, boy," three mouths said. Mal reached for his pocket with a quivering hand, and then another limb snatched his wrist, shaking it about until shotgun shells rained on the road.

"You had your chance to do that," Lanyard said. "I've chosen a different path now."

The Lanyard creature dragged Mal through the melee on the bridge, mindless of the combat all around them. With uneven rippling motions, the Witch made for the shadow-door at the other end, and the iris of the door opened slightly, smoke pouring forth.

"I'll dangle you in there," one of the Lanyard heads whispered in Mal's ear. "It'll hurt more than anything you've ever known. You'll beg me for death, like I begged you—and I won't listen to you either."

The battle was going badly for the Jesusmen. The Null emerged from under the bridge, scuttling back and forth to sweep its clapper head at both the Terminus and the failed sortie, and any magics they tried died on the tongue.

Bikes lay broken and burning. Birds struggled to disembowel creatures without bowels, and these Witches simply accepted the clawing, dragging the birds into themselves, swallowing them whole.

A crackle of defiant gunshots came from closer to the Terminus as those on foot retreated to the drawbridge. The assault was an absolute failure. Lyn was on foot, bloody and confused, still trying to drag the enormous machine gun. Mem was nowhere to be seen.

"Mal!" Tilly cried out. She was slowly being enveloped by a Witch who'd taken on the form of a grandfather snake. It had wrapped around her in thick coils, whipping her back and forth across the shadow-road. One of her arms was trapped in the loops of the beast, while in her free hand she held a knife. She struggled to find the heart of the beast, stabbing over and over.

Tilly met Mal's eyes, and he saw the moment that she gave up her own fight to survive as she found a better option.

"You fix this shit," she called out to him. "You're in charge of everyone now."

She threw the knife at Mal, as hard as she could, and it buried to the hilt in the flesh next to his face. Lanyard hissed as the Jesusmarked steel bubbled at his skin.

THE BRIDE & THE BIRDMAN • 251

"You're a disappointment, girl," he called out to her. "Your Marks barely hurt. I taught you better than this."

"You taught me enough," Tilly said, and then she bucked backward suddenly, her weight throwing her own captor off the side of the shadow-road. The snake unravelled like a rope on a boat. Mal caught the glimpse of one coil turning into a hand, scrabbling madly at the stone, and then the Witch plummeted to the distant ground.

"Tilly!" Lanyard snarled, almost shocked, and then seemed to compose himself. He peered over the edge of the shadow-road at the broken bodies below, hauling Mal along in his coils.

"You're still in there," Mal managed, the coils squeezing around him, tighter and tighter, each breath painful and hard-won. "I know it."

"Shut up, boy! You don't know anything!"

Lanyard started to move away from the sporadic fighting, dragging Mal away from Terminus.

"World's gonna end soon, boy," Lanyard said. "You heard what that golden bloke said. There's no good ending to this, so now we get to end things my way."

He writhed and wriggled along the shadow-road, closing in on the smoky gate, and Mal suddenly snatched at Tilly's knife with his free hand. Before Lanyard could stop him, he carved away with the blade, tracing out a Mark on his master's skin.

"Useless," Lanyard spat. "That's not a proper Mark! That's—oh."

Lanyard froze in place, and then he shivered and wailed, quickly releasing Mal and retreating from him, forming up multiple weapons to fire grey flame, but freezing in place at a gesture.

"I pay attention," Mal said, shaking lightly. "Saw just how you Marked your own pets."

"Fine," Lanyard spat. "We'll go back to the original plan then."

The sprawling Lanyard beast reformed into one Lanyard shape, a man who knelt at Mal's feet, bare-breasted and awaiting the blast of the holy shotgun to end his own unholy state.

"No," Mal said.

"But you have to kill me," Lanyard said, confused now.

"I don't think I do," Mal said slowly. "Not now that I've Marked you. You're mine now."

Impressing his will upon the Mark, he ordered Lanyard back. He kept eye contact with what was left of his father as he reloaded the shotgun.

"I'll come back for you one day, boss," he said to Lanyard. "We'll have a proper talk then."

"You strange boy," the Witch said, and Mal saw it then. Just a flicker, but it was there in that doughy face.

Pride.

"Your job's not done yet. Go," Mal ordered his master, driving back the pale white figure with a gesture. Lanyard was a sole candle in that advancing sea of waxy murder, watching his prentice. Silent, stoic. Considering.

"Mal's still over there!" someone shouted.

"Fuck him," another replied.

The Jesusmen were setting hands to the drawbridge, thoroughly defeated. They'd been routed, and they were going back into their last shelter to sulk and starve.

*You fix this shit,* Tilly had said.

Mal looked around desperately for the Null and heard the skitter of the creature on the road underneath him. Eyeing off the advancing tide of gibbering murder, Mal made an educated guess, and then pointed his shotgun straight down.

BAM. The overpowered god-cannon punched a hole through the fragile road, and there was the Null, its strange skull reverberating in what passed for a pained cry. It scurried over the lip of the road, bell-head ready to swallow Mal down to whatever passed for a stomach in that beast.

In that time, Mal had already fed in a fresh shell, and the gun glowed with the Marks engraved deep into the stock by long-dead hands. He jammed the gun into that reaching mouth and pulled both triggers.

The Null fell apart, the bell shivering into a dozen shards, and the rest was just meat riddled with shot. *Mission accomplished,* Kirstl thought. *Fuck that thing.*

Mal smiled, but his sense of satisfaction was short-lived. Turning once again to the gap in the road, he saw that his people were still pulling back the drawbridge, not waiting for him.

Snarling, Mal turned inward.

"Collybrock, I need you girl."

The bird capered forward, and once more she changed the body into a running machine, easily clearing the gap. She turned in fury against those who'd dare to harm her master, fists and boots punishing the Jesusmen on that side. When she found she no longer had a beak to peck with, a headbutt did the job. She was both bird and man in that moment, and when it came to beating the shit out of people, it turned out those two things lined up just fine.

Mal resumed control, looking on with a secret satisfaction at the injuries his body had handed out to those who'd tried to leave him behind. Even Lyn looked up at him with fear, wiping away a bloody nose.

"Stop being a bunch of sooks," he said, startled at how much of Lanyard came out of his mouth. "Get inside, *now*. We've got places to go."

The Jesusmen looked at each other for a long moment.

"I said do it!" he yelled. Responsibility fell across his shoulders, and in that moment, he understood the weight Lanyard and Tilly had carried from day to day. He no longer had the luxury of running from his problems—and now his problems were three dozen surly warriors who needed a good feed as much as they needed a solid kick in the arse.

"Do we have a problem?" he said as he fed fresh shells into Lanyard's gun. Correction, *his* gun, earned by blood and valour. And now the Jesusmen were his, down to the last pair of hands, the last bullet.

"No, boss," several of them mumbled. Bolts of grey fire from the Witches crashed near them, and he sent the laggard Jesusmen on toward Terminus with rough words and even a nudge or two from his boot.

"Boss," Lyn said, and Mal stopped short.

"What?" he snapped.

"You're bleeding," she said. He looked down to see an enormous shard of the Null sticking out of his ribs, lodged in there from the explosion.

"I don't have time to fucking bleed. Get inside."

"Yes, boss."

# — 21 —

## BILBENADIUM

When the Gravedigger finally carved a hole through the dimensions and out into the Now, Bilbenadium was waiting there for him. The obscenely fat spirit climbed out of his tunnel, coated with runnels of grey-blue mud from the Aether he sweated profusely.

"Their warriors are right behind me!" he gasped as the fallen angel drew him forward.

In the distance, a camp of desperate refugees cried out, pointing at the supernatural creatures. A motorbike kicked into gear, heading to the city walls.

"Good. The Giden will be needed here in the coming hours," they said. "Another called the Junkman will drive through there soon. Now come. You've one task left, and then I will release you."

"Thank you," the Gravedigger gibbered. Bilbenadium gripped him by the upper arm, and then they both were soaring up into the heavens, a brief flash of the purest white as they punched up through the sky and through the world veil.

Bilbenadium knew every step of the Impossible Stair and

understood the shift and flex of the path, the way the tilting galaxies adjusted where their feet would need to land.

"It's beautiful," the Gravedigger sputtered.

"Better than your hole in the ground," Bilbenadium agreed.

To the untrained, it could take weeks to arrive at the end of the stair, if they arrived at all, but Bilbenadium guided them through in mere hours. They then arrived at the final doorway, the entry point to the rest of the universe. Bilbenadium could smell the musk of the Most High here, the sense of entitlement, of unending bitterness.

Here was where it had drawn a line, declaring everything from this point to be the Severed Garden and anathema to the rest of its great creation.

"You are to dig through that," Bilbenadium instructed the Gravedigger.

"A big task," the spirit said, assessing the cosmic weight of the portal. A test with his shovel was not promising. "Even I will need a long time to get through."

"You say that every time," Bilbenadium said with a sigh. "And then you get through anyway."

"What happens then?"

"I don't know. I can't see anything past that."

Bilbenadium drew the Sworn Sword, a blade that ran through the centre of their spine. It was incredibly sharp, the edge honed enough to sever all things.

"This will only cut the once," Bilbenadium said. "But it will cut true."

"You don't need me then," the Gravedigger said, grunting with the effort of prying open the Most High's door.

"I won't waste it on what your sweat can also achieve. No, the Sworn Sword has a much higher purpose."

"To cut what?"

But Bilbenadium would not answer, and simply watched the Gravedigger scratch and pick at the universe's toughest door.

At the same time, instances of Bilbenadium scurried around in the footsteps of the Most High, finding holdouts of survivors from the god's furious destruction. Some were gentle creatures, wise races with advanced technologies and the grace to share them, but Bilbenadium ignored these.

Instead, they came for the predators, the world-eaters, the monsters that often crept through the world veil in search of food. Even these monstrosities were scared, but Bilbenadium lured them forth, offered themself as bait, or simply drove them out.

"Go here," Bilbenadium said. "There is food, and a safe place awaits you if you fight for it. Look for the gate. Take it!"

---

A long time before this, Bilbenadium walked invisibly through the dusty world of the Now. The angel had been spying on the powerful family of magicians ever since they'd destroyed their own world and escaped to this one.

Interesting. They showed great promise for the plan. It took some effort to view the timestream that far forward, but Bilbenadium could see the role of these magicians in the greater scheme. Pushing forward as far as they could manage, the angel tried to view its final moments.

This infamous Family was all there, and of course it made sense that Bilbenadium finessed events to make this so. They became a pet project of the fallen angel for decades, and Bilbenadium seized upon the fertility issues of Sol Goodface and Lady Bertha to drive in the first wedge.

*Of course you can use the Cruik to fix this! There's nothing you can't do!* the angel whispered to Papa Lucy, and the magician's eyes glittered with pride, hand gripping that foul staff tightly.

*Accept Lucy's help,* they told Lady Bertha. *He'll give you a baby. Sol is only resistant to the idea because of his own pride.*

*Your brother is not to be trusted,* the angel told Sol. *He has dangerous ambitions.*

And so on it went, Bilbenadium whispering in the ears of each magician, sowing the seeds of paranoia and fracture, and all along they only needed to repeat or echo the thoughts that they were already having. The angel was the true architect of Sad Plain. They were both pleased and saddened when Lucy finally stole the Boneman's bride, saw the Cruik quicken her womb and impregnate her.

Bilbenadium watched from Bertha's pillow during that dreadful birth, overjoyed as the Most High was reborn, a golden babe that could only live in flesh for a handful of moments. Of course, their own memory would not serve the plan, as the Most High would detect that Bilbenadium was the observer, and possibly laying a trap.

No, this necessitated the painful extraction of the memory from Baertha, centuries from now, and Bilbenadium saw that future moment with clarity, even as Bertha's horrified screams rattled the angel's spine.

*Goodbye, Rhiannon,* they thought, watching as the baby died in the sky. *You have served me most well indeed.*

# — 22 —

## RAY

He'd planned to go the long way, through the Edgemist and back into the lands of life, but fate had given him a shortcut. The criminal known as the Gravedigger had resurfaced, burrowing through to the outskirts of Crosspoint before vanishing with an angelic figure. *Bilbenadium*, Ray thought unhappily, and he eyed the tunnel with suspicion. After all, it had been planted there just for him, with all the convenience of a neatly delivered trap.

The Giden hailed Ray as he passed, the motley warriors from all of history pouring in through the tunnel mouth by the dozen.

"We have word from Lord Jesus and Lord John," a heavily armoured cataphract called down from horseback. "We're to go through with you. Guard your project."

The Many-Faced were arriving too, entire clans of the stones crashing and rolling forward. They flashed excited words such as *Battle!* and *Adventure!* as they joined the expedition.

Others came as well, though they kept their distance until the amnesty proclamation was read. Vampires joined this bizarre army, granted forgiveness for their sins in exchange for this one service.

Protect Ray Leicester, the Junkman. Guard the humans awaiting the construction of the gate. Destroy any monsters creeping through the weakened world veil. Hope like hell that the Family could stop the Most High from wrecking even this slim hope.

Into the tunnel Ray went, his muscle car coughing and misfiring. The Aurum supply in his car was running low now, the golden light spilling out only in fits and starts. Once that was gone, he'd be back to gasoline, or whatever he could fashion from the clouds behind him.

Once again, Ray pushed through that queasy moment between worlds, this time switching off the eight-track and cycling through the tuning on the radio until he found a countdown, his own voice playing out of the speakers.

Then he was racing through that narrow tunnel of earth and stone, complete with crude supports and flickering oil lamps that the Gravedigger had left to fight back the terror of those crushing tons above.

Behind him, a wagon train of wine-red clouds condensed themselves and followed him up to the surface, and then his tires bit into the honest dust of the Now.

His gate remained where he'd left it, protected by a handful of Boneguard soldiers. Two full tribes of the Taursi had come to offer their spears in defence of the gate, but the humans were forcing them to camp a full hundred yards downwind, suspicious of the sharp glass that the giants threw around liberally.

A refugee camp lay as close to the site as the soldiers would allow, and there were hundreds here, patiently awaiting whatever genius plan the Family was putting together. Still, dozens of refugee groups had abandoned the safety of the camp, fleeing in all directions at the sight of the small army of ghosts and strange beasts erupting from the hole in the ground.

Then came the red clouds, a sinister bunch of balloons trailing from behind Ray's car, and most of the camp fled, hoping for safety behind the walls of Crosspoint, or chancing the badlands, or facing the advancing range—anything but *that*.

The ghosts, vampires, and rock creatures followed Ray faithfully to the gate. To their credit, the Boneguard held firm, though the young man who greeted Ray was visibly shaken.

"They're here to help," Ray mumbled, already frowning over the

**THE BRIDE & THE BIRDMAN · 261**

mess of cabling he'd left here. It was a tricky problem he needed to solve, and he simply got back onto his task, mindless of the menagerie of strangeness around him.

"Junkman. Sir."

"What," he said, madly tightening a bolt with a socket wrench.

"Your ghosts are melting."

"Oh. Oh!"

The creatures of Gan-Eden were suffering under the direct sunlight, their forms wavering and wicking away by the minute. Ray moved into a panicked frenzy, ordering tents and shelters to be erected for his strange army.

Above, the clouds suffered similarly. They began to shed the red muck, the fluid from the Deep Insult pattering across the dust. The Boneguard were truly miserable in their small camp, fighting over the meagre shelter they had left to themselves.

Ray had to act quickly, and he fell into the problem with his usual calm. A puzzle to solve, and nothing more. He brought the last clouds over, the ones bearing the Shale mechanism. They'd only been able to bring the tip of it through, and it resembled a hypodermic needle.

This he set up as the entry point to a type of still, welding it to a mixture of copper twists and turns, but then it became a much stranger contraption, one that even then he was bringing into reality with his instinctive sorcery. This mechanism had slots to hang the Taursi hearts into, and a final pan at the end to catch any fuel they had left over.

"Quickly. I will need to bleed it out of you," he told the clouds, and one by one they came forward for a lancing. The spearpoint of dead Overhaeven pained them grievously, and they flashed lightning and shook as the Deep Insult drained out of them.

"OUR AGREEMENT WITH YOUR KIND IS NOT WORTH THIS PAIN!" the cloud rumbled.

The Shale mechanism had a deep throat, and Ray eyed his make-shift device with worry. He'd drained four clouds now, and none of the foul fluid had even dribbled into the still yet. The smell was staggering, and despite all his care during the lancings, a few spatters had landed on his hands. This stuff they'd brought back from the

Low Place made him feel anger, resentment, and the urge to lash out. Wicked souls, refined and now bottled up for his own use.

When he drove the lance into a cloud and killed it outright, the remaining handful of clouds scattered in fear, even as they dribbled their wicked payload across the plains and all over Crosspoint itself. In those final days there would be reports of dark and horrific deeds out in the badlands, these rain-drenched refugees exceeding evils beyond anything the Crooked Folk and their greypots could hope to achieve.

If there had been enough time left for the crops around Crosspoint to grow, Ray could only imagine what would sprout out of the ground now.

Under that rain, people had fallen into chaos. They fought viciously over nothing, and a spatter of gunshots rang out from the nearby town. It took a long moment for Ray to understand why he hadn't been overly affected by the powerful emotions in the rain: he had summoned up a bright yellow plastic mac, which faded into wisps of nothing as he realized the ridiculousness of the outfit.

"Watch out for the people. They've all turned angry," he said to the Boneguard, only to see them advancing upon him with rifles levelled and fury in their eyes. Bayonets fixed, they were preparing to spit him on those sharp points.

If he were his brother, he would've wiped them out with a Word, but all Ray had were his mystic inventions, and in his panic all he could summon was an oversized grease gun. He squirted it about in an attempt to delay the inevitable as he pleaded for mercy.

"NO! NOT HURT JUNKMAN! STOP!"

The House of Torana hit the mad riflemen like a hammer, scattering them like bowling pins. Then, the Giden surged out of their tents. Pale swords rose and fell, guns that chattered with a faint mystical echo popped, and then the survivors were pinned down and hogtied by soldiers from every era in history.

Understanding returned to their eyes after some moments, but the red tinge of rage never quite faded. The Deep Insult was in them now, and while Sol had only picked decent sorts to form his Boneguard,

**THE BRIDE & THE BIRDMAN · 263**

now they seemed base, men and woman of sneering sarcasm, cynics as broken as any town guard leaning on a pike for coin.

Shivering, Ray wiped the remaining red mess from his hands as best he could. There was nothing else to siphon, and he watched sadly as the raw fuel rained everywhere but where he wanted it to go. He fussed over the device, lifting up the sharp needle, and he could see the fluid behind the clear membrane, an impossible amount trapped in a small place. None of it was leaking through into the rest of the device.

"Why didn't it work?" he said in a small voice. His anxiety rose, and he looked at the teaming hordes brawling in the mud, the walled city that sheltered thousands of lives.

Everyone was relying on him, and when it mattered the most, he had simply failed.

"No no no no," he said, and then he was hitting himself in the head, and every failure, every misunderstanding, every low point of his confused life rose up to waylay him at once. It might have been better had the soldiers been allowed to murder him, and in that dark moment Ray truly believed it was all that he deserved.

Then he felt a bump in his leg, and another. Ray turned to see the House of Torana behind him, tongue lolling out of that grotesque mouth, and it nudged him again like a worried dog.

"NO NO NO," it joined in sympathetically. Ray let out a long, shuddering breath, and then another, and then he lowered his fist, unfolding his fingers. He knelt next to the car, scritching the flesh on its hood affectionately.

"Thank you," he told the car, his old nemesis looking up at him with something approaching love.

"DRIP," the car said.

"Excuse me?"

"DRIP DRIP DRIP."

Then Ray heard it too. The dripping of liquid as the Shale mechanism slowly began to empty out into the rest of Ray's device. It had been resistant, this weapon of the parasite gods, but it had finally connected to his piecemeal magical construct.

The first of the Taursi hearts turned into a red coal, the beautiful glass transforming into a lump of something evil and potent. Ray's anxiety faded away, replaced with the confidence he only felt when wrestling with tools and machinery.

He'd have the fuel to do the job soon. The next thing he needed to do was build the door.

---

He'd been left with only a fragment of the Shale mechanism, and it was transforming the spirit stuff slowly and sporadically. Ray found he could not watch the slow transformation of each chunk of amber, relishing his mother's old homily: *a watched pot never boils.*

He fussed over the gate instead, checking over the welds and measuring the right angles obsessively. When he found a patch of rust on a girder, he attacked it with steel wool and turpentine, bringing it back to a raw finish.

All of this was putting off the biggest problem: how would he open the gate? And how would he connect it to a suitable new world for the survivors to escape to?

Now that the Boneguard were less murderous, he sent them to bring whole wagons of material from his workshop. He tried to build control boxes with dials and switches, but without knowing what to measure or what he was even controlling, it felt abstract and frustrating at best. He tried attaching controls with wires to the frame itself, but he couldn't conceive of a connection, couldn't feel a way through to somewhere *else*.

"JUNKMAN MAKING TOYS," the House of Torana huffed at his elbow. "MAKE ME A TOY!"

"Here you go. Fetch!" Ray said, hurling one failed device across the dirt. The car roared and pounced on the machine, crushing it to bits.

"MORE!" the car said. Ray tossed another gizmo for the car, and with spinning tires the House of Torana got underneath it, batting the metal box away from its hood.

Ray smiled. His life had been strange in many ways, and playing fetch with a living car was one of the silliest things he'd ever done. He resolved then and there that he would do his best to find everyone the perfect world, a safe place where there was enough food for everyone, the paradise they deserved after suffering through the Now.

Ray's experimental control box bounced through the centre of the gate, and the car followed, pouncing on it like a fox. Then, for a split second, a glowing field washed down across the gate, glowing red and hateful, and a moment later this parted slightly to reveal somewhere else.

A verdant world, abundant and fertile. A lake wild with reeds and waterfowl reflected sunlight, and grasses waved in a gentle wind, small animals feasting on fodder that was lush and rich.

"Wait!" Ray said, and then the House of Torana crushed the device under its tires.

The gateway began to close.

"Get out of there!" he yelled at the car. "It's gonna cut you in half!"

The House of Torana was still jumping around jubilantly, crushing glass and steel and wires, but then it realized its predicament.

"Reverse!" Ray said, but in the car's panic it leapt forward instead. Wheels spinning, it whipped around in the loamy soil, but then it drew up short at the last minute.

The gap through to the Now was too narrow, and closing.

"NO!" the car yelled. "STUCK! HELP!"

"Pass me the box!"

The House of Torana nudged the broken control box through with its bumper, and Ray snatched it away as the gap closed to mere inches.

"I'll open this again. I promise."

"PLEASE HELP!"

The gateway closed, sealing the House of Torana in that perfect world. Ray saw that the first red Taursi heart had returned to an amber colour.

"Thirty seconds," he moaned. "It wasn't even open for thirty seconds."

---

Ray struggled to replicate the crushed mechanism. It was a mad box filled with switches and buttons, some of them wired to make small lights work, and others did nothing at all. He'd added an entire crystal radio kit into the mix. The whole thing was a costume piece to science, a miscellany, but it had been the only thing to open his gate.

As the glass hearts slowly refilled, Ray ran the numbers, and they weren't good. Assuming people and goods went through in an orderly way and there was no mad stampede, the gate could fit fifty people abreast. If each rank took two seconds to advance through the gate, they could move 1500 people per minute.

Crosspoint alone had a population of just under 30,000 people. Assuming that everyone marched through in lockstep without panic, it would take twenty minutes to evacuate the first city alone. Looking at the small stack of hearts slowly filling with that vile red power, Ray thought he might be able to hold the gate open for two, maybe three hours before the fuel ran out.

This was assuming he could even figure out what he'd done to accidentally open the door to a paradise.

"Junkman, sir," a Boneguard said gruffly, the chirpy helpfulness of Sol's handpicked squad long gone. This was a soldier speaking to a superior with the barest of manners, ready to answer any request with malicious compliance at best.

A sheaf of paper was thrust at Ray, which he took with puzzlement. "Telegrams, sir."

The man snapped a lazy salute, spun on a heel, and left. Ray looked over the dispatches and saw the soldiers had been sitting on these for days now. Everywhere with a working telegraph had been sending him panicked messages, requesting immediate aid or updates about the planned gate. Others were demanding that the criminal Papa Lucy be apprehended at once, while a message from Langenfell indicated they were under attack, the message itself ending abruptly.

Then a telegram from Graham's Wash, accusing Mawson of war crimes and insisting the Moot of Crosspoint send help. They also requested priority use of the Junkman's gate when it was operational, with a guarantee of a water supply for the evacuees. They were sending a huge contingent of their most important citizens to use the gate, guarded by a small army.

Mawson sent their own lengthy missive accusing the Water Barons of similar atrocities, including the butchery of the southern refugee cities. They denied giving any assistance to the fugitive Papa Lucy and claimed he'd destroyed their temple in a criminal act. Mawson also requested priority use of the Junkman's gate, with the proviso that the Water Barons be refused access. The refugees were reportedly streaming back north, and Mawson was sending their own hopeful group of citizens and soldiers to Crosspoint.

The more Ray read, the more his head hurt. All he wanted was to work with his hands, but he realized that with everyone off hunting Bilbenadium, he was the person in charge.

Of the entire Now.

He left the letters in a neat stack on the ground, the wind eventually scattering them in all directions. He did his rounds, checking the still, eyeing each glass heart to a minute level, and tinkering with the box that the House of Torana had destroyed.

"This thing is stupid," he declared, looking over the broken toy. "It's not even anything. Just junk."

Checking the welds on the top of the frame for the third time that day, Ray eventually heard the ruckus below. He wasn't the most observant of men, but from his vantage point he saw the commotion from the camps, and even the Giden and the other creatures from Gan-Eden emerged from their shelters and hidey-holes.

One of them pointed, and Ray followed the path of that arm to see the jag of mountains on the horizon, the Range finally visible from Crosspoint and moving fast. In front of the mountains billowed an enormous sheet of dust. Ray frantically reached for a telescope that wasn't there, and a moment later he was holding it to his eye anyway, real and functional.

Within the dust roiled a wave of monstrous shapes, shifting and squabbling, with more arriving by the second, the world veil tearing in dozens of places.

They were coming straight for the gate.

# — 23 —

## BAERTHA

Baertha drew her family in close, and they took their first ungainly step on the Impossible Stair. It was an arbitrary point in space, the dust of the stars around them gut-achingly beautiful, hanging thick in all directions. She chanced a glance over her shoulder to see the cosmos hanging in the void, a cross shape wrapped in gauze, and it flared with golden light as the Most High attacked the structure from within.

Aum, Greygulf, Realms left and right, and even Gan-Eden and the Low Place. Hunting for the mother of the golden babe, not knowing it was just a distraction.

"Nice bit of scenery, but can we please piss off to the next step?" Lucy said.

"I feel dizzy," Jenny said quietly, and shifted forward slightly. If she fell, she would never stop falling. Baertha caught her by the shirt and slowly drew her back.

"It's all about belief, the conviction that where you stand is the right place, a firm footing that won't give," Baertha said. "We are going to run through the wonders of the universe, and I want you to ignore all of it."

The magicians nodded.

"I'll count," she said. "Move in time, and don't overthink this. Just do it."

"One," she began, and they shifted as one through a blur of light, standing in a small solar system, each planet trailing moons like courtiers. She checked on everyone, and saw that John and Jesus were tightlipped, Sol struggling to keep his balance, and even Lucy was silent for once.

"Two."

This time they stood in an asteroid belt, the small but incredibly fast stones wearing down their defences, breaking across their shields with flashes of sorcerous flame.

"Quickly, three!"

Now they stood in a garden of light, with brilliant nebulae all around them.

"Don't look. Focus. Four!"

And so they went, on and on up the Impossible Stair. Some of the treads had been splintered apart by the Most High's recent descent to what it called the Severed Garden, and it took much of Baertha's energy to rebuild these platforms as they landed.

The Family were savvy magicians and had started to work out the process of each leap on their own. Jenny followed by instinct more than anything, and Baertha supposed that the Cruik part of her was powerful enough to make up for her own magical shortcomings.

Still, she soon drew up short, begging for a break. Jenny retched over the side of the stair, more sap than vomit, and Baertha ordered everyone to stop, widening the step until it was broad enough to sit on.

"I'm sorry," Jenny said, wiping her mouth. "Just got a bit of vertigo from all of those stars and things."

"Understandable," Baertha said. "Just lie down and let it pass."

Jenny was Lucy's victim but had emerged from her ordeals as a weird amalgam of ghost and artifact. In the short time she'd known the woman and her story, Baertha found she admired Jenny more than she pitied her. They'd given her every opportunity to go back to the Now with Ray, avoiding this conflict of gods and doomed sages, but she'd come forth willingly, donating the significant power of the Cruik to the cause.

Sol had started a small flame to heat up a mug of tea, and the merry little light gave their strange bivouac a homely feel. Baertha saw Jesus flash her a happy grin which she could not help but share. This was beyond anything the Collegia had ever thought possible, and here were the outcasts surviving even that stuffy institution, eclipsing the achievements of their long dead rivals.

She caught John surveying the constellations with a practiced eye, and she knew that the old special forces wizard was charting their location. If worst came to worst, he might be able to navigate their way home. She also knew enough of the soldier-mage to know that he was both planning their route home and committing to fight to the bitter end.

"You're doing that thing again," Lucy said to her, and she realized he'd been watching her the whole time.

"Excuse me?"

"Cataloguing us. Putting us in your mental rolodex. Oh, this one is a faithful friend. That one is a poor victim of Lucy's. Tell me, Baertha, do you exist in your own catalogue? Is there a neat place for you in your own universe?"

"You are such an arsehole."

"You didn't answer the question."

"Leave her alone," Sol warned.

"What? You'll break my bones again? Not fucking likely. All hands on deck and all that. Well?"

"I'm not without self-awareness," Baertha finally said. "We've got a complicated story, all of us. I'm in there too, for better or worse, but I'll own all of my fuck ups. Will you?"

"Says the brother fucker."

"Lucy!" Sol said, and the fire under his teacup flared, causing the liquid to spit. Baertha raised a hand.

"I can see what's going on here," Baertha said to Lucy. "You're jealous."

"Of you? Hah!"

"You're not the boss anymore. No one is. At the end of this, we all became equals, and you hate it."

"You think you're MY equal? I'm Papa fucking LUCY, bitch."

"Lucy, honestly, give it a rest," Jesus said. "I wish I'd never indulged you so much in the classroom. A bit of talent is no excuse for being an egotistical dickhead."

Snarling, Lucy cast a deadly bolt of magic at the professor. Jesus easily deflected it and did not even bother to retaliate.

"I used to think you were the greatest magician in the Family, but now? I honestly think it's Ray."

"Fucking RAY!?!"

"Careful," John Leicester warned. "He is everything that you are not."

Laughter, and the Family paused their long-entrenched squabble to see Jenny Rider howling up at the stars, laughing fit to burst.

"I—I used to pray to you," Jenny managed. "To the Family!" She clutched at her ribs, gasping and trying to stop.

"You're—you're completely dysfunctional!" Her laughter went on and on, and it was infectious. In the end it even brought a sardonic chuckle from Lucy.

Sol shared his mug of tea around their circle, and those of flesh and blood took a sip, an enchantment on the cup holding the freezing void at bay. Finally, Baertha handed it back to Sol, and their fingers brushed together for a moment.

"Baertha, I—"

"Sol, don't."

"No, I need to say this. I'm sorry about the baby."

"It was a long time ago."

"I should have been there. Should have said yes to Lucy using the Cruik on you."

"I'm right here, dickhead," Lucy scoffed.

"Sol, it would have all gone the same," Baertha said, ignoring Lucy. After a moment of hesitation she took Sol's hands in hers.

"It wasn't all bad though, was it?" he asked. "Us, I mean."

"No," Baertha admitted. "But it ended. It ended, and that's okay."

"After—after I threw the Cruik into the waters of Shale, I thought you were destroyed. I thought my arsehole brother lied to me about you being alive still, and it turned out to be true. I did horrible things to try to get you back."

"Sol, I saved *myself*. I loved you, I still care for you, but for pity's sake take off the hairshirt. It's really annoying."

"Bravo!" Lucy crowed with a slow round of applause that no one echoed.

"I can't help how I feel about you," Sol said slowly.

"We are about to battle for the fate of the universe. To take on Bilbenadium and maybe the Most High. And still you can make it about us, which is really making it all about you."

"Please, Baertha."

"It's the moping that got me in the end, Sol. Worshipping the idea of me and not loving the real version of me, the imperfect me. It was never about the baby or anything else really. So if you wanted closure, Sol, that's as good as I can give you."

He hung his head. Baertha gave his hands a good squeeze, and then let them go.

"For as long as we have left, we're family, with all the good and bad things that word means. Everyone here, even the *enfant terrible* over in the corner. And you, Jenny, you have earned your place in our story."

"And that, Papa Lucy, is my fucking catalogue," Baertha said, flipping the bird at her brother-in-law.

---

They came toward the end of the Impossible Stair, and Baertha held up a hand.

"In the next step or two, we will reach our goal. The Most High's door. If what Lucy says is true, that's where we'll find Bilbenadium. So what's our plan?"

Lucy answered immediately. "Run up the stairs. Kick the shit out of the rat. Open the gate and vacate the premises."

"What about everyone else?" Sol said. "We've got tens of thousands of people relying on us!"

**THE BRIDE & THE BIRDMAN · 273**

"We can find some beautiful world on the other side and go all Gilligan's Island over there," said Lucy. "I don't recommend trying to repopulate, given what happened last time, but we can see out our last few centuries fuck-eyed on coconut wine."

"That's not even approaching a plan," John Leicester said.

"Do you have anything?" Sol asked, and his brother paused.

"There's something off about this," Lucy finally ceded. "I've manipulated enough people to know that we're being nudged along this path. The rat probably knows that we realize this, too."

"Bilbenadium expects we're going to come after them with guns blazing," John said. "Why did they prod us to that outcome?"

"Because they wanted us to come here in strength," Jesus said. "I think we're about to be convinced to do something stupid."

"We could go back," Jenny said. "Take on the Most High."

"Don't see how we can win that fight," Sol said. "A god, and it's out there wrecking entire worlds. It will barely notice us as it wipes us out."

"Argh. Fuck this. I'm going dick first into this nonsense," Lucy said, leaping forward without a backward glance. With a curse, the others scrambled to follow him, and found themselves at the top of the Stair.

At the very edge of all things, they floated in a place just beyond the dim reach of the stars. A blank space here, the final door of the Most High, and there two figures awaited them.

The Gravedigger, that odious figure scratching and working at the door with his tools, struggling to pry it open.

Then Bilbenadium, floating serenely before them, charcoal grey perfection in the void, arms outspread in welcome. "You came, as you often do. I've had to fix the timeline more than once to guide you here."

Papa Lucy snarled, his savaged mouth twisted in hatred as he launched mystical energy at the angel, who merely twisted and shifted, anticipating each movement.

"Lucy, stop it!" Sol cried out.

"I can do this forever," Bilbenadium said.

"Well, I can kill *him* instead," Lucy said, launching a crackling bolt at the Gravedigger. Bilbenadium moved quicker than thought, reaching behind themselves to pull a shining length of steel from between their shoulder blades. The Sworn Sword.

The angel deflected the bolt of energy with the painfully bright blade, and then the next one, and then bounced Lucy's next magical effort back, inches away from his ear.

"Do I have your attention, Luciano Pappagallo?" Bilbenadium said.

"Fine, you piece of shit," he said in a huff. "I refuse to be manipulated. I'm leaving, and I hope these deadshits follow my example."

"You're not going anywhere," Bilbenadium said.

"Excuse me?"

"Because you're about to see what's on the other side of that door."

Bilbenadium floated closer to the Family, sword held down by their side.

"I tricked you by necessity," the angel said. "Everything I have ever done has led to this moment. Every nudge throughout history, every ripple in the waters of time, every evil and manipulative act that can be laid at my feet. It all meant the six of you, standing here on this precipice."

"I've nearly got it," the Gravedigger grunted, and the door moved another fraction of an inch.

"When you see what is on the other side, you will understand what you need to do," Bilbenadium said. "Why I ask of you what I ask."

"The theft of—" Jesus began.

"'The theft of our free will is your greatest crime,' you say, and then Baertha says she refuses to cooperate with anything I'm about to suggest, and then you all turn around and the Most High destroys you halfway down the Impossible Stair," Bilbenadium said. "That has happened too many times."

"The Most High is coming here?" Jenny whispered.

"Imminently. I did lay the trail of Baertha's baby memory all over the Stair, like a hunter laying down a scent."

Lucy swore, John Leicester let off a pointless shot at Bilbenadium, and Sol simply shook his head. They'd been used, led to their dooms.

"Come, the door is about to open."

"Not likely! It's still stuck," the Gravedigger said.

**THE BRIDE & THE BIRDMAN · 275**

"One more heave always does it."

"I'm serious, it's—oh," the Gravedigger said, and then his tools finally breached that powerful seal. Baertha flinched at the memory of the intense heat from her last visit, but this time around the Most High wasn't lurking on the far side.

They looked onto a scene of beauty and utter misery. While their home was a wildly grown universe with a failed garden bed at its centre, the Most High had been tending an ordered garden on the other side. As far as they could see were rows of endless cosmological formations, wrapped in the gauze of their own world veils. Each was a tree of realms, much like the one they lived in.

A junction world, a Greygulf.

Realms of living creatures, spreading around the centre like an axis.

A void, and then a realm for the blessed dead to live in.

Underneath this, a realm for the wicked to face refinement.

These structures bled out both the blue of Aether and the red mist of the Deep Insult into the universe. Each cosmos sat in a grid with its neighbours, and spreading endlessly, neat rows of prisons that were identical in every way.

Here there were no nebulae, no dust or wild meteoroid belts, nothing but the stars that the Most High had permitted for each structure to receive light and energy.

"You see this?" Bilbenadium said sadly. "The Most High seeks the love of all who live, and this is how it can get it. Slowly each spire breeds out the faithless while emitting the Aether of the faithful. The Most High measures love by how many die in its name."

Endless currents of Aether flowed between the structures, a grid of bright blue rivers that ran up and down, left and right.

"It wasn't always like this," Bilbenadium said. "At the start of all of time, the Most High was a prisoner, doomed to watch the birth and death of the universe it created, over and over. This was cruel, but it was necessary to keep the god chained up."

The angel gestured sadly to the stacked cosmoses.

"And now...now we see what happened the one time the Most High found a way to escape," the angel said. "The only place left that doesn't look like this is the Severed Garden."

"So why did you risk our worlds?" Sol said curtly. "That monster is destroying everything down there."

"The Most High is jealous and suspicious. This all had to be convincing. It loves humans and did not wish to destroy them utterly, but if it smelled a trick, it would have simply snuffed out this wild corner of the Garden."

"What happens now?" Baertha asked.

"We are going to try to slay the Most High," Bilbenadium said. "We will cast it through the door and destroy that abomination it's created. Then the Severed Garden shall be the only garden."

"What do you mean, try to slay it?" Baertha said. "Can't you see all of time?"

"This is where my vision stops," Bilbenadium said. "You ask that question, and then I see no more ahead. From here, my experience with time is the same as yours. It is disconcerting."

"So you want us to kill the creator of the universe?" Sol asked.

"You have no choice now. It's coming. I can feel its tread upon the stair. You are press-ganged into the most important battle of the universe. We must slay the Most High…or perish."

The magicians looked at each other for a long, considering moment.

"Shit yes," Papa Lucy finally said. "I am in like Errol fucking Flynn."

# — 24 —

## MAL

He was hopeless with names, always had been, and so Kirstl fed him this information as he paced around the Terminus, making everything ready.

"Lyn, snap out of it. You're needed at the window with that chatter gun. Yvette…"

*Yvonne!* Kirstl corrected.

"Yvonne, stand on that flagstone there. Concentrate. Do you feel that?"

The older Jesusman's eyes widened.

"Yep, just like on the shadow-roads. We can drive this thing. Julian, Isaac, and Foster, I want you standing there, there, and there. You lot, come upstairs now."

He placed the terrified survivors on all the nodes—or *stations,* as Lady Bertha named them. The Terminus shook from a concentration of Witch fire, and one lucky shot through a window had set a prentice aflame, screeching and dying in black, white, and grey agony.

"You lot! I want Marks on those guns," Mal said, surprised at how much of Lanyard fell from his tongue in the urgency. "There's nothing stopping our magic now. Make those bastards hurt."

Depositing more random bodies on station points, Mal climbed up into the crown of the structure. What they'd thought of as an attic or an afterthought was really a command post, and as he stepped on a worn piece of the stone flooring, he could feel a connection with everyone else standing on a station point. It was like a completed circuit, and now that the power was switched on, he could feel the structure come under his control.

Lights flickered on in the dome of the Terminus, a map of sorts. Amber points and broken lines depicted shadow-roads and shadow-doors. A brighter point flared at the centre; Mal could only assume this was the Terminus itself.

Mal switched out for Kirstl, who tried to figure out how to navigate the thing. It felt like moving a shadow-road, if that shadow-road was an unwieldy turnip that moved on a dozen axes. The mental load was simply incredible, and Kirstl staggered under the effort, even as spread out as it was through the network of magic-workers placed at each station.

The structure shuddered around them, and the stub of shadow-road still connected to it cracked away and fell. They moved up and away, still shuddering as a last fusillade of Witch-flame pummelled them.

Above them, the bright star moved across the chart. Kirstl recognized the pattern of the doors and aimed them toward the point that Lady Bertha had shown them. The door to Crosspoint, where they were most needed.

The Terminus moved in fits and starts. Below them, Jesusmen cried out as crates and supplies bounced around in the voyage. A brace of birds broke loose, screeching and causing havoc as the whole building shook around them.

Then the circuit broke, and they came to a halt. Riders rounded up the birds, and others tended to the wounded. Detritus and dust settled.

"What's going on? Report!" Mal called out after retaking control. Kirstl swirled in the background of their mind, grateful for the reprieve.

"Yvonne's dead!" someone called up to them. "She got crushed by a bird!"

"Move her out of the way. Someone else stand exactly where she was," Mal ordered. "Do it!"

The circuit reestablished, and Mal seized the controls.

*Let me do it,* Kirstl said wearily.

"It's just like driving a forklift," Mal said. "No trouble at all."

*You crashed the forklift.*

Sweat on his brow, he concentrated on moving the Terminus through the Greygulf sky. Even with the networked Jesusmen, the sheer effort was brutal, and he leaned against the railing, feeling his head thump with pain.

*You're going the wrong way.*

"No. It's the cluster of doors that looks like a diamond. The one at the top."

*No, no no! It's the one further left. The frying pan. We're going for the door that's the handle of the pan.*

*Frying pan,* Collybrock added.

"Damnit," Mal said and corrected their course. He felt like he was carrying the entire structure on top of his head. He grumbled every step of the way, but he did not put down his load, not even once.

---

It took hours in the end, the bright orange star of the Terminus moving dreadfully slow across the lit-up map in the cupola. Runners came with mugs of tea and what food they had left.

At least they'd figured out how to make Terminus move, and the vehicle slid more or less steadily across the silver sky. Mal saw some minor bleedthroughs appear in the distance, and from this high the Greygulf was beautiful in its own desolate way.

He thought of Lanyard and shuddered. He'd been very close to staying here forever.

At last the shadow-door came into sight, and Mal finally withdrew and let Kirstl take over for the finer movements. She slowly rotated the Terminus until one of the doorways lined up flush with the portal, connecting to it with a final faint bump.

*Thanks, love,* Mal said and swapped back into the body.

"All right, you lot," he said to the surviving Jesusmen. "We are about to return to the Now. That door leads to Crosspoint, and we have one job. It's the same job we always have."

He eyeballed everyone, wondering where his confident command was coming from. Then he realized it. When alive, Lanyard had been a shy, laconic man, broken in a dozen ways by life. Tilly was a girl robbed of her childhood, desperately trying to please the old man and constantly doubting herself.

Neither of them had been natural leaders. They'd been making do, motivated by the need to keep the work going, to keep their people alive. Brought down to these pure basics, command became an easy concept, while still being a burden as heavy as moving the Terminus — except on his heart, not his mind.

"Our job," he continued, "is to kill monsters. The Junkman is close to finishing his escape gate, and so there is a multitude of people there. The Range is closing in. All of this together means the world veil is about to break. There are going to be more monsters than we've ever seen. We will hold out for as long as we can and take out as many of those things as we can. That is our sworn duty."

"Yes, boss," his people chorused — and damned if he didn't hear one or two of them call him "Birdman."

Mal reached out and ordered the shadow door to spiral open.

"Go," he commanded, and the survivors pushed through in a rush of guns and bikes and birds, emerging into dust and chaos. There were shouts and pointed guns, and Mal stepped through to realize they'd emerged through the Boneman's gate.

"It's bloody Jesusmen," someone cried out, and Mal saw that the Boneguard were putting down their weapons, a moment later than he might have liked.

Taursi were there too, the indigenous echidna-people ready to stand in defence of the gate. Mal knew they had their own relationship with things of other planes and worlds, and he saw them as much like Jesusmen in many ways.

Monster enters your house. You kill that monster, and then you shut the door. The equation was simple enough.

Then he saw a further strangeness slipping out of tents and

shelters. Ghosts of warriors, walking in the lands of life, and it was his turn to shout at his own people, bidding them to stand down. These were the Giden, the warrior-ghosts that answered to John Leicester and Jesus. The Many-Faced were here too, rolling about and getting underfoot. They greeted him with excitement, butting him in the legs and flashing words like *B+N!* and *FRIEND!*

Clambering down a steel ladder was the Junkman, who rushed over in a distracted state.

"Jesusmen. Good. Where is Lanyard?"

"He's gone," Mal said. "Turned into a Witch."

"Oh," he said, a little crestfallen. "He was kind to me. That is sad. What about Tilly, can you point me to her?"

"Dead," Mal said.

"No, no no," the Junkman said. His hand came up toward his own head as if to slap it, and with a great effort he brought it back down.

"Who runs your group now?"

"I do," Mal said. "Tilly gave it to me with her last breath."

"You're Lanyard's boy," the Junkman said after a searching moment. "The Tontine."

He quickly showed Mal the bizarre mechanism slowly powering up the gate, an eye-swimming nonsense of sorcery and mechanics. Glass Taursi hearts were connected to a still, and they were slowly turning a deep red colour.

"The power is close to ready, but I'm still trying to work out the gate," the Junkman said. "But there's—there's that."

He waggled his hand by way of pointing, indicating the Range closing in and the enormous dust cloud preceding it.

"They'll be here soon," the Junkman said. "I need more time."

Mal looked closer and saw shapes moving in the dust-storm, a mile-wide front funnelling toward them. Every hair on his neck stood up at the sight, but he didn't need the senses of a Jesusman to know that nothing in that storm belonged in this world.

There were loping creatures on stilts that crashed left and right. Frog things the size of a house that lurched forward in fits and starts. Flitting creatures on wings that zipped above the dust from time to time, scouting. Soon, even the wind was carrying the excited yips and snarls of ten thousand predators let loose on the world.

He had a little over two dozen Jesusmen to his name. Ghosts and murderous little rocks. A surly Boneguard, and whatever assistance the militia in Crosspoint were prepared to lend them—if they ever decided to venture out from behind their walls.

"You'll get your time," Mal told the Junkman. "As much as our blood can buy."

"Thank you," he said, already puzzling over a small box in his hands with a screwdriver.

"Lyn, find us some food. The rest, with me," Mal instructed, and his half-starved paladins came forward. He issued commands, and they fell to, moving into the old caravanserai. Some of the refugees were hiding in their former enclave, and the Jesusmen simply worked around them, converting the structures into a fort.

He sent the prentices out with tar and brushes, and they painted Marks on the outer walls, signs to dazzle and confuse the enemy, and to draw them in. Runners brought cans of spray paint to the Jesusmen, and Kirstl came forward to teach some of the deadlier Marks to those who were ready to use them. Some were landmines in the form of symbols, and others were jagged fences ready to rise the moment a foot stepped upon them. Kirstl heard a stuttering boom as a Jesusman fudged his symbol, instantly detonating the magic and himself.

They were more diligent with their writing after that.

Lyn set the chattergun up top, ready to write mayhem, and then Mal felt a chill on his neck as the ghostly Giden arrived, ready to help hold the fort. He shared the battlements with the spirits of knights and riflemen, and gently glowing archers and crossbowmen took up positions next to his own gunners.

It took a long time to explain things to the Many-Faced, but eventually they gathered in a pile in the courtyard, ready to tear open the gates with their tentacles and roll out to engulf their foe.

As the vast wave of predators rolled closer to them, Mal continued to hold Lanyard's lessons to his heart. In a way he was glad to have finally conquered the old man, but he was even gladder he'd spared him. Even as a Witch, Lanyard continued to teach him, and the most

**THE BRIDE & THE BIRDMAN · 283**

basic lesson was this: fight with white-knuckled fury, especially when things were hopeless.

Jesusmen weren't allowed the luxury of hope, so Mal chose busy-work instead. He passed through the caravanserai, checking in on everybody, ensuring that their final stand was ready. It was the first day of his command, and possibly his last, but he meant to do it well.

Even now, he wanted to make Lanyard proud.

# — 25 —

## BAERTHA

They floated at that final threshold, six magicians, a liar, and a thief. Each awaited the tread of golden feet upon the stair.

"I need to know something," Baertha said warily to Bilbenadium. The angel was floating serenely, Sworn Sword in their hands.

"This is truly strange, a conversation where I know neither question nor answer," the angel said. "Talk then, and I shall do my best."

"I understand why you manipulated us. You showed us what the Most High did. It's a criminal and a despot. I don't have to look any further than Lucy there to recognize the type."

"Oi! Keep my good name out of your mouth, ya dumb slut," Lucy said lazily. He was laying a dozen sigils in front of him, the Marks glowing cheerfully in the gloom.

"But there's one thing I don't get."

"Go on."

"What do you get out of this?"

"I get nothing. I will likely die at my old master's hands."

"You've been plotting this for thousands of years. Setting up a gambit worthy of the ages. I think the servant wants the throne."

"Not at all. You've seen what that does to anyone with power. I can think of no worse nightmare than to rule the universe."

"Speak for yourself, ya dickless wonder," Lucy chuckled.

"Lucy," Sol scolded.

The Gravedigger floated up to Bilbenadium, broad-bladed shovel strapped to his back. Baertha could tell the grossly obese spirit had been gathering the courage to approach the angel.

"I did as you asked," he asked. "Opened the Most High's door."

"You always do."

"You said you were going to release me from your service," the Gravedigger said, a worried eye to the top of the stair.

"I release you," Bilbenadium said, making a theatrical gesture.

"Wh-where am I meant to go?" the thief said, darting around in a panic. "The Most High is coming!"

"I haven't seen this part, but I assume you follow one of three paths. Descend the Stair and face the oblivion you so richly deserve. Scurry into that well-ordered Garden where, in time, you will be snuffed out with the other pests. Or you reach into your satchel and pull out that rope of Allcatch you think is hidden from me."

The Gravedigger held one guilty hand to the satchel on his hip, but this turned into a determined grab. He snatched out a fat coil of golden rope, each strand formed from a dead Overhaeven being, the whole construct soaked in Aurum.

Without air, Baertha couldn't exactly smell it, but she ached for it all the same, just as an ex-smoker might pause at the stink of an ashtray.

Back in the glory days of Overhaeven, such ropes were crafted in secret, and the very owning of one meant a lingering and awful execution. Any being could be bound in Allcatch, their powers stripped from them, the powerful brought low.

"You cannot hope to catch me with that," Bilbenadium said cautiously. The Gravedigger feinted left, and Bilbenadium shifted in a dozen directions before settling back into the one place.

"Maybe not," the obese spirit said. "But I know things. Learn secrets. I know your one weakness."

"Do tell," the angel said, eyebrow arched.

"You can perish on a noose of Allcatch wielded by a Tontine.

These are your words, rat," the Gravedigger said, and then he made his move.

He threw the curled rope, which played out in space, the line halting within Baertha's reach. At the same time, he hurled himself at Bilbenadium, enormous shovel swinging, its sharp blade capable of piercing universes.

The angel parried the Gravediggers' shovel with the Sworn Sword, then with one deft move disarmed the spirit of his weapon. Looking down on it with bemusement, he suddenly darted forward, using the shovel's edge to separate the Gravedigger's head from his body.

The soul bled out for many long moments, a lake of stolen Aether tumbling out into the cold places between the stars. Bilbenadium clucked his tongue, even as the magicians looked at each other warily.

"There goes a parable in self-interest if ever there was one," Bilbenadium said.

"A waste," Papa Lucy said.

"Really? Him?" Jesus said.

"Fat fucker like that would have been a good speed bump for when our old mate comes tromping up the steps."

"Honestly. You're the very worst of us," John said wearily.

"Maybe. But I'll still be drilling snatch long after you kick the bucket."

"You are so gross," Jenny said.

Placing the Sworn Sword by his side, Bilbenadium considered something on the Gravedigger's shovel for a long moment. Then he set to it with his fingernail, scratching out a message that set the steel sparking and squealing.

His work complete, he hurled the implement through space, a shooting star that crossed the universe in the blink of an eye.

"A message," he explained. "Or an apology, perhaps."

"To whom?" Sol asked.

"Does your group have to know everything?" the angel said wearily. "I certainly don't owe you any answers."

"What! We are here to fight your battles," Baertha said. "You tricked us, over and over. You owe us everything we ask of you."

After a moment of consideration, she snatched up the Allcatch,

**THE BRIDE & THE BIRDMAN · 287**

rapidly looping it between palm and elbow, years of sailing instruction returning by muscle memory.

"Do you think to make me a new necktie?" Bilbenadium said.

"Don't flatter yourself," Baertha said. "I know you nudged this here, and I think you did it for a different reason."

Lucy laughed darkly and returned to his glowing sigils. The universe burned and twinkled around them, and all that was left was the waiting.

---

The Family got to work on their defences and made ready to kill a god.

After struggling for a while with the noose, Baertha gave the rope to John, who was experienced with traps and snares.

"It's a lariat. Knot slides up and down the rope. Much better."

"Thanks," she said, eyeing Bilbenadium, who had returned to a serene meditation, sword across their knees.

Lucy had placed a minefield of sigils and Marks around their position, hiding them with illusions. Sol and Jesus set to weakening the top few steps on the Stair, hoping they would give way and send the Most High tumbling.

Jenny considered the stars around them and reached out her hooking hands, tasting the universe like a creeping plant, looking for the best places to latch onto.

"Oh," she said, retreating a little. "Did you feel that?"

Beartha noticed it too. A faint reverberation, like the plucking of a web by a trapped fly, but then stillness.

"Come on," she urged. "Keep coming."

Now that she knew the trick of it, she could sense the nearness of her stolen memory, dabbed about like meat for the hounds. If she only had the time, she would pick up all of those hints of herself, hold them tight, stuff them back into her head.

She looked at the manipulative angel and felt nothing but rage in her heart. If she and the Family turned on the creature now, she was sure they would be able to subdue it long enough for her to slip the noose around its neck so she could choke it into oblivion.

"Why do we actually need you?" she asked Bilbenadium.

That was when the Most High came rushing out, not from the Impossible Stair but from a star system above them. The golden god was finally amongst them, raging, canny enough to sniff out their traps.

"TRAITORS AND SABOTEURS!" it bellowed. "THE IMMACU-LATE WOMB REVEALED!"

It paused, revelling in the moment of drama, the absolute knowledge it had outfoxed the enemy. Bilbenadium slowly unfolded, Sworn Sword in hand. Around him the magicians of the Family milled, unsure of what to do. The Most High drifted toward Bilbenadium, ignoring them all for the moment.

"YOU. I WARNED YOU. RETURN TO THIS DOOR AND PERISH."

"I disagree, my lord," Bilbenadium said.

"SCHEMES FOLDED INTO SCHEMES, BEATEN ON THE ANVIL OF TIME. IF ONLY YOU HAD WORKED AS HARD FOR ME, MY ANGEL!"

"In a way, I did," Bilbenadium said. "You tasked me with watching the humans, which I did. To protect your Gardens, which I did, and better than you. What *you* did to the Gardens beyond that portal is unforgivable."

"I AM THE SOLE ARBITER OF MY WORK!" the Most High shrieked.

"You gave us free will and judgement, and so we sit in judgement of you. You have failed. Give over and undo your manufactured cosmic cages. Do what you said you would."

The Most High looked back through the portal, to the neatly stacked Gardens and the rivers of Aether that connected it all.

"NO. IT IS A PERFECT DESIGN."

"I did not foresee this, but I am not surprised," Bilbenadium said.

"God fucking damn it!" Papa Lucy snarled in frustration.

The two powerful immortals turned to consider the upstart magician.

"I have never been so bored in my life," Papa Lucy said, "and I've sat through every budget speech my brother ever gave. Either fight or fuck already."

The Most High raised a hand to wipe out the offensive intruder, but the wave of solar heat that washed out from its palm merely undid an illusion of the mage.

"First mistake," Papa Lucy said, appearing behind the Most High's right shoulder. He sent out a lance of pure shadow at the god, but the magic could barely pierce its outer shell, sending a juddering, sparking scratch across its skin.

"Tough old bitch," Lucy said, a far-door sending him out of harm's way, and then he was with the rest of the Family, who now buzzed around the god like hornets, unleashing their magic upon their indifferent creator.

The years fell away for Baertha, and she thrilled at this moment where their cadre worked as one. Their fellowship had been forged in the final days of the Before, when they'd fought the authorities, and made tighter still when they'd conquered the Greygulf, side by side like this.

Even if they lost now, it was nice to go out this way.

The Most High was a horrifying opponent, devilishly quick, and Baertha knew that one stroke of its magic would undo any of them. The mages popped in and out of far-doors, struck and retreated, and kept the god in frustrated pursuit. It was a lightning-fast ballet, and the Family deployed every trick they had just to stay ahead of that great golden foe, who shifted about them with flowing ease.

As near as Baertha could tell, their magics were doing nothing to the Most High. She called out for madness and confusion, Lucy cast powerful sigils that it blundered through, and Sol reached for whatever skeleton the god had. Sol looked to Baertha with a puzzled frown, but then they were forced to fly apart, a blazing haymaker from a mile-long arm nearly destroying them.

She tried to deploy the Allcatch against the Most High, but the lariat's knot failed, and the rope merely uncoiled in space. The Most High saw the trap for what it was, and with a deep gust of breath, it blew the snare miles away, where it could tangle around the nearest star and choke it into darkness.

290 · JASON FISCHER

John Leicester called up brigades of ghostly rifles that chattered away, then a mortar that took away a small chip from the Most High's shoulder, but these were pockmarks at best, mosquito bites that bothered the god for only a moment or two.

Jenny Rider came at it like a forest of hooks, trying to snatch onto its lower legs. She found more success, her wooden claws leaving long, shallow scratches in that golden flesh. Even these healed, but more slowly.

"YOU!" the Most High screeched. "MY MOST UNFAITHFUL SERVANT. FALLEN IN WITH SUCH SCOUNDRELS."

It fell upon her like a striking snake, making to crush her between its hands like a troublesome fly. Jesus became a blue comet that flew forward, knocking Jenny Rider aside. As the god's mammoth palms crashed together, he was destroyed in her place.

"No!" Sol cried out. The Family stared in shock, their attack against the god broken and scattered. The Most High grinned, its smile a black curve against all that light, and it took a moment to taste the Aether pasted across its hands.

"AN EXCEPTIONAL SOUL," the god conceded. "YOU ARE RIGHT TO GRIEVE HIM."

At that utter boundary of life, a kind man had given his final lick of life in sacrifice of another, and it broke Baertha's heart as she realized the truth. It simply did not matter. They could not win here.

Their magical bee stings turned into a desperate retreat as one by one the Most High murdered them all. Sol was atomized with the heat of a breath that birthed stars. It swallowed John whole, then took pleasure in splaying Papa Lucy across the stars, spreading nerves and skin and innards across acres of the void, not allowing him to die for many long, painful minutes.

Jenny took the worst of the punishments. The great golden being froze her in place with a glare, its intense will shivering every fibre of her soul away until all that was left was the Cruik itself, which the Most High snatched up and broke across its knee.

All this time it ignored Baertha, suffering the stings of her magic, and it became apparent that she was to be the final victim, a great

**THE BRIDE & THE BIRDMAN · 291**

punishment awaiting her for daring to give birth to the Most High's twin.

Baertha turned to see Bilbenadium still seated, sword across their knees.

"Do something!" she screamed.

She'd been still for a moment too long, and the Most High pinched her between thumb and forefinger.

It could have snuffed her out like a candle flame, but she was taken away to suffer for an age as the Severed Garden burned and that final door closed behind them.

---

"Either fight or fuck already," Papa Lucy scoffed, and then the battle between the Family and the Most High played out much as it had before.

This time it occurred to Baertha to use the Allcatch against the Most High first, and when the god ambushed them, the Family trussed it up tight. They rejoiced as the god wriggled, impotent and undone.

Of course, Papa Lucy seized the moment to turn on his allies and destroyed Jesus and John before holding the others at a standoff.

"Just let me fucking leave," he snarled, deadly energies crackling between the feuding Family. "Keep your stupid Severed Garden, I'll have the rest."

"Do something!" Baertha screamed at Bilbenadium, who watched serenely, Sworn Sword in hand.

"It's not this one," the angel finally said, watching mournfully as the Most High finally snapped out of the Allcatch, butchering his captors in seconds.

---

"Do something!" Baertha screamed.

"I'm trying. Honestly."

---

"What do you mean, try to slay it?" Baertha said. "Can't you see all of time?"

"This is where my vision stops," Bilbenadium said, a lie as it always was. "You ask that question, and then I see no more ahead. From here, my experience with time is the same as yours. It is disconcerting."

The Family argued as they often did, and made their plans, and then the Most High surprised them and destroyed them utterly. The most disastrous outcomes came whenever Bilbenadium told the Family of the Most High's ambush, and so they chose to omit this knowledge, hoping to find the optimal sequence.

"You could tie me up with that," they offered to Baertha this time, when she threatened him with the Allcatch.

The Most High always broke through the rope, and this time the Family came up with a cunning trap. A spider web of individual Allcatch threads, surrounding and protecting them in all directions. Jenny proved deft at untangling that impossible rope into thin fibres, a hundred tiny hooks dancing rapidly while the Family quickly assembled the trap.

This time they caught the god, long enough to make *the discovery*, the one that Bilbenadium couldn't tell them for fear of the attempt failing. As always, they tried to destroy the Most High with their preferred magic, and the only outcome that ever mattered occurred.

"The Most High is missing a rib," Sol called out.

The Most High began to shred the Allcatch web around it, moments away from destroying them.

"Do something!" Baertha screamed, and this time Bilbenadium did. He drifted calmly over to Jenny Rider, who looked at him quizzically.

He raised the Sworn Sword and struck her down.

"Jenny!" Sol cried, and the Family turned on the angel, ready to destroy the betrayer.

Bilbenadium stepped aside, revealing the Once-Dead spirit of Jenny Rider, now separated from the Cruik. The shards of the Sworn Sword drifted away, the blade having perfectly severed the two.

"What did you do to me?" Jenny said, shocked and drifting. Bilbenadium ignored her and picked up the Cruik. He passed it to Lucy, who reached for it eagerly.

"Take it. I cannot hold it long," Bilbenadium said.

Papa Lucy snatched up the Cruik, laughing wildly as it filled him with power.

"Listen to me carefully," Bilbenadium said. "The Cruik is the Most High's rib. You have to put it back."

"Change of plans," Lucy said. "Sol and I walk into that other universe and shut the door behind us."

"Lucy, no!" Sol said. The Most High was almost free, and the threads were starting to snap. It began to inhale, and an awful heat danced just beyond its lips.

"It all falls to you," Bilbenadium said, and this was true. The Sworn Sword only ever cut the once, across all of time. It was this attempt or nothing. The others seemed to realize this, and they watched the tableau intently, none daring to speak.

"Lucy, I—"

"Sol, don't give me that bloody sanctimonious look."

"Listen to me. You've played at being a hero your whole life. Now you get to do it for real."

Lucy gripped the Cruik tightly.

"I don't think I can give this up," he admitted.

"Let me help you."

Lucy flinched as Sol reached his hands out, placing them over his.

"I know where bones go, how they connect. Come with me, and we'll set this thing to rights."

Sol was once more a Boneman of sorts, and Baertha watched sadly as he removed the outer layer of the Cruik, returning it to its original form.

A rib, as large as the keel of a ship. The others came forward then to lend a hand, the Family gripping the bone like it was a battering ram. Bilbenadium was the last to take their place, ready to lend their power to the charge.

"Be strong! Don't listen to it!" Sol cried out. The Cruik was trying to take them over, whispering seductive lies, even as the Most High fought free from the web.

From her place on the rib, Baertha felt the filthy corrosion of the

Cruik, the promises that it would be *hers*. In that moment, she faltered, as she knew they all were.

Then the feeling was instantly gone, and Baertha felt the moment that Papa Lucy asserted his control over the Cruik.

"You're MINE," Papa Lucy said to it. "Don't you bloody forget it."

Then they were driving forward at great velocity, each magician lending their power to the charge, the point of the rib aimed at the Most High's torso.

The Most High breathed out stardust and creation, enough to sear through even the most powerful of their shields. This was a suicidal charge, and each of them bent their backs to it willingly.

Baertha was behind the brothers, and she saw the moment that Papa Lucy looked over his shoulder to Sol. His mane of curls waved in that blistering heat, and he cracked open that winning smile.

"I bloody love you, mate."

Papa Lucy then used the magic of the Cruik to tear Sol loose and hurl him back down the Impossible Stair. Baertha's husband caught her eye in that last moment, his face open in a silent cry, hand reaching for her, and then he was simply gone, and they were as ended as they'd ever been.

Then there was nothing left but the impalement of the rib into the god, their unmaking in the Most High's breath, the momentum carrying them through the door into the other universe. As she saw the flesh melt from her fingerbones, Baertha reached out and traced a sorcerous Mark, spoke her last word, and closed the door to the Severed Garden behind them.

As the rib slid into place and connected, the Most High shivered and screeched and then burnt from within. A moment later it exploded, a cosmic exclamation mark that signalled the end of this stolen universe.

Billions of imprisoned souls died, their neat cosmic cells incinerated. Had Baertha been alive to see it, she would have enjoyed the spectacle, the funeral pyre that her Family deserved.

---

Jenny Rider saw everything up to the moment that Baertha shut the door, and even through that barrier the forces erupting from the dying god sent her hurtling back through the void.

It seemed that the Most High had built the garden wall strong, had made the gate fast for fear of something breaking in.

The Severed Garden had survived the gardener's death. Reaching out timidly for the top step of the Impossible Stair, Jenny began her slow descent back through the wild stars of her own universe.

With the loss of the Cruik part of herself, all she had left was willpower and determination. It took her many months, but the blue-tinged Once-Dead soul finally reached the bottom of the Stair, determined to find Sol, to share the story of what she had seen.

Jenny had prayed to the Family as a girl, had seen them at their worst, and finally seen them at their best. She was determined that their sacrifice would be remembered, their story told.

"Never meet your heroes, they said." Jenny laughed, teeth chattering against the chill of her fantastic journey.

# — 26 —

## MAL · RAY · SOL

Mal flinched at the blinding light in the sky, powerful enough even to pierce the haze of dust from the approaching Range. A moment of brilliance, come and gone, remarkable enough to draw pointing fingers and chatter from the defenders of the caravanserai.

*What the hell was that?* Kirstl asked.

"I've got no idea, love," he muttered. "Guess it's a good day for more trouble."

A chill northerly wind was washing over the Range and blowing millions of acres of thin Overland topsoil at them. Even Crosspoint was hard to see now, and the approaching horde of predators was nearly invisible in all that dust.

"Cover your faces!" Mal called out, and the living reached for kerchiefs and bandannas. The Inlanders among them were used to sudden storms and fitted their face covers swiftly, while others coughed away, cursing as they looked for something to use.

The Once-Dead spirits simply stood resolute against the scouring elements, glowing a faint blue against that sepia swirl. They were steadfast, veterans in life and death, and Mal hoped that his people could look up to this bizarre example, find some courage in these strange allies.

*BOOM.* An intruder had stepped on one of the explosive Marks, and something died in the gloom with an awful screech.

"Do it," Mal yelled out to his people, and they struck at road flares, setting the burning brands on top of the parapet. Mal meant for their redoubt to be the sole point of merry light in the gloom, an inviting target for the invaders.

He looked over his people, recognizing that eternal nervous moment, the defender waiting for the attack, the shield waiting for the sword to land. As the dust finally washed over the afternoon sun, he realized he could no longer see the far side of the caravanserai, and then he could barely make out anything beyond thirty feet.

The enemy was closing in, shepherded by the advancing line of mountains, and if they couldn't be seen they could definitely be heard. A cacophony of shrieking and yapping, metallic crashing, and the pinpoint crackle of creatures that could make their own fire and light.

Then, shapes appeared in the dust, large limbs supporting bodies overhead, underbellies swaying above the scurry of a beast with a thousand backs. Mal's imagination painted every flavour of horror to that surging shadow.

*BOOM.*

*BOOM.*

*BOOM.*

The defensive Marks fell silent.

"Be ready!" he shouted, and then Mal was at the wall's edge, aiming his enormous shotgun over the side. Bat-faced children with hook-hands were rapidly scaling the wall, unleashing an overwhelming, high-pitched screech at the defenders. Some of his people went reeling, hands held to their ears. One prentice fell to the decking with her mouth foaming, feet kicking at the sound.

*BANG! BANG!*

Mal ejected the spent shells as two creatures fell back into the gloom. He reloaded in two swift movements, feeding in two shells held between the knuckles of one hand and then slamming the action closed.

Two more down. Nearby, Lyn had opened up with the chatter gun, sending deadly spurts across the wall. She ran the weapon dry, the barrels finally spinning without firing and then falling silent. She picked up the entire apparatus and hurled it down at the climbers, caving in at least one skull and dislodging several others.

Mal shot two more, and then another two, and then the creatures were at the top of the wall, lashing out with their razor-sharp hooks.

"Fix bayonets!" he shouted. Mal fell into a savage place then, where there was nothing but the choking dust and the thrust of blades. He lashed out with the shotgun as if it were a club, holding it by the hot barrels, and then Mal fell completely into the dark.

Collybrock took over, lumbering in an awkward ballet as she stomped back and forth on the wall, legs kicking, swinging the gun in one hand like it was the extension of a wing. There was no mistaking that Mal carried a bird in his head.

When Collybrock fell into exhaustion, Kirstl climbed forward to a parapet slick with dead creatures, and with more on the way. They'd beaten them back, but others were still climbing. Suddenly a buzzing pierced the air, and flying creatures were all amongst them, diving and swooping, uttering truly alien sounds. Someone to the right screamed, and Kirstl saw a man murdered by a monster that resembled a bunch of pale grapes trailing a dozen stingers, driven forward by multiple sets of wings.

The parapet was lost, and she ordered a retreat down into the court-yard of the caravanserai. The Jesusmen had set up barricades down here, and they fired volleys at the squadrons of airborne monstrosities.

"Get ready to blow the gates!" Kirstl yelled. Large mounds of the Many-Faced clacked around in the dust, excited to sally forth and do battle.

*DEATH! CONTEST! TRICKERY!* the rocky creatures flashed as they signed to each other, no doubt bragging about the feats they were about to accomplish.

Kirstl wove Marks of misdirection as they were attacked from above, causing enough confusion in the ranks of the fliers that her sharpshooters were able to give them pause. Others good with magic bound the creatures' wings or popped their floatation sacs. Then the prentices joined the fray, fighting with the Many-Faced to finish off the surviving beasts.

Then the noise of the attackers reached a crescendo, and more creatures were cresting the parapets now, things of fang and hoof, scale and slime. A menagerie of creatures from a thousand different worlds, all here with murder in mind.

"Blow the gates!" Kirstl said, and the charges dropped the gates inward, an inviting throat for the invaders to funnel into. Once more the Jesusmen lit flares, as if setting candles on a monster's birthday cake. The beasts fought each other to gain access, frenzied by the nearby prey, and they created a logjam in the entrance.

The Many-Faced hit them from all directions, small enough that they could move and fight underneath the enfilade of shooters Mal had set up to one side of the doorway. Together they were able to pick apart anything that came through the gate.

"Keep coming!" Kirstl said, setting up jags of magical fencing on the parapet. "It's all about us. Just come on in, you hungry little bastards."

---

"Come on," Ray begged the contraption in his hands, willing the damaged casing to come back together. He looked away for a moment, and sure enough the casing was less crushed when his eyes returned to the job, the workings of it inside the box rather than a messy splay of wires and smashed lights.

The very concept that his willpower could create things, could have a real-life mechanical effect, was all too much for his brain to bear. If he dwelled on that thought for too long, he started to feel overwhelmed.

*Instinctive sorcery,* Sol and the others had called it, but the problem was that he had no instincts worth a damn. He had either routine or meltdowns and not much in between that.

Whatever he needed to do to make this gate happen again just wasn't coming to him. The more that he fumbled around the idea, the more stressed he got. It had been a happy accident, whatever he'd done to open the gate to that paradise. Repeating it meant trying to recreate the exact circumstances of that initial success, as he always did with a misbehaving machine or gizmo. This assumed the perfect conditions. A quiet room with a workbench and all the tools he needed. Model aeroplane kits for when he got stressed. A steady supply of baked beans, and—especially—no people around to bother him.

What Ray Leicester had was a cacophony of screaming people, barely held back from his gate by a Boneguard who were perhaps moments away from firing into the crowd. He also had dust and howling winds, moving mountains, and hideous beasts beyond counting. These were not the perfect conditions, and his brain simply felt stuck.

Then came the bright light, a flash from above, and the sight made him feel inexplicably sad. He wondered where his friends were now. If they'd found the Most High and gone on to do what all the magicians in his life did.

*John leaves me, they all leave me, and I stay behind.*

The still had filled up all of the Taursi hearts, and they hummed on the apparatus like fat, angry grapes. The refined slurry dripped out into the overflow pan now, and it was so potent that it burned at his nose and throat. He had enough fuel for the gate and then some, and all that was holding it back was him.

"Help us, Junkman!" someone screamed, and one of the Boneguard dropped the woman with a rifle butt. It was getting ugly now, and he looked at the box in his hands through the tunnel vision of panic.

"It doesn't make any sense," he muttered, looking at the nonsense box that had opened the gate. It was just dials and switches, a fidget toy, but he'd done *something* when he threw it that had opened it for the House of Torana.

"Come on!" he said, flipping things at random. He tossed it through the gate, and when nothing happened he walked through, changed the settings, and threw it again.

At the sight of his pointless tinkering, the crowd grew ugly. Brawls broke out. Worse still, others left the queue, heading south at high speed. Then the dust and wind fell upon them, scouring away at everything in the open, and visibility dropped. Ray could still hear the army of creatures closing in, and a wave of panic rose from the refugees waiting for his gate to open. The Taursi could be heard honking away in the dark, their spines clacking, and only they seemed calm.

Explosions from the fort. The Jesusmen had drawn the attack to the caravanserai. *They're fighting valiantly, selling their lives, all of it for a crazy old man whose idea didn't work!*

He started to cry with frustration.

"Why can't I make it work?" Ray sobbed. "What is wrong with me?"

He knew exactly what was different about him. His Asperger's, the prison where his thoughts misled themselves and where simple things became exhausting. The wiring of his brain, frozen in time by the Methuselah treatment, and even with centuries at his heels he'd never ever change.

Never would.

In minutes it wouldn't even matter. He would never see that perfect paradise again. The Family would fail against the Most High. Long before the Range could grind its way south to the sea, that golden god would end this entire cosmos.

Tears and snot running down into his beard, Ray the Junkman finally crushed the control box in his hands. He let the parts fall between his fingers, to scatter on the ground.

He stood before the gate, the only puzzle he'd never been able to solve, and in that moment he gave up. Relief flooded through him, even as the mayhem around him rose to a crescendo. Hands more comfortable with wrenches and hammers fell by his side. He reached inward for peace, hoping for a nice moment before the end.

There were good memories. The love he'd shared with his brother in the end. The kindness he'd found from neighbours in his old hometown, who probably didn't need their replaceable items fixed that badly. Finally, at the end of all things, he'd found respect. These people were lining up here in hope, knowing that Ray was clever. Ray had a plan.

Ray had seen paradise already today, so he knew it worked. His memory was near photographic, and so he revisited the moment that the House of Torana had slipped through the portal. The car

302 · JASON FISCHER

had broken the "control box" a split second before the gate opened. It had never done a damn thing.

A chill running through him, Ray raised his arms. He didn't have his tools to hide behind now, no misdirection from his mind to protect his worldview. All he had left was the impossible, and it came to him effortlessly.

He pictured paradise, and the door to it opened.

The red curtain between worlds rose up inside the steel frame, and it parted to reveal that verdant world as the energy machine hummed and pulsed power into the portal.

The crowd surged forward as one, and Ray was caught up in the crush, pushed through the gate and into that sanctuary world. The transition between the Now and this new place was flawless; none of those pushing through lost their minds, and they kept their language as they jostled and marvelled and fought to stay ahead of the stampede of escapees falling through behind them.

Ray did not have to struggle to keep his mind this time.

"I did it, John," he cried, pushing through the grassy meadow toward the lake as those around him wept for joy, some calling out his name and clapping him on the back. "It really worked."

---

Sol had never mastered the art of flying, but it was easy for anyone to fall, and he dropped through the heavens like a stone. He had one horrified moment to look back at the detonation of the Most High, the destruction of that other universe, and then the door slammed shut.

"Lucy!" he cried, arms and legs pinwheeling in space.

The force of that immense destruction sent him onward with no hope of return. All he could do was fumble for the steps of the Impossible Stair, desperate to grab onto one, but it was an awkward, spinning fall, each contact with a step both painful and frantic.

If he bounced away, he would be forever lost in the void.

He cried as he tumbled, cried for the brother who'd sacrificed his own life, cried over the injustice of the last dick move Papa Lucy had ever pulled on him. He told him he loved him, saved his life, and then took everyone else out with him in a grand fuck you against a great evil. His brother had left him with nothing but his life, and as with everything in their relationship, he had made that decision for him.

"I was meant to die with you!"

His Family, his family, and they were all gone now. Lucy. And Baertha, who'd regained herself at the very end only to fall. Jesus and John, dear friends, and Jenny, duped into their world but owning the Cruik that burned within her, doing much good with that corrosive force.

Sol grieved for their misspent centuries, felt relief that the Severed Garden had been saved, and roiled with an anger against his brother that he might never be able to resolve.

He was a comet falling through the beauty of the Garden, through the nebulae and whirling galaxies, bouncing from step to step. He could not slow his descent on the Stair, barely following the path back through the cosmos, to the Now and everything else wrapped up in the world veil.

Even as the Garden had been saved, Sol knew that the Now was doomed. Baertha had confirmed this. The destruction had been set into play by Overhaeven and could not be undone.

He needed Ray, and Ray needed him.

The last few steps of the Impossible Stair diverged to various parts of the planes. Sol aimed himself at the Now, and as he drew close he could see the pasty white of the Wastelands behind the Range, the knife of the mountains themselves, and the dust storm containing an immense army of murderous invaders.

Spotting Crosspoint, he threw as much magic around as he could spare to slow his descent, to save his life from a deadly impact with the world veil. He tore open a small hole at the last moment and bounced and tumbled across the ground, painfully sliding through the dirt and stones until he finally stopped.

All Sol wanted to do was lay there for a long time, miserable in both body and soul, but he climbed to his feet and headed toward the horde of people in front of Ray's gate.

"Ray, he'll need my help to—" and Sol stopped. The steel frame held a picture of another world, a green and lush place many had already fled to.

"Holy shit," he said, awed at the sight of this immense sorcery. The quiet mechanic wasn't likely to ever stop surprising him. For all of Papa Lucy's bluster, all he'd ever managed to achieve was a big gateway into the Greygulf, one that knocked the sense out of most who passed through it.

Without even setting foot in the Collegia, Ray was easily his brother's superior in terms of raw ability. At the thought of his old friends, Sol felt a painful twinge in his chest, and his eyes watered.

"I wish you'd all been able to see this," he whispered.

The escape was far from orderly, and Sol could see people knocked over and crushed underfoot. Some from Crosspoint were attempting to drive straight through the survivors with cars and bikes, and the Boneguard were firing upon them. It was an absolute mess, spurred on by the certain death closing in.

To Sol's left, flames burned on the parapets of the old caravanserai. The crackle of small-arms fire and the unmistakable boom of Jesusmen Marks told him the battle still raged.

Sol rushed to the nearest Boneguard, who saluted him sloppily. Recognizing the haze of the Deep Insult in the man's face, Sol made a mystical pass and undid the corruption in his veins.

"We need to restore order," Sol said. He spent precious seconds restoring his soldiers to a useful state, and then he passed near the gate, creating a small maze of glass and stone barriers in the middle of the crowd. His impromptu labyrinth reminded him of the winding pathways he'd seen at the banks and airports of the Before, and it served to slow people down.

He kept a laneway open for the vehicles from Crosspoint. Some who'd thought to bring cattle and livestock received higher priority.

Sol shook his head a little. Ray had discovered the way to transport people across the dimensions to a whole new world but hadn't given any consideration as to how to actually facilitate the crossing.

More gunfire from the fort. Sol left the escape to unfold as it should, and one of his soldiers raced him toward the caravanserai on a motorbike. They rode into dust and chaos, and this suited Sol's mood just fine.

---

Mal was the best marksman, and so he wore the skin of the Tontine. They'd run out of shotgun shells a few minutes ago, and so he'd taken a rifle from a pair of dead hands, sending bullets etched with killing sigils into the packed monstrosities.

A creature that looked like a wireframe ball that burned with magnesium intensity was hard to take down. It rolled all over the gunners stationed on the enfilade, melting them down into the clay of the yard. The Mark of Unmaking eventually worked, but it had killed half a dozen by then, Jesusmen that Mal couldn't spare.

"Keep at it!" he urged. "Make these bastards earn your blood!"

A lookout on the south wall had reported that Ray's gateway had opened, a green square just visible in the dust. People were escaping into some other world, and the longer they held out, the more would escape.

*Be brave, my love,* Kirstl urged him. *We're meant to be here.*

Then the invaders were in the yard in earnest, many with exoskeletons or distance weapons of their own. A large creature resembling a squid with segmented tentacles grasped the north wall in a dozen vice-grips and pushed and pulled and brought the whole thing down.

"Each one in here is one that's not out there!" Mal shouted. "Don't you dare break on me!"

He tried the Mark of Many Triggers on the squid, but this served only to stagger it for a moment or two. They spent the last of the mortar rounds on it, and then had to retreat against its flailing limbs, firing all the while.

Mal heard the rattle of the south doors, and he saw a frightened prentice shifting the bar, ready to flee.

He raised the rifle at the boy, knowing that he was expected to punish deserters. That this was their fiercest moment, and the last of his troop was a hair away from breaking. The open door would be the moment they fled, and that would put all the evacuees at risk.

The boy's eyes flicked between him and the throat of the rifle aimed his way. Tears cut lines down his dusty face, and he wet his pants, and his mouth worked silently.

This paladin, this guardian of the Now, was all of eight or nine years old. Had survived the siege in the Greygulf, seen every flavour of nightmare, and his young mind had finally just broken.

This was the legacy of the Jesusmen, the trauma passed down through the line of Bauer, master to prentice, and Mal wondered if the best mercy might be to pull the trigger right now.

*Don't do it,* Kirstl said. *Please, Mal. We don't need to be like Lanyard!*

He raised the gun.

"Get behind me," Mal finally told the boy. "Leave the bloody door alone."

The remaining Giden made ready to sell their second lives, and a man in an old military uniform reminiscent of the Leicesterites offered Mal a crisp salute. Then he raised a ghostly bugle to his lips and blew the charge.

These warriors of the ages carved through the creatures in the caravanserai yard and hit the squid with everything they had. Ethereal guns chattered, blades rose and fell, and an armoured knight crashed in on horseback, bloody lance lowered.

The tentacled giant swatted at the Giden, dispersing ghosts with every strike, but the assault chipped away at its flesh. The squid fell, and the Jesusmen celebrated with ragged cheers.

"Birdman! Birdman!" his people cheered, and Lyn was somehow still there and alive, clapping him on the back. The cigarettes came out, a small indulgence as they checked their guns and shared out the last few precious rounds.

A low chittering sound interrupted their respite, and another. Then a second squid slowly emerged from the dust, followed by a third, and shadows behind them indicated that a whole family of the things were closing in on their last stand.

*It's nearly over,* Kirstl offered. *We're letting the others escape. We did good.*

*Good,* Collybrock echoed.

The door behind them rattled again.

"I told you, kid, leave the bloody door alone. We're doing our job here."

"And you're doing your job well," Sol Goodface said. Mal turned, beaming as he hugged the man in a vice grip.

"Did it work?" Mal said as the survivors opened fire on the squids.

"Yes."

"Where are the others? Lady Bertha?"

"It's just me. I'll have to be enough."

The magician reached forward, flexing his will against the universe. The first squid's corpse slowly rose on its tentacles.

"Good thing there are always bits and pieces laying around," Sol said, and then he sent the dead squid against its brethren, limbs snatching and strangling the first two to try to enter the caravanserai.

Mal watched the giants entwining, the other squids trying to counterattack, but the dead squid drew no breath, and soon the others fell limp to the ground.

Sweat beading on his brow, Sol raised his hands again, and two more of the dead things rose under his control. He drew them all into the cramped caravanserai yard.

"You should go," he gasped. "Join the queue into Ray's gate. You can get away too."

"We don't do that," Mal said, reloading the rifle.

"No, I guess you don't," Sol said with a sad smile.

---

With the help of the powerful magician, Mal's Jesusmen held out for hours. When other creatures tore apart the resurrected squid monsters, Sol reached for more of their dead, raising phalanxes to hold off the immense onslaught.

"I'm so sorry, I'll need your dead too," Sol said, and Mal nodded permission. The fallen Jesusmen rose, tottering forward with fixed bayonets on empty guns.

The dust was beginning to dissipate, and visibility improved, but then lookouts on the walls reported the source. The Range was close now, mere miles away. There simply wasn't enough dust left for the wind to blow at them.

The refugee lines through the gate were thinning, and there were hundreds waiting to get through now, not thousands. The army of monsters now turned to this prey out in the open, the caravanserai abandoned as too tough of a target.

"Send up the fireworks!" Mal said, and they threw up a spatter of pretty lights in the early dusk, a trick to draw in the stupider of the beasts.

"You've done enough here, Jesusman," Sol said. He looked green and sickly, sweat slicking his hair to his head. "It's time to go."

Mal nodded, gazing over the thick field of the dead. He ordered the gates be thrown open, and both the living and Sol's puppets retreated from the caravanserai.

"Drop it. Drop the walls!" he yelled through a hoarse throat, and then the last Jesusmen through set off the placed charges. The yard was packed thick with the advancing killers, yapping and screeching and calling out for death in a hundred alien tongues.

The walls were tall and thick, and tons of stone crashed down on the horde.

"Quick! Forward!" he ordered the handful of surviving Jesusmen. "Hold them from the gate!"

Barely a dozen were left to his command, terrified and wounded. The boy he'd spared clung to his side, not daring to leave the protection of the Birdman.

Some of the creatures had reached the straggling line, feasting on evacuees as the last of the Boneguard gunned away at every type of strangeness, helped by the bare handful of surviving Taursi who hurled razor-sharp battleglass through the air. More monstrosities were turning from the ruins of the caravanserai to join the attack.

Mal flinched at a loud, sudden crack, and the Range surged forward, sliding south perhaps a mile in one second. Just like that, the city of Crosspoint was gone, swallowed up by the world's end.

The neat queues were forgotten in that final stampede, and Sol's magic finally failed, the winding maze drifting back into sand and

**THE BRIDE & THE BIRDMAN · 309**

dust. People began to trample each other in panic, pushing through into that green square, to salvation.

"Hold!" Mal said, joining his survivors up with the handful of Boneguard. There were perhaps two hundred people left in the queue now, trampling over the dead and dying, and any who lost their footing now were doomed to the same fate. It was a scene of sheer human misery, of desperate people casting aside their neighbours to save themselves.

They were surrounded on all sides now, a rearguard brought down to blades and grit, all that stood against that commonwealth of creatures.

Sol sent the foe backward with pulses of force and beams of crackling energy, and then he went down to one knee with a gasp. He'd been channelling his magic for hours now, and Mal didn't know what it was costing the magician to tap into these deep reserves.

"Stop it!" he said to Sol, yanking him to his feet. "We'll hold them off while you go through the gate."

"Mal," Sol said, squeezing his shoulder. He turned to look and blinked at the sight.

Those thousands of frantic escapees had finally made it through the gate, leaving behind a carpet of bodies. The Jesusmen and a handful of Boneguard were the only ones left, as the creatures increased the ferocity of the attack.

"Fall back!" Mal yelled. "We're leaving. Time to go!"

Then disaster. They were fully encircled by the army of monsters, cut off from the gate.

"Push!" he yelled. The Jesusmen threw out the last dribbles of their magic, blinding and wounding, and following this up with driving bayonets, but they were slowly falling, an island of humanity in a sea of terror.

*It's okay!* Kirstl said.

"I know, love," he said, knocking aside a serrated claw and caving in an enemy skull with the shotgun butt. "It's all over now."

*No! Look!*

Roaring out of the gate came a hideous sight. It was the House of Torana, with Ray leaning out of the window.

310 · JASON FISCHER

"YARGH! A FIELD OF FOOD!" the car cried out, wheels churning up human mincemeat as it slid out of paradise and into battle.

Ray held up a hand, concentrating, and a lance of white-hot fire burst out of his palm, impaling rank upon rank of the attackers. The House of Torana locked its wheels and drove in a tight donut around Mal and the others, bouncing over monsters, knocking down and savaging anything that tried to stand up.

Again and again, Ray swept his powerful sorcery across the attackers, and then the last of the defenders were clear. Mal pushed his people onto the gate as he helped Sol forward.

Then the House of Torana flipped, tossing Ray out of the window and across the ground, and the enemy spent a long moment destroying the vile car. Scrambling against the sluice of the dead underfoot, Ray waved off Mal's assistance and spent a moment checking over the workings of the gate.

"Shut the gate," Mal called out to Ray. "Don't let those things through."

Ray looked up in horror.

"I've made a mistake."

"What do you mean?"

"It won't close. It doesn't close!"

Ray summoned up a sledgehammer the size of a light pole, driving the creatures back. He trashed the power source, yanked out the cables, even smashed the Taursi hearts in one terrific blow, but still the gate stayed open. With the last of his strength, Sol tried to bring it all down with sorcery, but even he had to admit defeat. Ray turned the hammer into an oversized oxy-cutter to try to slice through the steel beams, but nothing worked.

"Forget it!" Mal said, and then the last of them were through the gate and into paradise. For many long minutes, that army of monsters poured through the gate and after them, predators of a thousand different species and just as many worlds.

The Range finally hit the gate and wiped it out, but by then the damage had been done.

By the end of the week, the cruising mountain range had smashed through the Riverland, and town after town was eradicated. First Graham's Wash, empty now as the Water Barons continued their fight to take Mawson. The besiegers fell, and then the walls, and then the Selector's Tower plummeted into the mountains. Jenny's old haunt splintered, shattered, and swallowed.

The Range rolled over the beach and then out into the oceans, swallowing walls of water. The scattered islands were subsumed, including Sol's stately old home, that place of bad memories lost to the crush of the world resetting itself.

Then there was nothing left but the elastic white of the Wastelands, the raw stuff of creation. This curled in on itself, rolling in from the edges, all of that clay compressing into a ball that might have been held in a hand, and there it waited in the darkness for someone to put form to it once again.

No one ever did.

# — 27 —

## A NEW WORLD

It went hard for the survivors of the Now. Those early months were spent fleeing through the richness of their new world, with little time to appreciate its beauty.

Survival was everything. They were hunted at every step by the monsters who'd slipped through the gate behind them. Whenever they attempted a settlement, the predators were there to tear down the walls and butcher those too slow to flee.

The last members of the human race formed councils and committees and squabbled and splintered. The main group of survivors was still led by Ray and Sol, and the Jesusmen were the army, the police force, and the sentries whenever they set up a nervous camp.

Mal led a group of scouts back toward their point of entry, watching for movement in the hunters' camp, and came back with curious news.

One race of the predators had called off the pursuit and was building a rough settlement by a river. It was a large group, maybe two hundred strong, arachnid warriors that hacked down trees with their great claws, webbing together logs into fortifications and walls.

It was a rich world, this one selected by Ray, but the humans found themselves pushed further and further from the best lands, with more settlements springing up in their wake. Every set of walls promised a future wellspring of foes, impossible to uproot.

The group led by Ray and Sol finally found safety in the places where the soil was thin and the watercourses dry. The survivors of the Now were used to tough lands, and here they started over.

One small settlement became another, and then another, each targeting resources or food, the whole pooled together and parcelled out under Sol's guardianship. Ray gave his powers and talents to the construction, sinking wells and raising walls and food silos, but these efforts were less and less successful.

"I'm afraid," he confessed to Sol and Mal one night. "It's getting harder to do the magic."

Even Sol had noticed this, his considerable powers atrophied and slowly fading. The remaining Jesusmen reported the same, and soon their limited store of Marks and Words began to fail altogether.

---

Two years later, a team of explorers found the Gravedigger's shovel.

The tool rested at the centre of a huge crater, miles of trees still lying flat all around it from the force of the impact.

It took Sol nearly a dozen far-doors to reach the site, and then he, Mal, and Ray climbed down into the deep pit.

"Bilbenadium sent this here," Sol said. "The angel said this was a message."

The shovel had been covered in a tiny script, neat words covering every spare inch of the blade and the haft. It was a Before-language, and Sol translated it for Mal.

*Thus my message falls into your hands, you the last of your race. The favourites of the Most High, as flawed as the hands that made you, and here will be your most painful lesson of all.*

*You are a worthy people. But you are not complete.*

*I have set these trials for you, scattered these wardens around your prison. If you had inherited this pristine world unopposed, you would have only repeated the same mistakes. War and inequality. The ravaging of your environment. You cannot be permitted to repeat this path.*

314 · JASON FISCHER

*But in privation, your race flourishes. Like a weed in a garden, you can be plucked out time and again, but you are always there, growing tenacious roots, raising your thorns and your ragged flowers to the sun.*

*So keep this privation well. Learn the lessons from the Before and the Now. Meditate on your failings and plan your path forward.*

*I lie and manipulate, but this manipulation is benevolent. I give you poverty and starvation, for generations to come, but I promise you this much:*

*There will come a time when your kind will reach an accommodation with your neighbours. You will not be the conquerors of your world or any other. You cannot be allowed to reach primacy. But you will be permitted to keep the best of the Most High's design.*

*Passion. Art and science. Reason and will.*

*You will be the advisors of others, the recorders and planners, the respected visionaries. The servants, as the Most High should have been. I see you there in a distant future, when the door to the Severed Garden opens once more.*

*When you are perfected and ready, you will step through the threshold with other companions. Then you will receive your inheritance.*

*You will not get everything, but you will get your share.*

*One last thing: magic is failing. It was derived from the Most High, and with the god's passing, so too does that miracle fall silent.*

*This implement will become your sole means of traversing the planes. Do not use it lightly, and keep this ability very secret. Only you, Sol Goodface, Ray the Junkman, and Mal the Birdman must know of this.*

*The world veil unravels. The worlds drift apart as they should. Let the Severed Garden remain wild.*

*I was ever your most loving adversary,*

*Bilbenadium.*

---

Only once did they ever make use of the Gravedigger's shovel, and Mal took it with Ray and Sol's blessing.

In a quiet glade, Mal cut a line through the air, and he climbed through the scar to stand once more in the Greygulf. Here he saw a marvellous sight.

The wreckage had all been cleaned up, neatly arranged in depots that covered many square miles. New shadow-roads spanned the skies, and the Terminus sat at the centre of all things, clean and repaired.

Moments after Mal's entry, the Terminus came rocketing along a shadow-road, and then it slowly descended to the ground. A door opened, and Lanyard emerged, the Witch standing before the man.

"You've a nerve, boy," he said quietly, and then Lanyard pounced at Mal, mouth spread lion-wide, teeth grown out into fangs like daggers.

He drew up short as if on a leash, and he yowled pitifully, batting at an unseen barrier between them. The Mark Mal had scratched into his flesh still held, but Mal could see this was fading, turning into something like an old scar.

"I will get you soon," Lanyard said. "I know it."

"I did this to you, boss, and I had my reason."

"Coward."

"Yes, but I have a plan for you. We have our world, a new place that isn't the Now. Our story goes on."

"None of you deserved to survive that," Lanyard said.

"Good. I want you to hate me, I want you to hate all of us."

"What is this, boy?"

Mal looked over the shovel in his hands, the story of their future engraved in the steel.

"We only ever had the one job, us Jesusmen. Guard the world veil. Spot the invaders whenever they try to break through. Kill them."

Lanyard lurched against his invisible chain, inching closer to Mal. He was a perfect wax figure of the old man, down to the stubble and the sour mouth. His eyes were orbs of blasted white, and he watched his prentice intently. Hungrily.

Mal said, "You're still a Jesusman, somewhere inside. So you don't get to finish doing that job."

Lanyard yowled.

"Soon, the world veil will fall. Then, this will be the only way to travel between the distant places. You and your kind, you're the last guardians. You will hold to your oaths and watch this place against the last true invader. Forever and always."

"Damn you," Lanyard said. "Release us."

"We are your last remaining enemy. If another human sets foot in your lands, kill them on sight."

"Gladly!"

"You will watch your gates for the next Papa Lucy, the next lords of Overhaeven, any with ambition and daring. Kill them."

"Yes. Yes, a thousand times yes!"

"If I come back, kill me."

"Wait a moment longer and your wish will come true."

"Goodbye, Lanyard."

Once more Mal swept the blade of the Gravedigger's shovel through the fading world veil, and turned to face his master, his father, the first person to ever show him love.

What he was faced with was the purest hatred, and the Witch shook with the urge to kill him, barely restrained by the Mark.

"I'll find you! I'll kill you!"

"I don't think so. Kirstl tells me that the shadow-doors are already sealed against you. The world veil is nearly gone. You'll have nothing but a void around you."

"Please," Lanyard said, sliding and slithering and reforming down on his knees. "I beg you, boy. Please kill me."

"You know I can't. You haven't finished your job."

"Argh!" Lanyard said, pounding on the ashen ground. "You damn bastard. I saved your life! I raised you!"

Mal stood there for a long moment and let the Witch rave at him, the Mark in Lanyard's flesh slowly dissolving. Mal took in every moment of the tirade, and then he stepped backward, sliding through the hole in the world veil.

His last view of Lanyard was the Witch darting forward, free of his spell as all Jesusman magic failed forever. Then the tear in the world veil closed, and Mal left Lanyard to wallow in his eternal vigilance.

---

Mal did not live a long life, but he lived a good one.

With the death of magic, the Jesusmen disbanded. Many became farmers or miners, and some turned to hunting for meat and fur.

They had no need of an army, and the best defence if ever their enemies came sniffing for them was to abandon their villages for a time and head out into the badlands. Any kind of resistance was disaster, and the human survivors had to abandon their old habits toward tribal violence.

The worst threats came from within. People carried evil in their hearts, and there were thefts and assaults, murders and worse. Mal became the head lawman and brought Lanyard's old lessons to his office.

He built a gallows for the rare times one was needed. Mostly the job was dull, and anyone who bucked this grim new social order was assigned to work in the mines or on the meagre farms.

Mal never took a wife, even though Kirstl gave her blessing. He lived with his entire family in his head, which was more than enough. Otherwise, he kept to his own humble lodgings by the cells.

He owned little but the clothes on his back, a native animal that served as a type of horse, and the old shotgun, the ancient Marks in the stock and the barrels slowly fading.

There was little left to the gun that had killed a god but old, rusted iron. It worked well enough though, a gun being a gun. Ray had set up an armoury and produced a limited amount of shells, enough for the hunters, and some for Mal and his deputies.

When two of these deputies turned outlaw, he fought them in a ferocious battle by a brackish dam. They filled him with lead, but he killed one man with gunshot and the other by a brutal blow to the head with the gunstock.

Mal bled out in the badlands, and he had many long minutes to make his peace.

"Kirstl. I'm scared."

*Don't be.*

"But we don't know what happens anymore. If there is anywhere for us to go. Maybe—what if we die and that's all there is now?"

*Then we have nothing to worry about, Mal.*

*Mal,* Collybrock echoed. *Mal. Mal.*

He died with a smile on his face, his lifeblood seeping out into the water. Mal was given a hero's burial, and he was laid to rest with the enormous shotgun. People told stories about him for many years, and then he was folklore, and then he was history, and then he was largely forgotten.

———————————————————

Sol put the first clod of earth on Mal's grave, and he cried the hardest. The Jesusman had been a force for law and had kept things going through the worst of their toughest days.

Above all, though, Mal had been one of the remaining touchstones of his old life. The one where he'd mattered, where he'd had friends and confidantes. Apart from Ray and some of the former Boneguard, the other villagers were strangers.

Life went on. Lyn was the new sheriff; the former Jesusman fell into sobriety, mohawk given over to neatly shorn hair. Gone was the wild twin, and Sol could imagine that their spirit of feral rebellion had died with her back in the Greygulf.

Ray fell back into mechanical pursuits and invented everything that kept their string of villages alive. Water purification. Ammunition. Automated irrigation gates. Fortified tunnels and other clever ways of hiding from the apex predators they shared the world with.

Sol had fallen far, and not a day went by that he didn't curse his brother for his final unwanted gift. His magic was the last to fail, and then he wasn't good for so much as a nightlight.

He was on the unkind side of middle-aged, body worn and never healed from his second flawed resurrection. He was little use in the manual works roster, and while he was always welcome in the councils, these other thinkers also laboured by day.

He felt superfluous. Worst of all, he felt *humoured*.

One hot day, he fell while threshing in the wheatfields, and Sol Goodface was forcibly retired from the workforce. All he had left to his days was endless ruminating, and he fell heavily into drinking the rotgut booze that was Ray's specialty.

**THE BRIDE & THE BIRDMAN · 319**

"What do I do now?" he asked Ray.

"Anything you want," Ray said. "Make things. Teach."

He taught at the schools for a while but found he could never connect with the children who'd only ever known this world, this way of life. He felt as alien to them as they were to him, and when he spoke of the human story, of the worlds of Before and Now, he felt his words falling on disbelieving ears.

Sol grew tired. When he was seen drunk and raving on the steps of the schoolhouse one morning, he was persuaded to retire totally.

This most esteemed citizen was given an equal share in everything and was asked for nothing. He simply sat on his porch, overlooking the humble settlement and drinking away his days.

"What do I do now?" he asked Ray on another of his rare visits. He was conscious of the way his skin was lined and worn now, his hair silver and thin, but Ray looked as hale as ever. The Methuselah treatment still ran in his veins, and he was likely to still have many centuries ahead of him.

"Write a book," Ray said quietly. "I wish I could do it."

He laughed at first, but then he did it. Clever Ray had reinvented papyrus and ink, and so Sol took to his memoirs with gusto. He poured out everything into those pages, and he spared no details, not even those that painted him in a poor light.

All of his heartache over Lucy, how he'd lost Baertha over and over, the tragedy of Lanyard and Mal, and how Bilbenadium had boxed them neatly into this world. He set aside the bottle while he worked, hating how it numbed his raw emotion. He needed every feeling to tell this tale properly.

By the time he was finished, he had enough for three large volumes, which Ray took away to bind in leather-stitched covers.

"What is it called?" Ray asked, handling the pages reverently.

"These are the *Books of Before & Now*," Sol said.

When Ray came back the next day with the bound volumes, he paused at Sol's garden gate, head bowed.

The broken old magician was still sitting on his porch chair. He'd died sometime during the night, and his dead eyes were fixed on some impossible distance past Ray.

Sol Pappagallo was buried next to Mal Birdman. His funeral was attended by many dignitaries, by former students, by the curious, but above all he was mourned by his only remaining friend.

Ray Leicester spent a long time by the grave, and he cried as he realized how utterly alone he now was.

---

When Ray had received the Methuselah treatment, the authorities' best guess was that it would extend a user's life to nine hundred and sixty nine years.

He'd lost many years to his fugue state in the Now, and their record-keeping in this new world had been sloppy. Quite simply, he did not know how old he was.

Ray Leicester was the sole steward of the human race, and he went about it in his humble way, improving lives with his home-taught engineering. Through the dragging decades, he was a constant in their lives, and as the tales of *Before & Now* fell into legend, he greeted new generations of children.

When he had a meltdown, the symptoms of his Asperger's were understood as the eccentricities of a god. He was treated kindly, attended by many who learned at his feet.

If another was born like him, the child was treated with reverence rather than misunderstanding, and this gave Ray the most hope. He let these little geniuses visit him often, trusting with them as much knowledge as they cared to pursue. He saw many of them grow into beloved members of their society, and he released whole generations of physicians and engineers and chemists into the world.

He knew respect in this second life, and the love of his community. He worked patiently and quietly on their problems, mostly because it kept him from dwelling too long on his own.

*What happens to me now?*

*Can I ever die?*

Decades passed, and then a century or more. He was everlasting, the living record of their history. He'd transformed their unfriendly stretch of land into an abundance of agriculture and civilization.

**THE BRIDE & THE BIRDMAN · 321**

They'd been left alone for a long time, but soon enough scouts came sniffing from the cities of their old enemies. Fearing the tales from Sol's memoirs, the elders advised hiding in the tunnels or withdrawing into the desert.

"I think it's time," Ray said. "Don't be afraid."

He went alone to the camp of the hunters, the spider creatures who'd once stalked them through these lands.

To his surprise, he found them civilized now, swathed in cotton shirts and hauling web-sacs of fruit and other goods.

These were traders, not fighters.

And so it went across the world. The humans had their place in this realm, and their ideas and technology were welcomed into every court. As long as they did not take up arms against their neighbours, humanity was safe enough now.

Bilbenadium had predicted everything correctly.

Working within the Polyglot—what passed for their council of nations—Ray oversaw a limited Industrial Age, this time tempered by environmentalism. When the Polyglot fractured briefly and there was a world war, humanity sought neutrality, and none molested their favourite geniuses.

Time passed, and Ray was saddened to realize he could no longer picture John's face. The rest of his old friends were more concept and shape than memory now. He'd known only the one Family once, and now he had thousands of families.

Centuries passed. The world was completely subdued by the Polyglot. The foremost of them developed their own magical science, a strange cousin to that wielded by the descendants of the Most High. They formed a Collegia like that in Sol Pappagallo's memoir and fostered similar desires.

An ambitious cadre pierced the Greygulf and did not return.

When pressed by the Polyglot as to how Mal Birdman had faced his master without magic, Ray refused to tell them. When a ruthless faction of this parliament threatened him, he still would not talk, but when they promised to take his prentices and visit woe on them, he owned up to the presence of the Gravedigger's shovel.

Returning from the wild goose chase he'd sent them on, the spider-warriors came into Ray's workshop just in time to see him destroying the shovel, bending and crushing it underneath a great steam-hammer.

They murdered Ray Leicester that night, and his ending was an awful and lingering punishment, witnessed by many in the powerless human tribe.

They'd learned the lessons, though. They did not raise a hand. They said nothing as they watched the grisly spectacle in their town square, watched their ancient one sell his life to protect the sanctity of the universe.

Ray's killers were found and executed by the Polyglot, who were ashamed of their actions. He'd been beloved by many throughout the nations, a reluctant leader with a gentle nature and no true ambitions of his own.

Most of all, the Polyglot was mystified by the reaction of the humans, a race with nothing but violence in its past, and how they'd reacted to this egregious crime with restraint and a quiet but damning judgement. The killers had fled from the withering glare of the village, knowing they'd broken something special.

Inspired by their unique servants, the Polyglot passed legislation protecting the human race in perpetuity. The Junkman's ending was the stuff of legend, and artists across the Polyglot wrote plays and great philosophies about the old man. Long after his death, his gentle ways guided the universe, and in his own fashion he had conquered far more than Papa Lucy and the Family had ever managed to.

Ray alone had known the truth of things. The Gravedigger's shovel in the hands of Lanyard would have caused the Witches to spill across the universe.

More so, no one on this world was ready yet to voyage forth and claim the Severed Garden, let alone whatever lay beyond the Most High's gate. They could not take shortcuts; they had to earn this great prize.

Bilbenadium had laid out the conditions so there could be no more Papa Lucys, no conceited conquerors. The Witches of the Greygulf would be the first great test of those grand voyagers, and the battle to escape this world would be bitter and hard.

It would be a long time until those new voyagers of the stars would be ready, and this was just and right.

———————————————

Ray knew terror and pain in those final moments as his greedy killers humiliated and destroyed him. They'd dragged him from his workshop and out into the village square, and he died, witnessed by those he'd delivered and raised, who did not waste their lives defending him.

They'd lost him, but in that moment, Ray realized they'd won everything. He died for them, this people who were the last remnant of the Most High, and they'd shown themselves grown beyond the golden god's poisonous example, formed into something new and beautiful.

Pain ended, and so did life, and as he slipped out of his broken body, he saw a new strangeness.

No longer was there a filter to process souls, a system of planes stacked together to direct energies for the Most High. He left the world, and for a moment he could see the Greygulf just beyond that reality, the final barrier between the living and the stars, and then he slipped into a void.

*It's just oblivion now,* he thought, and accepted this as what happened to souls.

Then he was suffused with light, and he opened his eyes.

He looked on a place of genuine joy, a place for the souls of the dead to gather, but they were not pale blue, nothing like the Once-Dead of the old system. They were white, and bright, and pulsed with life and goodness.

"We've been waiting for you," Jenny Rider said kindly. Mal and Sol were there, and so was the House of Torana, and Tilly, and Mem and Lyn.

There was a multitude of souls in this realm, a shifting place that was more dreamlike than the rigid Gan-Eden. Every fear and doubt he'd ever felt in his life was cast off, and there was nothing but joy and love for those around him, and the spirits of strangers didn't feel so strange.

The boundaries between himself and these others was paper-thin and joyous.

"Is Lanyard here?" he asked Mal dreamily.

"Not yet," Mal said with a smile. "He'll be with us soon."

The young man leaned against his sweetheart Kirstl, and his faithful bird Collybrock capered around them, playing some sort of game with the House of Torana, who was less horrifying here and more gentle, once more reunited with Gretel, the warlord smiling in gap-toothed ecstasy. Ray laughed at the sight.

"Ray, come this way," Jenny said, even though directions were pointless here.

A cloud parted, and then Ray stood face to face with his brother John, and there was Baertha and Jesus, and even Lucy was there, everything sinister about their old enemy reduced to an honest smile and a hug, with no more secrets or plots, nothing but the shared joy that defined this place.

"I thought you were gone," he said, gripping his brother fiercely, weeping happily. "Destroyed when the Most High fell."

"We were destroyed. Our Once-Dead souls were broken, and we were absorbed into the universe, and now we are here," John explained.

"Where are we?" Ray asked, a scientist even to the last.

"I know this one," Papa Lucy said with a smile.

"Where are we then, smartarse?" Sol scoffed.

"Turns out the bloody hippies were right. We're *everywhere*."

# — EPILOGUE —

At the beginning, the universe was empty, but a seed floated in its very centre, struggling to germinate in the cold and the dark.

No. Not a seed. An egg, iron and pitted, and it spun in place, struggling to remember.

"I remember," a voice said from within. Something worked at the insides of the shell with sharp teeth, and finally the baby emerged.

They were a large-eared rat, a golden pup that shed blinding light out into the dark. Remembering the failure of the Most High, the rat gathered the broken parts of their egg around themselves, weaving an impervious sac they could live in.

A permanent prison, from void to light and back to void again. They were meant to be both creator and observer. Prisoner and god. There could be no further interaction with the universe than this, and it was an ample reward for a plot that had quite literally hatched.

Birth was hard, and so the newborn spun in place, napping fitfully, finally opening their eyes to see the baubles they'd dreamt up to amuse themself during this sleep.

At the beginning of all things, Bilbenadium watched the cosmic eruptions as the universe began. They saw the flare of newborn stars, hurtling out from the bright nurseries of the nebulae. They observed every type of cosmic wonder from their prison at the centre of the universe, sitting up keenly and preening their whiskers.

Now the lights were on, Bilbenadium could see a hatch at the edge of this reality and knew that this whole time a part of the old universe had been sequestered safely away. The Severed Garden lay just beyond that door, and one day the perfected humans would enter this newly created universe, when the children of the Most High were finally ready to serve this glorious creation.

"Now this I didn't see," Bilbenadium said, grinning happily at the lightshow.

THE END.

# — ABOUT THE AUTHOR —

Jason Fischer is a writer who lives near Adelaide, South Australia. He has won the Colin Thiele Literature Scholarship, an Aurealis Award and the Writers of the Future Contest. In Jason's jack-of-all-trades writing career he has worked on comics, apps, television, short stories, novellas and novels. Jason also facilitates writing workshops, is an enthusiastic mentor, and loves anything to do with the written or spoken word.

Jason is also the founder and CEO of Spectrum Writing, a service that teaches professional writing skills to people on the Autism Spectrum.

He plays a LOT of Dungeons and Dragons, has a passion for godawful puns, and is known to sing karaoke until the small hours.